"Fiercely critical, ruefully funny, profoundly compassionate . . . humanizes the dire complexities inherent to a place fractured by perpetual violence, corruption, outside exploitation, bone-deep poverty, and fanaticism. A writer of charm, wit, conscience, and penetrating vision, Farah is a commanding and essential global writer."   —*Booklist*

"Farah has become the voice of the Somalian diaspora, telling stories of political, religious, and family conflict without sentimentality. . . . Like Conrad, Farah proves a master of his adopted language, enhancing his narratives with proverbs and instances of institutionalized irrationality."
—*Publishers Weekly* (starred review)

"Harrowing without resorting to sensationalism, this highly topical final volume in Farah's Past Imperfect trilogy should burnish his well-deserved reputation. [A] gripping but utterly humane thriller set in one of the least understood regions on earth."   —*Kirkus Reviews*

"Farah writes enthrallingly about his native Somalia. . . . Expect sharp insight into both human nature and sectarian strife, told in illuminating language free of cant."   —*Library Journal*

PENGUIN BOOKS

CROSSBONES

Nuruddin Farah is the author of ten previous novels, translated into more than twenty languages, and has won numerous awards, including the Neustadt International Prize for Literature. His work has been featured in *The New Yorker* and other publications. Born in Baidoa, Somalia, he lives in Cape Town.

NURUDDIN FARAH

CROSSBONES

PENGUIN BOOKS

PENGUIN BOOKS

Published by the Penguin Group

Penguin Group (USA) Inc., 375 Hudson Street, New York, New York 10014, USA • Penguin Group
(Canada), 90 Eglinton Avenue East, Suite 700, Toronto, Ontario M4P 2Y3, Canada (a division of Pearson
Penguin Canada Inc.) • Penguin Books Ltd, 80 Strand, London WC2R 0RL, England • Penguin Ireland,
25 St Stephen's Green, Dublin 2, Ireland (a division of Penguin Books Ltd) • Penguin Group (Australia),
707 Collins Street, Melbourne, Victoria 3008, Australia (a division of Pearson Australia Group Pty Ltd) •
Penguin Books India Pvt Ltd, 11 Community Centre, Panchsheel Park, New Delhi – 110 017, India •
Penguin Group (NZ), 67 Apollo Drive, Rosedale, Auckland 0632, New Zealand (a division of Pearson
New Zealand Ltd) • Penguin Books, Rosebank Office Park, 181 Jan Smuts Avenue, Parktown North 2193,
South Africa • Penguin China, B7 Jaiming Center, 27 East Third Ring Road North, Chaoyang District,
Beijing 100020, China

Penguin Books Ltd, Registered Offices: 80 Strand, London WC2R 0RL, England

First published in the United States of America by Riverhead Books, a member of
Penguin Group (USA) Inc. 2011
Published with revisions in Penguin Books 2012

10 9 8 7 6 5 4 3 2 1

Grateful acknowledgment is made to *The New Yorker*, where portions of this book previously appeared,
in slightly different form.

PUBLISHER'S NOTE

This is a work of fiction. Names, characters, places, and incidents either are the product of the author's
imagination or are used fictitiously, and any resemblance to actual persons, living or dead, businesses,
companies, events, or locales is entirely coincidental.

LIBRARY OF CONGRESS CATALOGING-IN-PUBLICATION DATA

Farah, Nuruddin, date.
  Crossbones / Nuruddin Farah.
    p.   cm.
  ISBN 978-1-59448-816-0 (hc.)
  ISBN 978-0-14-312253-1 (pbk.)
1. Americans—Somalia—Fiction. 2. Mogadishu (Somalia)—Fiction.
3. Political fiction. I. Title.
PR9396.9.F3C76   2011   2011018748
823'.914—dc22

Printed in the United States of America

BOOK DESIGN BY STEPHANIE HUNTWORK

FOR
CHARLIE SUGNET
&
ILIJA TROJANOW

CROSSBONES

A YANKEES-CAP-AND-RAY-BAN-WEARING BOY OF INDETERMINATE AGE gets out of a car that has just stopped. He climbs out gingerly, like a spider creeping up a crevice. He retrieves a carryall from the trunk of the car without help from the two men sitting in the front. The men are old army hands, and although they haven't said anything to him, he knows that they do not think highly of him.

The boy slings the carryall over his shoulder, nodding his thanks to the two men in the vehicle. They look away with obvious disdain; they do not wish to acknowledge his gratitude. He smiles with youthful bravado, betraying none of his trepidation. He does not want to fail; he cannot afford to fail. He is aware of the huge difference between martyring oneself and making a blunder of things and getting killed. Of course, he does not wish to die, not unless he has fulfilled his dream.

He is small in stature, huge in ambition. On his first day as a draftee into Shabaab, the instructor, upset with him, had pulled him up by the scruff of his neck, shouting in Somali, *"Waxyahow yar!"*—"You young thing!" The sobriquet stuck, and he answers to it now. The car reverses and he moves forward on the dirt road, his breathing heavy under the load he carries.

It is hot, and just before noon he meets a woman in a full-body tent going in the opposite direction. The woman takes an interest in him: a small-boned, four-and-a-half-foot-tall figure—a dwarf, she thinks at first—hoisting a carryall bigger and heavier than he is. She watches him as he puts the carryall down on the ground and sighs with relief. She waits for him to remove his sunglasses before she will consider peeling off her face veil or entertaining any question from him.

Deciding to be on an equal footing with him, she takes off her face veil and then crouches close enough to him, looking straight into his eyes in an effort to put him at ease. They exchange standard greetings, she addresses him in the may-peace-be-upon-you Somali greeting, *Nabad*, and he, in preference, uses the Arabic equivalent: *Salaamu Calaykum*.

"Can I help you?" she says. "You seem lost."

He asks her to tell him the way to the *qiblah*.

She takes her time, wondering if he is one of the young Shabaab *mules* assigned to do their dirty work. The poor sod must be mistaking the *qiblah*—the Arabic term for the direction in which a praying Muslim faces—for north, she thinks. She wonders if he is a grown man with the voice of a boy, or a boy in the body of a man. They stand on the dirt road, in East Wardhiigley, a rundown district of Mogadiscio, sizing each other up. The woman, Cambara, is on her way to the Bakhaaraha Market; she needs a few last items for the apartment she is preparing for her guests, Jeebleh and his journalist son-in-law, Malik, arriving on the morrow. Now she lights upon a thought, studying the young thing, that maybe he is passing himself off as someone he is not, just as she puts on the body tent before she leaves the house, as part of her disguise, like a theater prop. Somali women, who never used to wear veils, resorted to them when the strife began, in 1991—a protection from sexual harassment by armed youths. But lately, ever since 2006, when the Union of Islamic Courts took control of Mogadiscio, expanding their rule of Sharia law, veiling has become de rigueur. Women are punished if they appear in trousers or the less restrictive dresses that were common before the civil war.

His hair is the color of ash and is cursed with kinks that no comb can smooth out. From the little she has heard so far, his voice has not broken. Yet his face crawls with the deep furrows she associates with the hardened features of a herdsman from the central region, where all of Somalia's recent political instabilities have originated. Shabaab, the military wing of the Union of Islamic Courts, has been trying to terrorize the residents of the city into submission, and it appears to have succeeded to a degree. She assumes that he is one of the conscripts charged with "consecrating"—or rather, confiscating—a house in the neighborhood, from which he and his colleagues will launch attacks on their enemy targets. Cambara points south, sending him in the wrong direction, well away from the northeastern part of the city where she lives.

———

YoungThing lifts his carryall and walks in the direction the woman has shown him. He shifts the burden of his load from one shoulder to the other, breathing loudly through his nose. He plays at being tougher than he is; he tries to tread lightly, even if it is obvious that his attempt is a sham—he can't take two steps without faltering. Hampered by the weight he has to bear, he can no longer remember the details of the instructions he was given. No doubt he feels lucky to have been chosen for this delicate assignment cloaked in secrecy, his first mission. He will do anything to impress the commanders of the cell of which he is now a bona fide member. This brings a smile to his face, and briefly injects fresh energy into his gait.

He loses his balance just as he recalls picking up the carryall earlier that day. He had been sent to see a heavily bearded man known by the nom de guerre Garweyne—BigBeard. BigBeard manages one of the largest computer shops in the Bakhaaraha Market—a sanctuary from within whose labyrinthine warrens the insurrectionists initiate frequent offensives. The market complex confuses anyone unfamiliar with its numerous dead ends, bounded by shacks and stalls that take half a day to construct and only a couple of hours to dismantle.

In the carryall, BigBeard has put roadside mines, grenades and other explosive devices, small arms meant to make holes in airplane fuselages in the event of an Ethiopian raid, YoungThing assumes. In truth, BigBeard shared little intelligence with him directly, and Young-Thing knows that it is not his place to ask questions. He can't give in to curiosity, since any departure from instructions will earn him severe punishment. YoungThing understands this much: He is the advance member of a commando unit preparing the ground so that Shabaab can respond immediately to an Ethiopian invasion of Mogadiscio. He is an explosives trainee, but his job today is to consecrate a safe house.

———

There are two men in charge of YoungThing's unit—a select coterie of fighters sharing a central command. One of the leaders has the nom de guerre Dableh—FootSoldier. At the outbreak of the civil war, he was the commander of the largest weapons stockpile in the country, a colonel in the National Army appointed by Barre, the former dictator, himself. After the civil war began, the colonel changed sides and gave the warlord StrongmanSouth unfettered access to the arms cache, arming his ragtag clan militia and enabling them to run the head of state out of the city. Dableh has survived the civil war and changes in his masters' fortune. When StrongmanSouth died, he lost no time in switching his allegiance to the Courts, aiding in their final triumph over the warlords, in 2006. Now, a few months on, he is contributing his military expertise to the plan to invade Baidoa, the seat of the weak Transitional Federal Government.

The second man in the command structure is known as Al-Xaqq—"the Truth"—one of the ninety-nine names of Allah. A modest man, Al-Xaqq gives a more temporal meaning to his name and prefers to be addressed as TruthTeller. He is an explosives genius and a member of the high order of the Courts, a learned man, with expertise in people management. He takes pride in his formidable ability to identify potential suicide bombers. Al-Xaqq sleeps and eats with them—at times exacting harsh punishment and ordeals to test their dedication—cementing loyalty before the young men are sent out on their missions. At times, he is the only one privy to the details of a sortie, plotting operations to suit the martyr he has handpicked. A few months ago, after YoungThing failed to make the grade as a suicide bomber, Truth-Teller suggested he train in the explosives trade and seconded him to FootSoldier's unit.

YoungThing knows the protocol: BigBeard will have sent a text message to both FootSoldier and TruthTeller, confirming that YoungThing has picked up the carryall. Special events require special rituals, which are repeated many times over—each time an insurgent receives a cache of arms or a wad of cash from the men leading the insurrection.

Exhausted from lugging the carryall, YoungThing takes a long break, unsure that he's going the right way. According to the driver, it should have been no distance at all to the house. But either he has been going around and around in circles or he was misled by the woman in the body tent. He senses that he won't be on schedule. He quickens his pace, turns left, then right, and then right again. He happens upon two men conversing and decides they must be the two sympathizers who are supposed to give him further directions. The men do not pay him any mind at first, even though he stands close by. It seems to Young-Thing that they cannot decide what to make of him. Then he remembers the agreed-upon code. In the rehearsed voice of an actor reciting his lines, he asks, "Will one of you please tell me which way is north?"

That the two men do not exactly match the descriptions given to him by his instructors does not worry YoungThing. Tired and hungry, he is becoming hazy about the details of his mission. The older of the men is slim and very dark, with intelligent eyes; he is in a sarong. His younger, stockier companion is in Bedouin robes.

The robed man, his teeth stained brown, is the first to speak. He turns to his companion and, with the characteristic flourish with which a highly literate man talks to the unlettered, says, "This young thing wants to know the way north."

The older man replies, "What makes you think that he wants to know which way is north, when what he wants to know is the direction of the *qiblah*?"

YoungThing can no longer remember which stranger, or on what street corner, he was supposed to ask for directions, using the code word *qiblah*. From the tone of the older man's voice, he suspects that they are leading him on. A longer look at them throws him into a further muddle. The robed man is behaving curiously, as if he wants to reach out and open the carryall. Then, as if to prove his superior knowledge to the older man, he creates further uncertainty in YoungThing's mind. He says, "Does the young man think that the way north always points the way to the *qiblah*?"

Now doubts stir in the older man's eyes, and his gaze, too, focuses on the carryall. He tells YoungThing to go back the way he came until he finds a big house with a green gate bearing the freshly painted inscription *Allahu Akbar* in red paint.

"How far is the house with the inscription?"

The older man replies, "It is a hundred and fifty paces to the four-way road. Then you turn right, and right again. That's the way north, toward the *qiblah*, toward Mecca, the correct way. You can't miss the green gate or the inscription in blood red. That's the house you want."

YoungThing is barely out of earshot when the robed man bursts into derisory laughter, amused at the thought that they have sent the boy to the wrong property, which belongs to a business adversary of the older man's. The home owner is out of the country and has been renting it to a family from a rival clan with a questionable political history. "Two birds with one stone," he says.

———

As YoungThing searches for the house with the green gate and the inscription, he blames the frailty of his memory on the fact that he has eaten no breakfast, and that a young thing like him can't comprehend the intricate political games adults play. He suspects he is being used. Everything is a muddle. All at once, though, he finds the front gate with the inscription and he forgets his doubts. He walks past it and then takes a left turn. He wants the back gate, as per the directive. Here there is a high fence, which he must scale.

His heartbeat quickening, he sends a one-word text message informing his minder that he is at the back gate, and he receives a reply encouraging him to gain entry right away. He opens the carryall and takes out a light machine gun and a belt strung with bullets. He slings the collapsible gun over his shoulder, girdles the belt around his waist, and throws the carryall over a low part of the fence, then waits a few minutes.

YoungThing wishes himself good luck. As light-footed as a young dik-dik, he runs at the fence and shinnies up and over. He drops down on the other side with a quiet thud and remains in a crouch for a few seconds, his gun poised the way he has seen it done in movies.

An untended garden stretches before him, the shrubs low and scraggly, the trees stunted, and the wall of the house crawling with vines. He moves stealthily forward, as silent as the leopards in stories he has heard. He is certain his instructors at the madrassa would be pleased with him, assured that his training has turned him into a cadet ready to martyr himself in the service of the insurgency. He pauses for a startled fraction of a second when he picks out the sound of movement somewhere nearby. With purposeful speed, he retrieves the carryall and stands firm and unafraid behind the low shrubs—there are benefits to being of small size, after all, he thinks. But now he comes upon a shorter fence, of which no one has spoken. It goes to show, he tells himself, that even Shabaab's intelligence gatherers are fallible. Still, he doesn't look back, thinking that is the way of doom. Besides, there is no place for fear in a martyr. He'll use the gun, shoot and kill, if there is need.

He backs up three paces, breathing in and out quickly until he feels a burning sensation in his lungs. Having omitted mention of the second fence, the men may have missed something of a trickier nature; he must be ready for all eventualities. Unless, of course, the omission was deliberate, meant to test his mettle. His minder has impressed on him the importance of using his weapon only when it is imperative or in self-defense, and of using the silencer if he does have to shoot.

One nervous move follows another. He throws the carryall over the fence. He waits for a few minutes, then runs at it, vaults over, and, landing, gathers himself into a tight ball—he's learned this from watching videos on a jihadi website. In one video, the instructors encouraged young jihadis to retain the scalps of high-profile targets as trophies. YoungThing is uncertain that he will ever want to hang on to the head of a man he has killed. In fact, there is no chance in hell that he will want to do so, and in any case, he has no place to conceal a dead head; he has no home he can call his own.

Now he happens upon a second discrepancy in the directives given to him: he finds a half-open window, but it appears to lead not into a bathroom, as he was told, but into what looks like a kitchen.

He hides behind a huge tree with a trunk as big as a baobab's. He is still as a worshipper waiting for the imam to resume his prostrations. Then, committing himself fully to every move he makes, like a jihadi leading the onslaught on the enemy from the front, he gains the back porch in two swift, long strides.

He scans the area for evidence of habitation: the telltale presence of a wicker chair someone has brought out to sit in; a cat curled up in purring slumber; clothes drying on a washing line.

He enters the property by the kitchen window, squeezing himself through. Of course, no instructions can prepare one for every contingency. There are decisions one must make on the job, without help. As far as he can tell, all is quiet inside. He walks about the house a little, feeling triumphant, then comes out to retrieve the carryall and take it back indoors. He makes a phone call to tell his minder that he is in the house and that it is safe.

His minder asks him to describe the outside of the house he has "consecrated." In fact, he asks him several times to repeat how he got there. At first, YoungThing puts this down to a bad telephone connection. Then he begins to doubt whether he has gone to the right property.

He ends the call and embarks on a thorough reconnoitering, something he should have done first. He walks up the stairs and goes into the bedrooms. The rooms feel lived in: drawers ajar from recent use, socks black with dirt, a pair of underpants still damp from wear. He is in the wrong house, he thinks again. But what can he do about it?

The refrigerator in the kitchen is buzzing. He opens it and, seeing plastic containers full of last night's leftovers, he feels hungry, and angry, too. He hasn't had his fill of meat for a long time and is tempted to stuff himself with good food; he wishes he hadn't already made the phone call.

He hears movements coming from the front porch. He turns and sees through the open door an ancient man, unshaven and wearing only a dressing gown and flip-flops, tottering in the direction of the house. The old man seems equally surprised to see him. But the old man mistakes YoungThing for one of his many grandchildren and says, "Why, you are back early! You see, the wind pushed the door locked, and when I couldn't get back in, I fell asleep on the bench under the tree in the front garden."

JEEBLEH WALKS GROGGILY OUT OF THE FOKKER AIRCRAFT, JUST arrived in Mogadiscio from Nairobi, and down the wobbly steps pushed against its flank by a gaggle of youths who look like a prison work detail. As he descends, billows of dust mixed with the midday heat and humidity whip up at him in agitated vigor, the sea breeze from a mere half kilometer away hardly affecting the gooeyness of the amalgam. In addition, an irritating scrimmage of human traffic crowds the bottom of the stairway as porters squeeze through the descending passengers to offer their services.

Jeebleh is visiting Mogadiscio for the first time in a decade. His son-in-law, Malik, a freelance journalist based in New York, has come along, too, intending to write articles about the ancestral land he has never seen. Now, watching half a dozen bearded men in white robes with whips in their hands, Malik looks disturbed. Born in Aden, Yemen, of a Somali father and a Malay-Chinese mother, Malik was brought up partly in Malaysia, a most orderly country. He learned Somali as a child but has not spoken it continuously, and because of this, his hearing cannot accommodate the alien harshness of these bearded men's in-

flections as they bark instructions at passengers and porters alike. Jeebleh remembers his wife's refrain about Somalia: "That unfortunate
country, cursed with those dreadful clanspeople, forever killing one
another and everyone around them." Yet it is Judith, prone as she is to
speaking out of turn and making embarrassing gaffes, who suggested
that Jeebleh take Malik along and prevailed on their daughter, Amran,
to give her consent.

Now Jeebleh and Malik have become separated in the melee, as
the passengers shove one another in the rush to collect their luggage
or to get out of the way. Jeebleh steps aside and holds out his hand for
Malik, in the manner in which one stretches out a hand to a drowning
person. Malik acknowledges him with a nod and a smile, but declines
to take the proffered hand, so Jeebleh inches his way through the
crowd to rejoin him. "Let us head in the direction of the Immigration
and Customs down there," he shouts in English, and he points at the
hall, his hand striking someone in the face, an act for which he apolo-
gizes, although the man whom he has struck does not appear at all
bothered.

A man, seemingly in authority, even though he is not in uniform—
he is one of those wearing a white robe, Arab style, and a purple keffiyeh, Arafat style, but no whip—takes interest in the two of them
when he hears them communicate in English. He approaches with the
consummate confidence of the powerful, his hand outstretched toward
Jeebleh. "Your passport, please."

Malik mutters conspiratorially to Jeebleh, wondering who the man
is. Instead of answering the question, Jeebleh hands over his passport
and then, turning to Malik, suggests that he cede his own. The man
studies the passports, one at a time. When he has gleaned as much
information as he can, he returns them, politely gesturing them on toward Immigration and Customs. Jeebleh's Somali seventh sense alerts

him to some trouble ahead, even if he does not know its nature. But he takes care not to share his worry with Malik.

The terminal building is open on the side facing the airstrip and the ocean, and closed on the other, exit side. The airport reopened to traffic only a couple of months earlier, for the first time in sixteen civil war years. The repair job on the hall is not quite done, the scaffolding crisscrossing and impeding one's movements, nor is the work on the archways anywhere near complete. A rope is strung across the middle of the hall, separating arrivals and departures. In the departures area, some fifty or so cheap white plastic chairs are clustered in the corner, presumably for the use of passengers waiting to board their flights. In arrivals, a disorderly queue is forming as the first passengers scramble to clear the formalities. With no luggage carousels or carts, no trained personnel at Immigration and Customs, there is no knowing how things might pan out, no knowing what these robed, bearded men might or might not do.

Jeebleh and Malik start their own queue; apparently they are the only arriving passengers traveling on non-Somali passports. They are linked in intention, too. Malik wants to write about the city under the Union of Islamic Courts as it prepares for war. As a freelancer, he has signed a loose contract with a daily newspaper back home that gives it first right of refusal to any piece he writes. In return, the paper has given him a small retainer, from which he paid for his ticket to Somalia. But he is aware of the dangers involved in visiting the country; and knows, too, that his accompanying Jeebleh has pleased his father-in-law and eased his wife Amran's mind. For his part, Jeebleh intends to facilitate Malik's mission by introducing him to his bosom friend, Bile. Jeebleh and Bile were raised in the same household, their mothers almost interchangeable. Later, they went to Padua University together, Bile to take a medical degree, Jeebleh to write his doctoral thesis on Dante. They were even together in jail back in Somalia, where as political dissidents they occupied neighboring solitary cells. But now they live thousands of miles apart, and Jeebleh has heard that Bile's health is poor. He is eager to see his old friend, and to meet Bile's companion, Cambara, who has insisted they act as his and Malik's hosts in Mogadiscio. There are others to whom he can introduce his son-in-law, who will help him to adjust to his challenging surroundings.

Yet for all his good intentions, Jeebleh's anxiety about Malik's well-being is taking a toll on him, as he labors to anticipate the troubles that may arise, in hopes of allaying them. It doesn't help that Malik is already ill at ease with Jeebleh's solicitude. Having been a foreign correspondent in the Congo, Afghanistan, Iraq, and other of the world's hot spots, he appears certain he needs no telling what he must or mustn't do. Within half an hour of arriving in Somalia, the two of them are already erring on the side of reticence, neither saying what is on his mind.

The sight of a young man in his late teens reminds Malik of his nephew, Taxliil, who has recently disappeared from Minnesota, along with other Somali-American youths. Taxliil and the missing youths have reportedly gone to Somalia as volunteers in the ranks of Shabaab fighters. Ahl, Malik's older brother, will be coming to Somalia within a few days as well, in search of his runaway stepson. Unlike Jeebleh and Malik, Ahl will base himself in Puntland, the autonomous state notorious in the international media for its pirate hideouts. Malik remembers Jeebleh explaining that in the absence of verifiable reports in Somalia, given its statelessness, all one has to do is to circulate a *kutiri-kuteen* hearsay not traceable to any particular person, and you can be sure that once the word hits the street it will grow its own legs and will, in its wanderings, recruit more and more hearers, with each new hearer adding their bit to the roaming tale until it gains more speed and runs faster than truth. Now things are such that Taxliil is on the verge of being sent to Puntland, serving as a go-between from a top man in Shabaab to the pirates. Malik and Jeebleh intend to assist in tracking down Taxliil's movements in any way they can. With Jeebleh's extensive contacts in the city and the links Malik intends to forge with other journalists and whomever else he meets, they are confident they will find Taxliil.

Malik's skin is smarting from the sand now blowing from the sea, the breeze bearing more than a touch of salt; he is ceaselessly rubbing his eyes sore with the heel of his hand. The same white-robed man with the purple keffiyeh opens a window in the Customs cubicle and, after a payment of a visa fee of twenty U.S. dollars, stamps their passports, not a single word exchanged. Even so, Jeebleh's Somali seventh sense will not settle down.

They pick up their suitcases. Another white-robed man, this one with a single-tailed whip in his hand, asks if they have anything to declare. Jeebleh responds that they do not. The man says, "Welcome to the country," and adds, "Godspeed."

As soon as they are out of the building, Jeebleh starts across the no-man's-land of the airport grounds, giving himself the physical and mental space to calm his heightened nerves. Malik trails far behind, taking his time. No question there is a huge difference between this arrival and Jeebleh's harrowing arrival last time, at Casillay, twenty-five kilometers to the north. He quaked to his feet then, his heart pounding with fear. Those were the days of fierce armed confrontations between the warlords StrongmanSouth and StrongmanNorth. A Green Line divided the city in unequal halves, each warlord running his half. A boy not yet in his teens had been killed before Jeebleh even left the airport, as he and his mother boarded their Nairobi-bound flight.

Jeebleh knows that the internal wrangling of the Courts has prevented them from setting up a city administration, but there is no denying the semblance of order in the shape of the white-robed men with their riding crops or bullwhips. This time, there are no shifty men to waylay one, or unruly youths to use one for target practice, taking odds on the outcome. Even if there are no uniforms or badges, there are still activities associated with authority: men stamping passports, checking papers, holding back the spectators and those welcoming passengers. They walk past the boisterous, expectant crowd, taxi drivers waiting for fares, unemployed men offering to carry their shoulder bags, beggars begging. Amazingly, no one in this rowdy lot dares to step beyond the cord meant to keep them out, over which a man in a robe stands guard with a whip. Then Jeebleh spots Dajaal, who is waving, and he relaxes. His friend is an old pro who has lived through good and bad times in this city. Jeebleh met him during his 1996 visit and knows him to be brave, reliable, meticulous, and, above all, punctual.

Jeebleh hugs Dajaal warmly, and introduces him to Malik as "the man you want on your side when the chips are down." He introduces Malik as "my son-in-law, father to my only granddaughter."

Dajaal has with him a gawky, toothy young man with a long neck, whom he presents as Gumaad, a journalist. Jeebleh remembers the name, and how Dajaal characterized him on the phone as a "home-grown religionist-leaning fellow."

A crowd gathers around them, looking on curiously. In Somalia, crowds form quickly, maybe because people are hungry in many ways: hungry for news, good or bad; hungry and also hopeful that they may gain by standing close to where something is happening, to where two people are talking. But crowds change into mobs at the sound of a clarion call. Jeebleh recalls a couple of hair-raising incidents from his last visit.

As they walk toward the car, Dajaal says to Malik, "Gumaad will serve as your escort, your guide, and your researcher. God knows you will need someone with a handle on local politics, which is a minefield for a novice."

Even if Dajaal had not said anything in advance, Gumaad's accent would be a dead giveaway to Jeebleh. He hails from the same part of the country's central region as do Dajaal, Bile, and StrongmanSouth, as well as the man known among the in-crowd of the Courts simply as TheSheikh, the current ideologue and firebrand of the religionists. Jeebleh has often contended that you can trace all of Somalia's political instability over the past twenty years to this very district. Feisty and belligerent, its natives have between them contributed several of Somalia's most obdurate warlords, deadliest head pirates, and wealthiest businessmen, each in their way sworn to making the country ungovernable.

Jeebleh takes Dajaal aside and asks, "How well do you know Gumaad?"

"How well can you know anyone these days," Dajaal observes.

"Would you trust him? That's my question."

"I would string him from the rafters if he misbehaves toward you or Malik."

Jeebleh doesn't pursue the topic of trust, whether one can know another person in Somalia in these times. He knows that Dajaal means what he says.

Gumaad, finding himself alone with Malik, meanwhile, dispenses with formalities. "Be warned, I have strong views, and they are different from Dajaal's."

"I see nothing wrong with that," Malik says easily.

They get into the sedan, Jeebleh sitting up front with Dajaal, Gumaad and Malik in the back. Dajaal starts the engine but does not move, insisting that everyone put on his seat belt. Gumaad grumbles that "belting up" is un-Islamic; accidents happen and deaths occur when Allah wills them. "When will you accept that nothing happens without His express decision?"

"In my car, we wear seat belts," says Dajaal.

Even after he buckles up and Dajaal puts the car in motion, Gumaad doesn't let it go. "Listen to you. 'In my car, we wear seat belts.' This is Bile's car, not yours. So you can't say 'my car.'" A jet of his saliva strikes Malik in the face, and he wipes it away discreetly. Jeebleh, amused, shakes his head at this pointless altercation, looking from Dajaal to Gumaad. What relevance does the ownership of a vehicle have to do with wearing or not wearing seat belts? But Somalis, he knows, seldom admit to red herrings. It is typical of them to confound issues, mistake a metonym for a synecdoche. While there is always a beginning to an argument, there is never an end, never a logical conclusion to their disputation. Somalis are in a rich form when holding forth; they are in their element when they are spilling blood.

Now the car is slowing down. A man in a sarong and a T-shirt is standing in the middle of the road, holding a gun in his right hand. He flags them down.

Dajaal pulls to the side of the road and cuts the engine, as instructed. They alight, and the man gestures them to benches in the shade, an indication that they could be here for a long while. Gumaad asks, "Under whose authority?"

Dajaal gets a grip on Gumaad's elbow and leads him toward the benches, although not without Gumaad asserting loudly that he will make a call to TheSheikh and all will be sorted out in no time. He says to the man in the sarong and the T-shirt, "We thought that checkpoints manned by armed militiamen loyal to the warlords were things of the past."

The man pays him no attention at all.

As if to throw them further off course, another man arrives—an impressively large man, hairy of face, proud of bearing, slow of stride, with beady, penetrating, but unusually self-contained eyes. He has the longest, most unkempt beard Jeebleh has ever seen, reminiscent of a devout Sikh's. His immaculate, all-white attire, which he wears the way a police officer might wear a uniform, consists of a tunic and pajama-like trousers, cut wide at the top, narrow at the bottom, the legs short enough to allow him to perform his ablutions without rolling them up. He carries two mobile phones, a ringing one in his right hand, a silent one in his left. Maybe there is a third mobile phone in the pocket of his tunic, which droops heavily as he strides forward. Gumaad whispers to Dajaal, "What is *he* doing here?"

Dajaal says, "You never know with Garweyne. But tell me, is he no longer in the computer business? I thought he was doing very well lately, considering."

Gumaad says, "He is the rising star among those who have been inducted into the intelligence division of the military wing of the Courts."

"I'll be damned!" says Dajaal.

Malik overhears the conversation and thinks that, for all his size, the bearded man looks like a body builder, not an inch of flab on him.

Jeebleh is thinking about the change in the city's attire over the past decade. In the mid-nineties, for want of trained tailors, three-quarters of the men wore sarongs. Now Mogadiscio is awash in styles imported from as far away as Saudi Arabia, Afghanistan, and Pakistan. He is amazed at the variety of dress, both male and female, that he has seen in just the short time he has been here.

BigBeard makes a beeline for Malik's computer.

"Is that your computer?" the man asks Malik.

Malik stands firm, with his legs splayed and his body leaning back, as though preparing to shoulder in a resistant door.

He says to BigBeard, "I am a Somali journalist living in America and have come on a visit, inspired by the exemplary events here."

"For whom do you write?"

"I am a freelance journalist."

Malik recalls reading about journalists and writers visiting the

Soviet Union in its day of communist glory. Those who gave cagey answers met with official reprimand and would not be issued permits. He takes the plunge. "I hope to write about the peace that has dawned in the land, thanks to the Union of Islamic Courts, which has wrested it out of the hands of the warlords and their associates."

BigBeard speaks as though desert sand he swallowed a lifetime ago is interfering with his speech pattern, altering its rhythm, impeding its natural flow, like a drain blocked with an avalanche of sludge. He says, "Give the computer here."

Malik's eyes cloud with doubt as he realizes that the door he has meant to charge will not budge. But he remains silent, his expression stiffening. He furrows his forehead, more in confusion than anger, wondering why none of the others intervenes on his behalf.

"Why?" Malik asks, choking on his anger.

BigBeard has the astute look of a man who makes up his own rules as he goes along. Malik sees that there is no way he can force him to reverse the decision to dispossess him of his computer. He has met men like BigBeard before—brutes bullying journalists.

"Because I say so," BigBeard replies. His hands are busy in his beard, twining it; his tongue is plucking at his mustache. How Malik wishes he could strike the smirk off that face. Silence reigns. What can anyone do to forestall a crisis?

Then Gumaad asks, "What if we refuse?"

BigBeard almost achieves the impossible task of working his grin into a grimace. To Gumaad he says, "We—who is *we*? You and who else?"

Nervous, they fidget. A subtle nod from Gumaad encourages Dajaal to say, "I've always believed that the difference between your lot and the warlords from whom you took control was your sense of respect. Don't you think that our guests deserve respect?"

BigBeard is a master at taking his time. Up close, Jeebleh sees the whiskers on his cheeks twitching like those of an angry cat. He says to BigBeard, "Can we see some identification, please? That is what the young people are saying." He speaks with the politeness of someone needing not to lose both the battle to keep the computer and the war to recover it, if it is confiscated. There is no defeat in his eyes, only mild defiance.

With the desert sand no longer audible in his voice, BigBeard says to Jeebleh, "I represent the authority of the Courts. To date, the Courts have not supplied us with identity cards. We work as volunteers. Therefore, you have to trust me on this. I advise you to cooperate for the good of all."

Jeebleh says, "What if he refuses?"

BigBeard puts his hands in his pockets and knits his eyebrows together in the gesture of someone entertaining an unpleasant memory. At BigBeard's command, four armed youths emerge out of a cubicle to the right of where the group is standing. The youths fan out, each in a dramatic way, as if they are mimicking a movie they have seen or some jihadi documentary they have been shown. They raise their gas-operated AK-47s and, standing with their feet apart, push the selector switches to automatic: they are ready to shoot, if provoked or ordered by BigBeard to do so. But just at this least likely moment, BigBeard volunteers his name. "I am Abu Cumar bin Cafaan," he says, and he repeats that he is charged with ensuring that no objectionable computer software or pornographic material is imported into the country, in breach of the Islamic code of conduct.

Malik grudgingly hands over his computer.

Gumaad says to Malik, "Go in with him and type in your passwords so he can have access."

"There is no need," BigBeard says.

"No need?"

BigBeard says, "I should disabuse you of the view that just because we bear Muslim names from the days of the Prophet, may Allah bless him, and do not answer to Johnny, Billy, or Teddy, we'll have difficulty accessing a computer without a password. We are not as backward as you may think."

Dajaal says to Malik, "Give it to him and fear not what he might or might not do. We know how to deal with his kind."

Malik sits racked with despair.

BigBeard says, "Dajaal and I—fancy bearing a satanic name and being proud of it!—have known each other for a very long time. He knows what I am capable of, this ally of the devil."

As BigBeard walks away with the computer, leaving the four of them to exchange looks, none of them knowing what to say or do, Jeebleh remembers that, in Islamic mythology, Dajaal is the name for the Antichrist. Anyhow, he hopes that, as matters stand, the four of them will not blame one another for what has taken place. What Big-Beard is doing seems to have less to do with protecting against breaches in the Islamic code of conduct than with the settling of old scores with Dajaal. Malik is already comparing this latest experience with a long chain of previous encounters with the abuse of authority, from his detention by an Afghan warlord keen on Malik's companion, a female journalist, to the Congolese strongman who confiscated his car, cash, and an assortment of valuables.

Jeebleh calls, "Shall we wait?"

"I don't know how long it'll take," replies BigBeard. "I suggest you go and take a look around the city, enjoy your lunch, have a shower." Then, indicating Dajaal with his smug smile, he says to Jeebleh, "Send your driver and his sidekick to fetch your computer later."

Again, no one can think of anything to say.

AS HE DRIVES AWAY, DAJAAL REMEMBERS BIGBEARD'S CHILDHOOD epithet, "the father of all lies, an uncle to deceit." He drives fast, as though closing in on an elusive past in order to show the others what he has always seen. All he says, however, is this: "BigBeard is a man with more pseudonyms than anyone else I've ever known."

Dajaal is a military man; he speaks sparingly and is not given to emotional outbursts. He is cautious, concerned that his actions do not harm either Malik or Jeebleh. He and BigBeard go back a long way. He knows BigBeard and his family members for what they are: a self-destructive lot, the less said about them, the better for all. He is relieved that Malik and Jeebleh do not press him to speak.

Jeebleh sits in back with Malik now, but Malik won't respond to his solicitude. Jeebleh thinks how different people behave when their pride is hurt. Some sulk and withdraw into themselves, while others become jumpy, lose their cool. Where small sorrows make one incautious, Jeebleh reckons, big sorrows may render one tongue-tied. Malik is now entertaining a thoroughbred sullenness, neither looking in Jeebleh's direction nor talking. He doesn't even seem to be listening to

Gumaad, who, emboldened by the others' silence, blabbers away so excitedly no one can follow what he is saying. Mercifully, Malik hasn't said anything that he may later regret.

Unable to engage Malik, Jeebleh looks out of the window, sickened by the despoliation years of civil war have wrought on the city—as would be anyone who knew the metropolis in its "pearl of the Indian Ocean" days. The square mile of downtown, where at any one of five movie houses he watched Italian films in the original and other foreign films in their subtitled or dubbed versions, is utterly disfigured, and the historical districts are demolished. He thinks, There is no hurt worse than the hurt you cannot fully describe.

Malik, meanwhile, is replaying in his head a scene from David Lean's *Lawrence of Arabia*, which he saw recently on DVD. He is recalling in particular the harrowed look on Peter O'Toole's face when he emerges from the interrogation room, where he has undergone such suffering at the hands of his torturers. From then on, Lawrence is a changed man. Malik reminds himself that to be effective in his profession, he must not give in to personal anger. He must concentrate on boning up on everything Somali as speedily as possible, so that he can start writing about the place knowledgeably and without prejudice.

Jammed up against the side of the car, as far away from Jeebleh as he can get in the confined space, Malik looks past Jeebleh at the ravaged streets of the metropolis. Something in the shape of anger-as-madness sticks in Malik's gullet every time he visits a country in the throes of civil strife; but what makes this time unbearably hard to take is that this is his father's country, a land of which his father has seldom spoken with affection.

Both his parents were children of the British Empire, an offshoot of what Lawrence of Arabia had in mind to put together. His paternal grandfather, a Somali, worked as an interpreter and an accountant with his maternal grandfather, a Malay Chinese who'd been recruited to serve in Aden. Their children were schooled together, fell in love with each other, and married. Malik is of the view that perhaps an empire of a different thrust is now at work in Somalia. The Muslim world, from what he can tell, is at a crossroads, where several competing tendencies meet. One path is a burgeoning *umma*, a community of the faithful as conceived in the minds of Islamists who see themselves in deadly rivalry with both moderate or secularist Muslims and people of other faiths. The way Malik sees it, Somali religionists of radical persuasion are provoking a confrontation with the Ethiopian empire in hopes of pitting the Muslim world against Christian-led Ethiopia, even though Ethiopia, being militarily stronger and an ally of the United States, is very likely to gain the upper hand in the face-off. Elsewhere in Southeast Asia, India and Pakistan, two nations with nuclear potential, are locking horns. With Afghanistan turned into a theater and Chechnya haplessly caught in the fray, several countries' political and territorial concerns converge at oblique angles. And of course there is the never-ending conflict between the Arabs and the Israelis, which puts a large segment of the Muslim world in opposition to the Jewish state and the United States. Empires are no longer won by the musket, as that old imperialist Kipling argued Britain had done. An empire is won by those with the wherewithal to hold it, to subjugate it. Malik doubts very much that Shabaab can win a war, let alone, having won it, hold on to the conquered territories.

By now, Malik's dejection has spread inside the vehicle, like a contagion for which no one has a cure. Dajaal drives on; the car moves as though on autopilot. Gumaad appears troubled as he tries to get in touch with "someone" big in the Courts hierarchy to intercede with BigBeard. Each time, the line is busy (with optimism he lets everyone know), or it rings and rings and no one picks up (which he does not bother to tell them).

Jeebleh notes the absence of youths with weapons roaming the streets, or armed clan-based militiamen high on drugs, intent on threatening the lives of those who refuse to do their bidding. Since his 1996 visit, most of the youths have grown beards and donned those white robes, save for the odd youth in military fatigues or an ill-matched uniform assembled from various post-collapse loyalties. The general collapse is still the same, though; houses with their insides caved in, with a Lego-like look to them, the floor below or the one above entirely missing.

The great tragedy about civil wars, famines, and other disasters in the world's poor regions, he thinks, is that the rubble seldom divulges the secret sorrows it contains. The technology, the forensics to determine what is what, scientifically, is not available; the dead are rarely identified or exhumed. Often no one knows how many have perished in the mudslide or the tsunami. One never gets to hear the last words that passed their lips, or what, in the end, caused their death: a falling beam, a failing heart, a spear of bullet-shattered glass? Or sheer exhaustion with living in such horrid circumstances day in and day out?

Jeebleh cannot tell where they are in relation to the apartment, disoriented by fresh ruins from the latest confrontation between the warlords and the Courts, three months ago. One loses one's sense of direction in a city that has suffered civil war savageries; one is, at the best of times, in want of the guidance of those who have continued to live in it. Hoping to help Malik get the hang of the city's layout, he asks, "Where is Cambara's current home in relation to the apartment?"

Dajaal explains, "The Green Line marking off the territory between the two warlords is gone. But more roads have fallen into disuse and worse."

Malik says to Gumaad, "How do ordinary people with no cars move around? How is the transport here compared to other African cities?"

"I've never been outside Somalia."

"How do you move about?"

"There are ten-, fifteen-seater city hoppers-on. You flag them down and jump on, and pay your fare."

"Are they safe to take?"

"That is how I came to the airport, on a fifteen-seater minibus," Gumaad says. "I took it from close to where I live in Yaqshid, and then I took another from Makkal-Mukarramah Road to the airport. I had to wait long for the minibus that brought me to the airport, because the driver parked at a strategic spot and waited until there were enough passengers to make it worth his while to come. On the whole, there is peace, imposed through the Courts' goodwill. And taking the bus is safe."

Dajaal says, "The peace imposed needs a government to make it last, a government to provide the city and its one and a half million inhabitants with social services: schools, hospitals, and so on. I doubt the Courts have the experience, the willingness, and the wherewithal to provide us with these."

"Given time, the Courts will," Gumaad says.

Dajaal says, "With all the infighting, the clan-based rivalry, and the corruption among top cadres, the Courts are in no position to make peace work."

Gumaad explains how bad blood between various parties in the country has caused so many deaths and so much havoc. Dajaal and BigBeard, for example, have been enemies going back to when their families were neighbors and the two of them were young. "It's mutual loathing born out of personal jealousies," he maintains, then elaborates, "Dajaal here proved to be the more successful one, in every venture, while BigBeard's efforts usually met with disaster. Dajaal did well professionally, he was a major in the army and raised a loving family and was blessed with a boy and a girl, both of whom had their own children. BigBeard has married five times, no children; and until recently, he was not doing well financially."

"Yet he gives himself such airs," says Jeebleh.

"A self-assured man wears no airs," Dajaal says.

Gumaad goes on, "It is a well-known fact that BigBeard has lately targeted Bile, accusing him of living with Cambara in sin, to some an indictable offense, punishable by public stoning."

Cambara had alluded to a religionist who was fixated on her co-habitation with Bile when she and Jeebleh spoke on the phone the previous week; but she gave no name. Now Jeebleh realizes he's let himself be taken in by the hype about the Courts in general circulation among Somalis in the diaspora, who want to believe that the country has begun to turn a corner. It's been his folly to invest his trust in them. He reminds himself that the dodgiest words to pass the lips of a politi-cian are his affirmations of faith in God.

Dajaal slows down and turns left into a parking lot that Jeebleh remembers from earlier days. Dajaal and Gumaad help carry the bags up the stairs and into the flat.

———

There is something charming about the mess in the apartment, as if someone, with knowing chutzpah, has scattered books everywhere, making them appear to have fallen the way the petals of a geranium fall to the ground. Books—in a plethora of tongues and genres, about a miscellany of subjects—lie by the entrance into the apartment and sit orderly in the kitchen, spines showing. Books stand every which way in a metal rack; at the foot of the dining table; and in the toilet, on a low side table. Cleaned, dusted, the books are a great welcome to a professor of Italian literature and his journalist son-in-law. There is a TV set, too; from the wires showing, it looks to get cable as well.

There are flowers in vases and new curtains, and the rooms have been aired, the beds turned down—details that point to the delicate touch of a woman. In the bedrooms, there are hand towels, soaps, fly-swatters, and mosquito nets, along with notes of welcome from Cambara and Bile, saying among other things, "We wish you were staying with us, and maybe you will—eventually. We'll see."

"Wow, so many books," says Gumaad, who from the looks of him may never have read a book from cover to cover, and is amused at the excitement they have produced in the visitors, like children in a toy shop. He looks from Jeebleh to Malik, and then at the apartment, adding, "I've never known a place like this."

Dajaal insists on pointing out where things are, like a hotel bellhop. Here is the soap; here are the towels. The security system includes a metal plate huge as a door: you lock it from the inside when you are in and use the burglar bars on the windows and the one on the door when out. Jeebleh shows them how to work these contraptions, explains which metal extension is meant for which hole. He tells them how best to engage the locks in haste, in the event of an unexpected danger. "Securing the place is very important. You must be prepared at all times. Mogadiscio is a dangerous place, but you can make it less so. Please keep that in mind."

Lately, the apartment has been unoccupied. Bile has moved in with Cambara. Raasta, Bile's niece—a friend to peace, who liked to say that "in a civil war, there is continuous fighting, because of grievances that are forever changing"—and simple Makka—"who smiled, crying, and cried, laughing"—are now grown and in Dublin. They are attending university and remedial school, respectively, under the eye of Bile and Jeebleh's friend Seamus, who is spending more time in Ireland in order to be close to his bedridden mother. Jeebleh hopes to see them all there shortly, after he has helped Malik to settle in and hopefully helped to find the missing Taxliil.

Dajaal leads Malik and Jeebleh to the kitchen. He opens the fridge and points out the pantry, where the tinned foods are. Then he runs them through the mobile phones, which have local SIM cards, with prepaid airtime, as U.S. mobile phones are not compatible with those available here. He dials his number on each, to register it in electronic memory so that they may call him whenever they wish to do so. Then he makes sure that Bile's and Cambara's coordinates are there as well. Satisfied, he gives each of them a mobile phone, ready for use.

They all end up in a room with a sea view—it was Seamus's for much of the time he was in the country, and later it served as Bile's. Jeebleh offers it to Malik. Out of deference to his father-in-law, Malik declines, since Jeebleh is going to be in Mogadiscio for only a few days, but Jeebleh won't hear of it. "I want you to have the best there is in this city, my dearest Malik," he says, and they hug and touch cheeks.

From there, they go to Bile's former room, which will become Jeebleh's. Malik is looking more relaxed, realizing perhaps that he has been caught in the crosscurrents of a century-old quarrel between Dajaal's family and BigBeard's, and has simply stepped into a counterpunch. And since no one has said anything to cause a conflagration, there are no flames to douse. There is truth in the saying that the hearts of fools are in their mouths.

Malik wants to be alone in the room with the sea view. Jeebleh knows how keen he is on ritual. He wishes to get to know his room better in order to domesticate it, a concept that will barely make sense to a Somali pastoralist. Once, on a family trip, Malik refused to unpack his clothes until he had communed with his room's vital force and exorcised it of its past demons. Maybe communal and personal superstitions come to the fore and dominate when one is confronted with the foreignness of a place. Jeebleh understands this as the superstition of a man thrown into the deep end of a conflict, who has to consider every aspect of his surroundings. To get the others out of the room, he offers to make tea, and they leave Malik to his rituals.

As Jeebleh makes tea, Gumaad rattles on nervously over the telephone to a friend of his, and Dajaal silently plots his next move. Jeebleh hopes that when Malik reemerges, he will be in his element. One might consider today's incident as a rite of passage, even if Jeebleh cannot bring himself to say it. The thing is: How well does he know Malik? Does one ever have intimate knowledge of in-laws, with whom one is by nature formal?

Suddenly, Dajaal says to Gumaad, "Let's go."

Dajaal speaks like a man who has lit on a bright idea, on which he must act instantly. He won't hear Jeebleh's suggestion or Gumaad's appeal to stay for their tea, which is almost ready.

"What's the hurry?" Gumaad asks.

Dajaal says, "Tea later. Now we pick up the computer."

Gumaad is insistent. "What's the rush?"

"Have you ever heard of the proverb that asserts that where water recedes, crocodiles proliferate?" Dajaal asks.

Gumaad challenges. "What's your point?"

But Dajaal is at the door, waiting, and then out of it as soon as Gumaad joins him.

———

Alone, Jeebleh drinks his tea, and thinks back to the days when the former dictator ran the country, and when censorship was at its severest; when telephone tapping was common; when one handed over his passport to the immigration officer at the airport on returning from abroad and was expected to collect it from the Ministry of the Interior a week later. There is nothing new, is there? The present situation is nothing but dictatorship by another name. He leafs through an illustrated picture book of ancient Mogadiscio, thinking that Somalis, long familiar with dictatorships of socialist vintage, are now getting accustomed to a brand of religionist authoritarianism. But the imposition of will by religious fiat is still the imposition of will.

Jeebleh also worryingly remembers reading about the target assassination of several former army officers, peace activists killed at home

late at night in full view of their wives and children, intellectuals eliminated, allegedly, by Shabaab operatives, who saw them as threats to
their Taliban-inspired interpretation of Islam.

Dajaal telephones Jeebleh to inform him that they have picked up
the computer, no problem, and they are on their way back. Jeebleh
inquires whether BigBeard or one of his minions has bothered to explain what they have done to the computer, and if by any chance they
deleted files or found material of a pornographic nature and removed
it. Dajaal says, "He has deleted several files that were not complimen-
tary about the Courts and the photo of a nude girl serving as a screen
saver."

It rankles Jeebleh that BigBeard has deemed the photograph of his
one-year-old granddaughter, soaped and naked as she stands in a bath-
tub, "pornographic." It goes to show how much energy religionists of
the parochial variety squander on matters of little or no significance.

Malik joins him in the kitchen, refreshed and ready to take on the
world, Jeebleh thinks. He informs Malik that Dajaal has retrieved the
computer and is on his way back. When Malik asks for details, Jeebleh
tells him that some of the files have been deleted, because they have
been found to be uncomplimentary to the Courts.

"Is anything else deleted?" Malik wants to know.

Jeebleh tells him about the photo.

Malik says nothing. Jeebleh feels the sense of stress spreading, with
Malik biting his lower lip, too angry to speak. Jeebleh thinks how
stresses produce inexplicable results and he wonders how the stresses
they are all under, the strain that is bound to invade them—Malik, Ahl,
and himself—will affect them. What will they be like when they crack
up? What will Malik be like when the nervous tension makes him go
to pieces? He watches with worry as Malik steps away and stands
before the mirror on the wall in the living room and takes a good look
at his reflection. Jeebleh senses that even to himself Malik must look

older in a matter of moments, rugged and more wrinkled, his face careworn.

Dajaal returns alone and gives the computer without further explanation to Malik. Malik handles it with care the way a mother handles a sick child who is asleep. He takes it to the table in his future workroom off the kitchen, without bothering to open it.

Jeebleh asks, "Where is Gumaad?"

"He took public transport," Dajaal replies.

Jeebleh's mobile phone rings. It is Cambara, saying, "Where are you all? Bile and I are waiting, and the lunch is getting cold."

"We're coming," Jeebleh assures her.

AHLULKHAIR, KNOWN TO FAMILY AND CLOSE FRIENDS AS AHL, OLDER brother to Malik and the director of a Minneapolis-based center tasked with researching matters Somali, calls in sick, the first time he has done so in his long career as an educator. The truth is, the growing trend among Somali youths to join the self-declared religionist radical fringe, Shabaab, has thrown him off balance. Taxliil, his stepson, has now been gone more than six months, and is suspected to be somewhere in Somalia. In an earlier rumor, the runaway youth was seen in Kismayo, a coastal city that is in the hands of Shabaab and deemed too dangerous to visit. He was said to be training as a suicide bomber. But more recently they have heard, relayed to Ahl's wife, Yusur, via her close friend Xalan, whose husband, Warsame, received it from a man in the Puntland Intelligence Service, that Taxliil, along with a couple of Shabaab-trained diehards, is headed for Bosaso. Warsame and Xalan live in Bosaso and have offered to host Ahl when he arrives in the region in a few days, in search of Taxliil. Nobody is sure of the whereabouts of the other twenty or so Somali-American youths who have vanished from their homes (in various parts of the United States, but principally from Minnesota), but the rumor that Taxliil has been dispatched to Puntland, hurriedly promoted to the assignment of liaising with the pirates in a bid to build a bridge between them and Shabaab, is gaining plausibility. Taxliil is said to have served twice as an interpreter to a delegation from the Courts, to help them to communicate with hostages, some of them Muslim, held by Somali pirates.

Ahl's whole body has lately been out of kilter, so unbalanced that on occasion he has been incapable of coordinating the simplest physical demands. A month ago, he woke up just before dawn from a deep sleep, and, needing very badly to pee, sat up, ready to do just that. Only he never got to the bathroom; he wet himself, like a baby.

Malik and Jeebleh vowed to ask around about Taxliil when they reached Somalia, attempting to trace his movements in the country, but Ahl knew he must go to Puntland himself. Of course, there is no guarantee that Taxliil is in Puntland, or that any of them—Ahl, Malik, or Jeebleh—will locate him. Or that even if they do so, the young fellow will be willing to return with them to Minneapolis.

It is no easy matter preparing for a trip to Somalia these days. The country has been in the throes of unending violence for the past two decades. Moreover, Ahl and Malik, born and raised in Aden, were brought up to think of Somalia as their father's land—and even the old man himself never knew or visited the place. Even so, he made sure his sons spoke the language from childhood. Although the country is unfamiliar, Somalia's troubles haven't been very far from their minds.

In preparation for his visit, Ahl has taken the required vaccinations and has begun ingesting his weekly malaria tablets. He has also been collecting as much information as he can on Puntland, poring over maps and consulting others on what to do, where to go, and whom to contact. He has been in touch with Xalan, whom his wife, Yusur has known since childhood. Ahl knows from her that Xalan's nephew Ahmed-Rashid, her older sister Zaituun's son, has been missing for more than a year from Columbus, Ohio, vanished during his first year at a community college there. But because Zaituun, the boy's mother, doesn't seem bothered about his disappearance, Xalan and Warsame and the rest of the family act as if they are not worried, either. Perhaps this has something to do with the bad blood that exists between the two sisters, Xalan and Zaituun, although they both live in Bosaso. At any rate, Yusur has assured him, it won't affect his rapport with Xalan.

Ahl has trusted this and given the dates of his visit to Xalan in the hope that, with her husband's help, she will set in motion security arrangements for him. He prefers putting up in a hotel to staying with her and her husband for the first couple of days, if only to get an initial take on the place and a grip on his own priorities. He has his round-trip ticket to Bosaso via Paris and Djibouti. Xalan has offered to have Warsame pick him up from the airport and has confirmed that she has booked a room for him in a hotel.

Sitting with a book about Puntland open before him, Ahl has his cell phone by his side, willing it to ring; the landline is also within his reach. He is anxious to hear from Malik, who will have just landed in Mogadiscio. He wants to know if everything has gone according to plan. The night before, with Yusur on night shift, he stayed up late watching Al Jazeera, the BBC World Service, and CNN; and supplementing the information gleaned from these sources by reading American and European newspapers online. He wants to know the latest about the impending Ethiopian invasion of Somalia.

The phone rings: Yusur asks if he has heard from Malik. When he replies that Malik hasn't called, she lets out a whimper. Ahl reminds himself that he must remain strong for everyone's sake. His wife has a way of pulling him down with her to a point so low that there is noth-

ing but despair. Since her son left, she has been prone to long bouts
of depression; at times, she has found it difficult to hold down her
nursing job at a hospital. Of late she has been working night shifts at
an old people's home, and she seldom comes home even during the
day. There is always something to do at an old people's home, especially for a mother desperately mourning her missing son.

When Ahl arrived in the Twin Cities in the mid-1980s, there was only
one other Somali in town, a delectable young woman studying art. He
had been recruited from the UK, where he had taken his Ph.D. in
linguistics at the School of Oriental and African Studies at the University of London, to teach in the Education Department at the
University of Minnesota. He bought an apartment in downtown St.
Paul large enough to host Malik two or three times a year, between
assignments for the Singapore-based daily in which he published his
syndicated pieces. The two brothers set themselves apart from their
birth communities, hardly socializing with the Yemenis with whom
they had grown up in Aden, or with the new influx of Somalis with
whom they shared a loose-knit communality. Later, when Minnesota
became inundated with Somalis because the then governor offered
them better facilities than they could have enjoyed in San Diego,
Nashville, or other places where they had initially been concentrated,
the two brothers communicated in whichever language would exclude
those they did not wish to understand them: Somali when among
Arabs, Chinese when among Somalis, and English with each other and
when they wanted to be understood.

Malik made a name for himself as a foreign correspondent. Their
mother went back to Malaysia to look after her own aging parents,
and their father to Somalia, his ancestral land, where, bizarrely, he

melted into the rangelands of the north, tending hundreds of camels he had bought with the help of herdsmen in his employ. Their old man went totally native, as Malik liked to say, and married a woman in her late teens to produce additional offspring, in hope of making sure that his bloodline would not die out, a responsibility he no longer trusted either of his sons could fulfill.

Though neither had regular contact with either parent, the brothers went out of their way to keep each other abreast of one another's whereabouts, troubles, endeavors, and successes. Occasionally, Malik would disappear from view for months, covering some terrible war unfolding in yet another wretched, remote country. Then he would be back, exhausted from travel and needing Ahl to listen to his adventures and to read the pieces he had written. A run of intelligent women had fallen for him, and he'd had brief affairs with many of them.

Ahl was the first to marry. He met Yusur, a Somali woman seven years his junior, at a refresher course in public health meant for Somalis newly arrived in Minneapolis. He had given a lecture on teaching Somali grammar to non-native speakers of the tongue. He and Yusur struck a heartfelt amity immediately when they talked but maintained a deferential distance for quite some time, knowing that no closeness between them was possible. She was separated from her husband and lived alone with her infant son. Her marriage was troubled—she had an unemployed husband who passed his days chewing qaat with his likewise jobless mates. To a man, they received welfare benefits and, when possible, sponged off their wives. Yusur worked and attended classes part-time and so had to hire a babysitter. Not only was this expensive, but her husband's bad behavior reached new depths when he was arrested for sexually assaulting the babysitter.

Yusur's in-laws were furious when she declined to pay the lawyer who had been hired in an attempt to have the charge reduced from rape to aggravated assault. And when her husband was finally released and she wouldn't have him back, her in-laws made physical threats against her. In the end, his family, fearing he would continue to be a blight to their name, sent him off to Detroit to cool his heels and then helped him move to Toronto, where he submitted his papers as a freshly arrived Somali by virtue of a slight change to the order of his names.

Yusur and Ahl saw each other discreetly for a long time before becoming man and wife. Their wedding was private, known only to Malik and his parents. Their mother graced the occasion with her presence, but their father merely sent a terse telegram from Hargeisa: "You have my blessings."

The boy, Taxliil, and Ahl developed a father-son rapport, and while he didn't use the word, Taxliil behaved as though Ahl were his father. Ahl, in turn, made sure Taxliil was not lacking for anything. For most Somali children in the diaspora, he was aware, life was a chore: punishments at home; humiliation at school; mothers not assisted with the children, fathers seldom involved in raising their offspring. In many homes, relatives came and went from Somalia, bearing horror stories about what was happening in their country. The phones would ring at two, three, or four in the morning, the caller needing money to pay the burial expenses of a clansman killed in an intermilitia skirmish back home. With all the turmoil and the constant noise of the television, youngsters often lacked the will, the peace of mind, and the time to do their schoolwork.

But this was not the case in the home where Taxliil grew up, thanks to Ahl. The three of them lived as a nuclear family: a man, a woman, and a child, with Uncle Malik occasionally visiting, an ideal model, one would have thought, for a boy growing up. There was order and abundant love in the household. Ahl made time to supervise Taxliil's homework. Twice a week, Taxliil went to the neighborhood mosque to receive religious instruction from a Somali teacher with rudimentary Arabic, and often Ahl would subtly set Taxliil right without pointing out the teacher's failings.

On his first day of secondary school, Taxliil met a green-eyed Kurdish boy, Samir. The two became inseparable. They played sports and computer games together; swapped clothes; swam and took long walks on weekends. They spurred each other to achieve their ambitions. Neither admitted to knowing what the word *impossible* meant. Doing well wasn't good enough; they did better than anyone else.

One summer vacation, Samir flew out to Baghdad with his father to visit Iraq for the first time since the American takeover. He was sitting in the back of the car with his grandparents, his father in the front next to the driver, Samir's uncle, when an American Marine flagged them down at a checkpoint. Samir alighted speedily and waited by the roadside, away from the vehicle, as instructed. His father helped Grandma in regaining possession of her walker and held his hand out to her as she shakily stepped out of the vehicle. Meanwhile, his uncle bent down to assist Grandpa, who was still in the car, in retrieving his cane, and he took a long time, half his body hidden from view. Panicking that one of the two men would shoot him, the young Marine opened fire, killing everyone except Samir.

Back in the Twin Cities, Samir became morose. The two friends still spent time together, but their life lacked the fun and ambition they had previously shared. Then Samir began to speak of attending to his "religious responsibilities," and shortly thereafter he vanished from sight. A month or so later, his photo appeared in the *Star Tribune*, the caption reading: "Local boy turns Baghdad suicide bomber."

The FBI came early the next morning and descended with unnecessary force on Taxliil, Ahl, and Yusur, as if they had detonated the bomb that caused the death of the soldiers. They were taken in separate vehicles and fingerprinted, their histories together and separately gone

over again and again. Taxliil was made to endure longer hours of interrogation, with repeated threats. The FBI showed keen interest in Ahl
as well, because of his birthplace and because he, Yusur, and Taxliil
now lived in a house close to potential escape routes along the Missis-
sippi. An FBI officer accused him of being a talent spotter for radical
groups in the Muslim world.

The officers cast Yusur in the role of witness. They handled her with
kindness, in light of her history. In their narrative, she had gone from
a rapist to a man with a history of subversive tendencies, the older
brother of a journalist able to tap into jihadi resources because of his
connections. The officer asked Yusur if Ahl was likely to recruit Taxliil
as a suicide bomber. They suggested she get it off her chest; they were
her friends, and they meant her well. Who were *his* friends? Whom
did he contact, and how did he do it?

Eventually, all three were released by the FBI. Even so, they were
told to inform the agency of any suspicious activities. If they failed to
do so, they would be reclassified.

———

Ahl sits with his mobile phone close by, yet it does not ring. He thinks
that misfortune has followed the Somalis who fled their warring homeland; braved the seas; and put up with rape, daily harassment, corruption, and abuse. Just when they were on safe ground, they turned on
themselves, with their young setting up armed gangs, as if they were
out to prove that they could be better at cruelty than their elders.
Somali-on-Somali violence in the Twin Cities rivaled Somali-on-Somali
violence in their civil war–torn homeland.

The next time misfortune called, Taxliil was ready to follow. It took
him back to Somalia, his route an enigma, the source of the funds that
paid for his air ticket a mystery, his handlers a puzzle, the talent spot-
ters who recruited him a riddle. When Ahl decided that he would go

to Somalia, Yusur asked him why he would risk his own life in pursuit of the hopeless case of a young boy who had disappeared to God knows where. Ahl replied that he wished to reduce the number of unknown factors. He added, "I do not want to regret later that I did not go in search of our son. Taking the risk is the least I can do."

News arriving from Somalia is often no more than hearsay bolstered by scuttlebutt, fueled by rumor. Essentially this is what Ahl and Yusur have come to learn: Taxliil has joined the volunteer Somali youth brigade, recruited from within Somali communities in the diaspora and earmarked to train as jihadis. Ahl shakes at the thought that an innocent Taxliil, misled by an imam on whom he modeled his life, might come to harm. He doesn't know what would become of him and Yusur if something terrible were to happen to Taxliil.

When he has waited long enough and Malik has still not rung, he heads toward the Baraka Mall, to get additional phone numbers in Bosaso from a relative of Yusur's who owns a stall there. As soon as he gets out of his car, his gaze meets the stare of one of Taxliil's uncles, who rudely turns his back on him without so much as a smile or greeting. That the man does not bother to ask if there is news of his nephew disturbs Ahl. He probably wouldn't tell the man much; certainly not that he is off to Somalia in search of the runaway boy. Ahl is aware that Yusur's former in-laws blame them for what has happened, given that he and Yusur have had custody of Taxliil. He walks away downcast, then looks up at the sign that reads, WELCOME TO BARAKA MALL. He reads it softly in English, and then loudly in Somali.

The Somali mall in the Twin Cities has been open for a number of years. It was the idea of a Pakistani émigré who bought it dirt cheap when it was an abandoned auto repair shop, and subdivided it into ten-by-ten-meter shops and six-by-eight kiosks. He rented these out to Somalis who needed to establish businesses to supplement their families' meager incomes from the welfare department. The scheme worked to the Bangladeshi's advantage and he was able to recoup his investment. Ahl can't tell if the contention that he levies rents higher than market rate is true or just loose-lipped Somali talk, but clearly the venture has been successful.

In the warren of narrow passageways, Somali merchants sell clothes and memorabilia from Somalia, and goods imported mainly but not exclusively from the Arabian Gulf and the Indian subcontinent. Somalis, with no English or qualification in any profession, and no possibility of finding other work, have set up these stalls and opened restaurants, barbershops, music shops, and outlets for DVDs in Somali. This all-Somali mall has created a symbiosis, with many Somalis coming to exchange news about their country. The Somalis in charge of running the mall have agreed not to show TV news such as CNN or BBC, fearing this might cause flare-ups; they play only sports channels.

Ahl walks through the narrow hallway, bright with fluorescent lights. He passes a travel agency, a fabric store, and stalls specializing in jewelry imported from the Gulf. A large shop with metal bars in front of it promises to transfer your money into the recipient's hands anywhere in Somalia in less than twenty-four hours.

Up the steps to the first floor, two more shops down a shorter corridor, and Ahl enters a shop. The owner is on the phone, talking loudly—Somalis have the habit of speaking at deafening levels when they are making long-distance phone calls, as if the greater the distance their voices have to travel, the higher the volume must be. Every passerby stops and stares and then continues walking, many shaking their heads, even though they, too, shout just as animatedly as this man when they make long-distance calls.

As Ahl waits, the man's voice grows louder by the second, then suddenly he disconnects, and is quiet. He turns to Ahl, greets him warmly, and then opens a drawer and brings out a piece of paper with phone numbers written on it. The man's lips move, like a child practicing the spelling of a new word, and then he says, employing his normal voice, "Here they are, the numbers you wanted."

Ahl nods. "Thanks."

"I've just spoken to Warsame," says Ninety-Decibels. "All is well, as promised."

Ahl is relieved that Ninety-Decibels does not confuse him by naming the names of Yusur's relatives, whom he is expected to know but doesn't; he has no desire to get mixed up with the local politics, if he can help it, and he won't do so, unless the situation demands it. Staring at the names on the piece of paper torn from a child's exercise book, Ahl is aware that he is encountering a catalog of relationships entangled through blood, marriage, or both. This is where his upbringing in an insulated nuclear family fails him. To operate well in Somalia, one memorizes and makes active use, on a daily basis, of a multitude of details having to do with who is who in relation to whom. Most Somali speakers can't help but mention the clan names of everyone they talk about, and so he is often left utterly confused.

Ninety-Decibels continues, "Xalan and Warsame have been informed about your arrival, and one or both of them will meet your flight in Bosaso. They will take you to your hotel."

Ninety-Decibels's phone rings, and he answers it. To Ahl's surprise, though, Ninety-Decibels lowers the timbre of his voice to forty decibels. Ahl assumes the man must be speaking to someone local, maybe next door. When he hangs up, Ninety-Decibels asks, "Will you be looking for Taxliil?"

Ahl hesitates visibly, but says with a straight face, "We have no idea where he is."

"You say no news yet from your son?"

"We wait and hope," Ahl says.

When the phone rings and Ninety-Decibels's timbre escalates to 150 decibels, Ahl decides it is time to leave. As he departs, he mouths, "Thank you."

DHOORRE, WEARING A DRESSING GOWN AND, UNDER IT, A PAIR OF pajamas and slippers, shifts in the discomfort of his sleep on the garden bench. Then he awakens in a startle, badly in need of a pee.

It takes him a while to remember that he came out to the porch to take a closer, admiring look at a gorgeous bird with an immense beak and colorful plumage. Then a gust of wind shut the door and he couldn't get back in. The bird gone, he walked around the unkempt garden, where the trees, their bark like peeled-off skin, and the shrubs are emaciated from neglect. He feared he might come up against city riffraff camping out here, or someone fleeing the fighting, which has lately been ferocious. Property, after all, does not mean what it used to mean. He knows what he is talking about, he owned several houses, some of which were rented out. He was once an important man in Mogadiscio himself. Today he is a man without property, living in a house that his son himself is renting.

With no book to read and no one to talk to, he fell asleep on the garden bench. Now his bones are sore and the sciatica in his legs is extreme. He remembers he was having a sweet dream, in which he and a childhood friend were watching one of his favorite Italian movies, Vittorio De Sica's *Shoeshine*. He recalls the mesmerizing beauty of the camera work as it captured the two boys riding a horse through Rome. Two boys living in innocence until tragedy strikes. There is no innocence in this city. After all, every resident of this city is guilty, even if no one admits to being a culprit.

He gets up, yawns leisurely, stretching first his arms, then his legs until he feels he has overdone the stretching. For a man his age, he is blessed with a sharp mind, but his body is bent as the young branch of a eucalyptus tree. He feels the belt of his dressing gown loosening; in an instant, he'll feel exposed. Not that it matters—he presumes he is alone and his son, his daughter-in-law, his brood of grandchildren, and the maid are all out. It will amuse them to find him in the garden, unshaven, unwashed, in his pajamas and his dressing gown.

Suddenly his heart beats faster; he hears sounds from inside the house and realizes that this can only mean danger. He debates what he should do. He is on the verge of walking around the house to find out if there is a way of entering through a back window, when the front door opens. Out comes a young thing bearing a gun bigger than himself. The old man and the boy with the gun size each other up. Dhoorre thinks, What if he reacts as if the boy is holding a toy gun? What if he tells himself, even though this may not be the case, that the young thing does not know how to shoot and can't pose much of a threat?

He asks, "What have you been doing inside?" He speaks the way one might to a mischievous grandchild.

The boy says, "What are you doing outside?"

Looking at the two of them and listening to them, you would not be able to tell who is the guest and who is the host—the boy standing guard at the entrance to the house or the old man, befuddled and amused. Befuddled, because he can't figure out what to do; amused, because he can't imagine such a young thing frightening him. However, there is uncertainty in Dhoorre's demeanor when the boy says, "Answer my question."

Dhoorre tells himself that the boy is putting on a brave face, because he has a gun and this endows him with the hollow bravado of a coward. Is the boy the type who will beg for mercy when things turn nasty?

Hardness enters the boy's voice. "Answer before I lose my patience, old man. What are you doing outside, in near rags, in the garden?"

Dhoorre replies, "The wind locked me out, pushing the door shut behind me when I came out to enjoy a bit of fresh air outside, in the garden, and I couldn't get back in, so I napped on the bench. There." He points at the bench, his voice laced with a genuine tremor.

The boy is thinking, What if he is wrong about the old man, whom he first imagined to be a drifter with nothing more than the rags he has been lent by a kinsman? A typical tramp, come off the streets without his begging bowl, maneuvering his way in.

"The wind, eh?"

"That's right, the wind."

The boy is not convinced.

"And your clothes, where are your clothes?"

"Inside."

YoungThing considers his next move, and the implications if it does turn out that the Old Man lives in the house. He stares at the man, wondering how he can make him disappear before the advance team arrives. He could act like a trained insurgent—shoot first and explain later that he found this worthless hobo in the garden, insisting that he lived here. But the option of shooting the old man does not appeal to the boy. Yet how will he explain himself to the leader of the cell when he shows up?

The old man is saying, "My name is Dhoorre," and his outstretched hand waits, ready to shake the boy's. When the boy doesn't react, Dhoorre says, "At least tell me your name."

Then he takes one speedy step closer to the boy and another step closer to the door. The muscles of the boy's neck stiffen, his jaw goes taut, his whole attitude becomes more threatening. He raises his gas-operated AK-47 and presses the selector switch that turns it fully automatic. This action gives him the composure of a boxer who has just won a KO in the second round.

"I wouldn't act the fool if I were you," says the boy. "It is at your peril that you take me for a lamebrain. You make one foolish move, you are dead."

Fresh worries congregate in Dhoorre's head, where they huddle together like a clutch of poorly clad men suddenly exposed to unseasonable frost. This is the closest Dhoorre has been to danger in his seventy-plus years. His hand runs over his head, smoothing what hair there is, a head as bereft of hair as it is of new ideas. How can he bring his peace-making pleas to bear on a young mind that has known only violence? He moves nearer to the boy, no longer afraid.

"Go ahead," he says. "See if I care. Shoot."

"I won't shoot unless I have to," the boy says.

They embark on a badly choreographed, lurching dance.

"What's the matter?" challenges Dhoorre.

"One wrong move and you're dead."

In their gyrations for more favorable positions, Dhoorre now has his back to the door. All he has to do is move a step back and he'll be inside the house, the boy outside. But to what end?

"Why are you here, armed?"

"I am not authorized to tell you."

The word *authorized* coming out of such a small thing gives Dhoorre a jolt. Perhaps this is one of the boys he's heard about—the new order of youths trained for a higher cause, who, even though they receive their instructions from earthlings, ascribe their actions to divine inspiration. He has heard about boys such as this, whom Shabaab has kidnapped and then trained as suicide bombers, boys and a few girls who see themselves as martyrs beholden to high ideals. But what can this boy want? Or, rather, what can his superiors want? And why here, why him and his family? He must disabuse the boy of the notion that he, Dhoorre, harbors any resentment toward religionist ideals, it is only that he privileges dialogue, prioritizes peace.

"I am not an enemy to your cause," Dhoorre says.

Their eyes meet, the boy's glance anxious in its desire to make sense of the old man's sudden friendliness. Dhoorre's gaze takes on a more incisive shrewdness, his bearing grows more sanguine. He adds, "Tell me what you want done and I will do it."

"Just relax," says the boy. "That's all."

Dhoorre asks, "How can I relax when you haven't told me why you are here in our house, with a gun, threatening to shoot me, an old man, of the same age as your grandfather, if you have one?"

"You say our house? How many of you live here?"

"My son, his family, and I."

The exchange is interrupted by YoungThing's cell phone. He is aghast. Perhaps the advance team from the command center is already at the gate, waiting to be let in. His voice breaking, he says, "Yes, Sheikh," several times, bowing in deference to his absent commander. Dhoorre can sense an abrupt change in the boy's body language, as though he has just realized that he has made a major gaffe, maybe even disobeyed a command. From the little he can gather, the boy is being told off by the man he addresses as Sheikh.

When the call finally ends, the boy seems more agitated than before and barks orders to Dhoorre. "Follow me into the house."

When they are past the threshold, the boy says, "Go into the bathroom and bolt the door from inside. Be quick about it. And make no sound."

"What's happening?" asks Dhoorre.

"I'll do all I can do to spare your life," the boy says.

When Dhoorre goes into the bathroom, the boy bolts the door from outside, too, and then goes to welcome the men at the gate.

AHL FEELS ELATED, LIKE A MAN WHO HAS THE WORLD IN HIS sights, when he lands in Djibouti, in the Horn of Africa, forty-eight hours later. Relaxed, he walks over to the officer at Immigration to exchange brief banter with him, in Somali.

It's been a tiring journey, the longest Ahl has undertaken for quite a while. It has also been almost as taxing as when he used to fly from Europe as a student, across the entire world to visit his mother and other family members in Malaysia. But he was younger in those days, and there was a lot of excitement in planning and then executing his travels. Not so anymore, or not this time. Until his arrival in Djibouti, there has been hardly any joy in making the trip.

So far, everything has gone without a hitch. In Paris, he picked up his visa from the Djibouti consulate in time for his departure out of Orly. They hardly bothered to scrutinize his form once he started speaking in Somali, if hesitantly at first. Ahl put "tourism" where the form asked the purpose of his travel, well aware that many people do not think of Djibouti as a tourist destination. Of course, he was tempted to tell the truth: that he was on his way to the Horn of Africa in search of his missing son—there is no equivalent, in Somali, for *stepson*. Anyhow, from what he has read, Djibouti is worth a visit. Nature lovers especially are bound to admire the lunar look of the landscape, which boasts of geological wonders on a par with the best anywhere.

French was the operating language in the aircraft. In addition to a two-day-old *Le Monde*, Ahl found a copy of a day-old *Le Canard Enchaîné*, the French satirical paper, in his seat. He read the two papers, now one and now the other, since both had front-page pieces about a Panamanian-flagged, Norwegian-owned chemical tanker seized by Somali pirates in the Gulf of Aden, with the *Canard* providing more sensational copy about the seizure of the vessel and giving more inside information about the hostages' communication with their families. The 50,000-ton bulk shipper had a crew of sixty, many of them— almost two-thirds—from Korea, and the captain was Norwegian.

On a *Canard* inside page, the article claimed that the hijackers were treating the hostages well, allowing them to speak to their families once a week. From the conversation between the seamen and their families, it became clear how the pirates had captured the boat. They arrived in twelve-foot fiberglass speedboats with inboard motors, escorted by two smaller skiffs with outboard motors; a mother ship waited close by. The ship, weighed down with heavy cargo, moved slower than the small boats. The second mate had alerted the captain to the presence of the boats. But before the captain was able to organize a way of repelling the attack, a dozen armed men had gained access to the tanker before the seamen had a chance to lock themselves in. The leader of the pirates found his way to the captain's cabin, put a machine gun to the captain's forehead, and vowed to kill him unless he instructed his men to go where they were told to go and do what they were told to do. The ship was directed toward Garcad, which came within view the following day. There, the captain was allowed to make a call to the shipowners to inform them of their new situation. According to him, they wouldn't release the ship unless they were given $25 million.

Too tired to read any more, Ahl puts the newspaper away. But as he tries to sleep, he keeps thinking about the details of several other attacks—on luxury yachts, on an Israeli boat carrying chemical waste, on a huge Korean-owned tanker loaded with almost sixty tanks and other heavy weapons, destination unclear. Certainly the pirates received intelligence from an unnamed informant, who suggested that the buccaneers approach with only two skiffs and attack from the port side. No doubt the pirates would not know that the seamen keeping watch were likely to focus on the starboard side. One of the pirates would claim later that they knew the nature of the cargo as well, having received intelligence about it. He went on to say that they knew, too, that the cargo would in itself interest the world media, a shipment of weapons intended for Sudan, where it would fuel the civil war to flare between north and south.

Ahl is aware of another more recent hijacking. The Saudi-owned supertanker *Sirius Star* had been taken by a hardened lot of pirates armed with shoulder-launched antitank weapons, rocket-propelled grenades, Kalashnikovs, and other small arms. The pirates had taken the ship close to their lair, within view of Hobyo. Several men from the Courts entered the fray, claiming that the pirates would not be allowed to hold hostage a ship that belonged to a Muslim nation. According to reports received in Minneapolis, it was this delegation for whom Taxliil had acted as translator.

On another occasion, persistent rumor had it that Taxliil, whom "History" (the instructor of the unit to which he was seconded) looked upon with favor, because he had been teaching her English, was given the honor of escorting the envoys from the Courts to meet up with a delegation that had arrived in Kismayo following the capture of an

Iranian-flagged boat in Puntland. The ship moored near the ancient historical town of Eyl, along with several other ships held within view of the town. While the negotiations for the release of this ship dragged on for months, rumor spread in the town that the pirates assigned to guard it were starting to lose much of their hair and breaking out in rashes or suffering skin burns. One of the pirates spoke to the local press of exposure to radiation or heavy doses of chemical waste that the ship was carrying.

Ahl is about to fall asleep when he hears the captain announce that they will be starting their descent into Djibouti in a few minutes and that the passengers must make sure their seat belts are on.

––––––––

In his hotel room, Ahl lies on the bed, fully clothed and waiting for a local SIM card so that he can send a text message to his wife and to Malik, to let them know of his safe arrival. The air conditioner is on, and so is Al Jazeera, blaring in Arabic. As he listens, he thinks how every decade brings its own political troubles: Palestinians hijack aircraft for political reasons; the Italian Red Brigades kidnap Aldo Moro; the German Baader-Meinhof group assassinates bankers and top government officials. Just like Al Qaeda and its offshoots, of whom Shabaab claims to be one, are doing in Somalia. Despite the differences in their modus operandi, the differences in the provenance of their adherents, the use of terrorism for political gain runs through them. There was a time, in the sixties, when university-based movements engaged in agitations, albeit not as deadly. At present, entire regions are considered "terrorist territories"; entire nations are said to "host terrorism." Western commentators clued in on recent events add Islam to the equation, work it into the quandary, as if the idea to terrorize is in the Muslim's genetic makeup, forgetting that more Muslims than non-Muslims die at the hands of terrorism.

Now Ahl hears the maids in the corridor making a loud ruckus over a missing broom, nearly coming to blows over it. How he wishes Somalis in Minnesota showed the concern for their sons' disappearance that these women do about a missing broom. The Somali imams at the mosques in Minnesota responsible for the young men's disappearances go unchallenged. The feeling among Somalis is that it is a "clan thing." The curse of it, Ahl thinks. Somalis, adept at surrounding themselves with smoke screens, relish confounding issues. You are seldom able to corner them, because they know how to give you the runaround.

The phone in the room rings, reception telling him his SIM card has arrived. He collects it immediately, then sends brief messages to Yusur and Malik, giving them his Djibouti mobile number, which will be valid for only twenty-four hours. On learning that the airline offices reopen at four, he takes a nap.

In a dream of a clear quality, he meets a Somali woman unknown to him in a room in an unfamiliar city. They talk about nothing in particular for a very long time. Then they go for a walk, up a mountain, into a valley of extreme greenery, the leaves shiny, the shade of the trees delicious. To make him speak, a masseuse offers him a massage.

He wakes up, feeling rested.

In search of something to eat, Ahl walks out of the hotel and turns left. He has a cap on against the glare and the midday heat. Here the sun is very, very strong and, never weakening, bakes everything in sight, shortening one's shadow, almost obliterating it. He knows from having lived in Yemen that only after the sun has exhausted its stamina the afternoon shadows emerge.

Djibouti is a small country caught in the crosshairs of several tendencies—it shares a border with Somalia; is close to Yemen; lies along a stretch of an important waterway, the Bab el Mandeb; and exists cheek by jowl with Ethiopia and Eritrea. The eyes of the Western world are trained on it, and NATO has a prominent presence on its soil. It is a miracle that Djibouti continues to exist and fight for its corner in its own wily ways.

The country, rich in history, replenishes Ahl's sense of nostalgia, and he walks with the slowness of a hippo after a fight, taking in Djibouti's polyglot of tongues—Yemeni Arabic, Somali, Amharic, French, and Tigrigna. He's read somewhere that there is proof of sophisticated agriculture in the area, dating back four thousand years. Important evidence comes from the tomb of a young girl going back to 2000 BC or earlier. Now he is impressed with the city's cosmopolitanism.

The noise of children running in every direction attracts his attention: a dog is giving chase to five, six boys, one of whom has apparently run off with its bone, maybe to eat it; his mates are in the running for fun, but the dog wants its bone back. A Somali-speaking Yemeni who is standing in front of an eatery observes that the boys are not so much engaged in mischief as they are in finding something to eat. They won't let a dog eat its bone in peace.

Ahl asks the man if he is open for business. He asserts that he is, and they talk. It turns out that the man relocated from Mogadiscio to Djibouti after the eruption of the civil war there. Ahl orders a meal of mutton and injera, Ethiopian pancakes made from teff, the millet-like grain grown exclusively in the highlands of Ethiopia and ground into flour. Ahl loves the spongy feel of the injera, and its sour taste.

The Yemeni asks him where he is from, and Ahl says he is going to Bosaso.

"You must be in business, then," the Yemeni says.

"Do you know Bosaso at all?"

The Yemeni sings Bosaso's praises, describing it as a booming town. He claims to know a couple of people who are making a mint out of shady businesses such as piracy and people smuggling. Pressed, he won't give their names, only their broad identities. This is not of much help in a region more varied in hyphenated identities than even the United States. But the man is becoming suspicious, knowing that Djibouti is chockablock with spies from the United States, Ethiopia, and other countries. His conversation comes to a halt, and he goes away and returns with the bill, announcing that it is time for him to close up and join his mates. Ahl isolates the key word *sit*, which in Djibouti, Yemen, and everywhere else Somalis live means to chew *qaat*.

On the way back to his hotel, the streets are empty; everyone, it seems, is chewing *qaat*. Ahl comes across an abandoned building, with the paint coming off in layers, birds nesting in its gable, and a dog and its litter of pups sheltering in a quiet corner. The lintel is engraved with the Star of David. A huge lock the size of a human head, and an equally large chain, both brown with rust and old age, hang on the door.

In Mogadiscio, the cathedral was razed to the ground in the general mayhem at the start of the civil war, but here in Djibouti, the synagogue stands as testimony to peace. One of the first victims of the Somali strife was an Italian, Padre Salvatore Colombo, who lived in Mogadiscio for close to thirty years as the head of the Catholic Church–funded orphanage, one of the oldest institutions in the city. More recently, a Shabaab operative desecrated the Italian cemeteries, digging up the bones and scattering them around. To Ahl, the presence of a synagogue in a country with a Muslim majority is a healthy thing: cities, to qualify as cosmopolitan, must show tolerance toward communities different from their own. Intolerance has killed Mogadiscio. Djibouti is a living city, of which its residents can be proud.

At the hotel, he learns that the building served as a synagogue during the colonial era, but lately it has not been active as a place of worship. The man at the reception adds, "But do you know, there are Somalis claiming to be the true lost tribe of Israel."

"What's their evidence?" says Ahl.

"Their professional clan name—professional, because they work with metal and leather, and act as seers to other clans—sounds almost like a bastardization of 'Hebrew.'"

The pin drops. Ahl knows the name of the clan.

He watches some more TV news, and when the airline office has reopened, he buys the ticket to Bosaso, paying in U.S. dollars. Then he goes for a long walk, luxuriating in a day in Djibouti before flying out to Somalia.

To savor the city at night, he goes for a stroll without worrying about his safety. A clutch of men and half a dozen ladies of the night are at the entrance of a nightclub. He pays for a ticket and goes in. The music is terrible. There are four couples on the floor, only two dancing, the others talking and smoking. Despite this, he finds a corner table and sits. What has he to lose? He doubts there are nightclubs in Bosaso or that alcohol will be openly available for fear of what the religionists might do.

A woman with a cigarette between her lips, her dress tight across her chest, her cleavage showily pushing through, wants a light. Instinctively, Ahl feels his pockets, as if he might find a lighter there, or a box of matches. He shakes his head, and with the white of his palms facing her, shouts over the music, "I'm sorry, I don't smoke."

"No need to be sorry. But are you alone?"

He pretends he hasn't heard her question. Even so, she sits down, and as she bends down to do so, he gets a whiff of her perfume. Whatever else he may do, he mustn't lead her on. But how can he tell her that he is in the nightclub just for the experience of it? Granted, he hasn't had sex with his wife since Taxliil went missing.

"If you have no objection to sitting with me for a chat and no more," Ahl says, "then I can offer you a drink of your choice."

"I'll sit with you until I find a client."

He agrees to the deal. She orders hard liquor, a packet of cigarettes, and a lighter. The waiter insists on advance payment for the liquor. Then she asks, "Where are you from?"

"I am on my way to Somalia."

"Why would you go to a place everyone is leaving?"

"Maybe there is a purpose to my visit," he says, and falls silent.

The waiter arrives with the order.

"Why come into a nightclub when you are not drinking, dancing, or picking up a woman for the night?" she asks.

"As I've said, I am on my way to Somalia," he says.

"But I know many women like me from your country."

"But they aren't open about it, are they?" he asks.

"Like Arab women, they whore secretly."

He asks, "How do you mean?"

"Veiled in public," the woman says, "Arab women strip naked and are game faster than you think. Maybe that is what they do in Somalia these days. They whore secretly, covered from head to toe. You can't believe the stories we hear."

Ahl leaves when she spots a white client, and he suggests that the man come and take his place. He says, "All the best. Maybe we'll meet again."

"Take care," she says.

BIGBEARD, FOOTSOLDIER, AND TRUTHTELLER APPROACH THE HOUSE from different vantage points at the same time.

BigBeard wraps his purple keffiyeh around his waist, tucks in a revolver, just in case, and scales the back wall. FootSoldier, a black keffiyeh around his neck, accesses the compound from a neighboring garden. At the wheel of a pickup truck parked to the left of the front gate, TruthTeller, wearing a red keffiyeh, waits until the other men confirm that they are both in and it is safe for him to join them. He starts the pickup and waits for one of his mates to open the gate; then he maneuvers in the truck with caution, pulling a wheeled vehicle on which guns and other weapons are mounted, hidden under a tarpaulin.

The front gate securely fastened, the men assemble in the house to set up their operation center. BigBeard calls YoungThing over and without any warning punches him so hard in the face that he collapses in a heap on the floor. Everything is still for a while. The other two men watch as YoungThing pulls himself up, half kneeling, his cheek swollen, his lower lip bleeding. When YoungThing has recovered his balance and stands at attention, BigBeard says to him, "Do you realize that your negligence had the potential to cause the movement unnecessary loss of life?"

TruthTeller goes on, "We wouldn't be here if one of our sympathizers had not, by chance, informed our intelligence of your presence in the neighborhood."

"Imagine what would've happened if we had not been alerted to your grievous error," FootSoldier adds.

BigBeard, still angry, says, "Go. Off with you."

Then TruthTeller instructs him to stand guard at the gate while they have their initial meeting. With YoungThing gone, BigBeard assigns to FootSoldier the task of liaison duty to link the cell they are now forming to the principal cell in Wardhiigley District, where the presidential villa is situated. He charges TruthTeller with the responsibility of bringing in the gun parts. With FootSoldier on the phone to the command center, BigBeard starts to assemble the weapons.

Dhoorre, who is in the bathroom with the door bolted, eavesdrops on their conversation. When he hears all three men leave the house, he takes a hurried birdbath by letting the water drip into his cupped hands in the manner of somebody performing an ablution in an arid zone where water is scarce. In Islam, it is incumbent on a Muslim performing ablution to use even the sand if there is no water. Allah will look favorably on one if one is "clean" at the moment of death. He looks at his face in the mirror and confirms that he badly needs a shave—it's a pity that the blade is dull and he has no replacements.

Just then there is a sudden escalation of noise as TruthTeller returns, grumbling about the weight of the machine-gun and bazooka parts. Dhoorre hears weaponry being dropped near the door of the bathroom. It won't be long before one of the men invades the space where he is confined, Dhoorre realizes. Then he hears the sound of chairs pulled back from the table and the men sit down.

Straining his ears, he makes out the odd word. The arrival of these men, and their continued presence in the house, can mean only one thing: trouble. He surrenders to the wish to know more, if only to prepare for what is bound to come. He kneels down directly behind the keyhole, through which he can glimpse the faces of the men, discern their movements.

BigBeard, as the others call the one in the purple keffiyeh, is in his thirties, prodigiously built, hirsute, with a husky desert voice; his facial muscles knotted, forehead furrowed, he listens to his companions, now encouraging one of the men to speak, now dismissing another's comments. Dhoorre assumes that BigBeard is the leader of the group. His purple keffiyeh is folded almost in quarters, and wound around his forehead. His hand keeps coming into contact with the fold, caressing and readjusting it in a way that reminds Dhoorre of a vain young woman just returned from her hairdresser, whose hand keeps straying to her expensive hairdo. Dhoorre does not need to be told that keffiyehs have lately become fashionable among Mogadiscio's religionist elite. He remembers watching Peter O'Toole wear one as Lawrence of Arabia, and how in recent years Arafat turned it into a symbol of Palestinian nationhood. But Dhoorre can't tell if the color of the keffiyehs that these men wear points to their membership in a given cell.

BigBeard addresses a question to the wearer of the red keffiyeh—TruthTeller—a man with a big nose; he teasingly inquires, "What's bothering FootSoldier?"

TruthTeller replies, "He needs the bathroom. He's trying to get the door open."

BigBeard asks, "Has YoungThing come back without our permission?"

FootSoldier assures BigBeard that YoungThing is outside. "In fact, I can see him standing by the gate saying his rosary."

BigBeard now looks troubled. "Why won't the bathroom door open if we are the only people in the house?"

TruthTeller goes over to check if there is a key in the door on the outside. He pushes the door, kicks at it, and then puts his shoulder to it and shoves. But the door does not give. He says to BigBeard, "It's locked from the inside, I think."

FootSoldier asks, "Who is inside, then?"

BigBeard is growing impatient. He slaps FootSoldier, shouting, "What kind of a man are you that you can't hold your pee?"

He turns to TruthTeller and orders him to call YoungThing in. TruthTeller knocks into the furniture as he goes, kicking at chairs. From the door, he shouts to YoungThing. He asks, "Is someone in the bathroom?"

Dhoorre does not know what to do. He checks his face in the mirror—even a dying man wants to look comparatively clean. He realizes with concern that it'll be the end of the boy. One moment, he has a good mind to open the door and be done with it; the next moment, he feels inadequate to the task. He is dizzy, gulping air into his lungs, fearing that he will faint before he can open the door.

Then he hears the boy say, "Old man, open the door."

He unlocks the door and steps out. FootSoldier can't wait any longer and hurriedly pushes past him. Meanwhile, TruthTeller and Young-Thing step out of Dhoorre's way and keep their distance. BigBeard asks Dhoorre to come closer to him; his eyes penetrate deep into Dhoorre's fear. In a film, the old man thinks, BigBeard would be the one who pulls the trigger, a hard man with not one iota of gentleness.

With such a man you can never work out the cut and thrust of his intentions.

BigBeard asks, "Why are you here?"

"I live here," replies Dhoorre.

FootSoldier comes out in time to hear this. The eyes of all three keffiyeh-wearing men converge on YoungThing.

TruthTeller asks the boy if this is true.

YoungThing says, "He is a hobo squatting here."

FootSoldier, who is angry because he had to wait until he almost wet his robes, smacks Dhoorre in the face. "Tell us the truth."

The sudden upwelling pain overwhelms Dhoorre. "I am telling the truth," he replies.

TruthTeller, for his part, hits YoungThing, the strike splitting the boy's lower lip and making it bleed again. He asks, "Is he a hobo squatting here, or does he live here?" When the boy touches his lip, as if to wipe it dry, TruthTeller hits him again, twice.

BigBeard tells TruthTeller to stop pummeling the boy in front of a stranger. He adds, "Can't you see I am talking to the old man?"

Dhoorre says, "I am a guest, not a drifter."

"So who lives here?"

"My son," he replies, "whom I am visiting."

"What is your son's name?"

Dhoorre now realizes that he has inadvertently brought his son into focus. All that remains is for him to say his son's name. Dhoorre has two sons, and neither is in the good books of Shabaab. One of his sons, based in Baidoa, is a minister in the Transitional Federal Government, with which Shabaab is at war; the other son, who served in the National Army, is also a known foe of Shabaab, for he has declared himself a secularist and has often militated against the group in radio interviews. It is the latter, an American citizen living in Virginia, who has been visiting Mogadiscio with his family and is now hosting Dhoorre in this rented house. Too late to invent a false identity, Dhoorre gives his son's name.

BigBeard's expression is fluid, like dirty water going down a gutter, habitually moving in a downward direction. Dhoorre is aware that Shabaab would be only too pleased to grace either of his sons with immediate beheading, and that he is not likely to be spared, either.

Even though he is not sure that it will do the young thing any good, Dhoorre hopes that his statement will have in it the vigor of settling a matter in dispute. He says, pointing at YoungThing, "Let me say, for what it is worth, that this young fellow meant no ill to you or your cause. I would appeal to you to spare him. Islam is peace, the promise of justice. Because I may have misled him. Please."

Dhoorre discerns movement behind him, and from a corner of his eye he spots TruthTeller with his weapon poised, but not yet ready to shoot. He pushes Dhoorre down with the butt of the firearm. Sitting on a chair, the old man feels the harsh metallic coldness of the weapon against his nape.

FootSoldier says to YoungThing, "You've proven delinquent in your behavior. Why?"

YoungThing says, "I won't do it again."

BigBeard orders YoungThing to get his gun from the carryall. YoungThing does as ordered, without fear or sentiment. As he waits for instructions, he does not plead with any of the men to spare his life or that of the old man.

BigBeard says, "Shoot him."

Dhoorre says, "Please."

YoungThing can't determine if the Old Man is pleading with him not to shoot, or if he is saying, "Go ahead and shoot." He looks toward BigBeard, who is busy fingering his long, bushy beard, twisting it with the concentration of a philosopher deep in thought.

Dhoorre thinks that it is in such a scene, where violence gains the upper hand, that one can bear testimony to tragedy in all its registers: a country held to ransom, a people subjected to daily humiliation, a nation sadly put to the sword.

FootSoldier says, "What are you waiting for?"

Times passes, as slow as death.

TruthTeller shouts, "Shoot!"

YoungThing might as well pull the trigger and be done with it, he thinks, without a flinch or immediate regret, although he is aware, despite his young age, that his action will ricochet about in his brain and keep him awake at night, disturbed and jittery. He knows, too, that he is only postponing his own death; no sooner will he shoot the old man than one of the keffiyehs will make him pay for the crime of not wasting Dhoorre right away. He wishes he had listened to his older sister, Wiila, a flight attendant, who had offered him financial help if he agreed not to join Shabaab and to go to school instead. Or to his older brother with the alias Marduuf, who tried, without success, to recruit him as a pirate.

YoungThing shoots, using the silencer.

As the bullet strikes Dhoorre in the forehead, YoungThing is certain that he hears a seabird cawing, only he cannot interpret what it is saying, or whether it is foretelling his own imminent death.

Dhoorre falls off his chair, dropping to the floor in an uncoordinated heap of self-reproach; he is sad that he has had no time to alert his son, his daughter-in-law, and his grandchildren to the ambush that awaits them.

––––––––

From his posture alone, you can't tell if the old man is dead. He lies on his back, head to one side, eyes not wholly closed, his position suggesting sleep.

The keffiyeh-wearing men sit in the eerie silence that follows the shooting. The ringing of a cell phone startles them out of their immobility. They exchange bothered looks.

YoungThing glances around, as if trying to calculate not if but how soon one of the men will shoot him. The realization that he might die in a matter of minutes concentrates his mind, and he resolves not to be afraid. He walks over to where the old man lies sprawled, his legs splayed, his neck crooked, his hands spread out by his side, his nakedness embarrassing. As a token of his fearlessness, YoungThing straightens the man's legs and places his hands together across his chest, in the gesture of prayer. He moves back a pace and looks at what he has done, pleased that he has made the old man as comfortable in death as he can be. Then he waits.

BigBeard has anger etched into his features. Impatient, he is looking from FootSoldier to TruthTeller, as though wondering why they have not yet acted on his rage; then, even more furious, he watches YoungThing, as if he were expecting the boy to fall to his knees in terror. He says to YoungThing, "Have you anything to say before you die?"

YoungThing is defiantly silent. He glances from BigBeard to FootSoldier and then focuses his unrelenting stare on TruthTeller.

BigBeard says to TruthTeller, "Will you do us the favor of ridding us of this thing, this vermin?"

FootSoldier says, "I was hoping you'd ask me."

BigBeard says, "Fear not. You'll have your turn. But this is TruthTeller's turn. I've never seen him kill a thing before."

TruthTeller closes his eyes, winces like a child taking bitter medicine, and shoots YoungThing right between the eyes. Then he unscrews the silencer from his gun.

"Well done," BigBeard says. Then he orders FootSoldier to remove the two corpses, dump them in the garden, and report for duty, in double quick. He adds, "There is a lot of work for us to complete before nightfall. Remember, we have a country to liberate, a people to educate in the proper ways of our faith. Come; be quick about it, you two. What's holding you?"

TruthTeller volunteers to help FootSoldier, each of them dragging a corpse from the room before rigor mortis sets in.

WHEN THEY GET TO CAMBARA AND BILE'S HOUSE AND DAJAAL RINGS the bell, Malik and Jeebleh, to their surprise, hear dogs barking. Since neither remembers anyone mentioning the presence of dogs there, they look at each other and then at Dajaal. Dajaal explains, "The ringing of the bell activates the barking of dogs inside the house. Cambara imported the device from Toronto to scare off potential burglars. It's most effective because no one keeps dogs as pets or guards in a Muslim country, and virtually everyone is terrified of them."

Cambara receives Jeebleh and Malik with warmth. She has waited for them close to the entrance, the door open, her smile broad and beaming. She meets them halfway as they walk past the day guard. She hugs and kisses Jeebleh on the cheeks. She is formal with Malik; she takes his right hand in both hers. Dajaal takes his leave, suggesting that they ring when they are ready to be picked up.

On the way in, Cambara walks between the two men, Jeebleh's hand in hers in acknowledgment of their presumed closeness, even though the two have only ever spoken on the phone. He remembers that Cambara arrived here with the disquiet of a mother mourning, after losing her only son, her marriage broken and her life in tatters. Seamus, with whom he had spoken about her, described her as being equally suicidal and murderous. Then she met Bile, and he and Dajaal, with assistance from Seamus, helped her to deploy her strength constructively, in addition to helping her to reclaim her family and to produce a puppet play, the first of its kind in Mogadiscio, despite religionist threats. Eventually Cambara chose to throw in her lot with Bile's, and the two became an item, despite the dissimilarity in their temperaments. Their need for each other has set the terms of their togetherness.

Now Cambara says to him, "It feels as if I've known you ever since I met Bile. I am so pleased you are here."

With Dajaal gone, the features of the day guard harden and his eyes open wide at the sight of Cambara embracing and kissing Jeebleh and placing herself between him and Malik. Malik wonders if the man will report them to the religionist authorities for indulging in such un-Islamic intimacy.

Inside, Bile is lying prone on the couch in the living room, only a few days after his return from Nairobi, following surgery on his prostate at a clinic there. But when Bile hears them approach, he jumps up to welcome them. He and Jeebleh hug for a very long time, despite the tremor in Bile's grip. The storied house echoes with their words of joyous reunion, after which Bile hugs Malik, too.

Bile is a little shaky on his legs. Jeebleh observes how age has affected them differently. Whereas he is heavier around the waist, paunchier, with bags permanently under the eyes, Bile has grown thinner in the face, his chin oddly extending downward, the anemic skin on it wrinkly and sporting grayish sprouts of hair, stylishly trimmed. He ascribes this suaveness to Cambara. Indeed, Bile is dressed with uncommon flair, a linen shirt and a pair of trousers, tailored with sophistication. Cambara stands by, confidently wearing a plain caftan with a matching shoulder cover. Not wanting to take the luster away from their meeting, she allows the conversation to flow, seldom interfering, though she pays constant attention to the changes of mood when they get to the table. Bile asks questions about Jeebleh's family and grand-child as Cambara goes back and forth between them and the kitchen. Jeebleh remembers Seamus, their mutual Irish friend, commenting on how Bile, without two shillings to rub against each other, resisted hav-ing them take care of the expenses of his prostate surgery. "Typical Somali behavior," Seamus had said. "Such vacuous arrogance."

When the meal is served, they tuck into their food in appreciative silence. Malik has many questions about the country. However, it is never easy to talk fluently and without inhibition in a room where the sick are. Cambara notes that Bile is starting to display early signs of exhaustion from the small talk. She says to Malik, *"Et tu?"*

Malik says, "It feels bizarre that I am back in a place to which I have never been before."

Interested, Bile shifts in his seat and sits forward, his fingers close to his mouth in an effort to hide the ugliness of a front tooth with a tiny chip. He says, "Can one return to a place to which one has never been?"

Malik explains, "I meant that even though I have never been to Somalia, I know a lot about the country, because my grandparents and my father wished they could visit the country of their ancestors. In fact, my old man is living somewhere in the breakaway Republic of Somaliland, tending to his camels, married to a much younger woman and raising a new brood of kids."

Cambara lays her hand on Bile's thigh, and, turning to him, asks Malik if his mother is Chinese Malaysian. He nods his head. "She is. It is my father who is Somali."

Bile interjects, "You see Somalis everywhere."

"Stranded in an alien place, like flotsam," says Cambara.

Bile frowns and goes on, "I seldom imagine Somalis stranded.

Many do well wherever they end up." Then suddenly he holds his breath, as though he has the hiccups, and when he inhales he changes tack. "Have you ever heard of a Chinese female pirate, name of Mrs. Cheng?"

Malik, who has read a lot about the exploits of the Somali pirates in the peninsula and is equally familiar with other aspects of piracy, appears puzzled. "No, I haven't heard of Mrs. Cheng."

Jeebleh says to Bile, "Why did I think you would not be in the least interested in the question of piracy, either off the coast of Somalia or elsewhere?"

Bile replies, "Of course, I am interested."

Jeebleh is aware that among the Somalis with whom he has discussed the subject of piracy, many without reservation condemn the illegal foreign vessels fishing in the Somali Sea. They say that this unchecked robbery has caused joblessness among fishermen and led them to piracy. In fact, Somali fishermen appealed to the United Nations and the international community to help rid them of the large number of foreign vessels, estimated in 2005 at about seven hundred, engaged in unlicensed fishing off the country's southern shores. The country profile compiled by the United Nations' own Food and Agricultural Organization in 2005 confirmed that not only were these vessels plundering Somalia's marine resources but many of them were also dumping rubbish—nuclear and chemical waste.

Jeebleh asks Bile, "Why are you interested in the topic?"

"Because one of my distant nephews, a former fisherman, bought a skiff and set up his own piracy unit in Xarardheere after a Korean fishing vessel shot at him and his companions when they tried to discourage their presence near their own fishing grounds. Shot at, injured, made jobless, and very upset, they set up a cooperative and, together with some of his mates, formerly fishermen, now unemployed, they armed themselves to fight back. First, they hijacked a yacht, made a small killing amounting to a few thousand dollars in ransom, and then they took a Korean ship and crew captive. They received a ransom in thousands of dollars."

"Only a few thousand dollars in ransom?"

Jeebleh asks, "Do you think that vengeance is the motive behind these acts? They want to reclaim what is theirs by right, since the world cares little about the illicit fishing."

Bile says, "From what my nephew tells me, there isn't much money in it. Somalia loses more in the amount of fish taken away, in the continued degradation of the environment, and so on and so forth."

Malik wonders aloud, "You mean there are no lavish weddings being staged, no formidable mansions being built in Eyl, Hobyo, and Xarardheere? The entire region is not flush with funds and full of luxury goods?"

Bile replies, "All I know is what my nephew has told me. He speaks of ten thousand dollars apiece, much less than what the newspapers claim."

Malik asks, "So where does the money go?"

"I keep thinking something doesn't add up," Cambara says.

Jeebleh says, "Do you think then, Bile, that Cicero's often repeated description of pirates as the 'enemy of humanity' does not necessarily tell the whole story, when it comes to the Somalis locally labeled as the nation's coast guard?"

"That may have been the case when thievery at sea was common and when all the peoples living by the sea could've been described as pirates. Which they were, pirates," Bile says. "In fact, according to Thucydides, it was common among ancient Greeks to pursue thievery at sea as a lucrative vocation. Here, 'piracy' started only after the wholesale robbery of our marine resources."

Cambara says, "Truth be told, resorting to thuggery at sea and banditry on land have become normal as a result of two decades of civil war. Any other explanation is beside the point, as far as I am concerned."

Bile screws up his face, chews his food with the slow deliberateness of someone entertaining a nasty thought, and then says, "Anyhow, according to a book I've read, the Chinese female pirate Mrs. Cheng commanded a fleet larger than the navy of many countries in her day. She was some pirate, wasn't she?"

Malik says, "She must have been."

Cambara says, "Jeebleh tells me that your parents met and married in Aden. That's interesting."

A sudden exhaustion makes Bile's face assume a different shape, like a plant that has had too much sun and is now starting to wilt. His eyes droop, and his lips form themselves into an exhausted pout. When Cambara inquires if he needs help, whispering into his ear, Bile waves her off. Jeebleh thinks that Bile is behaving like a tired child refusing to go to bed.

Cambara says, "You would think that Somalis had invented piracy, from the way the Western media talk about their exploits, paying more attention to it than whatever else is happening in the country."

"Maybe because of the hostage-taking?" Malik wonders aloud. "And because of the dangers to shipping lanes."

"But that's not how the piracy started," she says.

Jeebleh says, "I am sure he knows that was not how the piracy started."

"Will you visit Puntland to write about the piracy there?" Cambara asks Malik.

"I am interested in writing about every aspect that touches on the lives of Somalis," Malik says. "The civil war and its repercussions. The Ethiopian invasion. The piracy and who funds it, where they get their intelligence before launching their attacks, how they receive the ransom payments."

Jeebleh says to Cambara, "I am sure I told you on the phone when we spoke that Ahl, Malik's older brother, is arriving in Puntland as we speak, to locate Taxliil, his runaway stepson. We believe he's holed up there with the militants."

Bile perks up when he hears all this. "You see, my dearest, everything happens for a reason. Illegal fishing in Somali waters and the resultant piracy. The Ethiopian invasion. The American involvement in Somali politics. Al Qaeda's presence in the peninsula. The Courts and their failings, apparent only to those of us who live in Mogadiscio. Somalis in the diaspora say, 'But at least they brought peace to the country.' Those of us who live inside the country and who know better say, 'At what price?' I doubt if that has been worth it. After all, the devastation being visited on the country following the Ethiopian invasion could have been avoided. If only!"

Jeebleh's gaze steadies and focuses on Bile, who is giving him a sharp look, as though urging him to level with him.

"I know that there are two or more sides to every story," Jeebleh says. Then he surprises even himself by blurting out, "We, too, have had a run-in with the capricious authoritarian nature of the Courts."

Malik, whose spoon is heaped with food, stops with it midway between his plate and his mouth, and stares at his father-in-law. His nostrils flare, touching off an alarm signal in Jeebleh. Malik is plainly unhappy that Jeebleh has chosen to speak about their encounter with BigBeard.

An uneasy hush descends. Bile purses his lips in self-blame. He says to Malik, "Time I retired." To Cambara, he adds, "Please don't get up. Stay with our guests." And he takes leave of Jeebleh, saying, "See you anon."

Self-conscious, they fall silent and look away. Bile takes a long time to get to the stairway and much longer to go up the steps one at a time.

When he has gone out of sight and she assumes he cannot hear her, Cambara explains, "Bile tires easily."

Jeebleh is understandably worried that Cambara may one day up and leave, as the younger partner in a couple often does, and he wonders what will become of his friend. He remembers a married couple younger than he and with whom he has been friends for years. The woman, younger than the husband by some ten years, opted out of the marriage just before turning fifty. Soon after, she entered a lesbian relationship, because the thought of a husband demanding sex after her menopause put her off men forever. She explained that she dreaded submitting to her husband's insatiable advances, and felt it would be easier with other women. Jeebleh never found out if that was the case, as he never dared ask her when they met in the common room at the college where they taught.

No one wants to eat any more. All three get to their feet, and Malik, eager to go on a tour of the city, gathers the plates and takes them to the kitchen. He returns to find Jeebleh chatting to Cambara about his family and, most touchingly, about his granddaughter and how bright-eyed she is. Jeebleh acknowledges Malik with a heartwarming smile.

Cambara says to Malik, "Be on your guard; journalists are under constant threat. There are fifth columnists, some working in cahoots with the religionists and others with foreign forces intent on destabilizing an already destabilized country."

Jeebleh thinks that Cambara has fallen afoul of the religionists because she is her own woman, unbending in her determination to do what she pleases. He recalls Dajaal informing him that she started wearing a headscarf and then the veil to minimize her unceasing quarrels with the men averse to seeing women with uncovered hair, or young women in trousers, or in dresses deemed to make men lust after them. Women must hide their bodily assets so that the men in whom fires of lust are burning may not be tempted into sin. It must be hard on Cambara, trained as a makeup artist and an actor, not to be able to express her womanliness, if that is what she has a mind to do.

No wonder some of the religionists want to run her out of the city where she has found the happiness that eluded her in Toronto.

Conveniently, Dajaal is at the door, ready to drive them back to the apartment.

Cambara stares into Jeebleh's eyes with great intensity. There is a hint of sorrow—of loneliness with depth, Jeebleh thinks, and he remarks that she runs her tongue repeatedly over her lips and seems to be holding back tears. She does not want them to go, even if she can't bring herself to say so; she wants the good-bye to last forever. Malik, for his part, thinks that there is nothing like the aloneness of a woman looking after a man she loves, in a city like Mogadiscio.

It is then that she comes out with it. "I wish you were staying here with us, both of you. Only we thought, or rather Bile thought, that Malik would want to have his own place, where he could do his writing and conduct his interviews in peace. Also, we have a young man staying in the annex, Robleh, the younger brother of a close friend of mine, a die-hard supporter of the Courts. He spends all his time in the mosques, politicking. I would love for you to meet him. He is some sort of talent spotter for the radical religionist fringe."

"I'd very much like to meet him," says Malik.

"Robleh is into everything the religionists do," she says. "Who knows, he may know someone who can assist you in finding what has become of the runaway Taxliil. What do you think?"

Dajaal, who has now joined them in the foyer, is pointing at his watch, indicating they are running out of daylight. Like a mother with a baby sleeping in another room, Cambara responds to a movement upstairs: Bile flushing the toilet and shuffling slowly back to bed.

"I must go," she says, hugging them, and they are off.

Jeebleh isn't keen on the city tour, but he doesn't fuss. He sits silently while Dajaal acts as tour guide, answering Malik's questions. Malik takes copious notes as Dajaal points out buildings, gives the names of streets, and spells the names of the districts through which they happen to be traveling. Dajaal has the sociology of it down pat. Malik writes in his notebook, "The heart sickens."

Jeebleh finds a generic featurelessness to the city's destruction, as if the impact of a single bomb, detonating, had brought down the adjacent buildings, or they had collapsed in sympathy. The city is oddly ostentatious in its vulgarity, like a woman who was once a beauty refusing to admit that the years have caught up with her. Dajaal says, "It's an in-your-face city, whose various parts, hamlets of no mean size, are less than the whole. It extends in many directions, in utter disorder, as if a blind city planner has determined its current shape."

Women in *niqabs*—veils—and body tents go past, treading with much care, in streets chockablock with minibuses speeding down the dusty roads. One loses one's bearings in a city with few landmarks, no road markings, and no street names.

Dajaal says, for Malik and Jeebleh's benefit, "The city has undergone many changes, in the residents it attracts and in the services it renders or doesn't render anymore."

Here, a set of dirt alleys leading into a maze of dead ends. There, hummocks of rubble accumulated over the years through neglect and lack of civic maintenance; kiosks, mere shacks, built bang in the center of what was once a main thoroughfare, now totally blocked. "How this city could do with the return of law and order in the shape of a functioning state!"

Malik writes away furiously, happy with the tour. Jeebleh suffers in shocked sadness.

Dajaal pulls off the road and stops. He asks Jeebleh if he remembers where they are. Jeebleh has no idea. He looks out in search of any distinctive features that might guide him, but finds none. Dajaal explains, "The Green Line dividing the territories of the two warlords during your last visit used to be here."

Satisfied now that he has filled several pages with his scribbles, Malik asks, "How far are we from the Siinlay?" He is referring to the spot where the fiercest battle between the CIA-funded warlords and the religionists occurred, ending with the religionists running the warlords out of the city.

"Siinlay is far," replies Dajaal.

"What about the Bakhaaraha market complex?"

"Too late," says Dajaal.

Jeebleh adds, "Besides, you need a whole day."

Dajaal looks at his watch and switches on the radio, just in time to hear a religionist announcing that the army of the faithful in control of much of Somalia is declaring war on Ethiopia.

Jeebleh says, "This is madness."

Dajaal says, "This foolish man declaring war on Ethiopia thinks, erroneously, that invading the strongest military power in this part of Africa will be a walk in the park. It won't be."

Silence reigns until they get to the apartment.

———

Nearly an hour after dropping them off, Dajaal telephones Jeebleh to confirm that he will be bringing Gumaad along, as Malik has requested. Malik is interested in hearing Gumaad's reaction to the declaration of war. He wants to know what an ardent supporter of the Courts will say.

Jeebleh is in the kitchen, improvising a light meal. He is troubled, because he has just learned from Malik that in addition to removing the naked photographs of Malik's baby daughter and several newspaper clippings and files, BigBeard has fed his computer a vicious virus that has effectively ruined the machine. At present, it works fitfully, coming on and then going off and sometimes balking when Malik attempts to restart it.

Jeebleh is sad that so far things have not worked out to his and Malik's expectations; he regrets that neither he nor Dajaal took preventive measures to avoid Malik suffering at the hands of a moonlighter claiming to be serving the interests of the Courts. Exhausted, his eyes closing as though of their own accord, Jeebleh is back now to the remote past, where he pays a nostalgic visit to his and Bile's childhood and revisits his student days in Italy with Bile and Seamus. Thinking about the visit with Bile earlier today, the memory leaves him dispirited.

Many years separate his and Bile's shared milestones, each representing a turning point in a life fully realized. Jeebleh still wishes to discharge his duty to his mother, on whose grave he will call at some stage, maybe alone, maybe with Malik—but only on the proviso that he does not write about it in one of his articles. He wants to protect his mother's memory.

A knock on the door of the apartment coincides with the ringing of Jeebleh's cell phone. Dajaal is outside. Jeebleh dismantles the security contraption, unbolting and then pulling back the metal sheet that covers the door. Then he pushes back the plating, which serves as a further impediment, meant to bar gunmen from gaining unwelcome access.

Gumaad is the first to enter, dressed to the nines, hands empty; he is all grins. He strikes Jeebleh as less of a finished product now that he is trying to impress. Dajaal follows, pushing the door wider. Malik joins them in time to see that he is carrying what looks like a platter wrapped in a handwoven shawl, the kind with which corpses of worthy Muslims are shrouded on their way to the burial grounds.

Once inside, Dajaal heads for the dining table, Gumaad on his heels to clear enough space for the platter. Dajaal sets it down with consummate care, as one might set down a soup bowl full to the brim. He says, "The best lamb dish Mogadiscio can offer. Compliments of Cambara and Bile."

"How thoughtful," Malik says.

"This is not homemade, is it?"

Dajaal replies, "Of course not."

As all four prepare to tuck in, Jeebleh remembers a Mogadiscio tradition, in which families would send food over to the rows and rows of rooms facing a central courtyard. Those were the rooms of the unmarried young men of the family, who had only sleeping provisions, but no cooking facilities. If they had jobs and could afford it, the bachelors would eat at restaurants in the evenings, preferring not to join the rest of the family in the evening's fare of beans and rice. There would be a glass of boiled and sugared milk waiting for them on their return home.

The lamb, soft-looking, juicy and cooked in the traditional way, is on the right side of brown, and sits on a bed of rice cooked in saffron and garnished with a mix of vegetables. The dish reignites in Jeebleh a memory of long-ago days at an institution called Jangal Night Club, famous for its lamb dishes. The restaurant got its name from its location in the bushes. You sat right under the acacia trees, trimmed into the shape of umbrellas, in the company of a young woman. Waiters flitted about in the semidarkness, bearing kerosene lamps to show clients the way to their private eating enclosures. You placed your order but the waiters would dawdle, allowing the couple sufficient time to "do their thing." When they returned, carrying a kerosene lamp in one hand and the food platters in the other, they would announce their presence and not enter the enclosure until you bade them to.

Jeebleh is certain that the religionists wouldn't permit such an establishment to function these days, but he asks anyway. "By the way, what's become of Jangal?"

Dajaal says, "This food is from Jangal."

Jeebleh says, "I am surprised to hear that."

"Jangal has recently reopened, with a new management, in a hotel," Dajaal explains. "The city's top-ranking religionists are the regulars there, so no fooling around in the bushes, necking or making love on the quick. The chef has not lost his magical touch, though—the lamb is still the best in town."

Malik says, "Let's eat. What're we waiting for?"

They wash their hands with hot water and soap, preparing to eat with their fingers. Malik remarks how expertly Jeebleh distributes the choicest lamb portions in the unmistakable manner of a patriarch presiding over a dinner table, ensuring that everyone gets his share and eats his fill. Jeebleh for his part observes how different Malik's style of eating is from theirs. He opens his palm flat, then forms it into the shape of a spade, picks the rice and some meat, and forms them into a ball before licking away mouthfuls of it. Maybe that is the way they eat where he originally comes from.

Malik showers compliments on the food after every second mouthful, and heaps accolades on Cambara for suggesting that Dajaal bring it. After dinner, when the others are busy stacking the dishes and washing them, he goes into his room and reemerges with a tape recorder. Again his heart is beating angrily, because he knows that until he has bought a new computer, he has to write everything down in longhand.

"Now tell me," Malik says. "Why would anyone threaten Ethiopia with invasion and claim that the army of the faithful is powerful enough to march all the way to Addis Ababa and take it?"

Gumaad cockily responds, "Possibly he knows something we, who are not privy to the secrets of the Courts, do not know."

Dajaal and Jeebleh say nothing; they listen.

"What do you think he knows that we don't?"

Gumaad then compares the statement the defense spokesman of the Courts made to the one Saddam Hussein made a month before the second U.S. invasion of Iraq, when he kept boasting that America would regret its action. Surprisingly, the Republican Guard, described as the fiercest and best-trained Arab army, melted away. However, once the United States occupied the country, the men from the Guard staged their insurgency on the occupying forces.

Malik is shocked at Gumaad's naïveté. "Why provoke a bully you can't defeat at a moment in your history when you are militarily at your weakest?"

Gumaad says, "We have Allah on our side, too."

The room fills with silence until Dajaal, slurring his words, says, "The defense spokesman is a fool speaking out of line."

Not wanting Gumaad and Dajaal to have a go at each other and derail his plans, Malik asks, "Do we know the number of men under arms, the strength of the Courts' fighting force?"

Gumaad admits he doesn't know.

"Do you know anyone who might?"

Gumaad says, "I'll ask around."

Jeebleh rises to his feet, saying, "Tea or coffee?"

In the kitchen, Jeebleh covers the remains of the lamb dish in aluminum foil and leaves it to cool. With Dajaal and Gumaad on the balcony, arguing vociferously about something to do with a drone over the city skies, Malik offers to dry and put away the plates for Jeebleh, whose hands are sudsy. As he does so, he fights hard not to allow his mind to wander away or to think about his computer; he has decided he will buy a new machine tomorrow, if possible.

Jeebleh says to Malik, "Perhaps you can serve the tea and coffee?"

"Sure," Malik says, and takes the tray out to the balcony.

Dajaal and Gumaad fall silent when Malik joins them. They each put several spoons of sugar in their tea. Then they sip, Gumaad making slurping noises as he does so.

He says to Malik, "Tell me, have you had a chance to read any of the articles by some of the local journalists, whom I hope you will get to meet and even interview?"

When Malik is hesitant and uncomfortable, Dajaal says, "Don't let it worry you. You may speak the truth to us. We know they can't be good, many of them. Gumaad and I know that none has had the kind of training that will make them professionals."

Gumaad adds his voice to Dajaal's, saying, "Go on and tell us."

Malik speaks with care. He says, "In my view, the writing is composed of ramshackle paragraphs sloppily conceived and shakily held together by a myriad of prejudices for which there is little or no supporting evidence. I suspect not one of them has done the background research for the pieces they've published. Moreover, the proofreading is atrocious, presumably because there are no trained editors or copy editors."

"You can't expect better," Dajaal says. "After all, they are self-taught and have taken up writing for these papers, which promote partisan, clan-based interests."

Gumaad says, "Come, come. Be fair, Dajaal."

"What training have you had?" Dajaal challenges.

Gumaad alters the thrust of their talk. He says, "I know some of the betters with whom I've worked. They have received several months' on-the-job training."

"Three months maximum, if that," Dajaal says.

As if to soften the blow, Malik says, "Still, I admire their courage, despite their lack of training or analytical acumen. They put their lives on the line, writing what they write. How many of us risk our lives on a daily basis for what we write? They are targeted, killed—and they continue writing. My hat is off to them."

When Jeebleh joins them, carrying his sugarless cup of coffee, Malik gives him the gist of their conversation. He nods his head in agreement but remains silent.

———

The night air is pleasant. The stars are aglitter, and there is a touch of salt in the wind. It's been a long day. Gumaad and Dajaal are still engaged in their long-winded diatribes. Dajaal has lost his cool twice, forfeiting his eloquence for short-term gain, almost resorting to abusive language. This is very uncharacteristic of him, Jeebleh thinks.

Jeebleh does not like Gumaad's cockiness, but believes it is good for Malik to hear someone who represents the religionist view, which constructs a world far less complicated than that of the secularists.

Gumaad confirms that Baidoa, the garrison town to which the Federalists are now confined, is under siege. The religionists control all the entry points; no trucks carrying food or fuel can go in or out. Twice in the past week alone, remote-controlled bombs exploded in the center of the town, causing casualties. The siege elevates matters to a riskier level and is bringing untold suffering to the town's residents.

"Do you expect an invasion soon?" Malik asks.

"The momentum is on our side, and we'll attack."

"Attack when the talks are ongoing?" Malik says.

Gumaad replies, "Because the Ethiopians, our age-old enemies, are liaising with the U.S., and the U.S. is providing them with intelligence from their satellites stationed above our city."

Malik says, "The Americans won't enter the fray. They have the Afghan and Iraqi wars occupying their minds and taking an enormous toll on their economy. Those two wars are enough to keep them busy for another decade or more. Anyhow, what's in it for them?"

They fall silent for quite a while. Then Gumaad gets to his feet. He pulls Malik up, then gestures to Jeebleh and Dajaal to join them. As the four of them stand side by side, their bodies touching, Gumaad speaks. "Can you hear it?"

"What am I supposed to hear?" asks Malik.

Gumaad says, "Look up at the sky."

"I am looking."

"Tell me what you can see."

"I see tropical stars."

"And what can you hear?"

"I hear city night noises."

"Listen. Take your time, gentlemen."

Jeebleh hears a distant drone.

"Can you see anything?" Gumaad asks Malik.

"What am I supposed to see?"

"A small light in the seventh sky, blinking."

Malik searches the sky. Nothing.

"More like a Cessna, from here," Jeebleh says, and points to a constellation of stars he cannot name. Then he says to Malik. "A lightweight plane, some sort of a surveillance drone, up in the sky. Can you not hear or see, Malik?"

Gumaad encourages him. "Concentrate. Please."

Malik at long last picks up a continuous drone, which reminds him of a child's battery-operated toy, the noise on and then off. An unmanned predator, operated by a ground pilot, or someone positioned on a carrier warship stationed ashore, flown in areas of medium risk for surveillance purposes, like the drones used in attempted targeted killings in Pakistan, Palestine, and Afghanistan. These unmanned predator drones have of late become a common feature in Mogadiscio's skies, because the United States suspects the Courts of giving refuge to four men it alleges are Al Qaeda operatives. The presence of high-flying spy planes here marks a significant departure, and makes the United States complicit if Ethiopia invades and occupies Mogadiscio. Or so Mogadiscians are convinced. They assume the drones, which they hear and see without fail from nine every evening until about four in the morning, are sufficient evidence that the Americans are gathering information.

Jeebleh yawns heavily, indicating he is tired; he wants Gumaad and Dajaal to leave. But before they do, he brings out the platter in which the food came, already washed and packed so that Dajaal may return it to its owner.

"See you tomorrow, about noon," Jeebleh says.

"Good night. See you tomorrow."

———

"Very good for a first day," Malik says.

"I'm glad things are working out, except for the computer problem," Jeebleh says. "But I know that you will not let that pull down your spirits."

Malik says, "I should have known what the reaction of a religionist with sex on his mind would be to a naked photograph of a year-old girl in her bath. Pornography, my foot! Not to worry. I will not allow it to color my judgment."

"What about the articles he deleted?"

"I have copies on a memory stick," Malik says.

Jeebleh says, "I should have alerted you to the possibility, and I should have been more supportive. I'm sorry."

"Don't let that worry you; you did what you could under the circumstances," Malik says, and he goes to embrace Jeebleh.

Jeebleh relaxes his features into a sweet softness, the night stars shining in his eyes. Just looking at him, Malik is so touched that he wants to wrap himself around his father-in-law yet again and to say how delighted he is to be here. Instead, he tells him about the mini-recorder he has in his pocket, which has registered everything. Malik makes Jeebleh listen to some of the conversation he recorded.

Jeebleh says, "Whatever else you do, please don't mention my name in any of your articles, lest it devalue your work or my input."

"I am proud of our association and will say so."

They embrace again and then go to bed, content.

AN AIRSTRIP IS A MISNOMER FOR THE SANDY PIT ON WHICH AHL'S plane lands in Bosaso. Close by, less than half a kilometer away, is Somalia's sea, in your face as always. Someone with a perverted sense of humor sited the airstrip here, for it requires pilots to perform some acrobatic feats on landing, and leaves only the most strong-hearted passengers unaffected.

With the plane now on the ground, the passengers rising to their feet in harried haste, Ahl looks in the direction of the flight attendant sitting across the aisle, her head in her hands, shoulders heaving. Earlier, she seemed morose, apathetic. He tried to get her to speak, to find out if there was anything he could do—not that he knew what he could do to help. When she didn't respond to his queries but kept staring at the photograph of a young boy and weeping, he decided to let her be. He listened to her sobbing for a long while before offering her his handkerchief to wipe away the tears. Now at the journey's end, he is still curious to know the cause of her sorrow. Is the young boy in the photograph missing or dead? He hangs around a little while more, taking his time to gather his things. Finally, she raises her head and looks up at him, the slight trace of a smile forming around her lips as she tentatively holds out the handkerchief in her cupped hand, as if uncertain that he will accept it back in its soiled state. Ahl suggests that she keep it, as he affords himself the time to read her name tag: WIILA. Nodding his head, he wishes her "every good thing."

The airstrip, now that he can observe it, has no barrier to fence it in; nothing to restrict unauthorized persons from walking straight onto the aircraft and mixing with the passengers as they land. A mob gathers at the foot of the stepladder, joining the man in a yellow vest, flip-flops, and trousers with holes in them who guided the aircraft to its parking position. He, too, chats up the passengers as they alight, asking for baksheesh.

The passengers, who in Djibouti fought their way onto the plane and to their seats, now scramble for their luggage, some hauling suitcases heavier than they are. Ahl stands back, amused, watching. He has all the time in the world to stretch his limbs and massage his back, which is aching after two hours in a plane with no seat belts. The pilot—Russian, Ukrainian, Serb?—joins him where he is, and behaves discourteously toward Wiila, whom he describes, in bad, accented English, as "fat-arsed, lazy, and weepy." Ahl is about to reprimand him when Wiila urges him to "stay out of it." Feeling all the more encouraged, the pilot dresses Wiila down in what sounds like a string of hard-bitten expletives. Embarrassed and feeling defeated, Ahl regrets involving himself in a matter of no immediate concern to him.

The breeze and the scent of the sea it bears help Ahl get purchase on his fractious disposition. Calmed, he tries to identify his hostess, Xalan, or her husband, Warsame, neither of whom he has met. He looks around sadly, quiet, like a pinched candle, wondering if he can recognize either of them from the descriptions his wife has given him. Then he tells himself that there is no happier person than a traveler who has arrived at his destination and feels the comfort and confidence to face the world before him with an open mind, without fear or tribulation. He is in no imminent danger, even though he is in Somalia. He has someone waiting to pick him up. And if no one shows up, he is sure he won't have any difficulty getting into town or to his hotel.

A couple of porters in blue overalls are bringing the baggage out of the hold and passing it around. Ahl receives his bag and remembers to offer a couple of U.S. dollars to the porter, thanking him. But he realizes that he is attracting the unwelcome attention of a loiterer, who follows him, persistently clutching at his shirtsleeve and computer bag. The man points to his mouth and belly. Ahl doesn't know what to do to rid himself of the beggar. Then he hears someone calling his name, and sees a big-bellied man duckwalking toward him. Ahl and the beggar wait in silence as he approaches.

"Welcome to Puntland, Ahl. I am Warsame."

Warsame wears his trousers low on his hips, like youths imitating jailbirds. But unlike the copycat youths, Warsame has on a belt, which is tight under his bulging tummy. As they walk away, he shoos off the pesterer, who stops bothering Ahl.

Warsame says, "I bring warm greetings from Xalan. She is home, cooking. But I'll take you to your hotel first, then home. Come now." Warsame takes Ahl by the forearm.

Ahl hates uncalled-for physical contact with other men in public. He faces the dilemma of reclaiming his arm from cuddly Warsame without undue rudeness so soon after their meeting. He doesn't wish to offend his kind host.

Warsame says, "Let me carry something."

"Thanks, but there is no need," Ahl says.

Warsame says, "You travel very light for a man coming from the United States."

"I love traveling light," Ahl says. "Less hassle."

"When Xalan returns from Canada," Warsame muses, in the long-suffering tone many men take when the discussion touches on their wives' luggage, "she requires a truck."

Ahl doesn't join in the wife-bashing, because while he knows some women who pack heavy suitcases for an overnight outing, he also knows men who wear more perfume than a Sudanese bride on the day of her wedding. He recalls Yusur telling him about a horrible incident involving Xalan and some of Mogadiscio's clan-based vigilantes—a most terrible incident, which, according to Yusur, Xalan's sister, Zaituun, accused her of provoking. In a bid to avoid spreading further bad blood, Ahl changes the subject. "How long has this airstrip been functioning?"

"Three years and a bit," Warsame says.

Ahl won't ask what's become of the funds the autonomous state collects as tax. He can guess where they have ended up; in someone's corrupt coffers. Nor does he comment on the shocking absence of an airport building of any sort, or even a runway. As if he has voiced his thoughts aloud, Warsame says, "We keep asking where the funds go."

It's never wise to make enemies of people on the first day you meet them, Ahl tells himself, especially if you don't know them well. He won't pursue the subject of corruption. Who knows, Warsame himself could be in on it, quietly receiving his share.

"Where's Immigration?" he asks.

Warsame points. "There."

Ahl looks around, his eyes following Warsame's finger. He spots a shack out to the left of a cluster of vehicles bearing United Arab Emirates license plates, on what would have been the apron of the runway had there been one.

"We'll get to our vehicle and someone from Immigration will come and collect your passport," Warsame says, "and return it stamped."

"Is that how things work out here?"

"Here, everything is ad hoc," Warsame explains.

Warsame leads Ahl to a waiting four-by-four with UAE plates, opens it, starts the engine, and turns on the AC full blast. A young man arrives to collect Ahl's passport. Saying, "Back in a minute," he disappears into the shed. Ahl thinks that until today he has never understood the full meaning of the term *ad hoc*: the heartlessness, the mindlessness of a community failing its responsibility toward itself; a feebleness of purpose; an inadequacy.

The young man is as good as his promise, though. He is back in a minute, ready to return Ahl's stamped passport on payment of twenty U.S. dollars. Warsame gives the young man a couple of dollars as well, thanking him, and then says to Ahl, "Now we may go." And they are off, raising dust and moving faster and faster, as if competing in a rally.

———

Like the airstrip, the city falls well below Ahl's expectations. Yusur and many other Puntlanders in the diaspora have talked up Bosaso, describing it as a booming coastal city bubbling with ideas, its gung-ho, on-the-go residents making pots of money, many of them from trade, a handful out of piracy. It is a city, he has been told, that has benefited from the negative consequences of the civil war, with thousands of professionals and businessmen who ancestrally hailed from this region returning and basing themselves here.

But the roads are not tarred, and the dust billows ahead of them disorientingly. The buildings within range appear to be little more than upgraded shacks. Cars are parked at odd angles, as if abandoned in haste. The streets themselves look to be assembled ad hoc, with temporary structures thrown up to house the internally displaced communities that have fled the fighting in Mogadiscio or have been deported from the breakaway Republic of Somaliland to the north. Now and then they drive past houses of solid stone, with proper gates and high fences. But there is something unsightly about these, too, because of the discarded polyethylene bags that are hanging, as if for dear life, from the electric wires with which the properties are surrounded.

Despite his attempt not to sound disapproving, Ahl's voice strikes a note of discord when he asks Warsame, "Has the city always been like this?"

As if in mitigation, Warsame says, "The state is autonomous, albeit dysfunctional. Our economy is underdeveloped. We are a city under siege, with immigrants from Ethiopia, Eritrea, and Tanzania. They all want to make their way to Yemen and Europe, courtesy of the human traffickers who exploit them as stowaways in flimsy boats—just to escape from here."

"Everyone comes because there is peace here?"

Warsame says, "There is of course the lucrative potential of piracy, given Bosaso's strategic location. Taken together, these features attract all sorts of riffraff."

"Do you have any idea what the population of the city is and what percentage of its residents are local?" Ahl asks.

"No one knows the number of its residents."

Ahl is aware that you need to put certain structures in place before it is possible to take a census. He says, "Because everything here is ad hoc."

Warsame nods and adds, "And life must go on."

Ahl asks Warsame to stop somewhere he can get a SIM card for his mobile phone.

Soon enough, Warsame obliges. He stops in front of a low structure with ads on its front walls for all makes of cigarettes and other products, and a few goats, in the absence of pasture, chewing a weather-hardened castaway pair of leather shoes, they are so hungry. Ahl buys a local SIM card and airtime with a ten-dollar bill. Still inside the shop, he inserts the SIM card in his phone.

In the vehicle, Warsame encourages Ahl to place his calls right away. "Go for it, please," he says, driving. "Make your calls. Tell Yusur or whosoever that you've landed, you've been picked up, and all is well."

Malik answers the phone on the first ring. They speak in Chinese and Ahl gives him his news. Malik asks Ahl what impression the city has made on him so far. Ahl responds that the city has more the look of a flea market than the prosperous metropolis he expected. He says, "I haven't been here half an hour and I am already wondering where the money said to be pouring in from piracy and hostage-taking has gone." Then he asks, "What about you, Malik? How are you doing?"

Malik is depressed, because, in the past day and a half, in Mogadiscio, three journalists have been killed—blown up—the latest an hour ago. The first two were radio journalists, killed dropping off their children at their nurseries or school before going to work. The third was on his way back from burying a colleague. A fourth journalist was wounded by a roadside device while walking, and hovers in critical condition, with little chance of surviving his injuries.

"Who is responsible?"

Malik says, "There are unconfirmed reports blaming shady fifth columnists who are believed to target anyone who writes anything the top men of the Courts don't like. They use remote-controlled roadside bombs or shoot their victims at point-blank range. Nobody knows much about them or their alliances. Except everyone points at Shabaab, which has an imprecise, albeit mutually beneficial rapport with the Courts."

Ahl says, "That's worrying."

"All good journalists are now on the radar of the assassins," Malik says. "It's sickening. This is killing me."

"Do you feel you're in danger?"

"I won't pack up and leave."

"Have I suggested you do that?"

"Amran has done just that every time I've spoken to her. I thought you might do the same," Malik says.

"What are your plans?"

"I may have to move in with Bile and Cambara."

"Would you feel safer with them?"

"I would."

Warsame drives past security at the hotel gate and stops in front of the building to let Ahl out, telling him he'll return for him later.

Out of the car, his gait wobbly, Ahl retrieves his bags and walks toward the sign that says, "Respecshin," amused that not one of the bellhops loitering in the parking lot offers to help. The muscles of his thighs a bit tight, he reaches the porch, aware that it has been a few days since his last workout. He thinks it unlikely that this two-star hotel will have a gym, and he imagines it would be unwise to go out for a jog or even for a swim.

At the reception, two young men are playing cards intently. One of them has a gap in his upper teeth, and the other is sporting a Mohawk. Even though neither is in uniform, Ahl speculates that Gap-in-the-Teeth is the one temporarily in charge. He is odds-on the son or other blood relative of the hotel owner. Back from school for the day, he mans the reception, while his friend is on an afternoon break.

Gap-in-the-Teeth asks Ahl, "What do you want?"

Ahl is not sure what answer to give, because he has discovered, now that he has searched for it, that Gap-in-the-Teeth and his stepson, Taxliil, share some remote resemblance: the manner in which they hold themselves apart, as if the world is synonymous with the dirt that prevails everywhere, and they wish to stay clean; and in their sweet smiles, as masterly as they are mistimed, smiles that often lead to misunderstandings.

"Has a room been reserved for Ahl?"

Gap-in-the-Teeth tells him he will be in room 15.

Ahl, unaided and unescorted, goes to his room, up the winding staircase with its uneven risers, pleased with the lightness of his bags, content that his needs are modest. He comes to a stop in front of room 15. The door is open, no need to make use of the key. He looks in and finds a vast room, the wall at the back of the bed tiled high and neatly in brown against a white background. A man is in the room, fiddling with the knobs and wires of the TV set, which is on, belting out a concatenation of what at first sounds like an alien language because the volume is so unbearably loud that the words are almost impossible to decipher.

"Please," Ahl pleads. "Turn the TV off."

"I am fixing your satellite TV," the man shouts loudly, in competition with the racket. He is chewing *qaat*, and his tongue, emerging from his mouth as he speaks, resembles a chameleon's—narrow, repellent.

Ahl repeats his plea, slowly this time, the better to be understood. The TV man stays on his haunches. He stares at a knob he is holding in his right hand, as if he might admonish it for its obstinate behavior— presumably this is the piece of hardware that is causing the set to malfunction. He shrieks, "I must fix the problem."

Ahl says, "Please do it later."

But the technician does no such thing. He has been instructed to see to it that all the rooms have functioning TV sets. Ahl feels that the din is making him lose touch with his senses or, worse, with his reason. But he has been warned that one must be circumspect in one's dealings with young Somalis. People out here are a nervy lot, quick to anger and to reach for their guns.

His voice calm, he says, "Please, please."

He ascribes the first *please* to the Somali part of his upbringing, which emphasizes considerateness to the point of formality, and the second *please* to fear of provoking that notorious Somali crankiness. He says, "I want to use the bathroom. Urgently."

At last the technician turns off the TV, disconsolate, clearly offended, and, as if to show his annoyance, masticates his *qaat* furiously. Just before he walks off in a huff, Ahl says, "Will you do me a favor, please?"

Rudely the man asks, "What do you want?"

"I'd like to eat if the kitchen is still open."

"What do you want to eat?"

"A fish dish and rice, if these are available."

"Of course they are available."

"I'd appreciate it if you could place an order."

And as a token of his appreciation, Ahl brings out a couple of U.S. dollars to give as a tip. But no, the man won't take the baksheesh, either because it is too small or because he doesn't wish to be appeased. He leaves in a fit of pique. Bemused, Ahl closes the door behind the man and goes into the bathroom.

Then, bizarrely, the TV comes on again, noisier than before. Ahl is incensed, assuming that the technician has returned and turned it back on. Ahl decides to finish peeing, and then deal with it. He is of several minds as to how he will achieve his aim. Kick the man in the butt and face the consequences, or kick the set to smithereens and pay for it? Or should he accept defeat? But when he comes out, there is no one in the room and Ahl is looking at an Arab in a suit and tie interviewing a Somali on Al Jazeera, with the ruins of the twelfth-century Arbaca Rukun mosque, destroyed in the 1991 fighting in Mogadiscio, serving as background.

The Somali interviewee is saying, "We, as mujahideen, martyrs of Islam, are ready to lay down our lives in the name of Allah. We'll help defeat Ethiopia and America, the enemies of Islam." Then, just as mysteriously as it came on, the TV goes off again.

———

The shower is very cold, despite the tropical heat. Ahl decides a bird-bath will do. He washes his face and armpits, changes his shirt, and rings Warsame and Xalan to find out when they are coming for him. No answer. Before going downstairs to eat the fish dish he ordered by telephone after calling the reception, he packs his computer in its bag, puts all his cash in its pockets, and descends the stairs with caution. When he walks past the reception desk, Gap-in-the-Teeth tells him he has a guest waiting for him. Assuming his visitor to be Warsame or Xalan, he asks where, and Gap-in-the-Teeth points to a small gazebo where a man is sitting alone at a table meant for four, with two of the untaken chairs tipped forward.

The man does not bother to introduce himself or even to greet Ahl. He has a down-turned mouth, very fine teeth, and bulging eyes, and he is dressed in a pleated shirt from another era. Even though he is the ugliest man Ahl has ever set eyes on, he is nonetheless a charmer, re-minding Ahl of a midget from Agrigento whose daughter Ahl once dated for almost a year, secretly, when he was at university in England. The woman was studying English, a pretty slow learner. She made up for it elsewhere: she was excellent in bed and a superb cook.

When the man in the gazebo asks Ahl how his room is, Ahl wonders if he is the hotel manager. But the man says, "As for *things* not work-ing? We have no plumbers to install hot water systems for hotels. Even though Puntland is in relative peace, we suffer from a shortage of trained personnel in all fields. Here we go about things with a trial-and-error and try-and-see attitude. Now things work, now they don't. Uncertainty reigns supreme."

Ahl decides there is nothing to lose by engaging in such banter in the middle of the day, with the security everywhere close, his mo-bile phone boasting airtime, Warsame or Xalan a touch of two but-tons away. "What's become of the trained personnel in these fields?" he asks.

"Those with good education have joined the exodus, and, fleeing the country, have ended up in refugee camps in Kenya or Ethiopia, and then eventually some have made it to the Arabian Gulf as low-paid workers, or gone to Europe or North America as refugees. Imagine— one and a half million of them, many of them destitute."

The arrival of food interrupts their conversation. "What will you have?" Ahl asks his guest, whom he does not want to leave. Who knows, this mysterious man may lead him to Taxliil.

The waiter says, "The kitchen is closed."

"This is enough for two. Please bring another plate and some more cutlery," Ahl says. "We can share this."

The waiter makes resentful noises but does as Ahl has requested, bringing a plate and more cutlery. The man tucks into the food with evident enjoyment.

"We haven't had the pleasure until now," he says. "I know your name is AhlulKhair. My full name is Ali Ahmed Fidno, but I am known among friends as Fidno."

Ahl asks, "How do you know who I am?"

Cautious like a feral cat defending its catch, Fidno bares his teeth and makes some sort of animal noise emanating from deep inside him. Taken aback, Ahl focuses his stare first on Fidno's hands, whose fingers now form into a fist, with the knuckles palely protruding, and then on his heavy jowls, which seem to expand, as if intimating impending trouble. Fidno looks away, and then, pulling from under him a large brown envelope on which he has been sitting, leans forward and says to Ahl, "Here. I have brought you these photographs."

Ahl's imagination runs off ahead of him: he envisions photographs of Taxliil posing in fatigues in some training camp close by.

"Photographs of who or what?"

"Of some boys doing their own thing."

Ahl hopes that Fidno is not taking him for a sex pervert. Does he think that Ahl is a fifty-something tourist after young things with whom he wants to play sex? Ahl has lost his appetite. He puts down his utensils and asks, "Of whom are the photos?"

Fidno favors the question with silence.

"Why, of all people, have you brought them to me?"

Fidno says, "Someone at the airport who saw you arrive has said to me that you are a Somali journalist, based in America."

"Let me have a look at them."

Ahl removes them from the envelope and takes his time studying them, a picture at a time, as he listens to Fidno's running commentary. They are all indeed of young men—in boats, in ships, manning guns, holding men, faces covered with balaclavas. Young men eating, sleeping, fooling around with one another, speaking on their mobile phones, some of them dressed in the jackets of which they dispossessed their hostages, of whom there are also photos. The names of the ships and their provenance are written on the sides: Ukrainian, Russian, Italian, Turkish, Israeli, Saudi, Filipino, Indian. The haul is big. But the young men wielding the AK-47s, the collapsible machine guns, are skinny, hungry-looking, many appearing as ill prepared for what life may throw at them as Paris Hilton might be going into the ring with Mike Tyson. Are these youths pirates? And if they are not pirates, then who are they, what are they? Six months is a long time in the life of a teenager, who may grow a beard or start wearing contact lenses.

Will Fidno, sitting at Ahl's table, stripping the last morsels of fish off the spine, be able to tell him more? Will he involve Malik? Can Fidno help him track down Taxliil?

"Where did you get the pictures?" Ahl asks.

Fidno is champing at a toothpick, taking his time.

"I had them taken by a photographer I hired."

It is a pity Fidno is not a pirate, a privateer, or even a buccaneer, because he has the charm that makes women lift their arms, place them right behind their heads, their armpits exposed and their breasts raised. Why do women find pirates charming, why do they giggle invitingly in their presence? Ahl recalls that the Sicilian woman did just that within an hour of his meeting her. Like a cat going on her back, waiting to be petted.

Ahl says, "In your capacity . . . as what?"

Fidno looks at their lunch things, not yet collected. Ahl beckons to the waiter standing close by to take the plates away and bring the bill.

"And coffee, if possible," Fidno says.

"Make it two coffees. Mine espresso," says Ahl.

Fidno says, "Make mine *lungo*, with lots of sugar."

The waiter gone, Ahl asks again, "In what capacity?"

Fidno responds, "I've had the photographs taken in my capacity as a mediator, a negotiator, an interpreter, and, most important, a go-between, when matters get too sticky between the pirates and the negotiators on behalf of the shipowners."

Ahl asks, "With whom do the negotiators deal?"

"They use intermediaries," Fidno replies, "often through middlemen based in Mombasa or Abu Dhabi."

"So they don't come to Puntland, and prefer assigning intermediaries to negotiate on their behalf?"

Fidno says, "They remain at their desks in London, Tokyo, or Moscow, wherever they are normally based. One of my jobs is to iron out unexpected difficulties when things get sticky, which they do a lot of the time. Each of these men—insurers, middlemen, facilitators—gets his cut, depending on his rank and his importance in the company hierarchy, without any direct contact with us."

"Too many people, too much money, and no direct communication—isn't that a recipe for possible disaster?" Ahl ventures.

Fidno says, "It is a recipe for deceit, double-dealing, and counterfeiting. And we are the marquee pawns of the greatest dupe. We're cheated, and yet there is no way we can prove any of this to the world, because they have the backing of the international media and we do not."

"Wait, wait. What are you saying?"

"Let's imagine you reading in your newspaper, wherever you are, that the owners of a ship hijacked by Somali pirates have paid five million dollars as ransom," Fidno proposes.

"Let's imagine I do."

Fidno says, "What if I told you that, to begin with, the largest bulk of the five million does not leave London, where the insurers are based, because no bank in Britain will countenance approving of so much money going out of its vaults to pay off a ransom?"

"That makes sense," Ahl concurs.

"What if I told you that in the end, after months of negotiations, proposals and counterproposals, broken agreements and delays, only half a million of the five million dollars will reach the pirates. First the negotiators of the insurers based in London, the middleman based in Abu Dhabi, and the intermediaries in Mombasa have each taken their huge cuts, so that the final payment is reduced to a pittance from which the funder financing the hijacking still has to pay the pirates holding the ship. You know the Somali proverb 'Mana wasni, warna iraac,' said to have been spoken by a woman suspected of having enjoyed lovemaking, when the man never even touched her. We're buggered, however you want to put it, and needless to say, we don't enjoy it at all."

"That's hairy," Ahl says.

"This utter disrespect makes us indignant."

Ahl says, "That is criminal."

Now Fidno is nervous, like a Mafioso not used to explaining the reason for his actions. In a telltale sign of confession, he leans forward, as though sharing a secret, and then changes his mind after policing the surroundings and seeing the waiter returning with the bill and the two coffees. Ahl settles the bill in U.S. dollars. Then they resume their conversation.

"What's your precise role in this business?"

Fidno replies, "Among the pirates, I am all things to almost every one of them. I am a link, a connector, an in-between man, an extinguisher of fires when fires need extinguishing. I am all things to the shipowners, the London men at their desks, bowler hats or not. I deal with insurance and safety matters with the captain, the crew, the ship, and the cargo, when held. I am all things to the men at the Suez Canal and many other men stationed at different ports in different countries, men privy to the secret details involved in the movements of the ships, the nature of cargo, whether legal or illegal, whether the cargo is chemical waste and who is carrying it and where it is to be dumped. I log in the departure details and the ships' destinations, too."

Ahl says, "You are something, aren't you?"

Fidno continues, "Sea banditry is a very risky business. It can get you killed easily in these lanes. You can make pots of wealth, depending on how you play the game. Questions to do with who gets to collect the ransom when the young Somalis hold a ship; who gets to receive the funds; who gets his due cut; who gets paid and who gets swindled. These pirates are not like the pirates of old, who got to keep a portion of their booty and share the loot among themselves—democratically! I am not in fact sure you can call the Somalis pirates."

Ahl wants to ask why not, but before he can say anything, Warsame is at their table, greeting Ahl and looking from him to Fidno. Fidno scrambles to his feet, almost knocking over his chair and coffee cup. Ahl introduces them.

Then Ahl asks, "Why don't you come with us?"

"Depends on where you are going."

Ahl turns to Warsame, "Can he?"

"Of course."

Fidno asks, "But where are we going?"

"To my home," Warsame says.

"Come along," Ahl urges Fidno.

They follow Warsame to the car. When Ahl tries to put the photographs in the pocket of his computer bag, Fidno extends his hand and, grinning, reclaims them from him. Then he walks over to his jalopy, parked across from Warsame's vehicle, to put them in his glove compartment.

Ahl thinks it will be easier to find out more about Fidno in the company of others. He tells himself that a liar seldom knows how to repeat his lies.

JEEBLEH STIRS AND, A LITTLE DAZED, PROPS HIMSELF UP ON HIS elbows, eyes still shut; he is wearing an airline eye-mask against the intense brightness of the hour. His head is aflutter with memories calling, the past revisiting in the shape of a monster, Bile's older brother Caloosha, a bully unlike any other; and the present raising its war-filled head, in the likeness of BigBeard, hirsute and ugly to the core, messaging vicious viruses, deleting files and baby photographs. Malik is in the other room, which once belonged to Makka and Raasta. As a rank rememberer, Jeebleh recalls his confrontation with Caloosha, which he compares with his vile encounter with BigBeard. This has left him traumatized, like an amputee suffering anew the agony of dismemberment.

Startled by a sudden clamor, source undetermined—the harshness of the noise suggests metal coming into unexpected collision with glass, breaking it—Jeebleh sits up, waits, and listens to the discordant sounds now banking up behind identifiable activities. He picks out what sounds like the wings of a bird flapping. All the same, the disjointed noises raise his sense of worry, almost to the point of fear, and he prepares himself for the worst. What can he do if an intruder tries to enter the apartment from the balcony?

He gets out of bed, ready to confront the trespasser and try to protect himself and Malik from harm. But he is unclear how he is going to achieve this. As he steps out of the room, wielding a broom—how ridiculous he must look, he tells himself—he is of two minds whether to activate the emergency procedure Dajaal instructed him in. But no sooner has he gained the inner security door leading to the balcony than he isolates the sound. It is the agitated squeak of a young bird in a flutter, flapping its wings—a medium-sized black-shouldered kite in mounting distress, caught in a small enclosure, struggling, now lifting its tail, now lowering it with animated vigor. Maybe the bird has erroneously flown in under the eaves, or through a chink in the window frame above the alcove to the left of the balcony.

Aware that his footsteps are heightening the bird's anxiety, Jeebleh approaches. Little by little, with consummate care, his tread soft and his forward motion purposeful, hands behind his back. He stops and sighs at length when he reaches the limits of the enclosure and then releases the catch, allowing the bird to fly free. Then he returns to the living room.

———

One reminiscence brings forth another, now replacing it, now supplementing it. He relives a confrontation in a hotel room in Mogadiscio, prostrate and in an eyeball-to-eyeball face-off with a chameleon, the reptile fearlessly making its way from the balcony into the room. The memory leaves him jittery, with anger welling up inside him. He paces back and forth, determined to shake off his rage. Again an ominous memory linked to Caloosha invades. Jeebleh thinks that there is undeniable similarity between Caloosha and BigBeard's methods, which both claim are in service to higher causes; the late Caloosha asserted his socialist ideals in the same way that BigBeard takes the sanctity of Islam as his mantra, asserts it is the beacon lighting his way to divine authority. Caloosha, in the end, got what he deserved, dying a miserable death. Jeebleh wonders when BigBeard will get his comeuppance, his just desserts.

Time to make tea. Slow in movement, Jeebleh picks up the metal kettle; not bothering to remove the lid, he fills it through its spout. Then he falls under the spell of a pleasant memory, the weekend he took his granddaughter's photograph, the one that served as Malik's screen saver until BigBeard deemed it pornographic. Jeebleh regrets that innocence provides no protection against a BigBeard with sex on his mind. Anyhow, it was the weekend before his departure. The whole family drove out to Port Jefferson on Long Island in a rental car. On their way back to the city, they detoured, stopping on the North Shore for lunch. He recalls his granddaughter's fascination with the beach sand, of which she took mouthfuls, in preference to the food her mother offered her.

He thinks that he should call home, and the thought brings forth another memory: of his first phone conversation with his wife, the last time he was here. A man with a portable machine bigger than a laptop came up to his room. Jeebleh could not figure out how the device worked, what the appliance was called or even how best to describe it. But it allowed him to speak to his wife, and that was what mattered then. He and Malik have so far only briefly texted their respective wives to let them know they have arrived safely, but have avoided speaking to them. Malik is worried that Amran might urge him to leave, if he tells her everything. Moreover, neither has found adequate words with which to describe BigBeard's depraved logic. No doubt, their guardedness has been intruding on their minds, disturbing their thinking. On the positive side, however, the two have remained at their most harmonious, and that is a great relief.

————

A quarter of an hour later, Malik emerges from his room, scratching with fury and cursing. The blood vessels around his eyelids have darkened; his eyes are smarting and bloodshot; his skin is torn and oozing in places.

"I itch all over," he says.

Jeebleh humors him. "It is human to itch."

"I dreamed I was itching and I woke up itching."

"Let's see." Jeebleh sees no bites or scratches.

Malik says, "I had a rash of dreams, a nightmare of allergies. In my dream, I broke out in eruptions, felt violated, intruded upon, invaded; the more the dreams infringed on my mind, the fiercer I scratched."

"An allergic reaction to food you've eaten?"

"I doubt it."

"Maybe bedbugs?"

"I turned on the lights and found nothing."

"Bedbugs strike furtively and hide."

"I upended the bed," Malik says. "No bugs."

Silent, Malik looks away, embarrassed. He touches his arm for bumps, sores, and swellings resulting from bites, but finds little that he can show to Jeebleh as one might show a trophy. He shakes his head in amazement.

"Can it be that Gumaad put it into your head?" Jeebleh asks.

"How is that?"

"Because Gumaad explained the derogatory term *Injirray*, which Somalis reserve for the Ethiopians. Maybe that is where your obsession with itching springs from."

Malik asks, "Why do Somalis allude to lice, when it comes to Ethiopia?"

Jeebleh tells him, "You see, the only Ethiopians that Somalis have met in large numbers are the ill-paid, ill-clad barefoot soldiers in the outposts of the Empire, extending down to Somali-speaking Ogaden. Unwashed and wearing the same uniforms for weeks on end, they itched and scratched. Ancient contacts between Somalis and Abyssinians shaped the terms each had for the other. 'Lice' defines the Abyssinian/Ethiopian foot soldiers in these outposts, the insect with which Somalis have associated these unwashed, ill-paid soldiers. For their part, the Amhara ethnic group refer to Somalis as 'ass washers,' or 'skirt wearers,' denigrating descriptors for Muslims who perform ablutions before their prayers, or who, like women, wear skirts. Nothing new in this. After all, the English call the French 'frogs,' don't they? No wonder then that you've dreamed of armies of lice invading."

Jeebleh recalls how, in the 1977 war between Ethiopia and Somalia, they found laughter in the treacherous nature of head lice, and discovered the punning potential in speaking figuratively about matters of political import. As a schoolboy, he came down often enough with fevers brought on by malaria and all sorts of other bites. His mother would use kerosene to rid him of the lice or shave his head.

Malik says, "A flea-bitten nation lying dead by a roadside, spotty, dirty, and armpits itchy, head crawling with lice. Battalions of bedbugs on the move and in fatigues, light green their carapace of choice. In my dream, I saw battalions of lice moving in an eastward motion, coming toward the Somali–Ethiopian border town of Feerfeer."

Jeebleh says, "The stakes are high and everyone is jittery, with the drums of war and the saber rattling, which are becoming deafening."

Jeebleh then recalls to himself a brief passage from Günter Grass's *Local Anesthetic*, in which the dentist describes tartar as "enemy number one" to the teeth. Imagine—tartar laying traps, ensnaring the tongue; and the tongue, busily searching for crust formations, rough surfaces that nurture tartar, so that it can destroy them. No wonder diseased gums are rich with pockets in which germs find homes; no wonder nations breed all sorts of persons, some of whom will cause the death of their own kind, betrayers, sellouts, subhuman suicides.

"Politics is a living thing, and you can never tell with living things," Jeebleh says. "Living things kill or are killed; they walk away, they change alliances; they bite, they are crushed underfoot. Lice or not, living things are the darkness upon the face of the deep."

Malik thinks, Nits, knocks, bites, and bellyaches, frets, furies, and mind-numbing fevers are little local pains. Little local aches caused by a chipped front tooth!

―――――

Breakfast is a simple affair: medium-size bowls of natural yogurt, a homemade gift from Cambara, eaten with two spoonfuls of marmalade for Jeebleh, who then makes an omelet with tomato and onion for Malik. Jeebleh has tea before joining Malik in coffee.

Dajaal telephones to say that, as Malik requested the previous night, he is bringing along Qasiir, his grandson, to try to repair Malik's computer.

"Give us half an hour," Jeebleh says.

Dajaal asks, "What about you, Jeebleh?"

Jeebleh replies, "I know that Malik wants to stay behind with Qasiir to work on the machine, but I would very much like to visit with Bile. From what she has told me, Cambara will be out shopping, and Bile will be alone, an ideal time to visit. He is expecting me, says he feels a lot better today, thank God."

"Then I can come and fetch you from Bile's after the business with Malik's computer?" Dajaal suggests.

"We'll arrange that when you come."

Barely has Jeebleh given a bear hug to Qasiir, whom he remembers fondly from his previous visit as "cool," using the idiom of the young, and introduced him to Malik, when it occurs to him that he must discuss with Malik the possibility of drafting Qasiir in their attempt to locate Taxliil. Jeebleh feels certain that Qasiir will have contacts among his former fellow militiamen, some of whom must be serving the current Courts dispensation.

By Jeebleh's recollection, Qasiir was quick, bright, and trustworthy, a levelheaded young man with a reputation for calculating risks before making a move; he was different from many of his peers. Today Qasiir has on a pair of ironed jeans, a shirt a size too small, and sneakers that look overused. His belt has a buckle the size of a fist and on his chin he sports a tuft of hair too sparse to bother with. He wears a shoulder holster, too, with a pistol in it.

"Look at you," Jeebleh says, "all grown up and with a family of your own. You have a child, don't you? Is it a boy or a girl?"

"A boy, such an active one he keeps us awake."

Jeebleh observes that Qasiir is physically and temperamentally different from the teenager on whom he had last set eyes a decade or so ago. He has put on some weight around the waist, but he carries it with ease.

"I am surprised you're still wearing jeans," Jeebleh says. "Don't your peers who have gone over and made common cause with the robed, bearded lot look upon a jeans-wearer with suspicion?"

"Many do, but those close to me know the score."

"You don't go to mosques wearing jeans, do you?"

"As if that matters," Dajaal says.

Qasiir says, "Not on Fridays, Grandpa."

Malik is momentarily distracted by the fact that Qasiir addresses

Dajaal, his granduncle, as "Grandpa." Then he remembers that the term *granduncle* has no equivalent in Somali. He knows from his own experience how taxing it can be to address Jeebleh in any tongue, for he cannot bring himself to address him as "uncle," as a Somali son-in-law might, but "father-in-law" is too awkward and formal. Maybe the problem of how to address in-laws is a problem nobody has resolved in any language, anywhere.

"You go to mosque only on Friday?" asks Malik.

"I want to be seen, don't I?"

"It's all part of the show," Dajaal says.

Malik asks, "If it's true that the religionists give women so many lashes if they are seen in the streets unveiled, how do you explain that jeans-wearing men are not penalized? I wouldn't be surprised if some thought you were sabotaging the Islamic way of life."

Qasiir is, as Jeebleh expects, quick on the uptake. "It is possible that they let me be because several of my mates are active Shabaab members, with considerable clout. I know these friends better than anyone, know that they exchanged their status as clan-based militia-men for a white robe and a beard because many are too lazy to bother finding razor blades and shaving daily."

Dajaal says, "Copycats, that's what they are."

Jeebleh remembers a French proverb that says that while a man with one watch knows what the time is, a man with two may become uncertain as to the precise time, because of the watches' disparity. He thinks that because Qasiir's peers, Janus-faced, look to both the past and the future, they may be likely to help.

"Received wisdom has it that everybody knows everybody's business in Mogadiscio," Jeebleh says. "But tell me, Qasiir. Has this wisdom become inoperative under the current conditions?"

"How do you mean?" Qasiir asks.

Jeebleh says, "We hear of unknown assassins roaming around the country, a group known as 'fifth columnists' creeping up on their prey and killing former senior army officers, intellectuals, journalists. Who are these assassins who operate by means of stealth and dare murder a man when he is coming out of a mosque?"

"We may think we know who they are, but we can't say for certain," Qasiir says.

Dajaal adds, "We suspect we know who is behind the killings, because we know who the victims are—mostly professionals."

Jeebleh asks, "Is it possible to know where the two dozen young recruits from Minnesota have ended up, or by which route they have come?"

"We base what we say on a *kutiri-kuteen*, on hearsay, no evidence," Dajaal replies. "In days of old, the functioning principle was the primacy of the clan. We knew that this was just a cover. Nowadays, the primacy is religion. The killer is described as a mujahid, who, if killed, becomes a martyr."

Malik says, "How are the victims described?"

"To justify killing them, the victims are defined as apostates," Qasiir responds. "I suppose there is nothing new in this."

Then Dajaal speaks knowingly about how the killers move in on their prey like cat burglars. Once they kill, off they go—unseen.

Jeebleh says, "We'll all have to be cautious."

"A small indiscretion can lead to death and disaster," Dajaal warns. "We'll all have to be aware of where we are at all times, conscious of how we go about our daily business. As a journalist, Malik has to remain alert. Every minute of the day."

"Caution at all times," Jeebleh says.

Malik assures them that he is used to all that.

Jeebleh looks at his watch discreetly and says to Dajaal, "Time we went, you and I. For my lunch with Bile."

"I'll wait by the car," Dajaal says, "and Qasiir will start working on

the computer, to repair it, if possible, or at least to recover the deleted files."

———

Jeebleh is becoming anxious that he will be leaving in a couple of days,
and may not bring the tasks he has set for himself to a successful end
in such a brief time. Still, he hopes at least to lay a foundation for
Malik to have help in searching for Taxliil, without sacrificing his resolution to pursue his writing. He joins his son-in-law in the room facing the sea before going down to join Dajaal. No sooner has Jeebleh
embarked hesitantly and longwindedly on laying out the strands of his
reasoning than Malik gently cuts him short, informing him that the
thought of involving Qasiir has already occurred to him; he will do it
at the opportune time.

Malik adds, "I'll discuss the matter with Qasiir, and then we'll firm
it all up in your and Dajaal's presence later. I'd like to receive Dajaal's
backing; it's proper to do so."

"Good idea," Jeebleh agrees.

WHEN JEEBLEH IS BUZZED INTO BILE AND CAMBARA'S HOUSE, HE finds the maid preparing to leave. Bile, seated, welcomes him with a warm handshake. He looks better. As Bile motions Jeebleh to a chair, the maid says, "Please, Bile, tell Cambara that you've asked me to leave early before I finished the job she asked me to finish. Please, please do so, because I don't want her to be upset with me."

Jeebleh thinks she can't be very good at her job, considering the unswept corners where the dust has gathered, the unwashed dishes in the sink. Surely jobs as cushy as this are hard to come by in a city with one of the highest unemployment rates in the world.

Bile says, "I'll tell Cambara that."

But the maid lingers until Bile shakes his head in annoyance and says, "We'll see you tomorrow."

With her gone, Jeebleh and Bile cursorily revisit their shared past, as childhood playmates raised like brothers in the same household through their years in Padua.

Now Bile gives Jeebleh news that pleases him no end: of the three lemon trees that Jeebleh planted at his mother's grave site, two have already fruited, and the mango tree is producing fruits the size of a monkey's head as well as providing shade to visitors at the cemetery. Bile says, "I've been there only twice in the past year, I am afraid, once in Dajaal's company, the second time in Cambara's."

"I will treasure the memory of your kindness."

"Come, come, she was *my* mother, too."

Moved, Jeebleh begins to blink away tears, and the palms of his hands reach upward, bloodlessly pale as a lizard's underside. Bile looks away, tracing the life line, the head line, the love line, the sun line, and finally the fate line of his own palm with his forefinger, as a blind man might. What a journey it has been, two friends taking parallel roads for a lifetime informed by the same ideals. Each served long prison terms as well, the last few years of Bile's in solitary confinement. Then their fates took them to opposing destinations: Jeebleh's, as a professor at a college in the United States and as a father of two daughters, one of whom has blessed him with a grandchild. Bile dedicates his life to the ideals of philanthropy; it is a great pity that civil wars do not admit the principle of charity toward others.

Bile is often off-kilter, prone to mood changes when he takes medicine and sick like a dog when he does not. His back and knees are the death of him, thanks to those years in cramped confinement. Today his shirt buttons are in the wrong holes, but Jeebleh won't draw attention to this, or to the sleep in the corners of his eyes, the dried toothpaste on his chin, or his unzipped fly. He'll only embarrass his friend; no one is else around, anyhow. He and Bile are no strangers to each other. Bile involuntarily issues a sound without being conscious of it. Jeebleh thinks, It happens to the best of us, like talking in our sleep, or snoring.

Taking their time, unrushed, they move to the kitchen. Bile sits while Jeebleh prepares a light repast for him; he must eat before taking his tablets. While Jeebleh prepares noodles in lemon and garlic sauce with freshly chopped chilis, Bile snacks on cheese and other delicacies Jeebleh presents to him. Unasked, Bile talks about the rapport between employers and employees in civil war Mogadiscio, pointing out that the maid is tetchy. Harmony between employer and employed is highly prized here in these troubled times, everyone fearing that things can quickly get out of hand when one party resorts to using the gun as the arbiter in the smallest dispute.

"Is that what she'll do if you tell her off?"

Bile replies, "If you have a dispute about the overtime due to her or, God forbid, fire her, a couple of youths bearing guns will turn up to waste you in less time than it takes to stub out a cigarette."

It has become a common feature of the civil war for armed youths to kill volunteer doctors working for Médecins sans Frontières or one of the UN bodies because of a spat over some paltry sum of money.

"Haven't the religionists put a stop to that?"

"Everyone, including the religionists, is playing a wait-and-see game," Bile says, "and no one has done anything about the firearms. Gun owners will bury them, stash their weapons, waiting to spot the weaknesses in the structures the religionists have put into place, in hope of exploiting them. The current situation is no different from that of 1993, when the U.S. Marines were first deployed. Then the warlords and their allies engaged in wait-and-see trickery until they identified the fault line in the indecisive ineptitude of the Americans. Basically, every gun-wielding youth wanted to know whether the Marines were peacemakers or peace enforcers. StrongmanSouth pursued the weakness of the U.S. rationale, and he maneuvered matters to his advantage when he played dirty, dragging an American corpse through the streets of the city. You can be sure the same will happen to the Ethiopians when they invade and one of their numbers is wounded or killed. They, too, will consider withdrawing—mark my words—just as the Marines did."

Jeebleh wonders if Bile has had the chance to see the movie *Black Hawk Down*, released since his own last visit to Mogadiscio, about the American attempt to deploy their post–Cold War "intravasionist" policy stratagem to "make the world safer."

Bile makes throaty noises, like that of a cat choking on a hastily swallowed fishbone, then sips at his glass of water and relaxes, ready to resume speaking.

"I would be tempted to reach for a gun, if I owned one, whenever I hear phrases like 'The Marines are here to serve God's will,' as the then U.S. president said, or when the religionists talk of having 'popular support' or of working according to 'popular will'—or when they sentence a woman raped and then falsely accused of adultery to death by stoning. I am displeased, too, when someone spouts the obsequious fallacy that all Somalis are Muslim, especially if this is meant to offer legitimacy to a clique of religionists determined to impose their will on this nation. Let's face it, the religionists are no different from the warlords they routed, or the Federalists. No one can convince me that the broad mass of Somalis will fall for the religionists' falsehoods. In any event, the religionists will sooner or later split into radical and moderate wings, whether Ethiopia invades or not. Although I itch with anger at the thought of provoking the bully next door, our age-old enemy."

Bile takes a bite of cheese, then adds, "I prefer a spineless secular state that is all-inclusive to a religionist one run by a bearded cabal."

"Are the religionists clan-based?"

"They are and they aren't," Bile replies. "When someone is earmarked to be eliminated, they assign the job of killing him to a close relative from within their ranks, to avoid anyone ascribing the killing to someone from another clan family. If they take a town, they appoint as governor someone with no roots or history there. It is a kind of affirmative clannism. Still, I am not impressed. That they suffer from infighting is evident in the fact that the Courts haven't set up a working administrative structure for the city, because they cannot agree among themselves."

Jeebleh feels like a man in a lean-to, sitting out a raging hurricane that is leveling homes and destroying lives. Is it safer to stay inside or foot it as fast as he can?

He dishes out the food and they eat. He asks, "What is your and Cambara's relationship with the religionists?"

Bile slowly rises to his feet, the fingers of his outstretched hand pressing against the edge of the kitchen table. He sways this way and that, his knees atremble; he looks askance at a world too shaky for his liking.

Jeebleh asks, "Where are you going?"

"My tablets are in the medicine cabinet."

Jeebleh gets them for him.

"I wish I didn't tire so easily," Bile says.

Jeebleh is relieved that his mother did not live into a sickly old age. How the body falters! Bile was such an athlete when he was young, never batting an eyelid when there was a chance to compete. Now, sickly as he is, he shambles on, preferring coping on his own to being dependent on the help of others. Jeebleh can't determine which category he would belong to if he were in such a state. Like Bile, he can't stand a spouse's overprotective fussiness. And his wife is of a fussier disposition than Cambara is.

When they've eaten their lunch, they move to the lounge, and more comfortable chairs, their knees almost touching, Bile drinking tea and Jeebleh coffee, both of them brooding.

Bile says, "If a city becomes the person who loves to live in it, then Mogadiscio befits me—and Somalia suits me more than anywhere else."

Bile has often said he'll leave Mogadiscio only on his way to the grave. His bullheadedness puts Jeebleh in mind of scenes from Margaret Laurence's *The Stone Angel*. In this unique novel, one of the most memorable in fiction anywhere, Hagar, named for the handmaid in the biblical tale, is imprisoned in her pride as well as in the confines of her enfeebled body. She is an ill-natured ninety-four-year-old woman, who has constructed her life on uncompromising certitudes. She hates being helped because she hates being beholden to anyone, and insists on surviving into her old age with dignity, refusing to be put into a nursing home. She shrieks walls down, she is so strong willed. Unlike Hagar, Bile is a mild-mannered man, yet he, too, is headstrong, and old age has only made him more obdurate. He sees himself as a cosmopolitan who refuses to quit the city when everyone else has done so. Jeebleh's thoughts are now edged with anxiety as he weighs how to encourage Bile to come to the United States to see specialists.

He says, "My wife, whom you've never met but who sends her love, wonders if you'll ever visit us in New York."

A touch of tenderness in Bile's voice. "But of course, I will visit you one day, even if I cannot say when."

Jeebleh thinks of Bile as a man drowning in discomfort, his eyes glazed over, his feet stretched forward, his body rigid. Maybe by their very nature, the sick and the elderly grow restive, depressive; they take up residence in that nowhere land, unreachably distant.

"What about you and Cambara?"

He says, "Commendably, she has invested in my worthless life, contrary to what often occurs. Many of my friends have been abandoned by their partners when they are ailing or in need. Cambara has stayed by me, a loyal, loving companion. She thinks of it as buying shares in the life of your partner, subject to capital gains and losses, as with all investments. 'You gain some, you lose some,' she says, in life and in love, too. She bought shares in my life when there was no working capital as such, and invested heavily in my recovery and stayed by me. I thought it was time I, too, made a commitment of a serious nature. So I proposed to her."

"What's been her response?"

"That she'll love me, but not become my wife."

Jeebleh is not surprised to learn this. The woman is formidable, a match for Bile. A man in the last lap of his life, too ill to matter—and she loves him.

Bile says, "She says *we* are the front line."

The image of young men departing for the front line, healthy and full of the joy of youth, sets off a panic button in Jeebleh, reminding him of the imminent invasion. He thinks how in movies young men going to war commit themselves to their sweethearts.

Bile says, "Cambara became a wife, on paper, to Zaak, soon after the eruption of the civil war in the early 1990s; he had just fled Mogadiscio. Theirs was a paper marriage and was never consummated, and they both knew it would not be. Several years later, she fell for and wed Wardi, a refugee in Switzerland, where he had no other chance of becoming a citizen. She married both her previous men to get them citizenship in Canada. Maybe she sees me as a man apart from her previous men, even though I, too, am in a war zone, equally damaged by the conflict. She doesn't wish to rush into marrying a third time, afraid it might not work for her. To a point, I can see what she means."

Jeebleh asks, "May I get on her case?"

"No point badgering her."

"That will get the religionists off your backs."

"She has no faith in marriage," Bile says.

They hear the voices of a man and a woman, a door opening, and Cambara and a young man walk in, laden with heavy shopping bags. Kisses, hugs, and then introductions. "This is Robleh, here is Jeebleh," says Cambara, kissing Bile on the forehead and then on the lips. Robleh looks ill at ease.

"Food to last us for months," Cambara says.

When Robleh and Cambara go out to the car to fetch in the rest of the groceries, Bile tells Jeebleh that their guest in the annex has been ratting them out to the Courts. He can't help it, the poor sod. He seems to hope that squealing on them to the religionists will lead him to the gravy train. "It is the thing to do in Somalia these days. No scruples. No probity. This is what's got us to where we are. Helpless."

"Why not show him the door?" Jeebleh says.

"It's Cambara's call, not mine," says Bile. "There's only one way of doing things. Her way."

The shopping in, Robleh says good-bye from a distance, but Cambara joins them.

"Why all this food?" Bile asks.

Cambara says, "In the event of an invasion."

Bile is exhausted. His eyes close, despite his valiant attempts to keep them open. When Dajaal telephones, Jeebleh tells him to come and get him in five minutes. Waiting, they discuss the inevitability of the war and agree on how the Courts have mismanaged the Khartoum talks.

"I hope to leave before the war starts," Jeebleh says.

"Will Malik stay on?" Cambara asks.

"He'll remain, whatever happens."

The bell rings, the dogs bark. The bells' ringing and the dogs' barking startle Bile from his napping. "Talk to you later," Jeebleh says, as he takes his leave.

AS SOON AS DAJAAL AND JEEBLEH LEAVE, MALIK AND QASIIR SET to work on the computer. And they talk at first about matters of no great concern to either. Malik asks Qasiir about what occupies his mind lately; how much time he spends with his family, his baby, and whether he goes to the movies, if in fact there are cinemas any longer.

"The men from the Courts have shut down all the movie houses," Qasiir replies. "Movies are *xaraam*—forbidden. Nothing, not even Bollywood; no music at teahouses. It is all serious religious stuff. This is resulting in young people becoming bored and in seeing life as very tough, tedious."

"What was it like in the days of the warlords?"

"Those were brutes, the warlords. And they perpetrated indescribable cruelties against the unarmed civilians."

"I meant, what was life like for the young? You were young in those days and a member of a clan-based militia, weren't you?"

"Despite the terribleness of the times," Qasiir says, "we had some fun, in our own way. We watched films, some of them Italian or American classics, played the music of our choice, we threw parties, we danced, we did everything the young everywhere enjoy doing. We even watched blue movies. There were a couple of places run by Zanzibari refugees where you could rent those. Of course, the warlords were terrible to most people, especially anyone who belonged to one of the weaker clan families or who wasn't armed."

When they hear the muezzin announcing the prayer time, Malik tells Qasiir that he doesn't mind if Qasiir stops working to pray and then gets back to work on the computer. But Qasiir doesn't pay him any mind, and with his head inclined, his whole body still, he focuses his attention wholly on typing computer commands, intently reading the results coming up on the screen. Malik leaves the workroom, goes to the fridge, and returns with a can of Coke, which he offers to Qasiir. Qasiir pops it open, takes a sip, and says, "Thanks."

Malik sees an opening and he takes it. "What is your rapport with your former mates, who served in the same clan-based militias as you?"

"Some currently occupy positions of power in the Courts, a few have joined Shabaab and are training their cadre," Qasiir says.

"Are you in touch with them?"

"I am in touch with a couple on a daily basis."

"Tell me, how are they able to distinguish the lies they told then, when they were supposedly killing in service to the supremacy and economic advancement of their clans, from the religious spin they propagate now as divine truth?"

Qasiir is comfortable holding his ground. In his early youth, from what Jeebleh told Malik, he was an aficionado of everything American, with a special fascination for eyewear of the Ray-Ban variety and Clint Eastwood westerns, which he watched so many times with his friends that he knows the dialogue from some of the movies by heart. He now gives thought to Malik's question, taking his time, and pauses in his typing.

"Are you asking if the militiamen formerly serving the warlords, who are now members of Shabaab, are true to their characters only when they are pulling the triggers of their guns, when they are roughing up innocent folks and killing, rather than when they are in the mosque praying? Do you doubt their sincerity?"

Malik remembers an audacious remark one of his journalist colleagues made when he was in Afghanistan, that honesty is not necessarily synonymous with truth. It stands to reason that not only is it convenient to do as your fellow fighters do but also, as a militiaman, you feel more secure in a crowd, less isolated. From the distant look in his eyes, Malik thinks that Qasiir may be reliving his younger days, when he considered it fun to hang around with other vigilantes and beat up any boy on the slightest provocation.

Qasiir says, "People change unrecognizably when the country in which they live changes. The civil war opens their eyes to areas of their lives to which they have been blind—the same way going to university and receiving a good education help you see things anew. People's attitudes toward life change with a change in their circumstances, more so in war than in peace. Nobody wants to feel left behind when others move on and do well, or to feel excluded."

Malik, emboldened by what he has just heard, asks, "What benefits, apart from being a member of a group of idealists, do the youths who join Shabaab receive?"

"Shabaab has plenty of money," Qasiir says.

"Where do they get it?"

"I can only repeat what I've heard others say." Qasiir resumes his typing. "That they receive large sums from religious charities set up by wealthy Arabs. I'm sure you know more than I do about this."

"Have you been tempted to join them?"

Qasiir's voice breaks for the first time, with fear insinuating itself into the crack that has opened. He says, "No."

"Why not?"

"I am not their sort of material," Qasiir says.

"What do you mean?"

Qasiir says, "Shabaab prefer their recruits to be much younger than I, greenhorns who know no better, who haven't developed their own way of looking at the world. They concentrate their efforts on recruiting teenagers from broken homes or young boys and girls to whom they can provide a safety net, a guaranteed livelihood after training. They brainwash them, then attach every new recruit to a trustworthy insider." He breathes hard, as though it hurts to get these things off his chest. He goes on, "I would be a risk to them, and those among them who know me are aware of this."

"Do you know anyone they've killed?" Malik asks.

"I do," says Qasiir.

"Who?"

"Let me correct myself," Qasiir says. "I knew someone who was assigned to bump off Grandpa Dajaal. He came and told me so himself, and as a result he ended his association with the organization and became a victim of targeted assassination."

"Why didn't he carry out the assignment?"

"He thought it unconscionable to kill a man who has done him no harm, and whom he has known for much of his life," Qasiir says.

"Why did he come to you?"

"He owed me a favor."

"What kind of favor?"

"We were mates, and one day when he was in a shoot-out, in which he could've been killed, I saved him. He and I were on different sides, fighting for control of lucrative turf. He was badly injured and I took him to Grandpa Dajaal's house and Uncle Bile treated him. Not one of his or my friends knew about this, but he remembered."

"Does Dajaal know about the contract out on him?"

"I chose not to tell him."

"Why not?"

"To what purpose?"

"So he would know."

"Grandpa wouldn't change his lifestyle, no matter what," Qasiir says. "He is the loveliest, the kindest, but also the most obstinate man I know."

"Do you know of any of your former comrades in the militia groups who carried out their assignments and who may be willing to talk to a journalist?"

"A Shabaab member wouldn't dare talk to a journalist."

"What would happen if he did?"

"Someone would follow him as he left the mosque," Qasiir say, "and would use a silencer to kill him. A passerby would stumble on the corpse nearby. The victim would be buried, no questions asked."

A sense of deliverance is evident in Qasiir's body language, which strikes Malik as that of an honest man speaking the honest truth.

Qasiir says, "It will be difficult to find an active member of Shabaab ready to talk on record. It's easier to find a disillusioned former member who will say his piece; or someone who's lost a family member to Shabaab. A new recruit or an active member won't want to talk. A talent spotter might. I hear rumors that Robleh, who stays at Uncle Bile's, is one. I can't tell if this is true or untrue. All I know is that he is very chummy with Shabaab. So why not speak to him?"

Malik feels a tug in his viscera when he hears this. Who knows, Qasiir may prove successful in tracking down Taxliil. He is the sort that can come up with the goods, if he puts his mind to it.

"Why would they want to kill Grandpa Dajaal?"

"Why have they killed the journalists? Or assassinated senior military officers, former colleagues of Grandpa Dajaal? Why have they murdered the peace activists? Shabaab view them as a threat."

"What kind of threat do these people pose?"

Qasiir says, "Why do tyrants do what they do?"

Malik can't think of an immediate answer.

When Qasiir says that he can do nothing to salvage the deleted files or restore the screen saver, Malik steps out to prepare a snack for them both. Meanwhile, he makes a detour to his room and brings along Tax-liil's photograph. He intends to show it to Qasiir only if he agrees to take the assignment.

Malik watches as Qasiir hungrily tucks into the warmed-up lamb dish, his fork knocking against his knife, with neither touching the salad. As they eat, they talk in greater depth about the recruitment stratagems of the various secular and religious groups vying for power in Somalia. Then Malik tells Qasiir, little by little, what is known and suspected about Taxliil's disappearance, and about the difficult mission that Ahl has embarked on in Puntland. The family, he says, would appreciate whatever assistance Qasiir can offer.

"In what way can I be of use?" Qasiir asks.

"What I have in mind is cloak-and-dagger stuff."

Qasiir says, "How very exciting."

"I am thinking the real clandestine article."

"Please explain."

"You could get hurt," Malik says. "Someone else may get hurt or blown up, badly maimed in the fragmentation blast of a roadside device."

For a brief moment, Qasiir looks at Malik with a mix of shock and curiosity that gives way to an expectant thrill. He says he is up for his share in this "cloak-and-dagger stuff, the real clandestine article," like in the movies. Clint Eastwood locating a runaway boy. As if to reassure himself that he can play the part, he touches the holster strapped to his shoulder.

"You still haven't told me what I would have to do."

"I'll give you all the details you need," Malik says. "When he was last seen and where—I'll provide you with his particulars."

"And a photograph. Photographs are important."

Malik says, "That goes without saying."

"OK." Qasiir nods. "Where and when do I start?"

"Here is what I'll want you to do," Malik explains. "Seek out any information you can get on him. We know that he is in Somalia, supposedly to join Shabaab as a volunteer trainee in explosives."

Qasiir has a hint of pride hovering around his eyes as he stares at Malik, his body relaxing into the status of a man with a mystery to solve, a runaway youth to locate, fearlessly ready to employ coercion if need be. But, in keeping with what is expected from him, he suppresses any outward show of eagerness.

He says, "I am game."

"We'll talk some more," Malik says. "We'll also let Dajaal and Jeebleh know, and lay down the terms of our agreement. Until then, mum's the word."

The doorbell rings twice, the first time gently; the second time rushed, almost discourteous, and a third time more agitated, with jarring harshness. It is as if someone being chased by a mob wants to gain entry.

Malik thinks. It can't be Dajaal, because he always telephones ahead; and such behavior is unlike Jeebleh. Who might it be?

He refuses Qasiir's offer to go and see.

"Be careful," Qasiir whispers.

Malik tiptoes softly toward the door, Qasiir on his heels. Both stand to the side, away from the spy hole, in order to avoid casting their shadows on it. Then carefully Malik puts his eye to the opening. He spots a figure in khaki trousers and rubber sandals. He gives himself time to get the measure of the person on the other side; he does not move or speak. After a while, he hears a mumbled exchange between the trousered man in rubber sandals and another figure out of view. After several attempts, Malik eventually catches a glimpse of the second figure: a man in a sarong, right hand hidden behind him, and wearing a pair of pink flip-flops. Malik looks around to make sure that the apartment's fortifications, including the metal sheeting and other security contraptions, are in place. Then, turning, he nods his head with his thumb up when Qasiir removes the pistol from its holster. Speaking in an assumed voice, he asks, "Who is at the door?"

The trousered, sandal-wearing figure that moves into the spy hole says, "It is I, Gumaad. Is that you, Malik? I know Jeebleh is out, because I spoke to Dajaal, but I thought I would bring you some news, the latest from the war front."

Malik is torn about whether to open the door, but Qasiir signals him not to. Then, improvising, Qasiir says, "Malik is not here at present. Any messages?"

"That can't be," insists Gumaad.

Qasiir asks, "What can't be?"

"He goes nowhere without Dajaal," Gumaad says.

"I've no idea what you are talking about."

"But who are you, anyway?" Gumaad wants to know.

Qasiir explains, "I am a plumber and am here fixing the hot water tank. I have strict instructions not to admit anyone in their absence." He waits, then says, "It's up to you. If you leave a message, I'll give it to them; if not, not."

"Tell him I may return later, if I am able."

When Gumaad and his mate are gone, Qasiir and Malik confer in the workroom. Qasiir, never one to give up easily, resumes feeding the computer a new series of commands and introducing small variants, in the persistent way of computer specialists.

Malik asks, "What do you think Gumaad is up to?"

"He is not always truthful," Qasiir says. "He boasts too much, claims to be a journalist when he is not trained to be one, but, because he is convinced he can write, he thinks he is a journalist. He has published very little, no more than half a dozen brief articles. I've known others like him, others who believe their own lies."

"But is he dangerous?" Malik asks.

"He is not bright," Qasiir says.

"I can see that."

"He is also a name-dropper and a liar."

"Still, you wouldn't think he is dangerous?"

"He isn't someone with whom secrets are safe."

Malik's phone rings. Dajaal is on his way; he will pick them up momentarily if they want to purchase a new computer and a printer.

Qasiir wants to have a word with Dajaal, so Malik puts the phone on speakerphone. "Grandpa," Qasiir asks, "have you by any chance spoken to Gumaad today?"

"No, I haven't spoken to Gumaad today. Why?"

"Because he says he has spoken to you," Qasiir says, "and that was why he knew that Malik was alone in the apartment."

"He is lying," Dajaal says, clearly agitated. "I haven't seen or talked to him today. But why? What is the problem? Are you and Malik okay?"

Malik reclaims his mobile phone to reassure Dajaal. He says, "See you shortly."

When he rejoins them, Dajaal is in an awful mood. He curses, mumbles imprecations, and, naming no names, showers all manner of damnations on men who have never fought a war and who are now having recourse to war, mistaken in their belief that God is on their side and will help them prevail. Inarticulate in his rage, Dajaal speaks of the harsh war of words exchanged between the Ethiopian premier, who announced "imminent retaliation for the provocation against the integrity of our country's borders and the sanctity of its security," and the provocative rebuttal from the Courts, whose executive director has said, "I trust to Providence that invaders of Muslim lands will be defeated."

Dajaal goes on, "The entire city has the jitters, many people are going to the mosques to pray, or preparing to go away; many more are buying a week's provisions, just in case. Now, tell me, one of you. Did Gumaad say he is leaving the city? Could he have been calling on you on his way out?"

"He said he would return later, if he is able."

Dajaal says, "I wonder what he was up to."

Qasiir volunteers, "Someone else was with him."

"Who?"

Qasiir shrugs his shoulders in silence.

Malik has had enough of their speculations. He says, "Shall we go and buy the computer?"

He goes into his bedroom to organize the funds. He counts out several hundred U.S. dollars in easy-to-carry, high denominations and throws in an extra, just-in-case hundred. Malik knows that there are money changers in the markets who sit at low tables, wads and wads of highly devalued Somali shillings on one side, and on the other, heaps of cash in several other currencies, including U.S. and Canadian dollars, euros, Saudi dirhams. Unlike many other countries, where movement of money is tightly controlled, in today's Somalia buying any currency you fancy is as easy as buying groceries.

When Malik reemerges from his room with the cash counted, he and Qasiir wait in apparent deference to Dajaal, who is still psyched up, not yet done with his tirade.

"I've known what it means to go to war and lose," he says. "I fought in the Ethiopia–Somalia war of 1977, as a major in the National Army. Somalia was much stronger then—we had an army, one of the strongest on the continent—and we lost the war, and were run out of the Ogaden. We haven't recovered from that debacle, and it resulted in the current strife."

"Grandpa, we are ready to go, if you are."

Dajaal remains fired up and says, "Men like Gumaad and the so-called defense spokesman of the Courts who have never held a gun in their lives have no right to invoke Allah's name in support for an ill-planned cause."

Qasiir drags Dajaal by the hand, and they make it to the car in silence. Qasiir asks if he should drive, to which Dajaal retorts, "I am not mad in the sense of being dangerous. I am mad in the sense of being angry with what these men from the Courts are doing to our nation, endangering its continued existence."

He sits at the wheel and sobers up fast as he prepares his mind for the next task. He reverses into the vehicle parked behind him as he drives out of his parking spot. It is unlike Dajaal to be so careless, and not to stop and check the damage he has caused to someone else's car. But that is what he does: the world is not what it used to be; Dajaal is not the man he was an hour before.

They have barely rounded a corner when they come upon a familiar scene, of men and women fleeing their homes, carrying their worldly belongings on their heads. Antlike, people are escaping ahead of the coming fire, not wanting to burn in it. At one point, Dajaal barely avoids colliding with a heavily laden donkey that resists the commands of the young girl attempting to pull it forward by the rope tied around its neck.

The columns of those in flight lengthen and shorten, like the long and short shadows that define the various hours of the day. As they approach the market, Malik taking notes furiously, they notice that people are streaming out of it, carrying what looks like days' worth of food. Some of the women, wearing expensive body tents, climb into the backs of SUVs. Qasiir observes that these are the people who are not likely to leave the city, out of concern that squatters might move into their properties and vandalize them.

Malik looks up from his notebook and stops scribbling as Dajaal brings the car to a stop, and they prepare to enter the market.

AHL SITS UP FRONT. WARSAME IS DRIVING, AND FIDNO IS IN THE back. Warsame speeds across an intersection and swerves to avoid a goat crossing the road, but catches her with the edge of the fender regardless. The goat sways this side and that, as if deciding whether to remain on her feet, her hips and ribs exposed, her breathing labored. Then she regains her balance and straightens up, takes a step, and halts again. Warsame has pulled over, and Ahl suggests they wait a minute or so. Even so, Warsame puts the car in gear, ready to move if the crowd milling on either side of the road looks likely to form into a mob. Ahl has his door ajar, preparing to get out and check on how the beast is faring, but at that very moment Warsame puts the vehicle in motion, and Ahl pulls the car door shut.

"I wish we had stopped," Ahl says.

"Hereabouts," Fidno says, "we're all fearful of making fatal mistakes. More than ever, one must be wary of the unruliness of crowds, living in a place where there is a total breakdown of law and order. You can get yourself into sticky situations if you aren't careful. I am speaking of crowds waiting at the behest of their unreasonable greed, a crowd turning into a mob."

Warsame, seemingly bemused, stays out of it.

Ahl challenges, "Crowd, what crowd? There was no crowd to speak of. There were people milling about, minding their own business, from what I could tell. Men and women selling or buying, young men standing in groups and bantering. I saw no crowd that was likely to turn into a mob."

"Do you know what would have happened if the car had run over the goat and killed it?" Fidno asks.

"We would pay what is due to the owner of the dead goat," Ahl says. "I see no problem there. Recompense the owner. What else is there to do?"

"How do you determine who to pay if as many as a dozen claimants present themselves, each saying he is the rightful owner of the goat, and several others, challenging these claimants, inform you that the goat's owner is a clansman and you should pay them?"

Ahl says, "That's altogether another matter."

"A goat is other than itself," Fidno says.

"I hadn't realized," Ahl agrees.

They come to a busy junction with throngs swarming around stalls, and Warsame stops. This moves Ahl to ask, "Where are we, and why are we here, stopping?"

Ahl is clearly wary of crowds.

"Warsame is getting his daily fix," Fidno says.

They have pulled up next to Warsame's favorite *qaat* stall, run by a woman from whom Warsame buys his ration of leaves of the mild stimulant he and millions of other Somalis chew daily. Ahl can perceive the craving in Warsame's eyes, the anticipation working its way into his body at the sight of the green leaves spread out within reach of his open window. The woman wears a *guntiino* robe, a bit of her breast exposed as she raises her arm to adjust the sacking around the bundles, which are wrapped in banana leaves and sprinkled with water periodically, to keep them fresh.

Ahl has read somewhere that Somalia boasts one of the highest populations addicted to *qaat*, a commodity imported from Ethiopia and Kenya at great cost to the national economy. *Qaat* is comparable in strength to cocaine, stronger if consumed in greater quantities for longer periods. The woman lifts a bundle to show Warsame how fresh her *qaat* is. The water sprays as she shakes the bundle, the leaves dancing, and Warsame's eyes brighten and his mouth moves as the hand holding the money trembles. He pays the woman without getting out of the vehicle, its engine running.

Just as they are ready to drive off, there is a sudden congestion of traffic, caused, one of the *qaat* sellers tells them, by a head-on collision between two cars up the road. A crowd pours into the street to watch. Patiently, they sit and wait for the blockage to ease, Warsame taking the opportunity to telephone Xalan to tell her what is causing the delay.

Meanwhile, an SUV comes into view. The woman in the front passenger seat smiles in their direction and then discreetly waves. Ahl smiles back, despite feeling that he is not the intended recipient of the woman's sweet grin and, bashful, looks about him to discover whether either Warsame or Fidno has chanced on the exchange. His wandering gaze encounters Fidno's, whose hand is raised in greeting.

Ahl adds, "I know the face, but can't put a name to it. Unless the two of you are acquainted and she is greeting you."

"Her name is Wiila," Fidno says.

"She is a flight attendant, isn't she?"

"What a small world. Maybe you flew with her!"

"Now that you've said the name," Ahl says, "I remember her. She seemed miserable, weepy for much of the flight from Djibouti."

Fidno explains, "She is mourning the death of her youngest brother, killed in Mogadiscio while on a special Shabaab mission."

"How come you know that?" Ahl asks.

"I know Marduuf, another of her brothers. We are close."

"Youngest brother dead and you know the other?"

"The one I know is in the pirate business."

"An associate of yours?"

Fidno says, "He is, as a matter of fact."

In the silence that follows, Ahl reflects that it is a pity he and Fidno cannot continue talking later. He could use a siesta. He didn't sleep well the night before, and he could do with a good rest.

Warsame throws a sheaf of *qaat* into the back of the vehicle, where Fidno is sitting. Fidno catches the bundle and selects a tender shoot to chew.

The roads are dusty and there is constant movement along them. Goats cross from one side to another, and humans carelessly walk across, impervious to danger, almost suicidal. Warsame drives with his foot an inch away from the brake pedal. He keeps the windows shut against the dust, and the air conditioner on. Even so, they can hear the music belting and recitations of the Koran blaring wherever they go. The buildings they pass, like those they saw on their way from the airport, have an improvised look, some whose walls consist only of zinc sheeting, others of corrugated aluminum, many unpainted. The sky is at times barely visible through the spaghetti of electrical wiring strewn between the structures.

"Do you want to chew some?" Warsame asks.

Ahl shakes his head no.

"I am impressed you never picked up the habit of chewing *qaat*, given that it is in Yemen. Especially as it's one of their main export crops," Fidno says.

Midly shocked that Fidno is so well informed about him, Ahl decides to be patient; he will find out at a later point how this is so. He says, "I don't chew *qaat*, never have."

Fidno asks, "Maybe your parents, as expatriates wanting their children to do well, discouraged it?"

"Chewing was not one of our pastimes as a family," Ahl replies. "We did a lot of sports as we grew up, we read a great deal, we played chess, we were never left wanting for things with which to occupy ourselves."

Out of deference to Warsame, his host, Ahl does not add that he finds the idea of wasting away the best part of a day masticating some green leaf and sitting doing nothing highly objectionable.

Warsame says, "Just like my wife."

"What about your wife?"

"She hasn't the patience to sit and chew."

Just as well, Ahl thinks, because he looks forward to getting to know Xalan, Yusur's best friend and almost sister. Yusur has described Xalan as a formidable woman, actively intelligent, with her heart in the right place, loyal. He will talk to her while the men enjoy their chewing.

Warsame says to Ahl, "I didn't know you had a friend here. What is his full name, and how long have the two of you known each other?"

Ahl says, "His name is Ali Ahmed Fidno."

Warsame says he doesn't recall ever seeing him in town. "He must be new to the city." Ahl finds it amusing that Warsame keeps talking about Fidno in the third person.

"Well, here he is, anyhow," Ahl says. "He is alive and well and sitting in your car, as your guest. He is coming with us to your home."

"I am pleased," Warsame says unconvincingly.

Ahl is uncertain what Xalan will make of him. Will she fall for him—a mysterious figure emerging out of the unknown and entering her life?

"Tell me more about your friend," Warsame says.

Ahl has a big problem. How does one introduce a man he hardly knows to the husband of one's wife's best friend, whom one has yet to meet? Like it or not, he finds Warsame down to earth, whereas, much as he likes Fidno, he hasn't met many men who are as shifty and hard to pin down. He says, "Fidno can tell you about himself better than I ever can."

"I come from Garowe," Fidno says. "Originally."

"But you didn't grow up in Garowe, did you?"

"I was sent to a boarding school in Qardho."

"Then where?"

"Then I went to university in Europe."

Warsame is attempting to locate Fidno's family tree and then identify the branch and clan trajectory. He asks, "Whose name or nickname is Fidno—yours, your father's, or your grandfather's?"

"Mine," Fidno responds.

Only now does it occur to Ahl that maybe Warsame does not wish to take into his home someone whose identity he can't vouch for. Xalan is bound to take him aside, accost him in the kitchen, or privately in the bedroom, and say, "Who is this guy you've brought into our house, our lives?"

"So where do you live?"

"Lately between Mogadiscio and Nairobi."

"What's your line of business?"

"I trained as a medical doctor in Germany."

"Where do you have your practice?"

"I've had some personal problems," Fidno replies, "and have been compelled to shut down my practice. But that is a complicated story. For another day."

Warsame repeats the name Ali Ahmed Fidno, as if the combination might fit some purpose, and then changes the order in which Fidno has given them and subjects them to a faster run, his tongue rushing at them, as if they might reveal a hidden secret. When they do not, he has several goes at them from different directions, each time to no avail. He says, "Every family name has its own story, and I doubt I know this story. Maybe Xalan will. She knows everyone's family and the stories that go with them."

Warsame stops in front of a gate and presses the horn. A man in military fatigues opens the gate and lets them in. Warsame enters with care. He parks to the side of the door and, getting out, gives a couple of bundles of *qaat* to the man in the fatigues, after he has locked the gate.

———

As Ahl gets out, he spots a woman stepping toward him, deliciously gliding, sweetly smiling, and getting ready to embrace him. Ahl is delighted, pleased that she has taken his hand. He mumbles his joy at being here.

Just as she leads him into the house, his hand in hers, however, she spots Fidno emerging from the vehicle. Xalan says to Ahl, "Who is your friend, dear?"

Before Ahl manages to get the words out, Warsame beats him to it, volunteering, "Our friend's name is Ali Ahmed Fidno."

But Xalan is uninterested in meeting Fidno, whom she assumes to be no friend of Ahl's but an acquaintance of her husband's, come to chew *qaat* with him. Warsame is in the habit of bringing along all sorts of men to chew with him. He says, "Wait, and let me introduce you to him," and she exchanges cursory greetings with the man. Then she walks off, dragging Ahl into the house and straight into the dining room, where the table has already been laid for company.

The room is large and pleasant. There are even flowers in a vase—God knows where she got them in Bosaso, of all places, this time of the year. The table is set for three, decked out with family heirlooms. Xalan has been planning this lunch for days—planned that she and Warsame will have Ahl to lunch, as a family. Of course, there is no family to speak of—only the two of them, with the children now grown and gone. The way she remembers it: Warsame at the head of the table, the children on either side of him, sharing their experiences. Like normal times. Peacetime in Mogadiscio. Short, sweet family get-togethers in Toronto, whenever Warsame visited them after she relocated there, to be with the children. But these days, loyal as they are to each other, they no longer form a family unit. Warsame knows how much she hates it when he locks himself away in his room to chew, but he cannot stop. For all these men care, she thinks, the world could be burning, their homes collapsing in on them. They must have their daily fix.

"Sit, dear. Sit." Xalan shows Ahl to his chair.

Ahl is uncomfortable; she can sense it. She assumes he has lost his way in the standoff between her and Warsame, each heading off in a different direction, she with him, he with Fidno. He blames himself for inviting Fidno and not making it clear to Xalan that he has done so. His fault; he has caused the embarrassment. He is to blame. There is no way around it.

He puts down his computer bag in a corner and says to Xalan's back, as she goes into the kitchen and opens the oven, where the food has been keeping warm, "Yusur sends her love."

His wandering gaze seizes upon several inhalers, stashed together in a little handwoven basket on the mantel, and a few others in easy reach of where Xalan is sitting.

She says, "It's your first visit to Puntland, right?"

"It is," he replies.

"From what Yusur has told me, I understand this is your first to the Somali-speaking peninsula," she says.

Ahl thinks that Xalan has just spoken Yusur's name not with apparent fondness but with a touch of amusement, as if she is holding back some information that she will reveal to him once she gets to know him better.

"Hard to believe, but true," he says.

She stares straight into his eyes, as if eager to detect the slightest intimation of duplicity. Xalan is the first woman he has met who has known Yusur for much of her life. So what is she telling him?

But Xalan doesn't talk about Yusur. She says, "Your Somali is excellent. Good for you, you've kept it up and used it. I am impressed. Yusur says you taught Taxliil how to speak it well. You have a northern accent."

"We spoke Somali at home. For Taxliil's sake."

"Do you know that ours don't speak it well?"

"It's worth the effort to teach them young."

She says, "Think about it."

"What?"

"If the hotel service is terrible, the food inedible, the noise unbearable, or if you feel unsafe, because you do not know where to put your cash," she says, "think about it. This is your home."

Ahl says, "I'll think about it. Thanks."

"The kitchen here runs daily. Come and eat."

"Thanks. I appreciate it."

A corner of her mouth turns up in amusement, then Xalan shakes her head, as if she is surprising herself. She says, "Would you like to move here?"

He doesn't know how to react.

"There's plenty of room, it is more comfortable than any hotel anywhere. The food we serve here, cooked by the same cook I had when we fled Mogadiscio, is of a higher quality than the rubbery and over-cooked stuff that passes for a meal at the restaurant."

What is there to say? He can say that he will think about it. In the meantime, he will have to get to know the two of them.

He hopes that he will not displease Warsame by staying and eating with her. It is difficult to gauge what someone like Warsame might do, a man married to a woman whose self-confidence seems limitless; a woman truly unafraid, sure of herself, and ready to take on the world. Ahl feels comforted at the thought of knowing her. He hopes that she will prove to be an asset in his search for Taxliil.

She brings the food out of the oven, a feast of it. There is so much of it Ahl wonders if she has meant to feed a battalion. Chicken, lamb dishes, rice done the traditional way, lobster, a variety of vegetables cooked in different styles, fruit juices. Xalan serves him a giant portion; she takes a small serving. "It is not that I am worried about my figure, no. After all, I've so far attained my age in good health, thank God," she teases.

She is long-necked and striking, with big eyes and a beautiful smile, owing to her fine teeth. She is in her early fifties, her every bodily gesture sure of itself and its meaning. He feels she knows well how to cope with all kinds of difficulties: impossible children, an impossible husband. He remembers Yusur telling him that Xalan—the name means "the cleansed one"—is a no-nonsense woman. Dressed in the traditional *guntiino* robe and a shawl and, as custom demands only of married women, with her hair covered, she does most things regally: the way she walks, eats, and uses her hands, dipping her fingers in the tepid water in the bowl. This is how Yusur described her: "Xalan does not block the sunlight when she comes into a room."

Xalan is saying, "It's tragic that our country has changed beyond recognition, because in the old, pre–civil war, pre-*qaat* days, when you invited a friend home for a meal, the entire family would be there to welcome the visitor. The civil war has put paid to all that, with hundreds of thousands quitting the country. Then, of late, *qaat* chewing has levied its heavy toll. *Qaat*: master disrupter of family normalcy, a costly demolisher of the social fabric."

He knows where she is going with this. He understands the frustrations of a woman who has gone to lengths to put a well-appointed meal on the table, only to find that her husband doesn't bother to take a mouthful in recognition of her efforts. Bosaso is no Toronto, where a hostess can entertain her guests with purchased foods tasting as though they were homemade. Here, Xalan bought the chicken live and had it slaughtered; spent days to find fresh lobster and fish. He regards her with a mix of wariness and admiration, feeling responsible for Warsame's absence.

"Welcome to our home, AhlulKhair," she says.

"Thank you, thank you."

"Your presence in our home cheers me up."

"Again, thanks."

He takes his first mouthful of the excellent lamb dish she has prepared; he can taste the love that has gone into the making of the meal. He talks as he eats, the better not to be self-conscious at how much he is consuming. He tells her everything to do with Taxliil, beginning with when he and his stepson first met, up until the day when he vanished. He also tells her about Malik and Jeebleh and how they, too, are doing all they can to locate the young runaway.

When Ahl has eaten his fill, Xalan offers him dessert, but he says he will give it a miss, and passes on tea or coffee as well. She says, "Go and see what the men are up to at the *majlis*. I'll ask the maid to clear the lunch things and will join you there in a couple of minutes."

At Xalan's call, the maid arrives: short, stocky, of indiscernible age; she has blue rings around her irises typical of Somalia's river people. Xalan says to the woman, "After you've done the washing, please prepare the guest room for possible occupation, starting tomorrow morning."

Ahl avoids looking at Xalan, fearing, perhaps, that one of them might say something that will upset the other.

When Ahl joins them in the *majlis*, Warsame and Fidno appear not to take notice of him. They are apparently wholly occupied catering to what their bodies crave. They slouch on the carpeted floor in sarongs, heavy cushions pushed against the wall, with incense burning at the far end of the room. Fidno is in an undershirt, Warsame in a singlet. They chew without interruption, chatting away about politics, piracy, terrorism, Shabaab, and every other topic that strikes their fancy.

He watches for a while as they stuff their cheeks and slurp water and Coca-Cola and sugared tea to avoid dehydration. After a while Ahl can no longer contain himself, and he yawns exorbitantly, complaining of his exhaustion after so much travel. Warsame calls to Xalan to arrange a lift for their guest. When she offers to drive him herself, he dismisses the suggestion. "There is no need. Ask one of the drivers to drop him off."

Eager to depart, Ahl reminds himself not to forget his laptop, and makes sure he has it before he hugs Xalan and says, "Thank you, and so long." The driver helps him into the vehicle, which is very high off the ground. Ahl is so tired that his eyes involuntarily close, and they stay shut for much of the trip. It is pitch dark, maybe because there is no street lighting, or maybe because of a power outage. But when they get to his hotel and through the security gate, the hotel generator is on and so are the lights, and he no longer feels as tired as he did in the car.

Back in his room, Ahl rings Malik. Malik is terribly agitated, his voice shaking and his diction rattled. He makes a jumble of statements, running his words together nonsensically.

"Wait, wait. Go back. Who are we talking about?"

"Dajaal," Malik says.

Ahl has never met Dajaal, but he knows who he is.

"Now tell me. What's happened to Dajaal?"

"They've made an attempt on his life."

Ahl knows who "they" refers to.

"When did that happen, and how?"

"He had given me a lift back to the apartment and then drove home, alone," says Malik. "Half a kilometer from the apartment block where Dajaal lives, a remote-controlled roadside bomb struck the passenger's side of the car, the side where I normally sit when I am a passenger. Jeebleh and I are not sure if *they* meant to kill *me*."

"How badly is Dajaal hurt?"

"Thank God, he is not hurt."

"But there is damage to the car?"

"We're taking it as a warning. To me."

"You're not planning to leave, are you?"

"No way."

"Will you move in with Bile and Cambara?"

Ahl can't help being cranky, the consequence of civil war crabbiness. He almost gives in to a tetchy thought that enters his mind, but thinks better of it, recalling that when they were younger and they could afford to be nasty to each other as siblings are, Ahl used to describe Malik as self-centered, someone who asked the world to come to him. But of course he won't say that now.

"And you," Malik says. "How have you been?"

Ahl tells him about meeting Fidno and his meeting with Xalan. For some reason he tells him about Wiila as well, and her connection to Fidno.

They agree to talk tomorrow. Malik gives him Bile's phone number, along with Cambara's and Qasiir's, just in case, and then adds, as if for good measure, "You never know how things may pan out here."

DAJAAL FINDS A DECENT PARKING SPOT IN A CUL-DE-SAC NOT FAR from the market, but Qasiir advises him to look for another, "safer" place, as dead-end roads pose unnecessary security risks. Dajaal concedes that Qasiir has a point and drives off, saying that he will join them.

Now Qasiir and Malik wait for him in the road. Malik has close to two thousand dollars in the front pocket of his trousers, and he can feel the lump of it as they speak. He is sure that the money is enough to buy a computer and a color laser printer. Even so, he is overwhelmed with the feeling that something is afoot; he smells it in the air. The sun is in his eyes, the breeze light, but his heart is heavy, very heavy. "Do you know where we are going?" Malik says.

Qasiir replies, "We'll go to a computer shop I know, and where a friend of mine works. He informed me that they have only one computer of this kind in stock and I've reserved it in my name, thinking it would be unwise to give yours."

"Tell me more."

Qasiir obliges. "Here is how things work at the Bakhaaraha. Traders bring in items for sale, items they describe as 'new,' 'almost new,' or 'as good as new.' What many buyers do not know is that someone else has bought these items singly in the Emirates, say, pretending they are for his own use, and then imports them 'sealed.' It's all part of the trading method here. When you buy a computer, the seller will not provide you, the end user, with a warranty, even if he sells it to you as new, almost new, reconditioned, or just resealed."

"They don't describe the true state of affairs?"

Dajaal joins them; he has found a convenient spot close enough. He and Qasiir agree that he will keep a discreet eye out, in the event someone is following them, or him. He vanishes into the melee of movement; Qasiir walks ahead, Malik on his heels, listening. They can make out Dajaal one second and lose him the next; both of them are watchful as they continue their conversation.

Qasiir says, "Someone buys a computer, a BlackBerry, or an iPod in Abu Dhabi for export and does not pay tax. This person then sends it with someone coming here to give it to someone living here. The gadget arrives in place of cash, as money sent home has come under severe scrutiny since September 2001. This way, no cash is being transferred, and no one will bother about it."

"Until someone discovers it," Malik says.

Qasiir pulls a face. He continues, "Moving money has become dangerous, and a number of the banks have been closed, accused of supporting terrorism. Some Somalis have ended up in Guantánamo or are currently detained in Sweden. The motto is this: Goods may move freely; money, because it may be dirty, may not."

"How come you know all this?" he asks Qasiir.

"I worked as a computer parts salesman."

"Nothing is as it seems," Malik says.

When Qasiir announces for his benefit that they are now at the junction where the market complex begins, Malik thinks that "market" is an inaccurate name for the Bakhaaraha, which has become an institution unlike any other. This market looks nothing like anyone's idea of an African market. It's more a mix of trading traditions, with stalls made of zinc sheets on one side, proper shops farther up, and low stands where women sell tomatoes and onions, all of it smack in the center of what might once have been a thoroughfare. Then, to confound the visitor more, one sees all sorts of people milling around, and many more gathered at corners, loitering, watching, gathered in groups, bantering, a few strolling about with whips in their hands and conversing with men bearing guns. Then Malik remembers the Spanish proverb—that not everyone at a market is there either to buy or sell. This strikes him as no truer anywhere than it is at the Bakhaaraha Market in Mogadiscio.

The labyrinthine culs-de-sac of the market continue to play a political role similar to the one the Casbah performed in the Algerian struggle for independence from France. In 1993, when the Marines were engaged in a manhunt for StrongmanSouth, the rumor mills were in overdrive that the general held his meetings openly at his redoubt in a basement at the Bakhaaraha, that he had been at a wedding, or that he had said his prayers at one of the biggest mosques in the city. More recently, during the 2006 routing of the U.S.-supported warlords, it was the popular support of the unified management of the market complex that made the difference. The fact that the market supported the Courts with weapons and funds tipped the balance in their favor. There is a complexity to the Bakhaaraha, given its history and economic potential. It offers immense profits in a country where business doesn't pay tax, as there are no state structures in place to levy or collect it.

Established in 1972 during the last tyrant's reign, according to the research Malik gathered before coming to Mogadiscio, the Bakhaaraha functioned as an alternative to the state-imposed structures of economy, and provided political brinksmanship to those opposing the status quo. Those who manage this institution are aware that war is at a premium these days, even if peace is in great demand. Here at the market, they sell either commodity, at exorbitant prices. Qasiir says, "When you've lived in a civil war condition and have not known peace, you become someone *other*, someone different from your natural self, as many of us have done."

The deeper they walk into the market, the more palpable the sense of excitement around them, an excitement brought on by a feeling of triumph. Maybe the Courts' announcement that they "will defeat the invaders the moment they set foot on our soil, a Muslim soil," is having its effect on the rabble. Malik catches snippets of conversation as they walk past, a couple of young men thrilled at the thought of volunteering to fight, one of them declaring that he is looking forward to drinking enemy blood. Malik finds it difficult to move forward, his feet leaden, his heart weighed down with sorrow. In his mind he plays host to many scenarios, in each of which he enterains similar premonitions: of terrible things afoot, of death making the rounds, of airplanes bombing cities, of tanks rolling eastward, of bullets, of lots of blood. A few young men gather into clutches near a stall whose owner offers to outfit anyone volunteering to fight with something that approaches a uniform—blue fatigues with a star in the center at the front and the back. Malik picks out Dajaal standing at the periphery of that group.

Malik says, "From what I've heard, many of the big businessmen are keener on war and funding it than they are on peace. Why is that?"

"Then they don't have to pay tax."

For an instant, he looks at Qasiir, almost unseeingly, because the sun is in his eyes. He squints and sees that Dajaal is joining them. Then he asks if in his opinion the invasion of the garrison town by the Courts is imminent.

"War is serious stuff," says Dajaal, who doesn't seem able to commit himself to a definite timetable, knowing the unpredictability of the men from the Courts, for whom he has nothing but disdain.

"But inevitable?"

"It does appear so."

It feels as if a hurricane has been forecast. No one is safe.

Dajaal, moving forward with the habitual sure-footedness of an athlete embarking on a marathon, once again lets Qasiir lead the way, followed by Malik, and again he takes up the rear, alert for unusual movements, for men in balaclavas, wearing tunics with pockets big enough to conceal weapons. He knows that in the Bakhaaraha danger is a neighbor, lurking at the end of the labyrinth into which they are walking. An assassin may emerge from any shop, any corner; every passerby is suspect and suspicious. Here, everyone is moonlighting as something they are not, and there are many men and women, Dajaal knows, whose job is to inform on any unfamiliar face.

Dajaal notices a young man whose eyes are following Malik. When the young man brings out his phone and speaks briefly into it, Dajaal slows down, the better to take note of any immediate changes in the surroundings. He notices movement at the edge of another cluster of young men, as excited as track fans waiting for a derby. Dajaal catches a familiar face but can't immediately place it from a distance. As he gets closer, he is surprised to see Gumaad, who is dressed in a motley combination of colors: his trousers a faded pink, shoes almost emerald green, the buttons of his shirt ranging from dark brown to orange and green. Yet neither Gumaad nor his mates seems aware of the clownlike clash of colors.

When Gumaad catches sight of Malik and Qasiir, then learns of their mission, he insists on accompanying them to the computer shop. He falls into step with them and his fellow revelers fall away. Dajaal waits. He checks the vicinity for hidden dangers and then assesses the situation before joining and walking alongside Gumaad.

He asks Gumaad, "What's this merrymaking about?"

"We are celebrating a victory," Gumaad replies.

"How can you think of celebrating the victory of a war not yet waged? This is war that has been lost before it's been launched," Dajaal says.

"We're celebrating the triumph of the Courts," Gumaad announces. He speaks loud enough for some of the passersby to overhear and approve of the sentiment he has expressed, by nodding their heads.

"Whom have the Courts defeated?"

"Ethiopia and her ally America," Gumaad says. But this time he keeps his voice low.

Qasiir says, "You are crazy."

"Why did I expect better of you?" Dajaal says to Gumaad.

Dajaal walks away, in truth because he wants to be alone with his thoughts for a few minutes. He is revisiting the three wars in which he served as an army officer, but what he pictures just now are not scenes of death in battle. The image in the forefront of his mind is of cattle running amok, chased by unseen lions; of goats driven by powers invisible from a place where peace reigns to a scrubland where nothing, absolutely nothing, not even cacti grow—a scrubland so barren and so waterless that the goats feed on stones that they dig from the drought-dry land. Close by, a short distance from where the cattle have now gathered to graze in the fenced-off brushwood, there are mines buried in the ground, mines planted by the various factions fighting for control of the scrubland. Now and then the goats unearth the mines and they blow up, slaughtering the goats that unearth them, as well as stray cattle; now and again, the mines blow up in the faces of humans, too.

As they make their way through the market, Gumaad asks Malik if he has received a message. Malik says that he hasn't, avoiding eye contact with Qasiir, whom he sees is listening in. Then Gumaad explains that he came to the apartment earlier and brought along a young former pirate, straight from Xarardheere, the coastal town where he is based. "I thought you would be interested in talking to him," he says.

"A pity I wasn't there," Malik says.

"A man whose voice I didn't recognize answered the doorbell," Gumaad says, "and he said through the spy hole that he was fixing the hot-water tank and you were out. Where did you go?"

Walking faster, Malik says, "Actually, I would be interested in talking to someone involved with funding piracy as well as a former pirate. I suspect a lot of the funders are based in Mogadiscio. Can you arrange that?"

"I know the very man to whom you can talk."

"A funder or a former pirate?"

"A funder. Then we'll see about a pirate."

"That'll be great," Malik says. "Looking forward."

They are at their destination, a little too soon for Malik, who wishes he had more time to take the measure of the market, now that he knows it is likely to serve as the center for the insurgency following the invasion.

———

The computer shop is sandwiched between Tawfik Bank and a mobile phone outlet, in a four-story building of stone. It is constructed as though to survive a heavy bombing, with walls so thick that Malik wonders if it once served as a bunker. The two tiny windows are both closed, but the air conditioner operates only fitfully, not wholly effective. The ceiling fans turn with the slowness of a headstrong donkey hauling a pulley. The shelves where the shops' wares are displayed are deep, but of cheap wood, with the few nails that are meant to hold them in place not hammered in properly. On the whole, however, it is a well-stocked shop, with all sorts of gizmos and gadgets, from computers and printers (both inkjet and laser) to the latest mobile telephones.

There are half a dozen young salesmen, some dressed in white shirts and khaki trousers, most of them bright-eyed and young, long-limbed, birdlike in the thinness of their chests. A family resemblance runs through many of them: the high cheekbones, the irregular shapes of their front teeth, their shovel-nosed appearance and their prominent jaws. Only one of them is in a long, loose shirt reaching down to his knees. The majority of the customers are young, too. A number of them are in jeans, and not a single one of them is bearded. A couple of them are there in search of a bargain, or have brought along an item to exchange. The salesman in the long shirt seems to be the head of operations in the computer section of the business, because the younger salesmen go to him with their questions and to ask if it is possible to offer a discount. Each time, he disappears through a door in the back, and comes back a few minutes later with a reply.

Dajaal has waited outside, to keep an eye on who is coming and going, and Gumaad stays close to Malik while Qasiir waits his turn. He spots his acquaintance, a hungry-looking, toothy youth. After exchanging a brief greeting, Qasiir requests Toothy to tell Sheikh-Wellie that he has come to pay for the item he'd reserved over the phone.

Toothy returns and goes back to serving customers, his eyes avoiding Qasiir's. Malik is taking notes for the article on the computer store he's already planning, but he sees that Qasiir is puzzled as to why Sheikh-Wellie is taking so long to come out. They wait so long that Dajaal sticks his head in to inquire if all is well. Malik, remembering that it's been their intention to make it look as if Qasiir, not he, is buying the computer, slips him the cash. Then he continues eavesdropping on a man haggling over the price of a BlackBerry and watching another man eagerly collecting his new purchase, packed in a big cardboard box, beside which an urchin shorter than the counter is standing to take it to the man's car.

It is not Sheikh-Wellie but BigBeard who emerges from the back of the shop. He does not seem to see Malik or Gumaad, but comes right to Qasiir and starts to engage him in computer talk. Malik feels a chill go down his spine at the sight of his nemesis. Qasiir is careful not to make eye contact with Malik, or in any way to acknowledge their having come together. To this end, he holds Malik's wad of cash in his hand and waves it close to BigBeard's face.

Eventually Qasiir and BigBeard arrive at a price, ten dollars more than what was previously agreed, and BigBeard returns to the rear of the shop. In his place arrives Sheikh-Wellie at last. A very dark, weak-eyed, timid fellow in his thirties, he is actually the deputy accountant at the computer shop, and he seems agitated and ill at ease dealing with a customer. He brings out the machine, deposits it before Qasiir, and abruptly requests that Toothy handle the sale. Then he, too, returns to the back of the shop.

After the obligatory, albeit perfunctory checks Toothy demonstrates that the machine is new and working properly, and Qasiir orders a color laser printer as well. Then he pays for both with Malik's cash, and they depart without further incident.

———

Gumaad accompanies them to the car. Dajaal is stewing over the incident at the flat, about which he is certain Gumaad is lying. He can no longer stand the sight of the man. Gumaad reminds him of everything that has gone wrong with the destiny of the country. He wants to be rid of him but doesn't want to pick a bone with him in public. So he says to Gumaad, "I would rather you found your way home from here, because we have other matters to attend to, Malik, Qasiir, and I."

"I was hoping to talk to Malik."

"Not now. Another time," Dajaal says, dismissing him.

Gumaad goes, but Dajaal's ire is not yet spent. His eyes, burning with rage, are now focused on Qasiir. He can't even wait until they reach the car before he vents his spleen at his nephew. "What's the matter with you, making us give more custom to BigBeard and then on top of that, striking an underhanded deal with your friend, whatever accursed name he answers to?"

"Let me explain, Grandpa."

"Your behavior puts me to shame."

Qasiir insists he can explain everything.

Dajaal says, "Don't you ever take liberties with our trust or treat us as if we are all fools. We'll talk, you and I. This is not the time and place."

"It was the only computer of its kind I could find in the city, and I received no cuts," Qasiir says, defending his honor. "Nor did anyone know I was buying it on Malik's behalf. Give me some credit, Grandpa. I am not *that* cheap."

"So what was BigBeard doing there?"

Qasiir says, "How would I know, Grandpa?"

Still clearly perturbed, Dajaal lets it go.

"Never a dull moment here, is there?" Malik says, hoping to lighten the mood. Malik wholly trusts Qasiir and is certain from Qasiir's behavior that he had no idea BigBeard would be in the shop. If anything, Malik thinks that it's Sheikh-Wellie who is guilty of "insider trading." Qasiir is clearly offended that his granduncle suspects him of dishonesty. He won't react to it angrily, not now, not in Malik's presence. He and Dajaal will have a quiet word or two about it in the car later, on their way home, after he has set up the machine for Malik.

They drive off in silence, passing people thronging the stalls to stock up on provisions. At some stalls, meat hangs from hooks hastily nailed into the wooden frames, buzzing with flies. Others display wilted cabbages, lettuce, and broccoli, dried-out carrots, and cassava pockmarked with fungus. The poor anywhere live the only way the poor know how: they buy food that is inexpensive. And the majority of the clients at these roadside stalls belong to this category.

Dajaal stops often to let pedestrians pass in front of the car, even when the vehicles behind him honk impatiently. He tells Malik and Qasiir that Cambara has already finished her shopping, buying enough food to last them for weeks if need be.

They pick up Jeebleh from Bile's house. Malik sits in the back and brings him up to speed, mentioning how much less the computer cost than it would have in New York. He notes with satisfaction that Dajaal has registered this comment, and hopes that it will ease his displeasure with and suspicion of Qasiir.

Jeebleh is neither surprised nor shocked to learn that they bought the machine from a shop presumably owned by BigBeard. After all, he thinks, Somalis are incestuous by nature, inseparable by temperament, and murderous by inclination; and such is their internecine closeness that quarreling is the norm—like twins fighting.

Malik asks, "What is your news?"

The news Jeebleh brings from his conversations with Bile and Cambara and from having watched the coverage on TV is just as unnerving as the sight of the hordes they are now passing along the roads, blocking traffic as they head out of the city, afraid of being caught in the impending war. He says, "There is a report of a most exasperating action of a Shabaab operative, who is leading a convoy of a dozen or so gun-mounted battlewagons to Buur Hakaba." Buur Hakaba is the town nearest Baidoa, where the president, the Federal Forces, and the parliament have their bases. "When asked why he needed to provoke a confrontation between the forces of the Courts and the FedForces," Jeebleh continues, "he said he meant nothing sinister by his actions, certainly not to do any harm to the ongoing peace talks between the two sides. He was paying a visit to one of his four wives. She lives in Buur Hakaba, as it happens."

It takes a minute or so for the significance of this report to sink in.

Jeebleh tells them that the incident has set off alarm bells in a number of far-flung cities: in Baidoa, of course, where not only the interim president of Somalia, but the provisional prime minister and the cabinet are based; in Addis Ababa, where Ethiopia's prime minister has called an emergency meeting of his cabinet and his military advisers; in Washington, D.C., where top functionaries at the Department of Defense and Department of State have called in those manning the Somali desk to brief them on the significance of this latest provocation. In Somalia, panic is everywhere, with everyone assuming that the garrison town of Baidoa will be attacked, if it hasn't been already.

"War jitters, wherever you turn," Malik says.

Jeebleh says, "Where will it all end? Will someone persuade the two parties to move away from the precipice, continuing with their peace negotiations instead of plunging this nation into an unnecessary, murderous war?"

"It's war, war—not if, but when," Dajaal says.

IT IS WITH TREMENDOUS WORRY, INEXPLICABLE THOUGH IT MAY seem, that Jeebleh stirs in his sleep, dreaming, and registers horses neighing, donkeys braying, cows mooing, the night darkening just before dawn breaks, the muezzin calling. In the dream, Malik and he are, surprisingly, among the worshippers. Malik sticks close to Jeebleh, looking anxious, as if he is suddenly unsure what to do, whether to place the right hand upon the left below or above the navel when standing; whether, with head and body inclined and hands placed upon the knees, he should separate the fingers a little or not at all. He is aware there are differences among the sects as to what to do when. But having not set foot in a mosque or prayed for almost twenty years, he is uncertain, and watches Jeebleh with intent so as not to embarrass his father-in-law.

A man standing nearby speaks of "morning madness reigning." Jeebleh doesn't understand what he is talking about. Nor is he bothered by the fact that he doesn't know who the man is until he discovers that Malik, with notebook in hand and pen ready to scribble away, is interviewing the man. Billows of dust stir in the distance, beckoning, and Jeebleh wanders away in the general direction of the vortex of sand, over the hills, farther east.

Then Jeebleh finds himself in a neighborhood with which he is unfamiliar, where virtually all the houses are leveled, the roads gutted, the pavements reduced to rotted ravines, with unexploded mines scattered in the rubble. In a gouged spot past a massive ruin that must have been caused by a bomb with the force of a meteor, there is a Technical, its mounted gun smeared with the blood of its victims; the Technical is still emitting smoke. When he touches it, it is as warm as a living body. Somewhere nearby are corpses left where they have fallen, some of them Ethiopians, from the look of their uniforms, others of them young Somalis. Then several of the dead Somali youths come to life and go into a huddle, as sports teams do. The huddle breaks and they take what appear to be prearranged positions, speaking in the manner of actors rehearsing a badly scripted play. Dressed in immaculate white and donning colorful keffiyehs, they sport long beards. Several women come out of nowhere, uniformly pretty, gazelle eyed, the very image of the houris of Paradise, to tend to the youths.

Now the youths separate themselves into units. One unit digs up an arms cache from the rubble: rocket-propelled grenades, light and heavy machine guns, semiautomatic weapons, an array of homemade explosives. A second unit waits by the roadside, bantering. But they go quiet when several armor-plated pickup trucks mounted with antiaircraft guns approach, and the youths get in an orderly fashion. A third unit, composed of the youngest, receives training in explosives from a short man with thick glasses, who consults a manual every time one of the pupils asks him a question.

Jeebleh has the feeling that he is not in a city but in a village somewhere in the hinterland. But he is not sure; Mogadiscio has lost whatever shape it used to have and is now as featureless as a ground-down cog in a broken machine. He is deeply disturbed that it is no longer the metropolis with which he is familiar, its current residents imported to raise a fighting force. Everywhere he looks, destitute men, women, and children in near rags wearily trudge by, many of them emaciated, their bellies swollen with undiagnosed illnesses, their eyes hosts to swarms of roaming flies. They seem exhausted, inarticulate with fear and vigilance, which imposes a further formlessness.

A mine detonates in the vicinity. Many people die and many more are injured. Jeebleh checks to see if any of his limbs are gone. Luck spares him this time. But he looks about in horror. Most of the dead and injured are young. There is little he can do to help. He meets a man as old as he is. When Jeebleh wonders aloud why the elderly have been spared, the old man says, "We are alive for a reason."

"Why have you been spared?" Jeebleh asks.

"Because I recruit the martyrs," the man says.

"You recruit them, they die, and you live on?"

"I blood the young brood of martyrs, suicides."

"The young die as martyrs and the old live on?"

The old man replies, "That's right."

"But that is absurd," Jeebleh says.

"On the contrary," the man says, "it is exemplary to die for one's country. There is nothing as honorable as martyring oneself, when young, for one's nation."

"Ultimately, it depends on the martyr, doesn't it?" Jeebleh challenges. "Has it ever occurred to you to give the young the choice whether to live on or to die for a religious cause in which they may not believe?"

The old man quips, "It is the martyrs' blood that helps keep the nation alive. Without that, there will be no country."

The old man walks away and sits nearby, pretending to pray. Jeebleh assists the wounded and then buries the dead in a mass grave, with no help from the recruiter of the martyrs. Then he leaves, and walks past a house caving in. He can spot human figures hanging from the rafters. He wonders if anyone will be charged with this mindless mass murder, if anyone will be made to answer for these crimes.

———

Jeebleh wakes up as exhausted as a wayfarer who has covered an immense distance to get here. His whole body aches, and his mind is weighed down with unidentified worries. He listens for sounds emanating from Malik's side of the apartment but hears none.

He is enjoying a leisurely breakfast of toast and coffee when Malik emerges from his workroom, saying, "Coffee. That is what I need."

Jeebleh says, "Good morning."

"Morning," Malik says.

"Sleep well?"

"I've slept little, but I've worked well."

Malik—indicating that he wants Jeebleh to wait for a moment— walks away in haste and enters the bathroom, maybe to clean his teeth before coffee. Jeebleh says to his back, "You can always catch up on sleep."

Malik is back before long. "Can I have some, please?" he asks, indicating the coffee.

Jeebleh replies, "With pleasure. And what else can I offer you?"

Malik says, "I agree that one can always catch up on sleep faster than one can catch up on writing when one has neglected it for some time." He takes a sip of his coffee and, as if defining the extent of his haste and underscoring that he is in no mood to engage in a lengthy conversation, says, "You won't mind if I leave you? I am itching to get on."

Jeebleh says, "Brilliant."

"It's time I met a journalist or two, time I set up interviews with people in the piracy business," Malik says. "But I plan to rely less on Gumaad and more on either Qasiir or Dajaal. They are plenty well connected."

"Good idea," Jeebleh says.

And Malik is off.

Jeebleh packs his suitcase and puts half the cash he has left in an envelope, to do with it what he will before he takes his flight early tomorrow—most likely share it out between Dajaal and Qasiir, giving the larger portion to the older man. Then he sits in the living room and catches up on his reading. He has brought along half a dozen books from New York, and he hasn't had the time to so much as look at them, much less read them. He will probably leave them behind; they could be useful to Malik for his research into the piracy question and the Somali civil war, viewed from the perspective of how the continued strife and the resultant impoverishment and desertification of the country may herald future conflicts in Africa and the Middle East.

But Jeebleh is restive and can't concentrate. It is unlike him to make hasty conclusions about what he has discovered so far about the men from the Courts, but from his brief encounter with BigBeard and the little he has gotten to know about Gumaad, he can't help concluding that they are an unhealthy procession of hardened, self-obsessed men who have been waiting in the wings for the opportunity to run the country their way. He worries whether Malik will fall victim to the particular cruelty Shabaab metes out to secular-leaning journalists.

He hangs up and dials Bile and Cambara's number. She picks up the phone on the first ring. Listening to her, Jeebleh realizes that he has taken to her more than he has been aware. He finds her voice not only pleasant but reassuring, and he is delighted that his friend is receiving the attention and affection he needs.

He says to her, "I wonder if it is convenient for me to visit? Malik is working, and I don't feel like reading."

"Yes, please," she says. "Do come. Anytime."

"How is Bile doing?"

"In bed, reading and occasionally napping."

"I'll see you shortly, then."

After he hangs up, Jeebleh telephones Dajaal to come fetch him.

After a light lunch with Cambara and Bile, Jeebleh is at the sink, washing up. Cambara is upstairs with Bile, who has packed it in, exhausted. Cambara has assured him she will come down once she has attended to Bile's needs.

He reads the Arabic writing on the bottle of dishwashing liquid: *Imported from Australia, via the United Arab Emirates.* Jeebleh thinks that the term *globalization* is misleading, a word that hardly describes all that is happening in businesses, big and small, the world over. His forehead is crisscrossed with furrows as he revisits his dream. He recalls that when he awoke, his hair stood out like the roots of a baobab tree battered by a tempest. He didn't tell his dream to Malik.

But his thoughts return to happiness for his friend. Granted, their current circumstances, within the prison of civil war that curtails freedom of movement, expression, and association, may not make for picture-book intimacy all the time. But they seem comfortable in each other's company. That they could live in these circumstances without giving in to acrimony indicates the depth of their commitment to each other. He couldn't care less if they occupy separate bedrooms, although he hopes that his friend, who spent so many years locked away and denied the opportunity to love, has had some opportunity to make up for lost time before the prison of sickness and old age closed in.

Just as he finishes putting the dishes back in the cupboards, Jeebleh hears Cambara coming down. He looks up and observes how the dust motes disperse in the sunlight at her approach, opening a way for her.

She asks him to make them espresso, and to retrieve a bottle of mineral water from the fridge. Jeebleh is pleased that she takes this sort of liberty with him; it makes him feel at home.

They sit at an angle, facing each other. Demurely dropping his gaze from her face, he notices that the front of his trousers is wet from standing against the sink. Cambara notices, too, and looks away, smiling, then bows her head slightly. She has had a shower and changed into a more casual caftan, and she seems revived; with her earrings in the clutch of her thumb and forefinger, she pauses and inserts them in her earlobes. Barefoot, she gives him the impression of a woman who intends to tiptoe through the remainder of the day, without a care in the world. He remembers how relaxed his wife used to seem after the children fell asleep. She takes a sip of her coffee and then unclasps her earring, after a bit of struggle, and removes it. She places the stud on her palm and takes a long look at it, then tosses it up, catches it, studies it again, and pockets it. She shifts in her seat, as if considering whether to unfasten the earring in her left ear, but seems to think better of it.

They talk at length about the early days of her return to Mogadiscio, when she had to get accustomed to the discomfort of a body tent, something she had never worn when she first lived there.

Jeebleh asks, "How does it feel, to be all covered up?"

"It makes me miss Toronto," she says.

Jeebleh senses she is comfortable with the figure she cuts, sitting confidently as she does now, her heels tucked under her. His gaze journeys from her heels to the firmness of the rest of her body. He doesn't want to know what Bile and she do for love, with Bile sick and she his junior by twenty-something years. Maybe the two of them take a long view of the matter, as life partners do, secure in the knowledge that there will be tomorrow and the day after, the way he and his wife have been doing since her menopause. It is the luxury of old age to have both a long- and a short-term perspective on sex. Jeebleh has known couples of disparate ages who seem to struggle to find topics that interest both partners. Bile and Cambara never seem to have a shortage of things to say to each other. But will Cambara continue to stay by Bile's side as his body weakens, as his health deteriorates? Himself, he has made a long investment in his rapport with his wife. They have a strong affinity, which will hold them together until their dying days.

"Are you still teaching?" Cambara asks.

He nods his head yes.

"Retirement not in sight?"

"Not yet," he replies.

"And your wife?"

"My wife thinks we'll be in each other's way if I retire and stay at home, as she does—she took early retirement. This is also because we've recently moved. We bought a smaller apartment for just the two of us when our younger girl left home."

"Retire and tour the world," she says. "Why not?"

Jeebleh bites down hard on his lips to keep mum, as he considers the difficulties Cambara and Bile would confront if they were to attempt a world tour. Cambara, younger and healthy and carrying a Canadian passport, wouldn't have a problem, but Bile wouldn't get far.

He says, spacing his words, "Ours is a problem of a different nature from yours. Judith was born in Manhattan to Jewish parents from Lithuania. She thinks that New York is the center of the world; she can't imagine why anyone wants to bother with the peripheries."

"Isn't it interesting that all the time I lived in Toronto," Cambara says, "I never fancied myself as residing in one of the world's centers? However, when I was younger and lived in Mogadiscio and knew no better, I thought of myself as residing in the center of the universe. How the world changes, and with it our perceptions of centers and peripheries!"

Jeebleh asks, "And what shape have your current perceptions taken now that you are back in Mogadiscio?"

"Every thought is centered here, on Bile."

"Are you saying that nothing else matters?"

"I am saying that my world is here, where Bile and I are, a world on the periphery that has become a center for me," she says.

"It's amazing—how *we* accommodate the changes."

She says, "I have been out of Mogadiscio only once since coming here, when I flew to Nairobi with Bile for his prostate operation. We had immense difficulties arranging for his visa into Kenya. I have no idea when or if I will return to Toronto. I can't see myself living there alone."

"You can't imagine my joy at meeting you."

"And I you."

He can't begin to imagine how she will respond to the thought that has just intruded upon his mind. He wonders if, in the midst of this easygoing conversation, this sudden question will encumber their rapport.

He asks, "What of your marriage prospects?"

He feels easy in his mind only after she laughs, his heart gladdening when she sighs and smiles. He is pleased to hear the jauntiness in her tone when she says, "You're bull's-eye direct for someone who is otherwise very refined in his manners."

"I am worried about Bile."

"How will marriage allay this?"

"It'll get the religionists off both your backs."

She says, "I doubt if marrying would achieve that goal. They lack goodwill. Why not think of me as a nurse caring for a convalescing man? They have outlawed contact between the sexes; soon they will forbid women driving. Where will all this end? Only male nurses for male patients? Female patients able to consult only female doctors? And this in a country short of female nurses to begin with, let alone female doctors?"

"How do they view it when Dajaal drives and you're in the car, sitting beside him in the front, lightly veiled and talking with him?"

She replies, "I lied once when a young nitwit stopped us and asked if he was my husband. I said he was. You see, these religionists are happier being lied to than hearing the truth. They are a hopeless lot, the sods, and I suppose they find me provocative, against the grain. After all, I am not one of the hordes of ill-clad women they recruit to sweep the roads. I'll say this about them: they know the type of women they prefer—the unlettered kind, who can't stand up to them. That's why they look to orphans and kids from broken homes to draft into Shabaab. They rely on the ill-informed and ill-supported to do their bidding."

"I wonder, are the women volunteering to clear the roads exempt from putting on veils?" Jeebleh asks.

She replies, "It is a class thing. A woman at the wheel of her own car, who lives with a man not married to her and speaks her mind— that they find provocative."

She falls silent now, and for the first time looks sad.

Jeebleh asks gently, "Where do you stand with Bile?" He waits until she is ready to answer.

"I love him."

"Let's call some people in," he says.

"Who and what for?"

Jeebleh abandons himself to a flush of shyness. Then he says, "So that you and Bile are declared man and wife, in the presence of witnesses."

He looks around, then at her, sighs heavily, sits back, closes his eyes, and rubs the bridge of his nose. Then he gazes at her, smiling. "God. I feel I am the one proposing."

"You're doing just that. Very adequately, I might add."

"As if I were his parent," Jeebleh says.

"Is that not how marriages are arranged?"

Jeebleh says, "If you wish, you may choose not to be present when the sheikh pronounces you and Bile man and wife."

"How very apt!"

"You know what I am doing, why and for whom."

"The trouble is I do."

"Then we'll say no more about it until the day?"

As if on cue, a bell rings, and a minute later, Dajaal comes in to fetch Jeebleh, as arranged. Jeebleh gets out of the chair, undecided what he will do. Dajaal senses that the atmosphere into which he has walked is heavy with others' concerns; he strides back out to wait in the car.

Cambara stands close to him, their bodies almost touching. Then she takes him in an embrace and kisses him, one cheek at a time. He feels a slight tremor in her body, as she withdraws from a full-fledged embrace. It becomes obvious to Jeebleh that she wishes to get one thing off her chest. She says, "There is no cause for worry on your part or anyone else's. Bile is in good, loving hands, and he won't be wanting for anything as long as I live. So don't worry about him."

They hug again.

"Go well."

"Be well."

Dinner is a hurried affair, because Malik hasn't got the time to talk; he is on a high, writing. Jeebleh retreats into his room. He is at a loss as to what to do, since he still cannot seem to hold the ideas of a single paragraph in his head long enough to make sense of it. It is his third attempt to read "Plundered Waters: Somalia's Maritime Resource Insecurity," a thirteen-page chapter by a political geographer named Clive Schofield in a book called *Crucible for Survival*. After several more failed attempts, he puts the book aside and, in his head, thanks the author for bringing the plundering of the Somali seas to the world's attention.

Jeebleh puts on a sweater, fearing he may find the breezy balcony cold. He gains the balcony without disturbing Malik, who is still at it, and he sits as fretful as a debtor worried about settling a bill. He wishes he could help Malik more; he wishes he had thought about how much closer to danger a journalist would be here.

The night is pitch black, the drone more fitful in its nocturnal re-connoitring. He tells himself that this will be the third time foreign forces have aided Ethiopia in invading Somalia. In the sixteenth century, Portuguese mercenaries fought on the side of Ethiopia—then known as Abyssinia—to defeat the Somali warrior Ahmed Gurey, Ahmed the Left-handed. In the late 1970s, the Soviets changed sides and the Cubans intervened, chasing the Somalis out of the Somali-speaking Ogaden region in Ethiopia. Will the third time mark the entry of the United States into this dark history?

Jeebleh sets himself the task of identifying the Mother Camels constellation, otherwise known as Draco the Dragon. He finds it, and the moment fills him with joy. He sits out there all night.

Perhaps he dozes, because at the first call of the muezzin, Malik makes a well-timed appearance on the balcony, with the quietness of a fellow conspirator. He brings a fresh pot of tea and cups on a tray.

"Two down, one more to go," says Malik.

The muezzins calling the faithful to prayers keep different times in their different voices. Some are sweet; some subtle, almost chummy; some throaty; others clumsy and heavy, like lumpy syrup; some strong, like the boughs of a baobab tree. Jeebleh's mother was partial to an Egyptian chanter of the Koran; she delighted in listening to his tapes again and again. Jeebleh wonders to himself when or if he will ever resume saying his prayers. But the susurrations of the breeze, which bring the morning's blessings from the mosques nearby, toughen his resolve that all will be well with Malik. And as the calls die down, the noise of the drone disappears from the skies.

Malik asks, "Would you like to read the articles?"

"I would be pleased to read them," says Jeebleh.

Malik offers the printout of the drafts to Jeebleh, in the manner that one gives a precious gift to a respected elder, with both hands and head slightly inclined. He says, "Here, please."

"Is it okay if I read them on the plane?"

"Of course it is. You may read them whenever."

That this is the first time Malik has volunteered to show him a piece before publication is not lost on Jeebleh. Maybe Malik is missing the camaraderie of being among fellow journalists, a situation he hasn't experienced with anyone in Mogadiscio so far. Or maybe he is making his peace with his coming isolation and the strain of their inability to discuss the possibility of his coming to harm is lifting.

The sun, rising, hits the balcony at an angle.

Finally Jeebleh says, "Time to shower."

Malik starts to put together some breakfast.

At breakfast, Jeebleh says, "Let's talk money."

"What's on your mind?" asks Malik.

"Dajaal and Qasiir are on my mind."

They eat in silence, both of them determined to push away every worrying thought from the forefront of their minds. Jeebleh's departure for Nairobi in a couple of hours will doubtless open up other avenues for Malik, even as it will expose him to unsettling unknowns.

Finally Jeebleh says, "Qasiir has in a very short time demonstrated how quick and useful he can be. I think it is worthwhile having him on board for all the time you are here. He is adept at fixing computers, well informed about the market trends, has contacts among his former fellow militiamen, some of them Shabaab operatives. He attends the prayers at the right mosques, and, unlike Gumaad, he is trustworthy." He pauses and then asks, "By the way, when were you last in a mosque?"

"I can't remember when I last prayed. Why?"

"Maybe it's time you went."

"Maybe I will."

Jeebleh says, "The mosque will remain the hub of opposition activities after the invasion, and those coalescing into the insurgency will meet there. Qasiir has the right credentials, as he is an active member of the mosques that are the nerve center of everything social, everything political."

"I'll attend prayers at mosques—discreetly."

"It'll be worth your while," Jeebleh predicts.

Malik says, "So what about money?"

"I meant to tell you that I will be arranging to send a hundred dollars monthly to Dajaal," says Jeebleh. "He's been loyal, bless his soul; he has no pension, no family to support him in his old age, and no guarantee that Bile will have the wherewithal to provide him with a monthly stipend, or if Cambara will want him if something happens to Bile and she returns to Toronto. A hundred dollars a month from me, and a similar sum from Seamus, will see him through these terrible economic times. But I want you to confide less in Gumaad, more in Qasiir. I am aware that Gumaad has set up an appointment for you with Ma-Gabadeh, a funder of the Xarardheere pirates. I suggest caution when you deal with him; be on your guard."

"I'll be vigilant."

Jeebleh says, "In addition, you must have either Dajaal or Qasiir with you, preferably Dajaal."

"I'll do as you advise," Malik says. "And I would like to contribute toward Dajaal's retirement, too."

Jeebleh's mobile vibrates. He reads the text. "They are here." Rushed, he says to Malik, "No need to come to the airport," in a way that allows no room for argument. "Stay behind and work. I'll call you from the plane when we are boarded and ready to take off, and from Nairobi as soon as we land."

Malik is up on his feet. He opens his arms to give a good-bye hug to Jeebleh, who's been waiting to receive it with a smile. He says, "I realize you may not want me to say it, but I will say it, nonetheless. I will miss you and I appreciate your coming with me and sharing a little of your life with which neither Judith nor your daughters are familiar."

Touched, Jeebleh says, "It's been my pleasure."

"Never have I had an introduction such as this."

They realize they could continue exchanging words in a similar vein all day, so they stop and hug and wrap their arms around each other, whispering endearments.

"Come, come," Jeebleh says. "I have to go."

"I know that you must."

But the way Malik tightens his embrace reminds Jeebleh of a child on his first day at nursery school, reluctant to let his parent go. Then suddenly Malik releases him, and breaks into a brilliant smile.

"Be good. Fear not, worry not," Jeebleh says.

Malik says, "We'll talk."

"Take good care of yourself."

ON THE DAY OF MALIK'S LUNCH APPOINTMENT WITH MA-GABADEH, Dajaal is indisposed, so he sends Qasiir in his place to drive. In addition, Qasiir has taken on the responsibility of setting up a special security detail before coming to fetch Malik. He has no doubt that Ma-Gabadeh will take his own precautionary measures. It is to this end that Qasiir has selected four of his trusted sidekicks, former lieutenants of his, who are prepared to remain inconspicuous and not to provoke a fight with Ma-Gabadeh's guard unit. They will situate themselves in the vicinity of the restaurant where Malik has rented a private alcove. Discreetly armed, they are to hang around and to report on any usual movements. One of them is to be stationed at the entrance to the alcove. The big challenge has been to keep Gumaad ignorant of the security detachment, given that he arranged the meeting.

Loosely translated, Ma-Gabadeh means "the fearless one." Gumaad has described Ma-Gabadeh as a major underwriter of a handful of daring piratical expeditions out of Xarardheere, hometown of both Gumaad and Ma-Gabadeh. In addition to sponsoring these "privateers," Ma-Gabadeh is allegedly bankrolling a string of activities in which his men collaborate with a Shabaab unit charged with bringing Yemeni and Pakistani operatives into Somalia by boat. It is rumored that the pirates bring the foreign jihadis into the Somali peninsula, and in exchange receive weapons and protection in the coastal areas under Shabaab control. It is all shady stuff. Gumaad has made it sound as if it will be a scoop, Malik's first, since Ma-Gabadeh has agreed to talk on tape.

Malik is not coping well on his own, with Jeebleh gone and Dajaal sick. He misses the certainty of these two men, one or the other always by his side and willing to answer his questions, challenge his decisions, or offer advice. Granted, Qasiir and Gumaad know things he doesn't about Somalia, having lived here all their lives. But he knows many things about Somalia of which they have no idea, because he has sought the information and obtained and read it, and he cannot take eiither of them as seriously as he would Jeebleh or Dajaal. But he has coped with worse situations before.

With Qasiir at the wheel, Gumaad is in a feisty mood. Unprompted, he says, "We'll singe the hairs off their heads if they come."

"Who are we talking about?" Malik asks.

"Who else, the Ethiopians of course, and their lackeys, the so-called Federal Government," he replies. "We'll teach the Ethiopians a lesson the Eritreans haven't taught them, when they invade."

Qasiir looks from Malik to Gumaad. "In times of war, you need to act grown up. There is talk and there is war. It is high time you tell the difference between the two."

"And I'll tell you what," Gumaad says.

"What?"

"TheSheikh has assured me that I'll be appointed to the position of spokesman of the Courts the moment the first bullet is shot by either party."

Qasiir roars with derisory laughter. "Get away. You can't be serious. How can anyone appoint you to the position when you have little

English, do not speak any other European language, and have only a couple of short articles to your name?"

"I'll make you eat your words one day."

"We've had enough of your fibbing."

Malik pleads, "Please. Let peace reign."

To Malik's relief, Gumaad desists from saying anything offensive or provocative from then on; Qasiir's behavior becomes agreeable, too. Malik, who doesn't see himself as a peacemaker, is relieved that so far his intercession has worked well.

As they approach their destination, Malik asks Gumaad to put Ma-Gabadeh in his civil war context, since nothing in Somalia makes sense until one places it in the "before," "after," and "during" of that frame of reference.

Gumaad obliges. "Ma-Gabadeh was a junior clerk in the Accountancy Department of the Ministry of Fisheries," he says.

"He was no junior clerk and you know it," Qasiir says. "He was a peon who worked his way by dint of coercion up to the rank of head janitor, and was eventually assigned an office. But he was no clerk. The fellow doesn't know how to read or write."

Dreading the thought of getting bogged down over whether Ma-Gabadeh was a junior clerk or head janitor, Malik urges Gumaad, "Please continue."

"Anyhow," Gumaad says, "he was at the desk managing the Somali-owned, Italian-funded SHIFCO—an acronym for Somali High-seas International Fishing Company—charged with exploiting Somalia's marine resources. SHIFCO, set up by the last central government, owned a dozen trawlers. A couple of them are still operational, although more than half the original number have been lost, several of them confiscated by Kenya and other countries for nonpayment of dues, others because of lack of maintenance."

After the collapse of the country's state structures, Gumaad goes on to explain, Ma-Gabadeh returned to Xarardheere, where he built a business partnership with an Italian fishing firm with whom he had dealt before in his Ministry of Fisheries capacity. He issued a back-dated license to the Italian firm, a license that was to be valid for three years. Then he relocated to Mogadiscio and, once there, struck an alliance with StrongmanSouth, who was on the run then. From the proceeds, Ma-Gabadeh established a frozen-food company centered on the fishing business, harvesting lobster and exporting it to Italy.

Following the death of StrongmanSouth, Ma-Gabadeh entered into a more lucrative alliance with StrongmanSouth's former financier, the man accused of killing the warlord and heading up a breakaway faction. Ma-Gabadeh then fell out with the Italian fishing firm, and to recover the assets in dispute, took two of their ships and crew hostage. He released the ships on payment of large sums of money, with which he funded an armed militia unit based in Xarardheere and specializing in the hijacking of the ships.

During the past few years, Ma-Gabadeh has diversified his business operations, branching out into the importation of *qaat* from Kenya and the exportation of charcoal from Somalia to the Gulf States. In addition, he runs other moneymaking ventures, many of them illegal. A heavyweight businessman with some fifty gun-mounted Technicals, he has lately thrown in his lot with the Courts, whom he backs with funds, and to whom he offers his thousand-strong armed militia whenever he is called upon to do so.

The car slows down and Qasiir heads into the hotel parking lot. He pulls around to the rear of the hotel and turns to Gumaad. "Since you know Ma-Gabadeh well," Qasiir says, "please go ahead. Malik and I will join you in a minute in the hotel foyer, as arranged."

Miffed because he senses Qasiir is making a point of putting him at a distance, Gumaad does as advised, but not without making his feelings known. "He's a busy man, Ma-Gabadeh is, and he won't want to be made to wait."

After he leaves, Qasiir goes over the security arrangements he has put in place and points out where a couple of his men are. He phones his men to make sure they are in their proper positions, then he cuts the engine and they step out together and walk side by side into the hotel, pretending to chat while Qasiir takes the measure of his surroundings, eyes darting this way and that. He nods discreetly to his two men at the entrance to the hotel, as they stride into the foyer.

Inside, there is a market feel to the place. The foyer is spacious and bathed in sunlight, yet it feels cramped, because it is thronged with people standing around and talking loudly, and it is also crowded with furniture that strikes him as belonging to a different period. When Qasiir moves, Malik follows him closely, but he finds he has to pause often to avoid colliding with people. Gumaad is standing with two other men in a huddle near the reception—a one-desk affair manned by three men, two of them in uniform and all of them focusing watchfully on the threesome's movements.

They join Gumaad and he makes brief introductions, naming them in order of importance. "Here is Ma-Gabadeh. Meet Malik. Malik, meet Fee-Jigan, a journalist."

Malik takes Ma-Gabadeh's short-fingered hand, and then his own hand vanishes in its entirety into Fee-Jigan's long-fingered shake.

Ma-Gabadeh says, "Shall we?"

Qasiir leads the way to the alcove. Following on his heels, Ma-Gabadeh duckwalks and sidesteps to make room for Malik to walk alongside him. He is a short man, balding, mustachioed, boasting a prominent paunch and a chinless face. His arms sway at his sides in rhythm with his hips. Ma-Gabadeh makes an immediate impression on Malik: that he is the type of man who comes to an engagement with a drawn face and leaves it with a smile when he has convinced himself that he has made a killing large enough to warrant the risk involved. Otherwise, what is in it for him to talk to a journalist? Despite the sweet expansive smile, which is probably part of a repertoire he deploys on occasions such as this, Malik finds nothing genial about him.

Fee-Jigan has on a baggy pair of khaki trousers, and his sandals are missing a buckle. Tall and slim, he is a big-eyed man in his mid-thirties, with ears almost as large as saucers. His handshake is firm, his smile charming. Malik is eager not to alienate him unnecessarily, assuming that he is an ally of Ma-Gabadeh's.

He asks, "Are you a print or radio journalist?"

"I am a recent returnee from Cairo," Fee-Jigan replies, "where I was a simultaneous interpreter in Arabic and English. Here I am a stringer for several Arabic wire services. I also report and do the occasional feed for Al Jazeera."

"I am delighted to make your acquaintance."

As if to further impress Malik with his importance, he says, "I have the ambition to write a book about Somalia. In fact, I've already done the first couple of chapters."

"But that is wonderful," Malik says.

Fee-Jigan has the habit of grinning every time his and Malik's eyes make contact. If there is something that unnerves Malik, it is this: Why does it feel as though he is in the company of a head of state with his retinue, not a mere funder of pirates?

At the entrance to the alcove, Ma-Gabadeh dismisses Gumaad and Qasiir with a wave of his hand. Malik notes the discreetly armed men loitering in the vicinity. In the alcove, the air conditioners are on, and three young men are working the table, the food already laid out, the colorful drinks poured, the large knives sharp as a butcher's. Ma-Gabadeh ejaculates, *"Bismillah,"* and, waiting for no further formalities, immediately takes his seat and heaps mountains of rice and mutton on his plate, then takes hold of a knife and begins to slice off mouthfuls of the meat. Time is money to Ma-Gabadeh; it is obvious he doesn't waste it on eating. Fee-Jigan keeps up with him, and begins eating just as quickly.

A slow eater, Malik lags behind, afraid of boring them.

Ma-Gabadeh teases Malik, "Why was I told that in America you do everything fast, eat standing and on the run, in buses, trains, and offices?"

Embarrassed, Malik gives up eating. The table is cleared forthwith.

Buoyed by the presence of two witnesses, Ma-Gabadeh is true to his sobriquet, fearlessly agreeing for their conversation to be taped, on condition that he receives copies of the interview when it is published. He explains to Malik that he has invited Fee-Jigan to join them to answer some of the questions, as he has done research on the topic. Anyhow, "Two heads are better than one."

Malik asks, "To what do you owe your success?"

"I *am* the success."

Malik is ill prepared for this sort of talk. Not only does he disagree with the intent of the statement, but he finds it smacks of cockiness with a terrible sting in its tail.

"Please explain your meaning," he says.

"I was born poor in a small hamlet," Ma-Gabadeh says, "to parents who hadn't a cent to spare for my education. Luckily, I knew I wanted to make it in the bigger world and had the ambition to match my wish. I started off as a junior clerk, and within a year was promoted to a section head in the Ministry of Fisheries, and within a couple more years I headed a service. I was on the verge of being made a head of department when the civil war erupted. I achieved what I achieved on my own, with little or no help from anyone. Let's face it: I, too, like many others, contributed to the creation of the crisis and then profited from the turmoil. Turbulence upsets things, sends the dregs to the top. We are enjoying the turmoil and are unfettered by tax laws, a parliament issuing decrees, a dictator passing edicts, a government declaring draconian measures: the ideal situation for growth of capital."

Malik asks, "Are you different from those born in the same hamlet as you, who were raised in more or less the same poverty?"

"There is no poverty worse than the poverty of many of the coastal areas in the northeast of Somalia," Ma-Gabadeh says, and then corrects himself. "Except for the places where there are deepwater ports. There are no tarred roads, no developed forms of communication, no transportation by land or even by sea. The region I come from has suffered total neglect, from the days of Italian colonialism onward. Since the collapse of the state, things have become much worse, because of the foreign vessels fishing illegally in our seas. So we have nothing to eat, no fish to fish. Think about it."

"Where were you when the state collapsed?"

"When the state collapsed, I was in Mogadiscio—a small, honest cog in a state machine, part of a bigger machine. I served my country until the engine of the state of which I was a mere cog ceased to run, because our president had fled in an army tank. Then I went home, depressed."

"What did you do then?"

"I sent my wife home to Guriceel, her hometown."

"Where is your wife now, as we speak?"

"She is in the States, an American citizen."

"And where are your children?"

"They are with her; Americans, too."

"What did you do after sending your wife home?"

"Jobless for several months, I contacted an Italian I knew and proposed he and I go into the lobster business together. I had at my disposal some of the old files, because I had saved them from the looters who were setting fire to the buildings after emptying them of computers and furniture. To cook up a deal with some of my old mates, I moved to Bosaso and linked up with them. We were fired up to provide employment for people, hired a thousand or so unemployed fishermen. Soon enough we started to export shiploads of lobster and other precious fish to Italy. When we became big enough to set up freezing facilities of our own, I moved my base to Mogadiscio. Not long after, we found that ships flying flags from faraway places—Korea, Japan, Spain, Russia, Yemen, China, Belize, Bermuda, Liberia, and a handful of countries you couldn't place on a map—were in our seas, plundering our fish and destroying their habitat. Bear in mind that our waters contained huge fishing potential—Somalia has the longest coastline in Africa."

Fee-Jigan interjects, "It is over thirty-three hundred kilometers long, and there are special features found in and around Ras Hafun, where there used to be an abundance of the largest variety of fish at certain periods of the year."

Ma-Gabadeh continues. "Anyway, upset by what these illegal fishing vessels were doing, we apprehended a trawler with a dummy registration in Kenya that was fishing inside Somali waters near the town of Garcad. The trawler was fined, the proceeds were shared out among the community of fishermen. After this, the foreign trawlers hired local militiamen, arming them, to protect their illegal fishing. The more numerous and the bigger the vessels, the more destruction they caused. We counted five to seven thousand professional fishermen, and not one of them could make a living. This was a no-win situation, and I quit."

Malik asks if Ma-Gabadeh has been engaged in funding some of the "piracy" acts taking place off the coast of Somalia.

Ma-Gabadeh replies, "I am an honest businessman, earn my money in an honest way, and spend what I must spend honestly. Granted, I give charitably to honest causes."

"Would you consider funding the Courts in their fight against the warlords a charitable activity worth funding?" Malik asks.

Fee-Jigan intervenes. "It would be unwise for Ma-Gabadeh to specify the institutions to which he contributes charitably. That is between him and his Creator."

Malik tries again. "What are your links to the pirates?"

Ma-Gabadeh replies, "I've said I am an honest man, I make honest money, and spend the honest money I make on honest causes. I have no links with the pirates."

"Nor with Shabaab?"

"Nor with Shabaab."

"Nor have you ever funded Shabaab?"

As if on cue, Ma-Gabadeh's mobile phone rings. He glances at it, then, turning, trains an angry stare on Fee-Jigan, who for his part is stagily looking away, fingers nonchalantly drumming on the table, his humming audible. Malik can't make sense of the goings-on, especially because Ma-Gabadeh behaves as though he is at once miffed, shocked, and disappointed. As if weighing his options, Ma-Gabadeh hands over his mobile phone to Malik and says, as if Fee-Jigan is not there, "Look at what this hapless fool, Fee-Jigan, is doing." He shakes his head in disapproval. "I hate his sort. Filthy cowards."

Malik turns to look at Fee-Jigan, who still acts as if he doesn't know what Ma-Gabadeh is on about. This in turn makes Ma-Gabadeh still more irate. He explains to Malik, "When he and I met in the hotel foyer before your arrival, Fee-Jigan suggested he would ring me on his mobile phone if you put an embarrassing question to me, so I might justifiably terminate our conversation and say that I was called away to attend an emergency business meeting. I told him to do no such thing and to make sure that he did not make a fool of us. Yet here he is and he has done precisely that—turned us into a laughingstock."

Fee-Jigan fidgets and, remorseful, narrows his eyes in sorry concentration. He lowers his head and then the rest of his body, as if going on his knees in apology. His voice almost a whisper, he says, "My phone was in my pocket and it must have dialed itself."

Ma-Gabadeh says, "You are a fool and a liar."

The tape recorder is on, registering every word.

Ma-Gabadeh then asks Fee-Jigan, "Tell it all on tape, you dishonest, filthy dog, if you do not want me to have my men slit your throat. Confess it on tape. Speak, and speak loud!"

"It's my fault," Fee-Jigan says. "Everything."

"Go on and tell him what I told you before we came here."

Fee-Jigan says, with abject humility, "You said that if you were displeased with a question the journalist put to you, you would exercise your right to refuse to answer, or might take the option of answering it on condition he rephrase his question."

Ma-Gabadeh turns to Malik. "You see, Malik, how very difficult it is to stay honest in a world that is becoming more dishonest by the second and in which those whom you trust continue to let you down. What do you suggest we do about the world? You are better educated and wiser than I am. What do you suggest we do about people's dishonesty?"

Ma-Gabadeh gathers his things, rises to his feet, calls his bodyguards on the phone, and tells them to have the car waiting in the rear of the hotel. Departing, Ma-Gabadeh says, "You'll hear from me."

Malik is not certain to whom Ma-Gabadeh's parting words are addressed, or what to make of them. They could be interpreted, if they are addressed to Malik, as meaning, "I'll get in touch with you." Equally, they could be communicating a warning—"I'll be gunning for you from here on," if Fee-Jigan is their intended recipient. But what if Ma-

Gabadeh is intending to warn Malik off, since he is the one who is asking sensitive questions about funding Shabaab, the very question that precipitated the set-to between Fee-Jigan and Ma-Gabadeh?

When he is gone, Malik sends a brief text to Qasiir: "All well."

Then Fee-Jigan leans forward, his hand outstretched as if in friendship, almost touching Malik's wrist. Maybe the man wishes to clear his name, Malik thinks.

Fee-Jigan says, "I am sure that was a piece of theater unlike any you've seen in your wanderings as a foreign correspondent. Not too bad, was it?"

"Frankly, I am still confused by it," Malik says. "Maybe you can enlighten me?"

Fee-Jigan is in no haste to get up. He says, "I deny categorically that the idea of bringing the interview to an end by dialing Ma-Gabadeh's number was mine. It was he who suggested it. I regret that I agreed."

If Malik does not counter Fee-Jigan's claim right away, it is because he remembers an Arabic proverb: that for the strong to impose their will on the weak, they must provoke them until they take an inadvisable course of action that will destroy them. Fee-Jigan, in other words, is in no position to call Ma-Gabadeh a liar.

Fee-Jigan continues, "Now to act as if he was innocent and I was the guilty party, and then to threaten me? I find that hard to take."

Malik is inclined to believe Fee-Jigan, but he says only, "Let's go get a cup of something."

———

The teahouse they find themselves in is a bit of a letdown after the hotel dining room and the private alcove. The waiters are scruffy, their white shirts stained with food and string holding up their trousers. The clients whom they are serving are no different from the folks one runs into in the street outside. Malik, cynical, thinks that maybe democracy has dawned here at last, after all. The men, pretentiously pious, wear lavish beards. They hush as Fee-Jigan and Malik go past them, looking for a free table. When they resume talking, they speak textbook Arabic, not the dialects native speakers would use. One of them is so pleased with his mastery of the language that he throws tongue-twisting gauntlets at them, like a teenager showing off.

As the waiter departs to get them the tea they have ordered, Malik cuts to the chase. He asks, "Does Ma-Gabadeh fund pirates?"

"In truth, the nexus between the pirates and Shabaab is hard to prove and much more difficult to discount," Fee-Jigan says. "Even so, I've heard it said by an associate of his that if there is a link in an expanding chain connecting the pirates to Shabaab, and Shabaab to the foreign jihadis, then Ma-Gabadeh is that link, because he has had extensive associations with all three groups. Moreover, he has been described as someone who has made deals beneficial to the pirates by lending them seed money, and to Shabaab by paying deposits on the weapons they bought from the Bakhaaraha. I know from one of my sources that he has collected tidy sums from the pirates as his percentage, and has paid protection fees to Shabaab. More significantly, he is related by marriage to TheSheikh."

"And he is wealthy on account of these links?"

Fee-Jigan says, with evident relish, "Ma-Gabadeh, a man from the shit creeks, is now so stinking rich from these illicit transactions that he can afford to bathe in tubs filled with the most expensive French perfume."

Malik asks, "What about Gumaad?"

"What about him?"

"What is his game?" Malik says.

"He is no journalist, I can tell you that."

"Precisely," Malik says. "So what's his game?"

"Rumor has it he has been lately recruited into the intelligence services of the Courts," Fee-Jigan says, "and we journalists do not trust him at all."

To Malik's surprise, Gumaad is again in the back of the car when Qasiir picks him up, but Qasiir merely says, "Belts, please," as usual, as he starts the engine and looks in the rearview mirror. Gumaad inquires how the interview has gone, but Malik is economical with his comments. He says simply that Fee-Jigan is the most interesting journalist he has met since his arrival—a clear putdown of Gumaad.

Clearly galled, Gumaad requests that Qasiir stop the car, then announces he won't be going with them back to the apartment. "I must help draft a communiqué to be released in the name of TheSheikh, in response to the imminent Ethiopian takeover of two Somali border towns."

Malik ascribes Gumaad's statement to similar self-important claims he has heard from him before. He is not sure when he will share with Qasiir, Dajaal, and Jeebleh Fee-Jigan's contention that Gumaad has been drafted into the Courts' intelligence services. He says only, "Good-bye and good luck," and waves Gumaad on.

Qasiir drives on and Malik looks out on the world outside, wondering if everyone on the road is in a greater rush today because they know something the two of them don't. Of course, he has heard about the Ethiopians invading and occupying Belet-Weyne, and all the news agencies are agreed that before long, the border town will fall. But how imminent is the real, final invasion of the country?

Malik asks, "What's the latest news?"

"My men on the security detail noted the curious presence of an explosives expert coming in and out of the hotel where you were conducting the interview," Qasiir says, "and we were rather worried. We wondered what he would be doing in the hotel."

"So what did you do?" Malik wants to know.

"I rang Grandpa for advice."

"What did he advise?"

"That we double the number of men on the beat," Qasiir says, "and that I change my parking position every so often; if need be, drive around and then come back."

It comes as a shock to Malik to imagine that he might become the victim of an assassination attempt when he has not published an article since he arrived in Somalia.

He asks, "The name of this explosives man?"

"His given name is Cabdul Xaqq," Qasiir says, "but it is possible that he has pseudonyms to which he answers. Even Grandpa can't be certain of this."

"What makes his presence curious?"

"Because he is seldom seen in public," Qasiir says. "His job is to put together roadside devices and analyze their performance. I can't understand why he was there, that's all."

"He did nothing to worry you, though?"

Qasiir says, "The entire country is on edge. Rationally, you would assume his plate would be full with matters of national importance, considering what is happening, but these are not normal men and you can trust them to behave abnormally. That was why we took the precautions we did."

Malik wonders whether the fact that his presence in the country rates a top explosives expert is a good or a bad thing. If he is a marked man, then it is high time he wrote something worth dying for. "How is your grandfather?" he asks.

Qasiir replies, "He is feeling a little better."

"Well enough to consult a doctor?" Malik asks.

"He doesn't bother with doctors usually."

"You can take him to visit Bile," Malik says. "Remember, he was a medic."

"Grandpa won't hear of it."

At the apartment, Malik takes the envelope with the money for the security detail and hands it to Qasiir, so that Qasiir can dole it out. He checks to make sure he has his tape recorder, then he waves good-bye and says, "Thank you, Qasiir. You've been very professional. And please give my best to your grandpa. I hope he feels better soon."

THE NEWS ABOUT THE RAID BY ETHIOPIAN AIRCRAFT ON TWO OF
Mogadiscio's airports comes early in the afternoon of December 26, an hour after an African Union delegation flew out of the country. It spreads like the wildest of fires. One couldn't help hearing it: the local radios broadcast it; total strangers meeting for the first time stop and chat about its consequences. Malik is in the workroom, licking a piece into shape, and doesn't hear of it until Dajaal calls him up. He thinks it is a risky action undertaken in broad daylight, by cocky men confident that they would get away with it. Somalis assumed they had in part the military intelligence garnered by the United States from the unmanned drones in the skies to thank for it.

"There were no fatalities as such in either attack," Dajaal says. "However, I hear that a young goatherd was hurt."

"What was the herder doing when he was hit?"

"He was pursuing one of his goats, which had strayed off the footpath and gone under the gaps in the airport security fence to graze," Dajaal explains. "My informant says that the beasts were close to the apron of the runway and he had barely chased the goat back when shrapnel from one of the bombs hit his side. It killed the goat."

Malik says, "Poor thing."

"The greatest casualty is neither the goat nor the boy who is hurt, but our national pride," Dajaal says. "The big mouths from the Courts, from TheSheikh down to the foot soldiers, feel no shame in provoking the bullies next door and exposing our vulnerabilities. Why talk big when you haven't the means, militarily, to defend the country?"

Malik senses Dajaal's anger. He prepares for an "I told you so" tirade, but Dajaal spares him that. After all, they are in agreement.

"How are you feeling, anyway?" Malik asks.

"I can't afford to be sick at such an hour, I am in such a rage," Dajaal says. "I am the proverbial man who chokes on water and doesn't know what else to drink. I am murderously annoyed with the men from the Courts and woeful, albeit homicidal, when I think about the raid."

Malik is of two minds whether to repeat Fee-Jigan's incrimination of Gumaad as an intelligence officer posing as a journalist when Dajaal inquires how his interview went. He thinks better of it, deciding that it no longer matters what Gumaad does for a job, since he won't excel at it. Malik will remain cordial but distant. He doesn't wish to make an enemy of Gumaad unnecessarily, since Gumaad can cause him much harm; all he has to do is heighten BigBeard's sense of paranoia and denounce Malik as an agent of the U.S. imperialists pretending to be a journalist. A journalist covering Somalia and holding a foreign passport must be careful what he wishes for.

He wishes Jeebleh were here. Neither he nor Ahl has responded to Malik's recent messages.

He channel-surfs, watching the news on the BBC and CNN in English; on Al Jazeera in Arabic; the BBC in Somali; then back to Al Jazeera, and finishing on the BBC. Apparently, between the time Jeebleh left and the bombing of the runway by the Ethiopian jets, a high-powered Arab League delegation on a fact-finding mission had taken off, and less than an hour later, a ten-man delegation from the Courts had returned from Eritrea. Local print and radio journalists had reportedly gone to the airport to interview the Arab League envoy before he departed for Cairo, and then waited on the tarmac to put their questions to the two most quotable members of the Courts delegation. Eritrea, Ethiopia's number-one enemy, is the principal ally of the Courts and the supplier of its weapons.

In his desire to know more, Malik tries Fee-Jigan, Gumaad, and several others. All to no avail, because their mobile phones are either busy or unavailable.

Cambara, who probably knows less than he does, is the first to call him—not to give him news, but to say that he is welcome to call or come whenever he is down, when he wants to reconnect, or when he is too tired to eat his own cooking, and to share a gossip or a laugh.

Sweetness, on occasion, brings out the bitterness in one. Malik starts to whine. "Everyone's phone is busy, or they do not answer."

"How has your day been otherwise?"

Malik gives her a rundown of his unsuccessful encounter with Ma-Gabadeh and then mentions that he has learned of the attack on the airports from Dajaal. Malik adds, "Gumaad claims he is to be appointed as the Courts' spokesman, and intimated he was off to meet up with TheSheikh, and to prepare a strongly worded statement about Ethiopia's moves along the border."

"Rather too late for that, I should think."

"Still, there is a need for a communiqué."

She asks, "Has Gumaad been of any use to you?"

Malik says, "Every bee with honey on its tongue has a sting in its tail and therefore its numerous uses. But not as much as I hoped."

"What are you saying?" she asks.

Then he tells her about his encounter with Fee-Jigan and repeats the journalist's incrimination of Gumaad as an intelligence officer. "I can't, I won't trust him anymore."

Cambara says, "It could be that because Dajaal, Bile, and I focused on Robleh, the snake in our midst, we missed the venomous spider. Have you shared this with Dajaal?"

"I thought he might take it badly."

"Anyhow, I don't think you need to worry anymore," Cambara says. "My suspicion is that TheSheikh and all the Courts' big shots, including TheOtherSheikh, will be fleeing the city in advance of the invading Ethiopians. Not one of them will relish falling into enemy hands or being taken prisoner and flown to Guantánamo for interrogation."

"I wish I could interview TheSheikh now."

Cambara, who is in a no-love-lost mood about the Courts, says, "TheSheikh won't be in any mood to chat to a nephew. I bet he won't stick around a second longer than necessary."

Malik imagines the robed men on the run as night falls, alive to the fact that defeat exposes them to ridicule, that their fair-weather friends will leave them to their own devices the second they lose power. Refuge will be difficult to find. One doesn't need to have read Machiavelli to know the tight spot the men of the Courts are in when or if the Ethiopians occupy Mogadiscio.

He asks Cambara, "How's Bile taking it?"

"To date, he is not aware of what has happened."

Malik, in his head, titles his article, "Sheikhs on the Run." Then he itches most furiously, as if a battalion of lice is advancing on him. He is so itchy he is tempted to suggest that they talk later.

But Cambara goes on. "This isn't an ideal country for someone on the run, especially if they are planning to stage a comeback, guerrilla style. There are no forests thick enough to hide a contingent of fighters preparing a hit-and-run attack, except in Lower Juba. TheSheikh won't dare cross into Kenya."

"Why not?"

"The Kenyans will hand him over to you-know-who."

"Why not take to the sea?"

She says, "You'd be surprised to know that even many coastal Somalis, born and bred in cities and towns on the sea, never learn to swim, or eat fish."

"Pirates not knowing how to swim? It's bizarre."

"It's strange but true," she says.

"I hear the Courts have planned a comeback."

She says, "Lately, the Bakhaaraha rumor mills have been abuzz with sightings of Shabaab cadres 'consecrating' people's properties with a view toward using them as bases from which they intend to launch their attacks on the Ethiopian forces invading or occupying Mogadiscio. Remember how the Republican Guard melted into the suburbs of Baghdad in the days of the U.S. invasion, and how they organized their comeback in a few weeks, with deadly results?"

"Is the plan afoot to do like the Iraqis?"

"They are planning a comeback."

"What will the cadres of the Courts do with the houses they are, as you put it, consecrating?"

"I've been told by a man related to my maid who is in the arms business that Shabaab have already moved heavy weapons into the houses they've consecrated," Cambara says. She goes on, "In fact, on the very day of your arrival, I met a young thing I suspected was on his way to set up such a safe house."

Malik, taking notes, presses her to recall all the details she remembers about the encounter. But just as they get started, she says, "Wait,

wait," and when she comes back on the line, she says, "Bile is calling me. Bye, I must go. But, really, you must come and stay with us. You'll be safer here."

"Let me think it over."

"Please come. It'll be good to have you around."

And when she hangs up, he remembers how often his wife interrupted her telephone conversations to attend to their daughter's crying. He reminds himself to phone home and say that he is well and safe.

———

All the major news agencies quote the Ethiopian government spokesman justifying, in a brief statement, the bombing of the two airports in Mogadiscio. "We attacked the airports so that no unauthorized aircraft may land at either runway in response to acts of aggression from the Courts."

Nothing sums up the foolishness better than the declaration the Courts' defense spokesman makes, when he vows that Allah is on the side of the Courts and it is his intention to lead an invasion into Ethiopia and to defeat the army of infidels. He says, "I promise that with God's will, the Army of the Faithful will conquer Ethiopia in less than three weeks, and it being Ramadan, the holy month, we will break our fast in Addis Ababa."

By all accounts, Malik thinks, this was the communiqué that had been fired ahead of the bullets. Here is where no-brainers meet clichés, where clichés make their acquaintance with lies, and where falsehood and hyperbole pile up, pyramidlike, until one can't tell the truth from a lie.

He sits on the balcony jotting down his notes, his mobile phone by his side, when he hears the muezzin's afternoon call. A monsoon rain in the form of a brief, localized drizzle is drenching the ground below him. Malik feels it when a single, huge drop wets his forehead, the moisture spreading. On impulse, he decides to step out of the apartment alone and head in the direction of the neighborhood mosque. He wants to get there in time for the after-prayer sermon.

Malik remembers traveling with a handful of Afghans crossing hostile territory into Pakistan. He was impressed with how these illiterate men mapped their exit out of Afghanistan and then back into it after doing whatever job took them there. Another time, he spent eight weeks with Rwandan commandos tracking a Hutu *génocidaire*. But he wonders if he is cut out for a visit to the mosque, where assassins may lie in wait. Still, at a mosque he should be inconspicuous. And mosques, as Jeebleh told him, are the nerve center, the ideal place to take the nation's pulse on a day such as this; mosques are the key with which to unlock the country's amped-up politics.

He changes into a sarong, a plain shirt twice his size, a shawl, and a cheap pair of sandals. Out of the apartment, he follows a group of men headed toward the mosque, talking, their conversation touching on the bombing. There is something unmistakably "alien" about his gait as he compares his way of walking to that of the other men: his stride is paced, his look averted, and not wanting to step into a hole or stumble against the rocks and debris scattered here and there, he lifts his feet carefully. He smiles sheepishly when his eyes encounter someone else's. He murmurs the Somali greeting "*Nabad*" to everyone he passes, and each answers, giving the full complement of the greeting in Arabic: "*Wacalaykumus Salaam.*"

The buildings on either side of the mosque are boarded up, with the odd door open, showing goats in full domicile there, their dry dung strewn like raisins. He holds back for a moment when he comes to the entrance, where a number of men are performing communal ablutions. Then he joins a queue at the standpipes, and begins to banter with a man about the day's events.

The man says, "I was told there were four planes. One of them dropped the bombs, and the other three were American planes show-ing it the way."

"Where did you hear that?"

"Someone reliable assured me there were four."

Another man contributes his bit. He says, "Yes, four planes. One on either side of the jet, the third leading the way to the airport, the fourth following."

Malik asks, "Leading the way? Where? How?"

"They are idiots, these Ethiopians," the man says. "I went to school in that country and know them very well. You see, they wouldn't know how to find their way anywhere, not even to hell, unless you pointed them in the right direction."

"And to whom did the other planes belong?"

"To the enemy of Islam."

"Who is that, specifically?"

"The Americans, of course."

The interior of the mosque is simply furnished; the ceiling is high, and there is plenty of space all around, with columns and pillars sepa-rating the prayer hall into uneven sections. Pushed and shoved, Malik is facing an impediment in the shape of a column as he joins one of the middle rows. As the faithful "purpose to offer up to Allah only," toward Mecca, he whispers the words of the prayer, inclining his head and body, with his hands on his knees, now saying, "Allah hears him who praises him," with his nose and then his forehead touching the floor, now prostrating, now kneeling. His knees hurt—he needs to pray more often, he tells himself, in the absence of a gym, and God will bless him more. His left foot bent under him, he sits on it, his hands on his knees. How excruciating the pain!

At the close of the prayer and the supplication, described as the marrow of worship, Malik is surprised that no one gives a sermon condemning the invasion. People just go their different ways, singly or in groups. Those that remain offer more prayers, while others gather outside and talk in low voices, seemingly unprepared to admit him, a total stranger, into their midst. Of course, they are talking about the attack, but they do not sound sufficiently incensed to make their feelings known.

Dispirited, because he hoped a visit to the mosque might supply him with better material, Malik returns home.

———————

As he lets himself into the apartment, his phone rings: it is Jeebleh, inquiring if he is all right. "For a moment, you had me worried," says his father-in-law. "I kept ringing and no answer. What's happened, and where have you been?"

"I've been out, and left my phone behind."

"Out where? Dajaal has no idea where you are."

"I've been at the mosque."

"Whatever have you been doing at a mosque?"

Malik is tempted to say, "What else do you do at a mosque except pray?" but stops himself just in time, out of respect for his father-in-law. Instead, he tells him he went to the house of prayer to take a measure of the mood in the country, as Jeebleh himself had advised. "I must have gone to the wrong mosque, because nothing unusual happened on this unusual day, the first of its kind in the annals of Somalia," he says.

"There is no wrong mosque," Jeebleh says.

"But you know what I mean."

"You chose the wrong day," Jeebleh tells him. "If you go to a mosque on a Friday, you are likely to hear an earful of condemnation from the pulpit."

"What's been the reaction in Kenya?" Malik asks.

"There is an air of incredulity here."

"No communiqué from the Kenyan government?"

"None so far as I know," replies Jeebleh. Then he says, "Wait," and Malik can hear him saying to a hotel maid, "I do not want my bed turned down. I am in it, can't you see?" Then he hears the slamming of a door, and Jeebleh is back on the line. "I've read the two interviews."

"I've just finished the draft of another."

"I loved them."

"Thank you," says Malik. "I appreciate hearing that."

"I've spoken to Bile and Cambara, too."

"I had a long, rambling chat with Cambara myself," says Malik.

Jeebleh says, "They suggest you move in."

"I'll think about it."

Jeebleh asks, "Do you want to hear my opinion?"

"I always like to hear your opinion."

"I would move in with them if I were you."

From where he is, the sky is streaked with orange clouds, turning brighter as the sunlight strikes them from several angles. The twilight is formidably picturesque, and Malik wishes he had the knack for photography.

"I'll call home and talk to Amran," Malik says.

The offer to telephone home is a masterstroke. It frees Malik from having to continue the conversation with Jeebleh, just as it reminds both that he will not consider moving in with Bile and Cambara, because it may upset his wife, who, they know, has the tendency to be raving jealous, no matter what she says. A spouse in denial is a difficult spouse.

Jeebleh says, "Do that," and hangs up.

The phone has barely rung a second time when Judith answers. Sweet and gentle, she speaks fast, saying that they are all well. Then she says, "Here is Amran. Bye for now. Love!"

Malik sweetens his words as best he can. "Hi, my dear, my darling, how are things? I miss you and miss my little one, too."

Amran is in a foul mood. "When are you coming home?"

He says foolishly, "The airports are closed."

Amran is furious that he has stayed behind instead of leaving Mogadiscio when her father did. When she is cross, she shouts; when jealous, she weeps; when loving, she is the sweetest thing there is. Amran has moods. Today, she is in a miasma of rage, she can't stop screaming. Malik holds the phone away from his ear and listens without interrupting. Her parents often shake their heads in sympathy with Malik, and say to each other, "But you know what she's like."

Amran is now saying at the top of her lungs, "The war has started— the foretaste of terrible battles to come. We're all worried sick about you. And all you can tell me is that the airports are closed. What's gotten into you?"

Malik says, "I am doing well, writing."

"I don't wish to raise an orphan on my own."

"What are you talking about? What orphan?"

"I want you to come home *now*," Amran orders.

"As I explained, the airports are closed."

"Then there is no point talking, is there?"

"But there is a point in talking, my love."

"You've always been unreliable when it comes to timekeeping, always untrustworthy when it comes to phoning and letting me know where you are and what you are up to or who you are with. Work, work,

work. Women, more admiring women, eating out of your palms the words of your wisdom. Who are you with now? What's her name? Why have a family if you work, work, and work? Why marry if you only want to entertain other women? While we wait for a word from you. While I worry how to raise an orphan on my own."

"Listen to me, honey," he pleads.

"Don't call me honey," she shouts back.

And, weeping, she hangs up on him. In a day or two, she will deny ever having said any of these things.

———

No more writing today, for sure. Knowing Amran, he may not be able to do any work the next day, either. She is a spoiler when she is unhappy, even if she also takes pride when Malik's work is in the limelight, earning praise or a prize.

Unable to think lucidly enough to write, Malik calls Nairobi to plead with Jeebleh to intercede; no answer. When his own phone rings and rings—maybe the journalists he has been attempting to contact are now returning his calls—Malik doesn't answer it. He takes to his bed, his heart heavy.

He gets up early and watches a series of pointless reality TV programs, involving housemates from a number of African countries living in an isolated house, with each contestant trying to avoid being evicted by viewers who have the power to vote him or her out. The last to be evicted receives a large cash prize at the end.

IT IS NOT TO AHL'S LIKING THAT HE HOSTS FIDNO FIRST THING IN the morning, but he does it with brio. Upset, Fidno rang him earlier, to complain that Ahl has not been forthright with him. "Why did you not tell me right away that you were not a journalist?"

"What time is it?" Ahl asks sleepily.

Fidno says he is down at the gazebo, waiting.

————

The waiter takes Fidno's breakfast order: tea, liver, and most Somalis' favorite breakfast, *canjeero* pancake and bananas. Ahl asks for *canjeero*, with honey on the side, and caffelatte, no sugar, please. He doubts he will eat much; he is still too exhausted. A mosquito buzzed in his ears last night from the moment he turned in. He had barely dropped into deep sleep when his mobile phone, which he'd set to vibrate, came to life against his ribs. At first he thought it was another mosquito, somehow disguising its tune—these having lately become more clever, resistant to everything modern medicine has thrown at them. Then Ahl realized that his phone was ringing and answered, believing it was

Malik. But it was Fidno. Now Ahl feels cheated of his fair share of sleep, and bullied, too. He is still in yesterday's clothes.

Ahl also regrets he hasn't brought his computer bag down with him: all his cash is in an envelope in it. He hesitates whether to go back and fetch it, but figures that no one will go into the room to clean until later in the morning. In any event, he has a few hundred U.S. dollars in an envelope in his back pocket, just in case. At least he can pay for their breakfast.

"You conned me," says Fidno.

"I did no such thing," Ahl insists.

"You made a fool out of me."

"Remember that Warsame arrived unexpectedly to pick me up. I had no idea what to say or how to introduce you, as I hadn't prepared him for your presence."

"And when we got to their home?"

"I had to talk to Xalan. She and I needed to sort out some family business. We had no chance, you and I, to talk alone."

"You could've said so to me. Plainly."

The waiter brings their food. Ahl decides Fidno has no right to heap guilt on him; he did no wrong. When the waiter returns to inquire how they are doing, Ahl brings out his two hundred dollars, as if testing the waiter's and Fidno's reaction to seeing greenbacks in large denominations. But if Ahl is hoping that the money will move Fidno to resume speaking to him as he had on their earlier visit—to tell him, perhaps, about the bagfuls of cash delivered as ransom to boats with crews held hostage—at least according to the international media—Fidno does no such thing. They eat their breakfast, neither saying anything. Yesterday, Fidno ate his and Ahl's lunch without embarrassment. Ahl thinks that no one with self-respect would do that. Maybe Fidno's pennilessness has canniness added to it, his impoverished state being of recent vin-

tage, comparable to a gambler's indigence—wealthy one day, impecu-
nious the next.

Fidno says, "Let's trade truths, you and I."

"How do you mean, 'trade truths'?"

"You tell me the truth of why you are here, like a man who wants to
pick up a whore but dares not, and I'll you the truth of who I am."

Ahl is startled. He doesn't like it when he can't fathom a person's
character from his knowable features. Fidno, however, is several steps
ahead of him. Fidno's daring suggestion that they trade truths reminds
Ahl of trading jokes with Malik. Malik knows thousands of jokes and,
what is more, knows well how to draw out the punch line, how to
mature it fully in the telling. Ahl has the terrible habit of ruining his
jokes by mistiming the narration, the way some women foul their fine
faces with the wrong makeup. Not wanting to fall for a ruse he does
not recognize, Ahl takes his time, eating his breakfast in concentrated
bites.

Fidno says, "I trained as a medical doctor in Germany, and had my
own practice in Berlin ten years ago. Then I messed up by having affairs with two of my patients, one of them a close friend of my wife's.
My wife denounced me to the medical board, which charged me with
malpractice; then she sued for divorce and won custody of our two
children, but not before she'd emptied all our jointly held bank accounts. I left Berlin and joined the practice of an Indian in Abu Dhabi.
He was not very good at his job; he knew it and I knew it. But he had
an advantage over me: he knew the truth about me.

"For three years, however, things worked out well. Then—what a
folly—I made another fatal error. I fell for a married Arab woman, my
Indian colleague's patient. When our affair went sour, she told him,
and he reported me to her husband, who in turn reported me to the
authorities. Because I did not want to face another case of presumed

malpractice in an Arab country, where the punishment would be severe, I came to Somalia.

"In Mogadiscio, an uncle of mine set me up as a financier. I put together half a dozen unemployed fishermen just as the Somali coast was being invaded by Korean, Spanish, Chinese, and Japanese 'sea bandits.' These sea bandits were stealing our fish, denying access to our fishermen, taking away their livelihood. In those days, there were no Somali pirates; there were only these foreigner sea bandits robbing our seas. As a last resort, I funded the hijacking of a ship belonging to a Korean shipping firm. We held the ship for three months, in return for which we received a fine for their illegal, unregulated fishing. We shared out the proceeds among the fishing community. I didn't make a huge profit, but I continued to advance the idea of taking any ship found fishing illicitly in our waters. That's how my involvement in the funding of piracy started."

He uses the recently coined Somali phrase *burcad badeed*, which translates as "sea bandits" and which is commonly employed as a sobriquet for "pirates." Ahl finds the terminology a bit confusing, banditry being something with which Somalis are familiar; in fact, in Kenya, the term *shifta* is a derogatory moniker for Somali. In other words, contrary to what is understood elsewhere—that Somalis are the pirates—Fidno seems to be casting the vessels fishing illegally in Somali waters as the true "sea bandits."

Ahl asks, "But aren't Somalis bandits, in that they exact ransom in the same way sea bandits do? You are unnecessarily obfuscating matters. Why?"

"Somalis are neither pirates nor sea bandits," Fidno says, his voice strong. "The world doesn't afford to Somalis a sinecure similar to the one given to those who sin against us. That is a fact."

"If not pirates, what are they, the Somalis?"

"Pirates are cruel seamen," says Fidno, "and they are out totally for their own personal gain. They rob their victims, using extreme violence. They torture their prey; they are no Robin Hoods. In all fairness, you cannot describe the Somalis as pirates, in that they do not behave cruelly toward the crew, use extreme violence, or torture their prey."

"But they are no Robin Hoods, are they?"

"There are only two cases in world history that I can think of when men described by others as 'pirates,' for lack of a better term, did in fact play a positive role in their nation's political history. You may not agree with me, but I would argue the Somali are a case in point. Even though described by others as pirates, it is fair to view them as conscientious avengers fighting to save our waters from total plunder."

"What's the second case?"

"The other case is the Dutch pirates."

"What Dutch pirates?"

"The Dutch pirates known as *watergeuzen*—'sea beggars'—set aside their sea banditry for almost two years, from 1571 to 1572, to fight alongside William of Orange to bring an end to Spanish occupation of their land."

Ahl waits for Fidno to continue.

Fidno obliges. "The Somalis are the closest in outlook to the Dutch *watergeuzen*, in that the Somalis initially set out to fight off foreign invasion of their sea in the absence of a functioning state, and then establish some kind of a coastal guard to protect our sea resources against continued foreign invasion."

But Ahl is not sure if they are anything like the Dutch sea beggars or privateers. He understands privateers as vessels armed and licensed to attack the ships of enemy nations and confiscate their property. Historically, many European sovereigns issued such licenses and they left it up to the licensed captains to determine the nature of the punishment to be meted out to the vessels they apprehended. A percentage of their catch went to the captain and crew, and the remainder to the license-issuing sovereign.

"What 'foreign invasion' are we talking about?" Ahl asks.

"I am talking of the inhumane assault on the coastland of Somalia, where the country's trawlable zones are located. A Somali scientist who specializes in fisheries said that at night, the lights of all those foreign vessels were so numerous that they could be mistaken for 'a well-lit metropolitan city.'"

"And who were, or are, the invaders?"

"They came from as far away as Europe, Japan, Russia, Korea, China, in vessels flying foreign flags—Belize, Kenya, Liberia, or Barbados," Fidno says. "They arrived armed, too, prepared for war, their speedboats at the ready whenever Somali fishermen reacted. And when they fished they made use of methods banned worldwide. In addition, they dumped nuclear, chemical, and other wastes on our coast. They never attempted to engage the Somalis in any meaningful dialogue. And they were unconcerned about the damage they were doing to the fishing environment. When Somalis complained, the world turned a deaf ear to our protestations."

"Is that when *you* entered the scene?"

"That's when I entered the scene as an avenger."

Ahl has difficulty here. He likes Fidno, whom he finds fascinating as one does a villain enacting his misdeeds elsewhere. Yet there is a part of Ahl that can't take to Fidno wholly or accept his claims at face value. He seems more likely to have arrived on the scene as a financier with a nose for profit rather than as a nationalist hero. Maybe his judgment is colored by the previous brushes with professional misconduct that Fidno has described.

"What was the first boat you helped them take?"

"It was a Kenya-registered trawler fishing in Somali waters, nearly a thousand nautical miles from Mombasa," Fidno says. But suddenly he is stumbling over his consonants, as though he has sprouted a forked tongue, the fork that tells the truth unable or unwilling to coordinate with the fork that tells the lie.

"Where did you get the money?"

"An uncle on my mother's side lent it to me."

"Does this man have a name?"

"He's known by his nickname, Ma-Gabadeh."

There is fire in Fidno's eyes at the mention of the name. It is as if a lamp has come on, lighting the peripheries of his irises. Ahl hopes the light stays. It complements his mischievous grin, and he looks cheerful. Ahl asks, "Is it your honest view that the Somalis aren't pirates?"

"It is," Fidno responds, the light not yet gone.

Ahl says, "Tell me why you hold this view when the rest of the world thinks otherwise?"

Until now Fidno has not smoked in Ahl's presence, but now he makes the gesture of a smoker flicking ash from the end of his cigarette, then issues sucking noises from his lips, as if inhaling smoke from a cigar. He says, "Let us separate the two questions. First, why do I argue that Somalis cannot be accurately described as pirates? Because pirates take pride in living outside the law and in pursuit of loot. Their presence invokes fear as a consequence of their crude treatment of their hostages. Theirs are stories of adventure, tyranny, mutiny, and they sail the wide seas, having no respect for borders. They stalk a ship for days, waiting for the right moment to attack. They fly false flags to dupe or conceal their intentions. They surprise their victims and then disappear without leaving behind a trace. These features describe the foreign invaders of our seas, but not the Somalis. The Somalis operate for the most part in their own seas. They torture no one, they harm no one, kill no one, not even their hostages, and they do not conceal their identities. It leaves me with a sour taste to listen to the aspersions circulated about us. We are cast as villains of the piece, and no one listens to our side of the story."

Ahl asks, "What of the millions given as ransom?"

"For starters," Fidno says, "what makes you believe that the 'pirates' receive millions of dollars as ransom?"

"Don't they?"

"That's why I want to talk to a journalist."

"You're not saying that they don't?"

Fidno says, "I would compare the pirates to pickpockets."

Ahl recalls a number of interviews with crews and captains of the hijacked vessels in which there was talk often of the pirates pilfering away their watches, their jackets, their telephones, and other small items. If Fidno is arguing that the pirates risk their lives for a pittance and do not receive millions of dollars as ransom, then it stands to reason that he compares them to pickpockets. After all, anyone making giant killings from taking tankers captive is unlikely to resort to pilfering. Unless the person is a kleptomaniac.

"Even though the amount that a man picking pockets makes on his best day may be more than a beggar's," Fidno says, "I know of no pickpocket who has become a millionaire. The Somalis receive little from the takings." Fidno pauses and then reiterates, "This is why I wish to speak to a journalist."

Fidno now has his nicotine-hungry look focused on the waiter, who is smoking nearby. As he takes the cue at last, Ahl orders a packet of cigarettes. Why, he thinks, if Fidno or the pirates were flush with money, would he need a near stranger to buy him a meal or a packet of cigarettes?

When he has lit his cigarette and taken a huge cloud of smoke into his lungs, Fidno continues. "In the absence of a central sovereign state, the community is the authority. Initially, the fishermen had the endorsement of the coastal communities that suffered at the hands of the invading foreign vessels."

"What percentage of the ransom did the community receive from those early adventures?" Ahl asks.

"Initially, the community received a lot."

"And lately?"

"Almost none." Fidno starts another cigarette.

"One question for my benefit," Ahl says. "Why would the UN Security Council pass a resolution authorizing countries to contribute to an anti-piracy coalition if this august body is aware that these same countries are fishing illegally and in an unregulated manner in the waters of Somalia?"

"Because the UN is at the service of the powerful veto-wielding countries that fund its programs and pay its electricity bills, the salaries of its staff," Fidno replies.

"What's in it for the nations footing the anti-piracy bills?" Ahl wants to know. "What do they expect to gain from their financial commitments?"

Fidno observes, "You might well ask."

Ahl says, "Is there truth to the media reports that insurers enjoying the support of European governments cite rampant piracy as a compelling reason for creating private navies to take on the Somalis?"

Fidno says, "Basically, a number of the nations contributing to the anti-piracy outfits or setting up private navies are keen either on safeguarding the ability of their vessels to fish illegitimately in our seas, or they are hunting down Al Qaeda."

"Your reply may not wash with others," Ahl says.

Fidno announces unnecessarily loudly that he is off to the bathroom.

Alone and sipping his coffee, Ahl jots down notes, aware that he will need to convince Malik that it is worth his while to interview Fidno. The stark reality, the dire conditions of most Somalis, the absence of food and environmental security, the never-ending conflict: each of these will have an impact on the future. From this perspective, Ahl views the future as one might view a troubled country marked by despoliation, devastation, and more poverty.

When Fidno returns, he orders another coffee and says, "It is your turn to tell truths. Why are you here?"

Ahl reminds himself that he has the right to edit his story, censoring portions of it and altering its general thrust for his own privacy as well as for Taxliil's and Malik's safety. However, he'll tell enough of it to stoke the fire of Fidno's curiosity. For now.

"I am in Puntland for a family reason."

Fidno says, "We're trading truths. Remember."

Ahl is about to elaborate on what has brought him here, when he suddenly feels ill at ease. He sits still and unspeaking for a long while, disturbed, his lips atremble, his breathing uneven, and his heart beating nervously faster. But then he senses Taxliil's presence stalking him and prowling in the outer reaches of his conscience. When he infers that Taxliil wants him to trade his truth with his man, his resolve firms up. What is there to lose?

He stumbles a bit, then begins. "I am in Puntland searching for Taxliil, my runaway stepson, a teenager, believed to be somewhere in Somalia, sent, the last we heard, to Puntland as a liaison between his religionist mentors and the pirates."

"Why Puntland?"

"Because it is his mother's ancestral home."

"Any other reason?"

"I've been told that he is in Puntland because it is a transit point for the religionists to Yemen and beyond. Would you say it is true that some of the pirates and some of the religionists, especially those with bases in Xarardheere, have struck a deal—that they collaborate? I've heard it said that some young Somalis pretend on the way out that they are migrants, and on the way back, escort the foreign recruits in boats that are virtually empty anyhow."

"You think Taxliil is one of them?"

"Do the pirates collaborate with Shabaab?"

Fidno says, "There is a rumor that some do."

"Do those that bring in foreign jihadis, who aren't necessarily young men, receive in exchange protection from the religionists?" Ahl asks.

"There is a lot of movement between Somalia and Yemen," Fidno says, "by means of dhows laden with goods, which return either empty or with illegal passengers. As for the human trafficking, that is part and parcel of the link; this is seasonal, with thousands of Ethiopians, Eritreans, Somalis, and other Africans trying their luck to get to Yemen in hope of making it to Saudi Arabia, where there are jobs, or Europe. I know some of the coastal villages from which they depart; I also know where the boats dock when they return. If you like, I can take you to some of these villages."

"I'd be happy to go anywhere to find my son."

"By the way, how old is Taxliil?"

Ahl tells him, and in addition, promises to provide him with a photograph of his stepson, taken a month or so before his disappearance.

"If he's in Puntland, we'll find him."

"I'd be grateful for any help."

Fidno says, "I'll get things moving soon."

For an instant, Ahl keeps at bay a clutch of worries snatching at his heart. It is as if he is in a fast-moving car, hurtling beltlessly down a ravine, moving perilously forward at an extraordinary speed, destination unknown, fellow passengers unfamiliar. It frightens him that he has been here for only a day and he has already formed a working relationship with a man who funds piracy, a man who, for all he knows, is on first-name terms with the owners of the dhows in the human trafficking business. Is it too late to withdraw? More to the point, is there any other means by which he may pursue his aim, to locate his stepson? After all, one devil knows another devil best—and it is best he gets to know Fidno, who may lead him to Shabaab's redoubts in Puntland.

He asks, "How will you get things moving?"

"For a start, I'll establish contact with the known big shots in the human-smuggling business and arrange for you to meet them," Fidno says. "I'll take you to a village called Guri-Maroodi, not far from here, from where the migrants depart. I have a mind to start with a man who has extensive connections among the top people in Puntland, the insurgents, the pirates, the lot. He is respected and at the same time feared everywhere in this country."

"Won't you tell me his name?"

"I'll give you the information only on a need-to-know basis," Fidno says. "And since I haven't been in touch with him yet, I can't tell you his name."

"Please explain how meeting a man in the human-smuggling business will help locate Taxliil, when what I need is to burrow into the underground structures of Shabaab?"

"You are going about the matter in the way God-fearing, upstanding individuals do when they are dealing with a straightforward problem, when what you require here is to know the mind-set of those with whom you are dealing," Fidno says. "If you are taking on men who operate outside the law, then you must approach the matter at hand from an equally shady angle."

"Men working outside the law?"

Fidno says, "Shabaab, the pirates, and the human traffickers work outside the law, they know one another; they collaborate in ways not too obvious to ordinary men. Because of this, one needs a new approach."

Ahl hesitantly asks, "Is the man you have in mind to contact, the human smuggler, capable of helping us to tunnel our way into Shabaab's hideout, and is he prepared to assist us—and if so, at what cost?"

Fidno does not tackle several parts of the loaded question. All he says is, "A few of his men are seconded to Shabaab."

"How is one to tunnel one's way in?"

Fidno answers, "One will start from the outside, unsuspected, unannounced, and unseen, and with help from my contacts' underlings, one will burrow one's way in."

"That way we'll find Taxliil?"

"If Taxliil is in Puntland."

"Why will he help us?"

Fidno says, "I've told you why he'll help."

"Because he owes you a big one?"

"Because he and I are friends."

"What about the Shabaab operatives?"

"Leave it all to me."

Ahl doesn't know if he wants to do that.

"You meet your side of the bargain, I mine."

Ahl looks away a little too timidly, determined to get their developing rapport on a firmer footing and to seal the deal with a declaration of his intent. Thinking that a thief believes that every man is a thief and can't be trusted, he decides to assure Fidno that he'll keep his word.

He says, "Malik will be very pleased to know of your help, and he'll do as you ask."

Fidno says, "I'm delighted we've traded truths."

"I know now who you are."

But Fidno is already dialing his mobile phone.

THE PROPOSITION THAT HE AGREE TO CONDUCT AN INTERVIEW with Fidno as a way of securing his help with Taxliil strikes Malik as a development of second-water grade, as far as diamond discovery goes, even if Ahl makes it sound as though he has uncovered a first-water-quality gem.

Ahl has called not only to share his breakthrough, as he puts it, but also to talk about the bombing of Mogadiscio's airports. Malik senses both Ahl's excitement at the thought of coming closer to locating Taxliil, and his worry for Malik's safety. Yet as they talk, Ahl can't bring himself to suggest that Malik should be quitting the country. It is curious, he thinks, that of the many ways humans express their affection for one another, worry is an effective one; worry about those whom you love. Ahl's worry about Taxliil is of a different weave from the twine threaded into his concern for Malik.

Now he says to Malik, "Maybe I am unjustifiably preoccupied, but do you think it is safe to remain while the city is bracing for more bombing?"

Malik is not the worrying type. Ahl has often teasingly pointed this out to him, saying, "It is because you are younger and you leave all worries to others." He is alluding to the Somali proverb that youngsters worry most about themselves, less about others, and least of all about their parents.

Malik has no similar fears about Ahl, in large part because Puntland, as an autonomous state, has maintained an amicable rapport with the Ethiopian regime following the collapse of Somali state structures.

When Ahl repeats at length the exchange between him and Fidno, Malik asks what it is that Fidno expects to gain, as Fidno is not asking for financial renumeration. "What is his game, really?" Malik wonders.

Ahl does not have a clear answer, but he emphasizes the professional gain to Malik from the deal. Finally Malik agrees to the plan. "Still, I can't commit myself to either the venue or the time where the meeting will take place," he insists, and then he excuses himself, because he wants to get back to work.

———

Malik stays in the workroom, taking notes and reading fitfully. He takes a break at some point and rings Fee-Jigan and a couple of other journalists whose names he has acquired; he is eager to build his base of contacts. No one answers, though. He is tempted to telephone Gumaad but thinks better of it.

In the broadcasts he listens to and the newspapers he reads online, there is general consensus that the big men from the Courts have fled Mogadiscio, a number of them returning to their home villages, where their clans reign. Moreover, every pundit is surprised that the Ethiopians are in no hurry to take Mogadiscio: they take one town at a time, and then assign the militias loyal to the interim president of Somalia the job of mopping up any resistance. So far, reports reaching the wire agencies say there has been no resistance as such. This, to Malik, has an uncanny resemblance to what occurred in Iraq, when the Republican Guard melted away in time before the American ground forces took Baghdad. They returned a few weeks later, having organized themselves into a resistance. Will the men from the Courts do the same?

In the broadcasts, there is persistent mention of Eritrea, described as the arms supplier to the men from the Courts. Eritrea is tarnished by her abysmal human rights record, one of the worst in Africa, and has the ignominy of being quarrelsome and of picking fights serially with all her neighbors: a bloody war with Ethiopia over a strip of cactus and sand dunes in which two million lost their lives; with Yemen, over claims to an island situated between them. Malik can't even recall what prompted Eritrea's confrontation with Djibouti. Now Eritrea is going out on a limb and fighting a proxy war with Ethiopia by aiding the Courts.

Hungry, he eats stale bread and hardened cheese. Then he makes a pot of tea, of which he has two cups. While drinking these, he prepares coffee. As usual, he makes more than he can finish. No wonder his wife often describes him as wasteful. It is his habit to boil more water for tea than he needs, to cook far too much and then not bother to check what is in the fridge before buying more; anyway, he seldom remembers to put the leftovers in the fridge so that they won't go bad. Feeling terrible about his profligacy, he decides he will force himself to drink all the coffee, one cup after another.

He is still upset at the way Amran responded to his enforced stay. True, he had wanted to remain for a few more days, but it is also a fact that the airports in Mogadiscio have been bombed and are now closed to traffic. Her tone when she is unreasonably upset irks him. She seldom applies her acute intelligence to situations before jumping to conclusions, and she tends to get carried away emotionally—like when she talks of raising an orphan if he doesn't fly home this minute.

He will have a word with Jeebleh, who will intercede. Or maybe his mother-in-law, often more levelheaded than her daughter, can calm matters down for the moment.

Insofar as the war front goes, HornAfrik Radio, indisputably Mogadiscio's best, reports from the border regions that the Ethiopians are entering Somalia from different border posts, and every hour brings talk of another town falling into their hands. With no open resistance, the Ethiopians won't need to defend or consolidate their hold on the territory they have occupied before moving on toward Mogadiscio. It is assumed they will be in the capital by as early as noon tomorrow. Meanwhile, the interim president, with half a battalion of Ethiopian soldiers and a smattering of Somalis in uniform escorting his entourage, has already arrived at the presidential villa, along with his own Ethiopian bodyguards and advisers, after receiving intelligence that TheSheikh and TheOtherSheikh and almost all the members of the Executive Board of the Courts have left soon after the bombing. What a tragic day it's been for both Somalia and Ethiopia, Malik thinks, then writes these words and underlines them twice.

Malik is drawing on his memory of other cities that he has witnessed on the verge of falling to enemy forces: in the Congo, in Afghanistan, and so on. He writes, "In most cases, it takes a long time for ordinary folks unaccustomed to bearing arms to work up an appetite for battle. There is more than one side to a fence, and peaceable civilians stay on whichever side makes them feel safer. Rather like young girls in countries with a tradition of arranged marriages, they will go with whichever suitor is presented to them."

He pauses, pen raised, and thinks how only later, after the occupation has been completed, a touch of cynicism will enter people's attitude toward the carousel politics of which they have become victims.

Now he writes, "Mogadiscians have met warlords of every variety; the memory of the trauma has cauterized people's suffering, minimizing it. They see the Ethiopian premier as just another warlord, albeit a foreigner, no less savage than their homegrown politico-sadists. To spare themselves more atrocities, the city will not show any open resistance to his advances. As one former senior military officer known to me has predicted, even the armed men loyal to the Courts won't attack the Ethiopians until after they've taken the enemy's measure." Yet Somalis everywhere are incensed by the invasion, he argues, including those who were and are against the politics of the Courts. "They'd wait for their payback day with due patience. And when that day comes, they will dance a victory dance in the dirt roads of the Bakhaaraha Market, dance around the enemy dead, singing and kicking the corpses and burning effigies, giving in to the debasing pleasure of poisoning themselves with the toxins of vengeance. They will, in essence, take self-debasing pleasure in poisoning their souls, as one proverb has it, with the toxin that is vengeance. The world is no longer what the world used to be. Besides, Mogadiscians have done it before: danced a macabre, self-dishonoring dance around a dead Marine, and nothing will stop them from repeating that."

He marks the article as "draft," prints it, and then puts it away for the time being. Maybe he can make a much longer piece out of it, he tells himself. A pity he doesn't know many ordinary people in Mogadiscio. But walking the streets with a tape recorder, a camera, and a microphone isn't an option in a city where journalists are subject to death threats.

He pours himself another cup of coffee and turns to a new piece on the tendency of defeated armies to wreck cities before leaving them, and why. Before he puts pen to paper, he works the piece in his head, remembering parallel instances from other figures and places he has covered: the Afghani warlord Gulbuddin Hekmatyar, the Congolese faction leaders Laurent Nkunda and Germain Katanga. The HornAfrik commentator, one Mohamed Elmi, is confessing to being "impressed with the grown-up manner in which the Courts have handled their withdrawal," and Malik finds himself agreeing. Mr. Elmi imagines that "it can't have been easy to leave the city they wrested from the warlords only six months ago. Now they've had to abandon it to the crueler hands of the Ethiopians. True to the wisdom that a parent must not strike in anger the child whom they love, the Courts quit without ransacking the city, promising to return. When they come back, better armed, will they bomb in anger the very people whom they claim to love?"

The phone rings: Dajaal is on the line. Malik puts a couple of questions to him, most important, what he thinks about the Courts quitting the city.

Dajaal has nothing kind to say about the Courts. "When they first arrived on the scene, they entered the city with cannon, purportedly to oust the U.S.-supported warlords. But they damaged the morale of the residents by indiscriminately bombing a number of the districts, totally destroying ordinary people's lives. Why are they in such a hurry to abandon the city to the Ethiopians now? Cowards win no friends."

Malik knows well that during the war with the warlords, the Courts commanders inscribed the phrase *"Allahu akbar"* on the bazookas they launched, which fell in the most populous area of the city, killing hundreds. Still, he says, "At least this time they did not sack the city, or subject it to looting, as I have seen the Congolese and Afghan militias do when they fled."

"Still, where are they when the city needs them?"

Malik says, "But they quit without firing a shot."

"Why do you accept weapons as a gift from Eritrea, a pariah state, when you won't fire a shot at your mutual enemy?" challenges Dajaal. "Rest assured that when they return, calling themselves 'resistance fighters' or 'martyrs of the faith,' they will resort to bombing the very people whom they claim to love."

Anyway, according to Dajaal, only the men who are the known public face of the Courts have quit the city. The rest have stayed behind, supposedly to organize the resistance from within. Malik supposes that they have not yet released any statement because they must feel secure somewhere before doing so.

Dajaal goes on, fuming. "Shabaab, meanwhile, have assassinated three former military officers who came to Mogadiscio in advance of the interim president's entourage, to prepare the way for the Transitional Federal Forces, such as they are." One of the men killed was a former colleague of his. "But why provoke the Ethiopians, then flee the city? Nothing makes sense."

Malik says, "If you weren't under the weather, I would ask you to come straightaway. I would very much like to talk to you in more depth."

"You know what?" says Dajaal. "I can't afford to be ill on a day such as this, a day in which the city braces for the arrival of our archenemy. I'll ask Qasiir to fetch me. We will be at the apartment shortly."

Dajaal has barely entered the apartment when Qasiir says, "The Kenyans have caught the first big fish in their net. That's the news we've just heard on the car radio."

Qasiir is in a T-shirt and jeans, and he has on an elegant pair of painted leather shoes. Maybe he was on his way somewhere when Dajaal rang and requested a lift, Malik thinks. As for Dajaal, despite his claim that he is feeling better, his lips are swollen, as if freshly stung by a bee, and his eyes look dull, too.

Malik asks, "Who is this the Kenyans have caught? Does the big fish have a name?"

The big fish is Saleh Ali Saleh Nabhan, Dajaal says. "He's considered the third most wanted on a list of so-called international terrorists and is suspected of planting bombs in two U.S. embassies and of attacking an Israeli-owned hotel in Mombasa. The Americans have always insisted that he lives in Somalia and enjoys the protection of a highly placed Courts individual." But he ascribes the supposed Kenyan "coup" to rumor.

Malik, too, doubts if such a big fish will have fallen easily into Kenyan hands on the very day the Ethiopian invasion has started. The only fish, big or small, that are likely to fall into Kenyan nets will be those who might be fleeing the fighting or who will present themselves at the closed border between Kenya and Somalia, either as bona fide travelers or as asylum seekers. Since Saleh Ali Saleh Nabhan fits neither description, he has more likely thrown in his lot with the top Shabaab men said to be in the forest in Ras Kamboni, and it will take a few days to flush them out.

Malik makes tea for them, and as he passes them milk and sugar, the discussion resumes.

Dajaal says, "What worries me is not what they will do with the big fish they catch—the so-called terrorists and high-ranking Courts officials—but all the small fry, hundreds of them. When you send big trawlers into waters where a war is raging, you can't help overfishing. The Kenyans have been fishing in troubled Somali waters for years now. In addition to the pirates who have been handed over to them to bring before their corrupt courts, the Kenyans have benefited in many ways from the collapse of Somalia."

Malik knows from his research that Kenya is raking in millions in hard currency from the foreign embassies and all the UN bodies working on Somalia-related projects, all of which are currently based in Kenya, because of the chaos here. But he doesn't understand all of what Dajaal has said. "What small fry are you talking about?" he asks.

Dajaal says, "Many Somalis who had left the country earlier and established citizenship elsewhere returned during the Courts' reign, to lap up the milk and peace that was on offer. I worry what will happen to them now as they head back to their respective homes, bearing their foreign passports. The Kenyans will exploit the situation."

There is a knock at the door. "Who is it?" Malik asks.

"It is I, Gumaad."

Malik doesn't ask if Gumaad has come alone or if he has again brought someone with him. He opens the door.

Gumaad is alone, but he is clearly not happy to find Qasiir and Dajaal with Malik. He looks as if he has been in a fight, and lost. His shoes have lost their buckles, and the back of his trousers are stained. His shirt is dirty and rumpled, and some of the buttons are missing. There is straw in his uncombed hair. In addition, he seems to be shedding dandruff at an incredible rate, as if he is suffering from some sort of skin disorder.

Qasiir asks, "Where have you been roughing it?"

Gumaad is noncommittal. "Here and there."

Dajaal says, "You've been on the run, haven't you, holed up with TheSheikh in a rat hole somewhere and preparing to sneak out of the city, like thieves in the night."

"It's been tough," Gumaad says to Malik.

"A towel for your shower," Malik says, handing him one. "And then we'll talk."

Dajaal is a model of restraint and says nothing more until Gumaad vanishes into the bathroom. Then he repeats the rumor circulating in the city, that TheSheikh is on a plane heading for Asmara, where he will be a guest of the Eritrean government. TheOtherSheikh, who is considered to be a more moderate force within Shabaab, is believed to be headed for the Kenyan border to seek political asylum.

As soon as Gumaad emerges from the bathroom, Dajaal asks where TheSheikh is. Malik thinks that you might as well ask a Mafia minion to tell where his boss is.

Gumaad replies calmly, "Somewhere in the city."

"You're lying," Dajaal says.

Malik wonders if Gumaad is the kind that lies as unconsciously as he sheds dead skin. He has known pathological liars in his day, not all of them men.

Gumaad challenges, "Why would I be lying?"

"The city is small. Where in the city is he?"

"I can't trust you enough to tell you."

"If he is in the city," Dajaal says, "I'll bet he is secreting himself somewhere like a dog gnawing on a stripped bone. Imagine TheSheikh, on whom the hope of the nation has rested, hiding his face but showing his fear. Is that what you are telling us?"

Dajaal no longer seems ill; he is full of energy born out of rage—rage at the assassination of his friend, rage at what he sees as the Courts' senseless provocation of the invasion.

"Please, Grandpa," says Qasiir. "Why are you torturing Gumaad?"

"His lies upset me."

Gumaad says, "I've told no lies so far."

Dajaal says, "The foreign news agencies all place TheSheikh on a plane headed for Asmara."

Qasiir says, "Why believe them and not Gumaad?"

"That's right. Why not believe me and not them?"

"They have a point," Malik intervenes.

Up close, Gumaad's appearance bespeaks his true mental state.

Tears well in the corners of his eyes. He does not seem to be lying, and perhaps he isn't. After all, StrongmanSouth, when he was warlord, hid out in Mogadiscio for several months without the foreign "invaders" apprehending him. In fact, he used to throw parties within a mile of where the U.S. Marines were garrisoned, and they never found him. Will TheSheikh do the same with the Ethiopians if it turns out that he has stayed put to lead the resistance?

"Why is he here?" Dajaal asks, speaking not to Gumaad but to Malik. But it is Gumaad who answers. "I've come to arrange an interview."

Silence, in which they all exchange looks.

"TheSheikh wants to do an interview with Malik."

"How very grand!" Dajaal says. "One minute he bides his time in concealment, like a bank robber keeping his loot company, the next instant he acts the role of royalty, granting an interview to a foreign journalist."

"It's Malik's prerogative to accept or not accept the offer," Gumaad says. "It is not my place or yours to decide." He turns to Malik. "You make up your mind, if you will or won't."

"An interview by phone or face-to-face?"

"Depends on what we can arrange," Gumaad says.

"I'd like to do the interview face-to-face."

"As matters stand, he wants a phone interview."

Dajaal says, "If I were you, I wouldn't do it face-to-face, as there is always the risk of him being blown up. The drones are more active than before. They might pick up his movement and go for him."

There is a spell of jumpiness, Gumaad shifting in his seat. Then he cries, "Malik has no reason to fear being blown up. What nonsense!"

"*They* blew a former colleague of mine sky high with remote-controlled roadside bombs," Dajaal says. "*They* have perfected their art of killing. If I were you, Malik, I wouldn't do a phone interview, either; a drone might mistake your number for his, and strike you dead."

Gumaad has gone nervy and sweaty again, and a new layer of scurf coats the back of his neck and shoulders.

"Please, Grandpa," Qasiir begs. "Stop this."

"Why? His men have killed my colleagues."

"Someone may hear you."

"It isn't long before they kill *me*, I know."

Gumaad mumbles something inaudible, his words colliding discordantly. He mixes his tenses, trips on his adverbs, stops making sense. Malik's stomach goes through the complete life cycle of the butterfly. He is remembering a fragment from a dream he had a few nights ago, in which Gumaad betrayed him, handing him over to a group of freelance militiamen, who took him hostage. In the dream, Malik pleaded with Gumaad not to break faith with him. But all he says is, "Enough now, Dajaal."

For the first time, Malik thinks that maybe Dajaal's days are indeed numbered. He also wonders if an interview with TheSheikh would be a scoop worth the risk. Then he picks up a foul scent. It is Gumaad's breath—not so much ordinary bad breath as the scent of his fear, which Malik thinks he can smell in the same way that he believes he can smell Dajaal's rage.

"Please, all of you," he says abruptly.

Everyone looks at him, mildly shocked.

"I want to be alone."

After they have gone, Malik telephones Jeebleh and asks his opinion about whether the interview with TheSheikh is worth the risk. In truth, what he really wants is for Jeebleh to be aware of what he is up to, in the event that something happens. In his head, Malik can hear Amran harping on about his taking needless risks.

Jeebleh acknowledges the professional benefits of doing the interview, but believes that it is not worth it, given the imminent Ethiopian occupation. "You may become an easy target for both the Transitional Government and the occupying force."

"What if I use a pseudonym?"

"Don't do it," Jeebleh says. "Please."

Next, Malik calls Ahl. Ahl, too, advises against it. He says, "TheSheikh is a man on the run, for crying out loud. Think of this: The FBI will be on your tail once it becomes known that you've talked to a wanted man."

"But it would be a big scoop for me," Malik argues. "And earlier you were all for my interviewing a funder of piracy who is by all accounts a crook. How is that?"

"That was different," Ahl says.

"Different? What do you mean 'different'?"

"We all want to get Taxliil to come home safe," Ahl says. "What you are proposing poses danger to us all. Look at it from that angle. Please think again and do not do anything that might jeopardize our chance of recovering Taxliil."

Malik is not convinced that he agrees with Ahl's reasoning. But he opts not to speak, apprehensive that his brother might think that he places his professional advancement far above family loyalty.

"It's been a long, eventful day," Ahl says.

"You're right. It's been long and eventful."

Ahl says, "Sleep on it, and let's talk tomorrow."

"Good night."

"Good night to you, too."

THE SKY IS DARK; THE NIGHT IS STARLESS. IN A DREAM, A TOTAL eclipse has just ended, and Malik ventures out of the apartment for the first time in twenty-four hours. He is on his way to a hospital, walking; Dajaal is indisposed. Roadside mines, tanks, and four days of fighting between the insurgents and the Ethiopian army of occupation have made the city roads impassable, turned them unsafe.

When he finally reaches the hospital, he encounters more ruin; the main building has been hit and reduced to rubble. Radio reports place the number of dead at five hundred, and those critically wounded at over a thousand. A large number of the hospital staff figure among the dead and the missing, perhaps buried in the debris. To the left of the main entrance, a huge crowd is raising an unearthly ruckus. It takes Malik a few minutes to work out the nature of the conflict. The remaining Somali medical staff and several Europeans, no doubt flown in at huge expense by the World Health Organization to help save lives, are engaged in a heated back-and-forth debate with some bearded Shabaab types. The debate centers on whether dogs may be used to save human lives from the wreckage of the hospital. A Gumaad look-alike describes the use of dogs to rescue people from the ruins as an affront to Muslim sensibilities. He is saying to the Europeans, as if from a pulpit, "Dogs are unclean, and we as Muslims are forbidden to come into contact with them."

But someone is calling from below, deep down in the ruins. It is a man pleading for someone to help rescue his daughter, who is buried in the rubble. The man wants the medical team to use their trained dogs to bring his daughter out, alive.

The WHO team is led by a large woman with a red face, red hair, and skin the color of beetroot from a combination of anger and the tropical sun. She shouts at the Gumaad look-alike, "I'll beat you up if you don't get out of the way of the job I've come to perform." Frightened by her outburst, he backs down sheepishly and quietly leaves the scene.

Meanwhile, another member of the hospital medical staff is engaged in his own shouting match with one of the other bearded men. The doctor is saying, "Do you think that Islam condones the desecration of cemeteries, even if the dead were once Christian? I view the desecration of Mogadiscio's Christian cemetery as heinous and a more serious crime than permitting the use of dogs to pull a living girl out of the rubble. I feel certain that you will have to answer to the Almighty on Judgment Day for dishonoring and debasing the dead bodies of Christians, whereas I am convinced that as long as we mean well and save lives, all will be forgiven by the Divine. Not that I agree with you that Islam forbids the use of dogs to save human lives."

The row continues, and Malik moves toward the cottages sprawled over an acre and a half in every direction. With the main building destroyed, the cottages now serve as the hospital. The sickening sights are reminiscent of the carnage from World War I, with the wounded lying everywhere on the floor, writhing in pain for lack of morphine or enough doctors and nurses to attend to them. The uniforms of the nurses are dyed in blood.

A nurse, her hands dripping with blood, asks Malik to undo her bra; she explains that it is the only one she owns. Clumsily self-conscious, he suggests she turn so that he can unclasp the catch from the back. But, no, the hooks are in the front. He doesn't recall ever taking so long to undo a woman's bra. He sweats so liberally that a drop of perspiration from his forehead almost blinds him.

He remembers that he has an appointment with a doctor, but not why. He asks himself if he is ailing or if he is seeking help for someone else—and if so, for whom? Then he remembers that it is Dajaal who has been hurt in the blast from a roadside bomb, driving. And that when he failed to arrange an appointment with a doctor for Dajaal, he used his press card, describing himself as a journalist interviewing the victims of this ruthless bombing of civilians. To get what he wanted, he remarked that Ethiopia had atrocities to answer for, and that someone was bound to submit a case to the International Court of Justice for this reckless bombing of the city's residential area.

A phone rings somewhere. At first it sounds as if it is ringing in his head, the way telephones ring inside the head of a dreamer—distant and yet so near, persistent, doggedly insistent, almost otherworldly. Malik listens to the ringing, but can't be bothered, as if imagining that it is ringing for someone else.

Then he isolates the tone, which is coming from the kitchen counter, where he left his phone to recharge when he fell asleep in the small hours. He infers, eventually, that it must be his. Cursing, he gets out of bed to answer it, his head aching.

———

Cambara has very bad news. Dajaal is dead.

Malik asks, "Dead? How?"

"Killed at close range by an unknown assassin," she finally manages to say. "I am told the murderer used the most powerful handgun available on the market—I can't remember the name, but Bile has described using such a weapon as literally overkill."

Malik wants to know the time, as if this has something to do with Dajaal's death. As he searches for his watch, instant guilt preys on his mind. He wishes he knew if Dajaal was killed at the very time he, Malik, was dreaming of visiting him at the hospital, as if this might lessen or intensify his own sense of self-reproach. Cambara tells him that Dajaal's passing occurred at dawn, as he was on his way to the mosque to pray. Tearful and choking, she adds, "Nobody remembers Dajaal ever going to the mosque for the dawn prayer."

Malik's watch reads almost eleven.

He says, "When is the burial?"

"He's already been buried," says Cambara.

Malik can't believe it. When he finds his tongue, his words run in pursuit of one another; there are gaps in his thinking, which doesn't keep up with the speed of his speech. He says, "Dajaal died at dawn. So why the hurry?"

"Because the gun that the assassin used hacks into its victims, tearing them apart with formidable force. Given the state of his body, it was deemed best to bury him right away."

"A death meant as a lesson to us all, perhaps?"

She says, "One hated or loved Dajaal."

"His friends and family loved him."

"We'll miss him, Bile and me."

An alien disorder seizes Malik by the throat and renders him speechless. Plenty of words come to him, but somehow his tongue won't let go of them.

"Are you still there?" Cambara asks.

He is barely audible when he says, "Yes."

"Qasiir made the arrangements," she explains. "He sent the diggers out early, called the sheikh to lead the Janaaza-prayer and community to prepare the body for interment, rented the bier, and organized the other burial rituals."

"I wonder why he didn't call me," Malik says.

"He said he called," she says. "No answer."

Malik says, "Where will all this end?"

Cambara says, "I doubt it will ever end."

"Do we have any idea who killed him?"

"Bile—he answered the phone—asked Qasiir to come over, and the two of them were locked in the upstairs bedroom for a long time. I am not privy to their conversation. Frankly, I doubt if anyone other than Shabaab was behind it. And you can be sure Dajaal's murder will lead to more bloodletting."

"I'd talk to Qasiir if he were still there," says Malik.

"He left earlier, and Bile took to bed," she says.

Malik senses sickness spreading through his entire body. He is remembering the last altercation between Dajaal and Gumaad, and the sensation he'd had at the time—that Dajaal would pay with his life for what he said about TheSheikh.

"How is Qasiir handling it?"

"He's devastated," Cambara says.

"Any idea what he is planning?"

"Qasiir won't do anything in a mad rush," she says. "Bile says that he is very much like his grandfather in this way."

They talk for a few more minutes. Cambara tells Malik that, in between attempts to reach him, she spoke to Jeebleh and Seamus to let them know of Dajaal's passing. She goes on to say, "Seamus thinks that you should base yourself in Nairobi, where you can get all the news about Somalia by the minute. Things will get much worse here before they get better."

"What did Jeebleh say?"

"That he expects you to know what to do."

"Jeebleh hasn't suggested that I relocate to Kenya to cover Somalia from there, like all those European journalists do?"

"He says he will trust you to know what to do."

Before hanging up, Cambara presses him to at least think more seriously about moving in with them, and she reminds him that if he needs transportation anywhere, both Qasiir and the car are at his disposal.

He thanks her and they hang up.

————

Depression sends Malik back to bed. From there he makes several attempts to reach Qasiir, but each time the line is either busy or disconnected. Despondency overwhelms him.

Later, when he rises, a strain of unfamiliar sorrow stirs him out of his depressive lethargy. But he doesn't know what to do with himself. The day stretches ahead of him. He goes to the bathroom to clean his teeth, but he cannot bear the thought of looking in the mirror, worried at what he might see.

In the kitchen, he makes breakfast for two. Then he rings Dajaal's number, just as he used to, aware that Somalis are unsentimental about death and certain that someone will have taken over Dajaal's mobile phone and will use it until it runs out of airtime, and then decide whether to top it up or not.

A woman answers.

"This is Malik," he says. "To whom am I speaking?"

She replies, "I am Qasiir's mother," and weeps.

Malik pays his respects and tells her how much he will miss Dajaal. "He's been very dear to me," he says. "I wish I had been there for his burial. But you know!"

"It's God's will that he is gone," she says. "I loved him more than I loved my own father, because he raised me, supported and stood by me when the attacking Americans hurt my daughter. Allah will bless him."

"Please tell Qasiir that I called."

"I will, I will," she assures him.

"I hope to come around and see you before I leave."

"May Allah be praised," she says.

Speaking to Qasiir's mother does him good, helping him remember his responsibility as a journalist and as a friend to Dajaal and men like him, who are often murdered for the views they hold, risking their lives for their stands against tyranny. Dajaal loved the country, and has been killed by men who cannot love Somalia until they turn it into a different country, in which they prosper and their opponents perish. He will pen a piece about the tragic eradication of a generation of Somali professionals, of whom Dajaal was a prime example.

He gets down to just doing that.

Ahl calls. Malik tells him about Dajaal's death. Ahl, however, is consumed by the thought of the newly appointed Ethiopian ambassador to Somalia lodging in Somalia's presidential villa as though it were an upmarket hotel, not only as a guest of Somalia's traitorous interim government, but on the false pretext of safeguarding the state and its interim president, who was escorted to the villa with a heavily armed detachment of Ethiopian and a hundred or so Somali soldiers.

Malik is conscious of his gauche failure—giving importance to the death of an individual when he should be concerned with the current state of the nation, in apparent contrast to Ahl, who, being physically distant from the scene of the bombings and having not known Dajaal in person, can afford a wider perspective in his assessment of these events. Maybe when one lives in a city riven by civil war, one is obsessed with the immediate situation almost to the exclusion of all else, whereas when one is operating outside these stressful conditions, one has the luxury, as Ahl does, to take a broader view and to study the matter from an entirely different perspective. At the moment, Malik is so preoccupied with Dajaal's death—with thinking and writing about it—that he needs reminding that the Ethiopians are spreading their tentacles into strategic locations in Mogadiscio.

Malik ends the call and returns to his writing. Barely has he completed an initial draft and saved it when Qasiir calls.

After offering his heartfelt condolences, Malik says, "I suggest you take it easy for a couple of days. You need the time to grieve, to mourn your grandfather. He was a wonderful, wonderful man in my view, too."

Qasiir says, "I would be failing Grandpa and dishonoring his memory if I did not get on with my life in the same way I had always done before his death—and perform my responsibility toward the jobs at hand."

Malik is shocked and impressed: shocked, because he can't imagine being able to function so soon after the untimely death of a beloved grandfather; impressed, because only pragmatists, who value life for what it is—a loan that is borrowed and, as with all loans, must be returned—appreciate every moment of it, conscious of the need to put food on the table, draw water from the well, graze the beasts, tend the sick—so that other people may go on living. He feels humbled, as he doesn't think he would have done for anyone what Qasiir is doing.

"Then why don't you come," he says.

———

Qasiir arrives: hugs, condolences, and regrets.

He tells Malik about Dajaal's death in a more succinct way than

Cambara had done. Apparently a man stalked him as he walked to the mosque. Fifty meters before Dajaal reached the house of worship, the gunman pulled out his Magnum 55 and hit him in the back of the head; a professional killing, no room for error, and death was instantaneous. Malik is relieved that Qasiir spares him the gory details. He says purposefully, "Grandpa is dead. I know who will pay for it: a life for a life. We'll have to do what we must do today, and then sometime in the future, the assassin will pay for what he has done. Meanwhile, I'll bide my time and live my life in the way I see fit, and as Grandpa would have been happy with if he had been alive, relying on the guidance of a Somali wisdom—that the shoes of a dead man are more useful than he is."

Malik isn't familiar with Somali poetry or proverbs. But he is conversant with the Arabic tradition, having been brought up on a rich diet of Arabic poetry, especially of the pre-Islamic period, otherwise known as the Jaahiliya—the time of ignorance. So he recites in his head a couple of verses from Imrul Qays, indubitably the best Arab poet of any era, the son of a sultan, who uttered his most famous riposte on the assassination of his father, giving air to words of cynicism that have since entered Arab folklore. Asked when he might avenge his father, Qays replied, "Tomorrow is for drinking, tomorrow for vengeance." Malik wonders if Qasiir will do the killing quietly, in his own time, since, according to Cambara, he is not the type to rush matters.

Malik finds himself discomfited to be alone with Qasiir, now that he has learned the shape of Qasiir's thinking. Malik's eyes wander away; he cannot bear to focus on Qasiir's palsied features, his evasiveness a testament to his own desire not to bear witness to a mourner's pain. In the long silence that follows, he fidgets, then makes tea and, to keep busy, offers to prepare a meal. When Qasiir tells him he has no wish to eat anything, he suggests they go for a drive. He finds the apartment too small to contain the two of them.

Qasiir asks, "Where?"

Malik has been wondering what changes the carousel of politics, with the Courts now departed and the Ethiopians and the Transitional Federal Government replacing them, has brought about. He thinks that there is no place better than the Bakhaaraha to study them.

"Let's go to the Bakhaaraha," Malik suggests.

"What do you have in mind?" Qasiir asks.

Malik says, "We may run into people we know."

"And of what benefit is that to either of us?"

The thought of running into BigBeard so soon after the Courts' authority has been dismantled perversely excites Malik. But he chooses not to speak of this wrongheadedness to Qasiir now, lest Qasiir think him deranged. He simply locks up, making sure that all the security contraptions are in good working order. Then he follows Qasiir, who leads the way, down the staircase, through the passageways, and finally to the parking lot.

In the car, Malik says, "Maybe we'll run into Gumaad."

"Gumaad is on his way to Eritrea," Qasiir says, "appointed as the spokesman of the exiled Somali community in Asmara. The group includes the Courts and several other Somali associations opposing the Transitional Federal Government and Ethiopia. He was on the radio, giving an interview at the top of the hour."

"How did he get there so quickly?" Malik asks. "I wonder if he is lying again, claiming to be speaking from Asmara when he is right here in the city." It feels like a long time ago when Gumaad suggested that he interview TheSheikh. A lot can happen in a day in a civil war. Dajaal is dead and buried; Gumaad is in Asmara. What else has he missed? "And where is TheSheikh?"

"Gumaad escorted TheSheikh on a special flight that took him straight to Eritrea," Qasiir says. "Presumably, they were flown out of an airstrip still believed to be in the hands of the Courts. The mystery now surrounds TheOtherSheikh. One rumor places him in a village near the Somali-Kenya border, another speaks of the possibility of him going to the Sudan or Libya, where he was schooled."

"What's become of the other Courts members?"

"Some are headed for Iran, some to the Gulf."

"Is it fair to assume that every single Somali politician has a different paymaster outside this country from whom he receives instructions, and whose interests he serves?" Malik is remembering that a UN annual situation report on Somalia, published the previous year, claimed that there were twelve countries involved in the Somali conflict—Eritrea, Ethiopia, Iran, Libya, Egypt, Kenya, Iraq, China, Italy, the United States, France, and Britain.

"That's right."

Outside, pedestrians are crossing the busy street in no hurry at all, as if daring the drivers to run them over. Some of them stop in the center, as though saying, "Hit me. See if I care." Malik observes that already more women are walking around unveiled than when the Courts ran the city.

Qasiir says, "Please tell me where we're going."

"Maybe we'll visit BigBeard's shop," Malik says.

"What's the purpose of our visit?"

"Must there be a purpose?" Malik says.

"In an ideal world, we do things for a reason."

Malik says, "Well, then, I can pretend to be looking for an iPod or, better still, we can say we are there to price a BlackBerry. We can say anything that will allow us to take a good look at him, unobserved."

Qasiir doesn't seem convinced it is a good idea. But he doesn't say anything.

"Are you opposed to us paying him a visit?"

Qasiir brakes for a pedestrian walking backward, but still the pedestrian collides with his front bumper. The pedestrian, unhurt, signals his apology and backs away into oncoming traffic. There is a ruckus, with drivers stopping all of a sudden, and one of the cars smashes into the one ahead of it. Instantly, crowds gather on either side of the street. Then a man breaks away and Malik observes the surfeit of interest in the eyes of many in the crowd. It is as if everyone is watching and waiting for the opportune moment to go for broke. In his travels, Malik has known of mobs on a Nairobi main street beating a man nearly to death as he was running after a minibus, mistaking him for a thief. A man nearby, just then realizing that he had been dispossessed of his wallet, shouted, "Thief running, catch the thief." Another man echoed the phrase—"Thief running"—and then another and another joined the chorus. Before the runner had reached his bus, a fourth tripped him. Turning into a mob, the bystanders fell on the man, raining deadly blows on him. By the time the police arrived, the man had also lost his front teeth to a kick, and his own wallet and documents were gone.

But no such incident occurs just now. The traffic eases and they move on.

Malik says, "Tell me what you really think of my plan."

"There is no benefit in provoking BigBeard unnecessarily," Qasiir says. "Grandpa, who knew him all his life, always advised me to give him a wide berth."

"He ruined my visit on my first day, and I won't forgive myself if I do not do a little to disrupt the flow of his life and then write about it," Malik says.

Malik thinks that if civil wars are an affront to common sense and Qasiir has known nothing but the affrontery resulting from civil wars, then he may not understand why it matters to see BigBeard a day after the Courts have been ousted. No need to reiterate that in the old dispensation, when the Courts were in charge, BigBeard doubled as a customs officer in addition to running a computer shop. He is Malik's idea of a corrupt Courts bureaucrat, although it occurs to him that, along with those determined to profit themselves, there must also have been a core of well-meaning, hardworking, honest individuals.

"I hope we find him at the shop," Malik says.

Qasiir says, "I hope we don't."

"You think talking to him may put us in danger?"

"Not immediately," Qasiir says.

"But it might put us in danger eventually?"

"It might," Qasiir says.

Still, Qasiir's warning doesn't deter Malik. Maybe he is making up for missing out on interviewing TheSheikh when he had the chance to do so. Once upon a time, he did what he pleased. How he loved the lure of danger when he was younger, when he had no wife and no child. "We've become a father," he said when his child was born, a smile adorning his lips. In a way, he thinks, war correspondents have no business being family people, since that will deter them from pursuing their vocation without worry or fear. Isn't that what journalists do when they cover wars—endanger their lives? Malik recalls an Austrian poet and editor who described the breed as "heroes of obtrusiveness." Is there anywhere on earth where the intrusive, inquisitive, danger-courting journalist is as conspicuous as he is in Somalia? Yes, we've become a father.

"We'll just have to be careful with BigBeard. That's all," Qasiir says, and he reverses into a parking spot that has fallen vacant.

It takes them longer than necessary to walk to the computer shop, in part because Qasiir drags it out, clearly opposed to the idea of the encounter. He doesn't have daring in the marrow of his bones. But neither is he bold enough to challenge Malik outright, reminding himself of his responsibility to Grandpa, who is still warm in his grave and would be upset if Qasiir upset Malik. He remembers, too, that Dajaal was fond of the militaristic motto "Orders from high up are orders from high up, and they must be obeyed." He stays in close contact with Malik, who is reflecting that life here is built on quicksand. Alive one minute, dead the next, and buried in the blink of an eye, no postmortem, not even an entry in a ledger.

The shop is busy, with lots of customers standing around, ordering items and waiting for them to be delivered from the back. When it is Malik and Qasiir's turn, Malik says that he wants to see BigBeard. At the mention of the nickname, a hush descends among the staff. A tall, thin man separates himself from the others.

He asks Malik, "Why do you want to see him?"

Malik says, "I bought a computer from this shop a few days back and it is malfunctioning. The manager told me to come and see him personally anytime if there was a problem with the machine."

"Where is the computer?" the man asks.

But Malik only repeats, "Is BigBeard here?"

The man stands statue still, as if reflecting on Malik's request, and then he is gone for a long time. Meanwhile, the shop empties, and one of the younger salesmen posts himself at the entrance to tell people wanting to enter the shop that it is no longer open for business that day, and to bid them to come back tomorrow.

A man emerges from the back of the shop. He is identical to Malik's memory of BigBeard, except that he is wearing a suit and he is beardless. He waits for one of the salesmen to point out the person who has asked for him, even though Malik and Qasiir are now the only customers left.

"What can I do for you?" BigBeard asks, not a trace of recognition in his eyes, no tension in his body, no fear or worry evident anywhere in him.

Malik says, "My computer is malfunctioning."

Then, as if he recognizes Malik's face or remembers the sound of his voice, BigBeard's easy composure wears off. He starts to look hard-pressed. He stares at Malik, as if taking his measure in an effort to determine what course of action is open to him. His eyes prowl the shop, like an eagle on the lookout for prey to pounce on. But when his wandering eyes land on Qasiir, he seems to regain his composure with a forced effort. He says to Qasiir, "I hadn't realized you were here, in the shop. No one has told me. Please, please accept my condolences. And, please, please greet your mother and tell her how sorry I am to hear of your grandfather's death."

A quiet hush descends. He turns to Malik and asks, "Did you bring the machine with you that you say is now malfunctioning?"

Malik shakes his head.

BigBeard says, "Bring it and we'll fix it."

He turns to go.

Malik calls him back. "Haven't we met before?"

BigBeard pauses briefly, then replies, "I am often mistaken for other people with whom I share a family resemblance. Maybe you've met one of my cousins. He used to work here."

Qasiir, meanwhile, has put a bit of distance between himself and Malik, the way teenagers stand to one side and look away in embarrassment when their parents start plying their friends with stories about them.

Malik says to BigBeard, keeping his voice low, "I am not mistaking you for anyone else. I know who you are: you confiscated my computer, deleted the photograph of my daughter, and then poisoned my machine with a venomous virus, which ruined it. Do you remember any of that?"

"You're mistaking me for someone else."

They look hard into each other's eyes, neither blinking. It is as if they are testing each other's mettle. BigBeard seems almost buoyant, though, as if a victory is nigh; Malik's confidence is fueled by his rage.

"What exactly do you want?" BigBeard asks at length.

"I would like my machine back."

In the silence that follows, Qasiir rallies his inner strength and says quietly to Malik, "Please let us go."

But nothing will move Malik from where he is.

BigBeard says, "You are an impetuous man and a fool and you do not know what is good for you. If you value your life, you will go out of here this instant. If you don't . . . !"

"What, if I don't?"

BigBeard pulls his coat aside to reveal the butt of his Magnum. "You'll die a painful death. I will make certain of that. And remember, I know where you live. I know everything about you."

Whatever he expected, Malik did not think their conversation would end in a cul-de-sac of such naked threat. His calm exterior and his steady stare now conceal an inner tremor, and he startles this time when Qasiir touches him and says, "Shall we go, please?"

Malik wonders how much of what was said could be heard by Qasiir, or whether he, too, caught a flash of the Magnum.

———

Back in the car, Malik is impressed at how Qasiir restrains himself from prying or from reprimanding him. He knows he is given to keeping his foibles under wraps, making a point not to publicize them. He has a bad sense of direction, for example, which makes him doubly grateful for Qasiir. On his own in other locales, he sometimes goes to the venues where he is to meet someone a day ahead, reconnoitering, to avoid making a fool of himself.

Qasiir says, "One of my mates drafted as a Shabaab cadre has informed me of a young thing who died at BigBeard's instructions a couple of days ago. He is a ruthless man, BigBeard."

"Can I meet your friend, the Shabaab recruit?"

"I asked him if he would meet you."

"What was his answer?"

"He prefers that you meet the brother of the young thing."

Qasiir explains that the dead boy was part of an advance team, sent out to "consecrate" safe houses close to the presidential villa from which they intend to launch their war on both the interim head and the Ethiopian invaders.

"Do you know where to find him?"

"He is a former pirate, now jobless."

Malik asks, "What's his name?"

"Marduuf."

"How bizarre," Malik says. "Named for a large measure of wrapped *qaat*."

"He is partial to *qaat*, and wasted the money he made from piracy chewing it."

"Where does he live?"

"He came to Mogadiscio soon after his brother was buried, and has spent a great deal of time gathering as much information as possible about his late sibling," Qasiir replies. "I hear he has built a case for vengeance."

"And he is biding his time?"

"He is waiting for a good opportunity to act on his rage," Qasiir says.

"Is he willing, do you think, to come to where I choose and do the interview?"

"That's my understanding," Qasiir says.

"What about a time of my choosing—will he agree to that, too?"

Qasiir says, "I believe he will."

They part without saying more.

AHL HEADS FOR HIS ROOM TO MAKE SURE THAT HIS PERSONAL effects, including his cash and passports, are safely locked away before going off to Guri-Maroodi, the village where groups of young men congregate—would-be illegal migrants bracing for a sea trip to Yemen and then Europe. He puts the key in the door, but the lock won't engage. The TV in the room is blaring, but he doesn't recall turning it on before going down earlier. He pulls the key out and inserts it a second time, and a third. Still, it won't turn. He is about to go down to the reception desk to ask for help when the door opens a crack. He sees that a young man with a familiar face—the TV programmer—is in the room.

Ahl asks, "What are you doing in my room?"

As soon as the words leave his mouth, he asks himself if one can say "my room" when one has only temporary access to it.

"I am programming the TV. For you."

"With the door locked?"

"Does it matter whether the door is or isn't locked when I am in the room, programming your TV?" the young fellow says with incorrigible cheekiness.

Ahl stares in silence at the young man—the door open, the key in the clutch of his hand, his eyes washing over his suitcase and shoulder bag, uncertain if they are where he left them. Do they seem a little disorderly, as if someone has tampered with them? Ahl recalls opening the computer bag before he went down to breakfast. But did he leave the bag unlocked? No point asking the young man anything. People out here are jittery, their tetchiness priming them to jump to the wrong conclusions.

He says to the young man, "Get out!"

Alone in the room, the door securely latched from the inside, he unplugs the TV. The sealed envelopes with Taxliil's photograph and the cash are still in the computer bag—there is no time to make sure that nothing else is missing. He decides to carry these valuables on his person, unable to think of a better way of keeping them safe. He wears the cash belt and carries the laptop with him. But for the sake of form, he locks his suitcase, in which there is nothing but his dirty clothes.

Back outside, his eyes clap on a pack of young crows with feathers so shiny they look as if they've been dipped in black oil. Some strut around, as if daring him to chase them; others take off as he approaches, then alight on the tree branches and descend to the patch of garden. They make a racket, clucking and pecking at one another.

Ahl goes to reception to complain about the TV programmer. An unfamiliar middle-aged man who is missing one eye is at the front desk. He hesitates, not sure if he wants to discuss his grievance with this man, whom he assumes doesn't work here.

"Where is the manager?" Ahl asks.

"What do you want?" the one-eyed man demands.

"I'd like to submit a complaint about the young man who has made a habit of locking my room from the inside, and rummaging in my stuff. He claims he's the TV programmer," Ahl says.

The one-eyed man scratches his stubbled chin. He says, "I am afraid we do not have a TV programmer in our employ. We fired the last one who worked here three days ago precisely because he was found routing about in a guest's room."

"But he was in my room just now," Ahl says.

"He has no business being in your room."

Ahl asks, "How does he gain access unless he has a master key, or collects one from reception? I chased him out a few minutes ago."

"He has no business being in your room, or collecting a master key from here," the one-eyed man insists. "I'll report him to the management. Action will be taken against him soon."

"Please do that," Ahl says, although he doesn't believe for a moment that the man will take any such action.

———

A car horn honks, and the outside gate opens to admit a battered jalopy. Fidno is at the wheel. Ahl wonders whether it makes sense for him to carry all his cash and his computer with him when Fidno evidently thinks the village they are driving to rates no better than the bucket of bolts he is driving rather than his usual posh car. But what else can he do? He puts his faith in his good fortune, trusting that all will be well for now. Maybe he will check out of the hotel at the first opportunity and move in with Xalan and Warsame, if the offer still stands.

Barely has Ahl clambered into the four-wheel wreck, placed his laptop at his feet, and put on the seat belt when Fidno squeals out of the gate and steps on the gas, as if eager to be clear of the place. Within half a kilometer they are in a poor neighborhood on the out- skirts of the city, where the huts are built of coarse matting rein- forced here and there with zinc, or from packing material bearing the names of its manufacturers, although they are moving too fast for Ahl to make out the letters. The doors to the dwellings, which are impro- vised out of cloth, blow in the wind. Everything about these huts and the lean-tos that serve as their kitchens has an air of the temporary about it. The residents are those displaced by the fighting in the south of the country. They have come to Bosaso because there is peace here.

Fidno climbs through the gears in quick succession, the clunker rattling so loudly that neither man talks, not even when Fidno nearly runs over a couple of pedestrians loitering in the center of the road. At the last second, they scatter, and Fidno roars on, like a race-car driver participating in an autocross relay through an uninhabited countryside. The ride is as disagreeable as mounting a bad-tempered young male camel that spits, kicks, and foams furiously at the mouth.

Straining to be heard over the ruckus, Ahl asks, "Why the rush? Are we late?"

"Our man is restless," Fidno says. "We may not find him still there if we delay."

"What's his name?"

Fidno responds irritably, "If you really must know, he is known by his nickname, Magac-Laawe. A no-name man."

"Have you spoken to No-Name yourself, then?"

"I've spoken to his henchman."

Ahl wishes Malik were here, Malik who knows how to deal with this specimen of humanity, the dirt no one dare clean up, in a land with no laws, in a country where brute force earns high dividends. If war-

lords have deputies, and presidents their vice presidents, then it follows that, in a world in which coercion is the norm, a human trafficker
must have underlings as well.

"What have you told No-Name about me?"

"That you are my friend."

What does that make him? Ahl wonders. An associate of a known
criminal? Is this what children do to you, knowingly or unwittingly,
make you into an accomplice of outlaws? He prays that Fidno does not
run afoul of the authorities while they are together, especially not with
so much cash and his laptop on him, in this beat-up vehicle on the way
to Guri-Maroodi, a hot spot with few equals in notoriety, even within
Puntland.

"What else did you tell him?"

"That you are looking for your runaway nephew."

"My nephew—why nephew? He is my son."

"Makes no difference. Nephew, son, stepson!"

Of course it does make a difference; but Ahl says nothing.

Fidno says, "I was worried that No-Name might think you would
become too emotional, irrational, or hard to please if things do not go
the way you want them to. 'My son' is different from 'my nephew.' I
don't know if this makes sense to you, but that is what I thought. I did
it for your sake. To make things happen."

Again, Ahl thinks that he is not suited for this kind of assignment
the way Malik is, having interviewed Afghani drug lords as well as
Pakistani Taliban warlords. It requires a familiarity with the criminal
mind that is beyond his experience. Ahl worries that once he's en-
dorsed a lie, he will be open to telling more, and there will be no end
to it.

He says, "I'll set No-Name right on this. A lie does not run off my
tongue easily, and I'll have to beware of what I say all the time."

"Do what suits you," Fidno concedes.

They go through a drab-looking hamlet that boasts of only a few low shops built of stone, atop a wood foundation, the zinc roofing painted in different colors, mainly blue. Billboards advertise cigarettes, soda, milk, and other products, Ahl guesses more for decoration than because they are actually available. They have slowed to a snail's pace, and Ahl can see people in clusters of three and four, with their curious eyes trained on the jalopy. He can even hear them: they are speaking a babble of Swahili, Oromo, Tigrinya, broken Yemeni Arabic, and Somali. A microcosm of the Horn, a cosmopolitan misery marked with unforgiving poverty.

Minibuses ply the road to Bosaso, and young men and women walk along the road, hitching a ride or footing it; almost everyone here is young, and there are more men than women.

"I could hear Amharic, Swahili, and Tigrinya as we passed," Ahl says. "How on earth do they all get here?"

"The Ethiopians, Eritreans, and Somalis from the south of the country walk for several days to get here," Fidno responds. "Some of the Kenyans and the Tanzanians arrive by plane or by boat. But only a few make it to Yemen. The owners of the fishing boats have been known to throw three-quarters of their passengers overboard before they make it ashore to avoid the possible confiscation of their boats."

There is a group of young men gathered around a pickup with the back open. A woman has set up a stall close by selling *qaat*. Ahl sees one of the youths carrying a bundle and a number of his mates following, some clearly asking him to give them a share.

"Tell me how you described Taxliil," says Ahl.

Fidno says, "A bright young fellow with excellent language skills, impeccable manners, assigned to welcome foreign Shabaab recruits here to join the insurgency in Somalia."

"In what capacity does No-Name enter the scene?"

"It makes business sense for the boat owners not to return empty after transporting the migrants to the shores of Yemen," Fidno explains. Ahl considers how this works to the advantage of several groups operating outside the law. Likewise, it makes sense for the pirates and the religionists to work together, not only for profit but also for mutual security.

They have reached the outskirts of the village. As they continue south, the landscape turns desolate, burned. Then there is a sudden change in the wind, which picks up and brings along with it a cooler breeze from the sea. The vegetation is sparse, much of it of the thorny sort, with a few trees to provide shade to humans and fodder for camels. A young boy, shirtless and in a sarong, with a chewing stick in his mouth, looks lost as his camels chomp away at one of the treetops. Ahl says, "There is a world of difference between the young Somali nomad looking after his beasts and the migrants wanting to cross the sea, isn't there?"

"Do you suppose the young nomad is content because he knows no better life?" asks Fidno.

"I would imagine that many of the migrants, being city born and city bred, are unhappy with their lot and eager to seek adventure elsewhere," Ahl observes. "Perhaps because they've seen too much TV and believe that life elsewhere is more comfortable."

"What about your son? He had the possibility of a successful future ahead of him. Do you know what made him leave Minneapolis to return to this desolate place?"

"I wish I knew," Ahl mumbles.

They enter another enclave. The sea breeze is now stronger as they pass men sitting around or lying in the scanty shade of the trees, chewing *qaat*.

"Who are they?" asks Ahl, pointing out a group of young migrants, half lying and half sitting, as if they are too tired even to sit all the way up.

"Migrants exhausted from waiting."

"What are they waiting for?"

But Fidno does not answer Ahl's question. "We're here," he says instead, and he turns in and stops at a metal gate guarded by armed men in khaki uniforms. A young man with large eyes and a thin, half-trimmed mustache comes forward. Fidno waves his hand in greeting, and the youth acknowledges him with a broad smile.

One side of the gate opens, and the young man steps out, just as another youth with a small head and wearing huge spectacles emerges from the gatehouse and stands by a second barrier that needs to be removed manually. The first young man approaches the car to check out Ahl.

"We're expected," Fidno says.

The gate opens, and Fidno drives in.

———

The grounds on which the villa is built are extensive and surrounded in all directions by a high fence. The house itself, set far back, is two stories high, with French windows and a glassed-in balcony large enough for a sumptuous party. The sea is visible behind the house. An awning extends almost to the gates, providing shade as they drive in. Fidno parks, and Ahl picks up his laptop and follows him toward the pair of uniformed young men who wait in front of the awning. The entire structure looks new and well made; the railing on the upper story is shiny with fresh paint. The loud humming of a heavy-duty generator comes from the back.

There is order here, the order of a corrupt autocrat imposed through coercion, Ahl thinks. One of the uniformed men leads them up to the house, his pace measured. He knocks on the door in a rhythmic knock, presumably a code. The door opens. Fidno and Ahl enter; the uniformed youth stays behind, bowing.

"Welcome, AhlulKhair. I am your host."

The voice Ahl hears has something magisterial about it: distant, assertive. He identifies it as belonging to a little, lean man of advanced years sitting in what looks like a child's high chair, with a full, graying beard and penetrating eyes. How very odd that such a small man, almost a midget, can produce such a commanding voice, Ahl thinks. He can't be more than four feet tall. He reminds Ahl of pictures he has seen of Emperor Haile Selassie, and because of this, he somehow expects a Chihuahua to be imperiously perched on No-Name's lap. Ahl wonders if No-Name is a cripple.

"How have things been?" he says to Ahl, in a tone of surprising familiarity.

"Everything has been good so far," Ahl says, although this is not what he feels inside.

"What about you, Fidno?" No-Name asks, his voice sounding a notch more authoritative, its timbre more full-bodied.

Fidno says, "Everything is according to plan."

"Excellent."

"How have you been yourself?" Fidno asks.

No-Name appears a little offended. He says to Fidno, "Give us a few minutes, will you? You may join the others outside. You know your way around here."

The caller of tunes, No-Name expects to be obeyed, and Fidno takes his leave. "Thank you for seeing my friend," he says.

"We'll see you later." Ahl notes the royal *we*.

When Fidno opens the door to leave, the hall is awash in the intense brightness of the midday sun. And once again Ahl wonders if he is doing the right thing, liaising with criminals.

As Ahl approaches, No-Name frowns, like someone used to wearing spectacles. It's plain he's not accustomed to anyone doing anything without his say-so. The closer Ahl gets to the high chair No-Name is sitting in, the weirder it all looks. Almost hilarious.

No-Name says, "Please sit."

But there is nowhere to sit, save a lounge area at the other end of the hall, furnished with an ottoman and a plush carpet dotted with cushions propped up against the walls. Is this where No-Name chews *qaat* with his pals? Does an emperor have pals?

What a day and what humiliation! Ahl crouches down, knees creaking, wondering if children have any notion what troubles one goes through for them.

With a trace of a grin around his lips, No-Name says, "Tell me everything about your nephew."

"My son, actually."

"I am sure Fidno described him as your nephew," No-Name says.

"That may be so, but he is my son."

"That changes my perspective on things."

"I am not his father. His mother is my wife. But I raised him."

No-Name takes all this in. His right foot shakes as though it has its own mind.

"What else did Fidno get wrong, before we move on?"

Ahl shrugs his shoulders in a search-me gesture.

"Tell me about your son, all that I need to know."

Ahl tells him.

"Have you a photo of the runaway youth?"

Ahl produces it.

"What's his date and place of birth?"

Ahl tells him.

"What are his mother's and your full three names?"

Ahl supplies him with these, wondering how No-Name can possibly remember such details without taking notes or having a secretary do so. Is he being made a fool of, or does No-Name already know where and who Taxliil is?

"What is the name of the imam at the mosque in Minnesota who recruited him?"

Ahl answers the question fully, with details.

"Do you know the names of his fellow jihadis?"

Ahl shakes his head.

"He didn't know the twenty other recruits from Minnesota and nearby?"

Ahl says, "I don't know; we don't know."

"How do we reach you if we wish to do so?" No-Name asks, and Ahl provides him with a host of phone numbers.

"How long have you been here?"

Ahl tells him.

"When do you leave?"

Ahl shrugs. "It all depends on my success."

"Or lack of it," No-Name says. Then, "Fidno has mentioned that Malik, a journalist, is in Mogadiscio."

"What about Malik?"

"Is he likely to come here?"

"Why do you ask?"

"Because I'd like to meet him."

"He hasn't said he will come and visit here, but I will make sure to introduce you to him if he does."

"I look forward to that."

Ahl finds himself sitting uncomfortably forward, supporting his body on his knees, like a devotee at an ashram.

He says, "If I may ask a question, please?"

"Go ahead."

A current of worry goes through his body, lodging for a moment or so in his heart, then in his head. One indiscreet question from him might jeopardize everything. Nonetheless, he asks it. "Why did you agree to see me?"

No-Name presses his forehead and winces, as if thinking of the reasons or sharing them with Ahl is causing him pain. His eyes closed, he says, "One, because I am doing Fidno, my pal, a favor."

"That's very good of you."

"Two, because sometime in the past few days someone spoke three names in my presence—I cannot recall in what context. But Taxliil's name was one of them, and the name stuck, as I have never known anyone else with it. So when Fidno came to me, I agreed to step in and to assist. I'll do all I am able to help you find Taxliil."

As if on cue, a mobile phone rings in another room. No-Name shifts in his high chair in a manner that suggests to Ahl that their conversation is at an end. The uniformed young man enters from the back, and offers Ahl a hand to help him straighten up. Then he leads him out to where Fidno is waiting in the jalopy.

———

Fidno takes off in the direction of Bosaso, driving even faster than before and appearing agitated. He wants to hear Ahl's impression of No-Name. Ahl thinks that extortionists, like whores attempting to collect up front the fee for services not yet rendered, and then to render them speedily, are prone to presenting their bills much too fast.

"I don't know what answer to give," he says.

Fidno says, "No-Name has extensive connections among top people in Puntland and beyond—insurgents, pirates, the lot."

Ahl feels a little reassured by this, but he is not at all certain that he is any closer to locating Taxliil than before. Partners in crime: Fidno, No-Name, and all their associates! Then he adds, "Let's say I am more optimistic than before."

"All will work out well, you'll see."

Ahl senses that Fidno is now softening him for a hit; he can't wait to hear it.

Fidno says, "Please ring Malik and let him know."

"Don't worry. I will. Later."

"*Now*, please. Ring him *now*."

"What do I tell him?"

"Ask him if he'll see me, when and where."

"I'll call him later."

Fidno's voice takes on a threatening tone. "Please call him. Now."

Ahl opens his window to a blast of wind and sand. The land they are driving through is more desolate than he remembers from the journey down. The truth is, he has been hesitant to call Malik since they disagreed about the wisdom of his interviewing TheSheikh, with Ahl insisting that family trumps career. Given the choice, Ahl would prefer to make the call in the privacy of his hotel room, alone, but he feels he has no choice but to telephone Malik now.

He dials and lets it ring. The line is busy and he disconnects, promising Fidno that he'll try again shortly. Then he switches on the car radio, and they catch the tail end of a news bulletin. There has been fierce fighting between the Ethiopian occupying army and the insurgents, with high civilian casualties. He tries again, and this time Malik answers on the fourth ring. Ahl puts him on speakerphone so that Fidno can hear the exchange. He tells his brother about the meeting with No-Name and assures him that it has made him feel optimistic. Then he asks, "Have you thought when you might have time to meet up with Fidno? You could interview him here in Puntland. If you are unable to fly out here, he is willing to come down to Mogadiscio."

But Malik is in no mood at the moment. He's just learned about the death of yet another journalist, thanks to yet another roadside bomb. "Why don't we speak later in the evening," he says, "and we'll figure it out then? Looks like he'll have to come to Mogadiscio, as I won't be able to come to Puntland."

"Good."

"I'm delighted things are working out."

"But tell me about yourself, Malik," Ahl says anxiously. "Are you hurt or anything?"

"Just shocked, traumatized—out of sync."

They agree to talk more in the evening, and say good-bye.

After he hangs up, there is silence for long enough that Ahl assumes Fidno isn't going to speak. But just then Fidno says, "It'll give me joy to go to Mogadiscio. Because I am so eager, maybe I'll take the first available flight. But I won't book it until I hear from you. And there is a small possibility I'll want to bring along a friend to the interview."

"That's the first I've heard of a friend going with you."

"We'll talk, you and I," Fidno promises. "There is time yet."

Ahl stares at Fidno in anger and mistrust. Of course, Malik will be upset at this development. But Malik is family, and he will do what is best for Taxliil in the end. Or, at least, Ahl hopes he will.

———

At the hotel, Ahl alights, bones aching, eyes smarting from the day's heat and exhaustion. He is about to bid Fidno farewell when a young woman, demurely dressed, head covered, face veiled, but only cursorily, comes out of the reception. She makes a beeline for Fidno, whispers to him, and stands to the side, waiting.

Fidno says, "If you have a moment, let me introduce you to Wiila." I believe you met her on your flight. And then you'll remember we saw her together at the *qaat* stall, with Warsame."

Tired, but thinking it too impolite to walk away, Ahl takes the hand Wiila is holding out for him to shake. But even decked out in traditional garb, her bearing takes him back to the nightclub in Djibouti, when the prostitute tried to chat him up. Wiila has the same knowingness. And, given that she is a friend to Fidno, Ahl decides to be wary.

Ahl says, "I'm delighted to make your acquaintance. As Fidno said the other day, some of us make the world smaller than it is in reality."

But when he makes as if to leave, Fidno grips his hand. "Come and buy us some coffee, some tea. We're your guests. Where are your manners?"

Aware that it won't do the business of locating Taxliil any good to decline, yet conscious, too, that he will be courting unnecessary danger by putting too much trust in them, Ahl opts for a middle way: cooperation and vigilance.

They sit in the gazebo. Fidno and Ahl order coffee, Wiila a soft drink. While they are waiting for their order, Wiila explains why she was tearful on the day she and Ahl met. "My younger brother had been killed by Shabaab earlier that day. I am still mourning him."

Ahl recalls that brief encounter and wonders why Fidno has the look of someone who has unearthed a gem to present to him.

He asks, "What do I have to do with any of this?"

"You don't."

Fidno nods his head in Wiila's direction, dismissing her. Ahl catches the slightest trace of a smile that makes her lips twitch and her eyes brighten slightly, like someone who has fulfilled her part of a contract and is now free. She gets to her feet, bows her head a little to both men, and with her soft drink untouched, she walks away.

"What game are you playing?" Ahl asks Fidno when she is gone.

Fidno says, "This is simple as home cooking, labor intensive but worth it, worth every pound in the mortar, every grain of salt."

Ahl presumes he is being duped the moment Fidno resorts to fancy words. But still, the man has him in a corner. So he lets himself sound only mildly annoyed when he asks, "Where are you going with all this?"

Fidno says, "My intention isn't to involve you. But I want to bring in Malik. Dangerous, yes, but worth the effort."

Ahl's voice strains under the weight of his worry. He says, "Do you want him to talk to Wiila?"

Fidno can't help putting on airs, like a student straining to be more clever than his mentor. "There is her older brother, Muusa Ibraahim, a former pirate, who worked with me. I'd like Malik to interview him. Muusa comes as part of a package. Malik will have spoken to a funder of piracy, and he has agreed to speak to me—I, being all things to pirates and piracy, Muusa is the real article, and he has a lot to say about Shabaab."

This has been a day of emotional chaos, in which Ahl's hope of locating Taxliil has been raised, then jeopardized unless he caters to Fidno's extortionate greed. When will it all end?

"I'll talk to Malik later today," he says.

Then Fidno brings out his mobile phone, turns it on, and searches for a number, which Ahl presumes to be Muusa Ibraahim's. Ahl takes down the number as Fidno dictates it.

The day's business done, as if he and Ahl are jolly companions deep in their cups, Fidno says, with a mischievous grin spreading down to his chin, "Wiila has told me that she won't be averse to be of service to you, if you are in the mood to be entertained in this dreadful hotel. Say the word and I'll send her over."

Ahl is at a loss for the appropriate response, but then it comes to him. He says, "I had no idea you were into pimping, too."

Fidno doesn't take offense. He says, "Just checking. Just offering. These are tempting times, and I know family men who won't say no to Wiila."

And then Ahl is up and off, and Fidno, for once, settles their bill.

AS BEFORE, THE DOOR TO AHL'S ROOM IS LOCKED FROM THE IN- side. After he knocks on it repeatedly, the TV programmer lets him in. Ahl can't help but feel amused at this point, especially once he has reflexively checked that he still has his money belt, and felt the weight of the laptop he is carrying. Then, as if to prove a point, he pretends to check on the state of his suitcase, which has had its lock torn off. Without waiting for the TV programmer to leave, he telephones his wife's cousin, Xalan, to ask her to please come for him as soon as she can. He doesn't explain why, he just wants to leave. *Basta!*

He moves about the room, picking up a towel, running the tap, and with the luxury of a man who has a lot of time to kill, washing his hands and his face. Seemingly unperturbed and unflustered, the TV program-mer stays in the room, fiddling with the knobs and taking no notice of Ahl's presence or his need for some privacy. Maybe the never-ending conflict in this country won't tail off until its burglars master their art, Ahl thinks. Maybe the foolishness displayed by the nation's politicians, its so-called intellectuals, its clan elders and imams, and its rudderless youths is contagious; everyone in the land seems somehow lacking in horse sense.

His mobile rings: Xalan is downstairs, waiting. Ahl awkwardly picks up his suitcase with the broken lock, not bothering to check if any of his shirts, pairs of trousers, underwear, or sandals are missing. He leaves the door to the room open, the TV man still tinkering with the set, the volume high, then low.

Xalan is a joy to behold: she is dressed in a caftan, arms showing, her figure handsome and her smile beautiful. She meets him halfway and they both laugh when their attempt at a hug fails and they both stumble. She carries his laptop down and leaves him to struggle with the suitcase with the broken lock.

There is no one at the reception, so they decide to put the suitcase in the trunk and wait by the vehicle, in the hope that one of the receptionists will show up and alert the manager to bring Ahl the bill. As they wait, Ahl tells Xalan all that has transpired so far.

"It's shocking," she says. "He's still in the room? In any event, I am delighted you are moving in with us."

Then they have a laugh about it.

"I don't look forward to having further altercations with the hotel staff, including the hotel manager. Most likely, he won't believe me if I tell him: it's my word against the TV tinkerer's. And I suppose his coworkers will gang up against me, an alien guest, never mind that I speak Somali."

When the manager arrives with the bill, Xalan studies the squiggly figures, frowning; among other things, Ahl is being charged for TV repair, along with the use of sheets and towels and meals he did not order. The combined shakedown comes to a lot, but Ahl knows that you do not negotiate with extortionists, and this price is par for the course for a diaspora Somali visiting home from the "dollar countries." If he refuses to pay and reports the rip-off to the authorities, he stands little chance of success. Later, he'll be made to pay at gunpoint, possibly with his life. Woe betide the man who denies his bodyguard's request for a loan, or the journalist whose newspaper refuses the ransom asked when his kidnapping happens to occur on the day he is scheduled to leave for home.

But Xalan won't be cowed. "What if he says he won't pay?" she asks.

"I'd advise him not to take that route," the manager says, in a tone meant to intimidate.

An argument ensues when Ahl points out that he had already reported the programmer's misdemeanor to a one-eyed man at the reception and the manager denies that any such person works in the hotel.

"Well, that's something," Ahl says with a sigh.

Inevitably, Xalan and the manager exchange harsh words, after the manager accuses Ahl of lying. She threatens to call the police and the manager retorts that the police are in his pocket and, in fact, he'll have her arrested if they don't pay up and leave.

Meanwhile, the heat has grown unbearable. Ahl's shirt sticks to his back; even his hair is damp with sweat. He hasn't the proper hardiness for this situation. He remembers hearing of an incident in which armed youths, too weak to carry their loot home, forced their victims to load the plunder into their own vehicles and, since the thieves did not know how to drive, to chauffeur them home with it. He doesn't want to lose sight of why he is here, and to him the sum demanded is paltry. He insists on paying it in full, in dollars, and adds a tip for good measure. At last they are free.

———

Out of the hotel grounds, Xalan tells him the harrowing story of a Somali friend visiting from Nairobi. "Our friend visits Puntland. He's invested a great deal of time and money here," she says. "In fact, he is a founding member of the autonomous state, a highly revered homeboy and a businessman of great intelligence and cunning. He rents a car to travel from Bosaso and Gaalkacyo, and they make several detours. With him are two armed escorts the rental company insists he takes along, and two other men, both relatives of his, getting a free ride home.

"Well, you know what an amazing landscape Puntland has. At one point on the journey, our friend stops to gathers a handful of rocks with exquisite shapes. You see, we Puntlanders are of the unshakable belief that our region is rich in oil, gas, and minerals, and that even our stones are precious—if only we had them analyzed. He puts several stones into his bag, announcing to everybody within hearing that these must contain some treasure more precious than gold. He'll take them to Nairobi; then, depending on the outcome, maybe to Europe, to find out their value.

"He returns to Nairobi with the samples. He shows the rocks around, and resigns himself to the fact that they are not worth anything. His wife and business partner finds a use for them in her office as paperweights.

"Several months later, our friend returns to Puntland. And guess what—three of the men who were with him when he gathered the rocks present themselves at the friend's house where he is being put up and demand their share of the money he made from the sale of the rocks. He tells them off. They take him hostage and hold him incommunicado for a couple of days, accusing him of shortchanging them. The clan members intervene to set him free."

———————

Ahl's phone rings, but when he sees Fidno's number on the screen, he decides not to answer. He hasn't told Yusur about his dealings with the man, for fear of raising her hopes and dashing them, and so far he hasn't told Xalan much. He will tell Yusur when his efforts bear fruit;

he will share the news with Xalan only when he is certain there is no possibility of a setback. He worries that keeping all these secrets will eventually get to him, especially when he is under Xalan's roof—make him ill, complicate matters.

He fears Xalan's tough loneliness, though—the aftereffect of her horrible experience in Mogadiscio, which Yusur described to him in some detail. She can be moody and difficult to please, a woman of discomforting character, the sort Ahl would prefer to avoid. Since Warsame is seldom in the picture, either running his business or chewing *qaat*, he'll have to become skillful at navigating her troubled waters.

The phone rings again, and again Ahl doesn't take the call. Xalan trains her gentle eyes on him, grinning. Maybe she is thinking that it is a woman who is calling, and Ahl does not want to take the call in her presence. He's about to say something to correct that impression when a small, colorful bird alights on his side of the window and then, unfathomably, manages to hang on, staring piercingly into his eyes. He falls under the spell of the bird and watches it, mesmerized, as the bird does the figures seven, eight, nine, one, and three. Is this feathered friend communicating mysteries he is unable to decipher? He is jolted out of his reverie when the car swerves, and he realizes that Xalan has almost run over a pedestrian ambling along in the center of the road.

She stops the car, digs in the glove compartment, then fumbles in her handbag and takes out an inhaler, inhales, exhales, and then sits back. Apparently her asthma, the consequence, probably, of the trauma of rape, is acting up. He waits, averting his eyes and staying silent.

She drives for a quarter of a kilometer and then turns the car around and, back at the scene of the near accident, pulls over and puts her hand in her handbag. This time she takes out a thick wad of cash, opens the door, and before Ahl can say or do anything, dashes over to the pedestrian, who is now walking alongside the road, to apologize.

The man is embarrassed himself, and apparently thinks that he was as much at fault as she was, as he initially refuses the cash. At her insistence, though, he finally accepts the gift with both hands, demonstrating his gratitude for the unexpected windfall.

Ahl thinks about the bird's appearance. An epiphany? He feels that things are falling into place. He takes the bird's performance as a herald of Taxliil's imminent arrival, the nearness of his hour. He doesn't share his feeling with anyone, not least Xalan, not wanting to interpret wrongly, or to tempt fate.

On returning to the car and taking the wheel, Xalan mumbles something about "going crackers." Ahl pats her on her wrist, as if to reassure her that everything will be all right. She relaxes her grip on the steering wheel, but doesn't move: she needs more time to gather herself.

She says, "One minute I feel absolutely positive about myself and comfortable within myself, and the next minute everything goes haywire."

She starts the car and drives on in silence for a few minutes, then stops in front of a gate and honks. A man in fatigues opens it. Driving in, she is a different person again: a woman in charge. She gives instructions to the man to carry in Ahl's suitcase and computer bag. She calls to the maid, inquiring if the room she has prepared for Ahl is ready.

———

In the upstairs guest room, Ahl checks his phone. Three missed calls from Fidno, and two from an unknown caller. What can all these calls mean? He anchors in his mind the thought that whatever happens, he will try to save Taxliil from his own foolishness. Otherwise, what is the point of this mad expedition?

His attempt to suppress a sneeze starts to sound like a cat choking on a fishbone. He wipes away the moisture from around his mouth with the back of his hand. He sniffs repeatedly, like a man with whom the snuff he has just taken doesn't agree. He quotes to himself one of his favorite lines of poetry, to hold at bay the waves of anxiety that he fears will engulf him: "'I am everything that is around me.'"

He unpacks and sits on the edge of the bed, repeating the line several more times. Who was the poet, Wallace Stevens or Robert Frost? What is around him but the misery of a nation down in the dumps? He paces the room like an undertaker measuring the size of a coffin for a corpse, but he can't bring himself to make the call to Fidno, afraid he will hear bad news. Again he thinks of the bird landing on the side of his window; and again he can't decide if its arrival is a harbinger of good or ill.

There is a heavy knock on the door but he doesn't answer at first, still gripped by a sense of foreboding. Then he hears Xalan saying, ". . . food on the table."

———

He joins her in the dining room, not to eat, but to be with her—simply as a gesture of goodwill. He wishes he could bring up the subject of her missing nephew, Ahmed-Rashid, but he doesn't want to upset her. Still, he thinks it odd that she hasn't alluded to him at all, even when they are discussing Taxliil's disappearance.

"Where is Warsame today?" he asks.

"Chewing *qaat* at a friend's home," she says. There is a glass of grapefruit juice at Ahl's place. He takes a sip but says that he cannot eat because his stomach is upset. As if to prove it, he squeezes his stomach, which makes ugly noises. Xalan finds this amusing, and she laughs.

"You haven't eaten since breakfast."

"Maybe later," he says.

"Maybe the water here is hard on your stomach," she says. "Would you like a glass of bottled mineral water?"

"I've no problem with the water," he says.

"Let us have tea, then."

She instructs the housekeeper to make tea for three. Tea for three? But who is the third? Again a line of poetry, this time from T. S. Eliot, intrudes—"'Who is the third who walks always beside you?'" Ahl continues the poem silently, allowing his mind to be hostage to it, keeping him away from worrying thoughts. How curious and also how interesting that Xalan hasn't shared with him who this third party might be. He decides, however, not to quiz her, as that would be bad manners. He senses that something out of the ordinary, something of great value and help, is taking place. First a mysterious bird, and now a mysterious third. Ahl's heart beats, now not so much with anxiety as with expectancy.

Then, as though on cue, they hear a loud banging on the outside gate, and the sound of it opening and closing. Ahl waits, looking up at a spot on the ceiling, avoiding Xalan's gaze. The visitor enters, a young man. Xalan jumps up and wraps herself around him as though he were a long-lost son. She weeps with joy. Then the visitor embraces Ahl.

He is a young man a few years Taxliil's senior, tall and gaunt, with considerable facial hair. His bodily movements are extremely anxious, like those of someone on the run, and there is an untamed wildness to his eyes. Despite the joyful expression etched on his features, he also has fear written all over him. His disquiet is immense.

Ahl suffers anxious moments as he stares at the two of them touching, an image that instantaneously brings tears to his eyes and the memory of little Taxliil falling asleep in his arms. Ahl is utterly confused, so confused that he asks himself if either Fidno or No-Name, in their wish to keep their side of the bargain, have sent this young fellow to him in error. And because he cannot decide either way, he waits in hope that a framework in which he can make sense of all this will emerge out of the muddle.

He sees that Xalan is gripping the visitor by the wrist, as if he might run off. Now she pulls him forward, his elbow in her clasp.

No longer able to restrain himself, Ahl asks Xalan a run of questions. Who is this young man, where has he come from, and why is Xalan excited to welcome him, embrace him?

Xalan says, "His name is Ahmed. Ahmed-Rashid. This is my nephew."

The young man pulls away, as if offended. Then he stands apart from Xalan and puts some physical distance between them. He says, "No, my name is no longer Ahmed. It hasn't been Ahmed for a long while now."

"To what name do you answer, then?" Ahl asks.

"My name is Saifullah," the young man responds.

Something resembling clarity is beginning to emerge for Ahl, a clarity that allows him to see the young man for what he is: a religious renegade, a zealot with a vision.

"Is Saifullah your nom de guerre?" he asks.

Nodding, Saifullah says, "I'm no longer the person I used to be."

"How did you get here?"

"I traveled incognito," Saifullah says.

"From?"

"Nowhere in particular."

Saifullah's evasiveness strikes a warning chord in Ahl.

"And where are you going?"

"I am going to my heavenly destiny."

An expression of fresh dread steals over Xalan. She looks from Ahl to Saifullah. Then once again she wraps herself around Saifullah, embracing him as if he is her beloved embarking on an arduous journey from which he may never return. Weepy, she clings to him and says, "Does my sister know you are here?"

Saifullah says, "My mom knows everything."

Xalan stops crying. She dries her face, wiping away her tears. Then she lets go of him, sniffs, sits down, and asks, "What did she say?"

"You know what my mother is like."

There is hardness to her voice when Xalan says, "Tell me how she is. We haven't seen each other for a very long time."

Ahl prepares to leave in order to give them privacy. Xalan, however, beckons to him not to go. Instead she says, "Tell me what your mum is like now. I know her to be a devout woman, reclusive, prayerful. But what is her position on you deciding to go to your heavenly destiny?"

"I'm afraid you'll have to ask her yourself."

"She doesn't approve, does she?"

"I suggest you get her to tell you her thoughts herself."

Ahl senses that it is his moment to step in with his burning question. "Do you happen to know my son, Taxliil?"

Saifullah stares at Ahl, as if he does not appreciate the interruption. He catches Xalan's eyes, but she looks away, and down at the floor. But then he says simply, "Yes, I do know Taxliil."

Ahl reacts in silence, more in shock than relief, at Saifullah's admission. His eyes dim, as if in concentration, but he cannot get any words out. After a long pause, he asks slowly, "Where and when did you last see him?"

Saifullah says, "We've served together, he and I, in the same contingent in a training camp close to Kismayo when he first got there."

"How was he when you last saw him?"

"He was in good health apart from the trouble he was having with his eyes. He had broken his glasses within a week of arriving. Meanwhile, his sight has deteriorated."

"And when and where did you last see him?"

"I can't recall when and where. We moved a lot, went back and forth between camps, slept somewhere one night and then off at dawn, after the Subh prayer."

"Otherwise, you reckon he is well?"

Saifullah replies, "He has some other personal problems, which have caused him trouble he could do without."

"What is that?"

"He is a soft touch, that's what."

"In what way is he a soft touch?" Ahl asks.

"Please, no more questions," Saifullah says. "I'm not authorized to speak of this or other related matters."

As he turns as if to go, Xalan says, "How about a bowl of spaghetti with Bolognese? Faai will make it."

Xalan explains that Saifullah has known Faai, her maid, from childhood, and he was a great favorite whom she plied with delicacies and sweets. Now it is Ahl's turn to watch, as the two of them visit a nonpolemical aspect of their past.

Saifullah is excited. "Where did you find her?"

"Here in Bosaso, at a camp for the internally displaced," Xalan replies. "She lived in a shack and we found her just by chance."

"How I loved the Bolognese she made!"

"She's just made some."

"First tea, with lots of sugar," Saifullah says.

"Then spaghetti with Faai's Bolognese?"

"Where can I have a lie-down?" he says.

"Upstairs, in the spare room."

Just before Saifullah goes upstairs, Faai enters the living room, her hands stuffed into her apron pockets. She stares at Saifullah, and then at Xalan.

"Look at him, our Ahmed," Xalan says.

Saifullah doesn't bother correcting her. Instead, he takes one long stride toward the maid, who does not recognize him at first. Then recognition lights her features and he lifts her off the floor into a warm hug. They are a funny sight, he double her height, she twice his girth. When he lets go of her, she picks up his thin wrists and then cups his gaunt cheeks with her hands.

Faai says, "Look at you. Have you, too, been in a refugee camp or a detention center? Why, you are a beanpole, so thin!"

Xalan hastily changes the subject, not wanting to upset Saifullah or prompt him to flee. But Faai insists on knowing. "Where have you come from? Not from a detention center, where they hardly feed the inmates on proper food?"

"I am all right, actually," Saifullah says.

Faai, ululating, says, "A miracle is at hand."

Ahl shares Faai's sentiment, but doesn't say it.

Xalan says to Saifullah, "Ahmed was your grandfather's name on your father's side and Rashid your grandmother's name on your mother's side, two beautiful Muslim names. Why drop them for Saifullah?"

"The name is a perfect fit," he says.

Faai clasps him more tightly and calls him by his old name several times, until tears run down her cheeks. Then she asks, "Now, what kind of name is Saifullah?"

No one answers and everyone looks at her as though she has made an unpardonable gaffe.

Then Saifullah says, "I am tired. I am off to bed."

Xalan says, "That hungry body needs some food."

"Where is the Bolognese, then?" Saifullah says, and at last Faai goes back to the kitchen to fetch it.

Rationally, Ahl doesn't know what to make of all this, but he has the strong sense that it augurs well that he has met Saifullah, and he can't wait until all is revealed. But he thinks worriedly that whatever else he may say or do, Saifullah's behavior is going to prove unpredictable. And if this is true of Saifullah, what can he expect of Taxliil?

———

With Saifullah upstairs, Ahl and Xalan sit in weighty silence, assessing the significance of what has just happened. Ahl wonders if his expectations should be inflated or deflated by what he has heard about Taxliil.

Xalan repeats for his benefit a few salient facts: that Saifullah has been missing longer than Taxliil, and was rumored to have died in a failed suicide bombing. Or been court-martialed by Shabaab and executed.

Then one or the other of them changes the subject and they speak of how bizarre it is that the Shabaab minders choose such archaic names.

Ahl says, "I am delighted to hear Taxliil's news, even if I can't decide what to expect next."

Xalan says, "For a second, I thought Saifullah might bolt out the door like a frightened horse. Or that he might seize up and not speak, or run off and disappear as mysteriously as he appeared."

A brief silence follows.

Then Ahl says, "Funny, him saying that he is not authorized to speak on the matter. What manner of bureaucratese is that?"

Xalan says, "You know what is worrying me?"

"What's worrying you?"

"He has the look of someone not meant to last."

Ahl concurs, "As if he is on a mission."

"I can't bring myself to think about it."

The thought troubles Ahl and he tries to fight it off by taking the opposite view, if only because he wants to believe that he will see Taxliil, too. "Maybe once he has slept off his nightmares, Saifullah will be more willing to talk to us."

Xalan says, "I must visit his mother."

Up in his room, Ahl makes several more attempts to reach Malik and Fidno. The messages he gets are identical: the subscriber is not in range. What on earth can that mean? At last he reaches Malik, and brings him up to speed, summarizing all that has happened.

Malik sounds optimistic. "I am sure everything will work out in the end. Taxliil will return, as runaways often do, unexpectedly, apologetic, and promising not to do it again. Look at Saifullah."

Ahl gains courage from listening to what Malik has to say and is delighted and relieved to find his brother in a more receptive mood than he expected. It is then that he says to him, "Fidno has offered to introduce you to one Muusa Ibraahim, otherwise universally known as Marduuf, a former pirate, who also has it in for Shabaab, because they killed his younger brother, a teenage conscript of the group. Are you interested in talking to him?"

Malik is enthusiastic about the idea and takes down Marduuf's contact details, although he cannot say when he will meet or talk to him.

MALIK RINGS THE BELL NEXT TO THE OUTSIDE GATE AT BILE AND Cambara's, and then looks back at Qasiir parked within view of the gate, waiting. Qasiir wants to make sure that Malik gets in before he drives off.

While waiting for someone to appear or for the lock on the gate to be released via the intercom, activating the dogs' barking, Malik recalls watching *101 Dalmatians* on DVD with his baby daughter in his lap. At one she was too little to understand it, even though she points at real dogs excitedly, and imitates their barking. To amuse her, he likes to run through a repertoire of different breeds' barks: he can yelp like a collie, woof like an Afghan hound, and bay like a husky.

Cambara's arrival reminds him of where he is. She calls to tell him that she is on her way to open the gate manually, because of a power outage. Approaching, she walks cautiously, as if avoiding puddles, and affects a frown that is really a smile. She has on a pair of indoor shoes and a *guntiino* robe that flatters her, showing bits of flesh and a flash of cleavage when her garment fashionably slips off her shoulder. As she approaches the side gate, though, she pulls up the patterned summery shawl as if to make sure there is no misunderstanding on Malik's part. He turns to wave at Qasiir in the departing car. Cambara passes the bunch of keys to Malik so that he can open the gate from the outside. Their fingers touch accidentally and this produces static electricity. Malik looks away, embarrassed, although Cambara appears unruffled. She walks ahead of him, and neither speaks until they are inside the house and Cambara has restored the key ring to the hook behind the door.

In a rehearsed voice, Malik says, "That death comes early and snatches away our best is a wisdom that many of us do not appreciate until someone dear dies. Of course, it is worse if he is murdered."

Waiting for him to finish, with her hands outstretched, maybe to embrace him, Cambara has the look of someone with fog in her eyes and who can't therefore see more than two feet ahead of her. For an instant, Malik stands so still that it feels as if bits of him have stopped functioning.

Cambara puts life back into him, saying, "Yes!"

Malik goes on. "I've known Dajaal for a short time, yet I will miss him. His death makes me think, What if I die when I have less than a page left to write? Dajaal had plenty of work to do, and some evil person cut his life short."

Just when he had said his say and they are at last ready to embrace, she pricks up her ears and pauses in mid-movement, like a ballerina stopping before completing a pirouette—and backs off. Instead she takes his hand and together they walk forward, she leading, he keeping pace.

"No doubt a difficult man to please, at times harder on himself than on others, Dajaal was a man of such high principles. He was loyal, truthful; he was reliable. We'll miss him terribly. He is *our* story, Bile's and mine. He made our world go around a lot of the time, making our living together easier, even though occasionally he came in between us, causing mild frictions between Bile and me. But I was fond of him, very fond."

Malik says, "I often think how, in fiction, death serves a purpose. I wish I knew the objective of such a real-life death."

———————

Cambara makes two tall drinks and a short one, adds a drop of something to one of the tall glasses—Malik is unsure what, maybe a drop of medicine, for Bile? She gives him one of the tall ones and raises her short one, saying, "To your health."

He asks, "How's Bile been?"

"He is coming down shortly," she announces.

And soon enough, Bile joins them. He is looking much better, if a little nervous; his index and middle fingers rub against his thumb in rhythm with his slow tread, his every step bringing him closer to his goal—a soft chair with a hard back set between Cambara's and Malik's seats. They can't help but be conscious of his gradual progress, but neither wants to focus on it. Malik rises to his feet to offer him a hug.

Cambara offers him the untouched tall drink and she says to him, kissing him on the forehead and then on the lips, "Your drink, my dear, with a drop of your medicine in it."

He holds the edge of the glass to his lower lip and takes a sip, his Adam's apple visibly moving, then another thirsty swallow.

Just then a single rocket falls close by. The house trembles slightly, the windowpanes shaking in their frames, the bulbs of the chandelier lightly knocking against one another with a tinkling sound that, to Malik, distantly recalls one of his daughter's windup toys.

"Well, what do you say to that?" Malik says.

Bile, who obsessively keeps abreast of news of the fighting by listening to HornAfrik, has heard that some of the rockets are aimed in the general direction of the villa where the Ethiopians and the interim president are based. "Earlier, we could feel one of them flying overhead. Some of those interviewed on the radio talked of being able to identify the house where the insurgents firing the rockets were holed up."

"Then what happened?"

"Then they heard the response coming from the direction of the presidential villa, with the Ethiopians employing heavier bombs, deadlier and causing more damage."

"I've known rockets to miss their targets in the wars I've covered," Malik offers. "And as a consequence there are civilian casualties."

"Here neither of the warring parties cares," Bile says. "The Ethiopians delight in causing more Somali deaths, and the insurgents, as religionists, by their very nature, are equally unpardonably brutal."

"According to the radio reports, many of the bombs did in fact miss their intended destination," Cambara says. "They cause enormous civilian casualties."

"I am sure that it will interest Malik to visit some of the homes destroyed, and learn about the people whose lives are cut short," Bile says.

"Shabaab assassinated Dajaal," Cambara says.

"And the Ethiopians bomb and kill civilians."

Cambara then adds, "Indiscriminately."

Meanwhile, Bile, adjusting in his seat, unwittingly pushes away one of his slippers and then his feet search blindly for them, only to kick them farther, rather than bring them nearer. Malik is quick to get up and help recover the slipper slithering out of Bile's reach.

Bile says, "Thanks."

Malik offers his condolences for Dajaal, and Bile stammers a few almost inaudible words in reply, nearly spilling his drink as he says them. "Here I am useless and living, and there he was very useful— and dead. We have the tendency to self-destruct as a people."

"He was wonderful to me, generous," Malik says.

Bile inquires about Malik's writing, the research and interviews, and if Qasiir is working out well so far. Malik's positive replies delight Bile, and he drinks to everyone's health.

"We want you to move into our house," Bile says, "now that the two-room flat is empty of its troubled occupant."

"What's become of Robleh?" Malik asks.

Cambara answers. "He's gone."

"I'd say good riddance," Bile says.

"He'll get his just desserts," she says.

"He was nothing but trouble," Malik says.

Bile says, "Yet Cambara wouldn't throw him out."

Malik is thinking about changing the subject, when they hear another bomb exploding in the vicinity that makes the house shake. But Bile won't leave the topic alone. He pursues it with vengeful venom. Malik thinks they are living on edge, amid all the bombs falling, and because Dajaal's death has brought their own mortality home to them.

Bile says, "Robleh had the habit of bringing home neophytes from the mosques, and of telling them right in our presence that he has frequently advised us to 'take the vow.' A lie like any other, one he couldn't say to us alone and, what's more, didn't. I would have killed the fool if I could."

For a moment, Cambara resembles a cat in the gaze of a snake and she makes a hissing sound. Then, finding things to do in the kitchen, she departs, visibly annoyed. Malik is convinced that it won't be the end of the stories about Robleh. He has a mind to pursue a tangentially related theme: Somalis with foreign passports leaving the country in the wake of the Ethiopian invasion. He wants to write an article about how they are treated at the Kenyan border, and he is sad that he has to give the topic a wide berth for now. Maybe Qasiir can find him someone to interview.

Cambara serves them a light repast of clear lemongrass soup and prawns. They eat right where they are, balancing their plates in their laps—Bile's on a tray, so that he does not have to move, as his knees are bothering him. They sip their soup with hardly a sound, not even the clink of a spoon against a bowl. Malik has a worry knocking about in his head.

"I've meant to talk about Dajaal," Malik says.

"What about him?" Bile asks.

Malik says, "Before Jeebleh left, he and I agreed that we would set up some sort of remuneration—on a monthly basis, the equivalent of a year's pay—for Dajaal. Now that he has been murdered, I do not know what to do about the remuneration. I should have asked Qasiir, but it would be helpful to have the view of someone outside the immediate family circle."

"What are you trying to ask?" Bile says.

"Did Dajaal have any family who could benefit from the funds, if I set it up?"

"We were his family," Bile says, as if to preempt any further discussion of the matter. "I wouldn't want you to bother," he adds.

"I owe him his pay, though."

Bile says, "You're our guest, so don't worry."

"Jeebleh and I . . . ," Malik starts, and trails off.

"Please," says Bile.

Cambara turns to him. "Let's hear him out."

Bile says firmly, "You stay out of it."

Malik thinks that if the herdsman takes delight in talking of his camels, the Don Giovanni of his exploits, the statesman of his political savvy, the war correspondent of the risks taken, then those like Bile and Cambara, who have known nothing but strife, for lack of something else to focus on, risk turning on each other. Again he changes the subject in an effort to avoid an argument.

He says to Bile, "How did you and Dajaal meet?"

There is a rough edge to Bile's tone when he speaks, as if he were clearing his throat after swallowing a fishbone. He says, "Dajaal and I met a day or two into the civil war. The gates of the prison where I had spent almost two decades, half of it with Jeebleh, had been flung open. Knife-brandishing street urchins were threatening to seize the car I was traveling in, and the money I had stolen from the house where I had taken refuge after my escape. As luck had it, Dajaal drove by just then. He was in military uniform and armed. He suspected the urchins were up to no good, and he intervened. Then he helped me find Shanta, my sister. And when I set up the Refuge with the stolen money, I made him my factotum. I loved him: he cultivated to perfection the uncanny knack of being just where his timely intervention was needed."

Cambara drops her spoon. Bile and Malik look at her, and she blurts out, "Me, too!"

"You, too, what? What're you saying?" Bile asks.

Cambara replies, "Dajaal's first words to me were, 'Are there any problems with which you need help?' I had just fought off the menacing advances of several boys who pulled up alongside me in a car as I was on my way to this property, which at the time was home to a minor warlord. They'd offered me a ride and then tried to force themselves on me, saying, 'Don't you want it?' I met Dajaal at the very moment I had managed to get them to drop me off, and I knew instantly that my life had taken a decisive turn. Dajaal would go on to help me recover the property."

Malik feels he doesn't need to add his own experiences with Dajaal, although he could sing the man's praises for hours. He says, "I wonder why it never occurred to me to ask him if he had a family. It's embarrassing, isn't it?"

"He was so discreet," Cambara says, "one hesitated to ask him questions about his private life or to ask if he had financial or other troubles. Unlike many employees, he never pestered you for a loan or absented himself from work."

"He wasn't an employee," Bile says. "He was family."

"Except he wasn't family," Cambara says.

Bile's eyebrows arch with visible indignation.

Cambara asks, "Do you know what Dajaal did when he left us after dark, darling?"

"No idea," Bile answers. "He was a private man and he wanted it that way."

"Dajaal was, toward the end, a changed man," she says.

"You two didn't always get along well," he says.

"He got touchy," she says.

Bile says, "So is the entire country—nervous, self-murderous, on edge." He raises his voice a little, stressing his points. "Admit it, he was more exposed to the daily menaces than we were. Also, thanks to him, we felt protected. For all we know, Dajaal may have died protecting us."

"It's not that he had ever talked back to me, or showed any dissent to me openly," she says. "He was deferential to me, but I could feel a change in his behavior, his anger toward the world, toward life in general. It was as though he felt the times moving past him."

Bile says, "You would be a changed person, too, if your life was under constant threat and you didn't know when a murderer in a balaclava might come out of the shadows to assassinate you." He pauses for a long time, then asks Cambara, "What is it you're not telling us? Something has eaten into you; something has turned you against Dajaal. What did he do to upset you so?"

She sits up, looking miffed, and then stands, but at first does not seem to know what to do; then she sees Malik holding the plates and disposseses him of them, motioning to him to sit down.

"There is no love without jealousy," she says, addressing herself to Malik. "I wonder if it has ever occurred to Bile how often I've felt redundant when I saw him and Jeebleh together, so relaxed in each other's company, never exchanging an unkind word, their dialogue flowing seamlessly. No question about it: I've felt inessential. Bile looked younger, happier, and more alive chatting to Jeebleh. He appeared more ebullient in Jeebleh's company than in mine, as if he finds me irritating, like a small child with insatiable demands. Alone with me, I sense he is less energetic and talks much less about life-and-death matters, only of what ails him and where. Often, he behaves as if I were his hired nurse."

Then, in the silence that follows, she murmurs a few words, as if to herself, and for an instant she appears embarrassed. Too late to regret her inapt outburst, she strides off toward the kitchen, the plates clattering.

Malik blames the stresses under which Cambara and Bile have been living for her outpouring. Civil war makes excessive demands on those who suffer it, and many snap under the strain.

The silence lasts until she returns to ask if Malik or Bile wants tea or coffee. She gives her profile to Bile, indicating her annoyance.

Bile asks Malik, "Were you present at the last altercation between Dajaal and Gumaad in the apartment? Did you think that Dajaal went too far in provoking Gumaad?"

Thinking that one witness is no witness, and that in any case he can't tell if that altercation led to Dajaal's death, Malik asks Bile, "Does anyone have any idea who murdered him?"

Bile replies, "Qasiir claims to know."

"Does he suspect Shabaab?"

"That's what I gathered from talking to him."

Malik asks, "Does he have concrete evidence?"

"His opinion is based on mere conjecture," Bile says. "Not that that will stop him from acting on it, I fear."

Cambara continues to seem uneasy. She shifts in her chair, then says, "Yet Shabaab and their allies claim to be jihadis, when they do not even behave like Muslims." Then she gets to her feet, as if to leave their presence.

Bile says, "You can't determine that. Only God has the privilege to decide if they are or aren't Muslim."

"Why kill in mosques or in the vicinity of mosques?" she asks, as if the answer to the question might unravel everything.

"The murders are political," Bile says.

"Are these assassinations commissioned by fifth columnists allied to the Courts?" Malik asks.

"According to what Qasiir has told me, they are."

"Is he implying that Dajaal set himself up for it, describing himself publicly as a secularist?" Malik says.

Bile ventures, "Shabaab knew all along where Dajaal stood. He needn't have called himself a secularist. If anything, he was a democrat and therefore a secularist. It is a mystery they didn't kill him sooner."

Malik takes a furtive look at Cambara, assuming with little evidence that unless she occupies center stage, where she is appreciated, pampered, loved, and praised, she is the type who will stand apart, as she does now, listening to their banter as if it concerns someone she doesn't know. He attempts to bring her back in.

"What's your feeling, Cambara? The Courts are out—we know you weren't enamored of them or their hard-line position. Now the Ethiopians are here. What would you say if I asked you what your feelings are today, as matters stand?"

"A plague on both their houses," Cambara mutters.

Bile says, "As the Somali saying goes, 'Drinking milk is unlikely to help you when you choke on water.'"

Cambara says, "Aren't you saying the same thing I am saying, only with proverbs?"

"Perhaps I am saying more than that," Bile says.

"Peace, please!" says Malik.

"I am saying that the Courts will have learned their lesson," Bile retorts. "And if they get a second chance to rule Somalia, they won't be as arrogant and unreasoning as they were the first time. Of course, there will be those who will insist on having an Islamic state at all costs, and there will be splinter groups, this faction against that faction and so on."

"You can't do much with a bad egg. That is what the Courts are, a bad egg," Cambara says, pleased with herself.

"What are the Ethiopians, then?" Bile asks, amused.

"Pollutants farting against the wind," she says.

There is a long silence.

Then Bile says, "The bad-egg image of the Courts is apt. But there are at least possibilities of negotiation. They are now in the political wilderness. They were wrong to assume that weapons from Eritrea would help them defeat Ethiopia here and march all the way to Addis, and take and occupy it. Easier dreamed of than done."

Cambara stares at her fingers, thinking. She says, "You surprise me, darling. You have a soft spot for the Courts. I would never have thought that of you."

"I so loathe the Ethiopian occupation and this interim president who engineered it, I would have the Courts back any day, in their place," Bile says. "Still, I would choke on the water that I may have to drink."

On another day, Malik might stay and enjoy bantering with Bile, especially as he seems to be in better health today. But he retreats into the bathroom to send Qasiir a text message asking him to come for him in a jiffy. When he rejoins Bile and Cambara, he says, "It's past your siesta time, and I have plenty of work to get through. So I'll thank you for the wonderful lunch and company."

Bile says, in a tone of command not to be challenged, "I'll ask Qasiir to bring your things from the apartment. I want you to move into the annex. It's safer here."

"We have everything you require," Cambara says.

Bile adds, "Please, no back talk from you."

"I will move in," says Malik, "but not until tomorrow."

"Why not right away, or tonight at least?"

"I am in the middle of something," Malik says.

"We'll tell the maid to set it all up."

"Tomorrow, then."

———

En route to the apartment—Qasiir at the wheel—Malik notices several missed calls, many of them dating back to last night, and one very long SMS.

In the SMS, Ahl, who says he has sent the same text in an e-mail format, shares his latest with him: that he confirms that he feels more comfortable putting up at Xalan and Warsame's, indirectly suggesting to Malik that he move in with Cambara and Bile—but not clearly spelling it out. Ahl ends with, "Be on guard at all times."

Malik can tell that Qasiir is excited: his eyes keep narrowing, like a shortsighted person concentrating on a faraway spot, and his lips are constantly moving. Malik asks him, "Is everything okay?"

"I've found Marduuf, the former pirate," Qasiir says. "We met at a teahouse. He is a very angry man."

"Do you know where he lives?"

"I know what he does for a living, too. He sells rugs," Qasiir says. "He told me that since he discovered there was more risk than money in piracy, he bought a small pickup truck with what money he had made and set up a rug-selling business."

Malik asks, "When can I meet him?"

"Whenever you like, really."

"You mean as soon as now?" Malik asks, excited.

Qasiir says, "But of course."

"I am a bit exhausted."

"Tell me what suits you, and it'll be done."

Malik thinks it over. A former pirate who has a lot of venom toward Shabaab is a good prospect. He says, "You'll drop me and then fetch him."

They fall silent. Then Malik ventures the question that has been on his mind. "What was your grandfather's home situation? Is your grandmother still alive?"

Qasiir drives in silence for a while, in the attitude of someone taking the measure of a challenge. Finally, he answers, "Grandpa lived alone in a house that was in first-class shape when he bought it. Lately, however, it's begun to fall apart, the roof leaking, the paint flaking, water gathering in puddles, the drainage not functioning. He kept saying he would deal with the structural problems and either rent it out or, if peace came, sell it and buy a one-room apartment. He didn't want to bother fixing it piecemeal."

"Did he have dependents?"

"Not if you're speaking of a wife and children."

"You were his only living relative?"

"May I ask where these questions are leading?"

"You see, before leaving, Jeebleh informed your grandfather that he would set up a monthly check. Did you know about this?" says Malik, who doesn't mention his own discussion with Bile and Cambara, who were also of a similar mind, ready to put some money aside for Dajaal.

Qasiir asks, "That is very good of Uncle Jeebleh. But tell me, what is your question?"

"Did your grandpa have dependents, like a young family—you know, men in this part of the world continue producing until they are dragged off to their graves."

"No, he had no young family."

"None at all?"

Qasiir broaches the subject of his own younger sister, deaf from the noise generated by the helicopters of the U.S. Marines when they invaded the district in which StrongmanSouth had his base. He goes on, "She was a baby then. Sadly though, she hasn't spoken since and can't look after herself. Grandpa was her lifeline after I started my own family. She was dependent on him."

"Let's talk in more detail about it when we have the time," says Malik, seeing that they are nearly at the apartment. "In the meantime, I need to ask: do you know anyone with firsthand information about what happens at the Kenyan border to Somalis with foreign passports who are suspected of being sympathetic to the Courts? Because according to a HornAfrik commentary I heard, there are a handful of FBI officers present when the Kenyan immigration officers conduct the interviews."

"That'll be easy," Qasiir says. "In fact, I know a man, one Liibaan, who served in the National Army with Grandpa and who owns a fleet of buses that I think ply the route between Mogadiscio, Kismayo, and the border crossing. Maybe he will help find us someone, or better still, he may be prepared to talk to you. Leave it with me, and I'll find somebody."

What a beautiful phrase—"Leave it with me"—Malik thinks, especially when spoken with such confidence. He takes comfort in it and delights in its meaning: "Trust me, and everything will be done to your satisfaction."

"You'll call me if you can't find Marduuf?"

Qasiir says, "I know where he lives, I know the mosque at which he prays, the teahouse at which he plays cards with a couple of his pals. I'll get him. So see you shortly."

———————

While waiting for Qasiir to return, Malik wanders aimlessly around the apartment and ends up in his workroom. He picks up a piece of paper from the floor, and a few lines in his own hand catch his eye, part of a longer piece he has completed and sent off to some editor, he cannot recall which: *Somalis are a people in a fix; a nation with a trapped nerve; a country in a terrible mess. The entire nation is caught up in a spiraling degeneracy that a near stranger like me cannot make full sense of. It is all a fib, that is what it is, just a fib.*

On second thought, the scribbler has run a hesitant line through that last sentence and continued with these words: *This conflict has nothing to do with clan or religious rivalries. Rather, it has everything to do with economics. There is a Somali wisdom that it is best that the drum belongs to you, so that you may beat it the way you please. If not, the second best thing is for the drum to belong to someone close, like a relative, who will share it with you. In other words, the Somali civil war has a lot to do with personal gains and personality conflicts.*

———————

Qasiir waits in the TV room, watching sports, while Malik gets down to the business of interviewing Muusa Ibraahim, aka Marduuf.

Marduuf has the deportment of a man whom, if he walked into your home and declared himself the owner, you wouldn't feel fully entitled to challenge. He is of medium height, with a broad chest and the fists of a pugilist. Veins run all over the back of his hands, and they move as he gesticulates. He is soft-spoken, though, for a man his size, and his smile is disarming.

Malik asks him where and when he was born, how many siblings he has, and where, if anywhere, he was schooled. Marduuf's voice is so soft that Malik brings the tape recorder closer to his mouth and adjusts the volume. There is something of the hillbilly to his accent as well, and Malik has to pay a great deal of attention to catch his nuances.

"I was born in Daawo, the twin sister to Eyl," Marduuf says. "I am the firstborn. My family started large, but became reduced to three. Five of my siblings died before they reached the age of four; there were deaths from diseases like TB and malaria, or because there was no doctor in our village to cure a cough. Very few of the children born in our area survived. You had to be very strong from birth to live."

Malik cannot decide if it is nerves or anger, but something makes Marduuf pause every few words, like a reader who has come late to literacy.

"How old are you?"

"I am thirty-five."

"Where are your remaining siblings now?"

"My sister works on planes, as a stewardess."

"And your brother?"

"He is recently dead. Shabaab killed him."

Malik wants to ask why, but he doesn't want to get diverted from his real interest in Marduuf's story.

He asks, "How old was he when he died?"

"He didn't die. He was killed," Marduuf says, with emphasis.

"But how old was he?" Malik says.

Marduuf bristles slightly, then collects himself and says only, "He was small for his size. He had the face of an old man, but the body of a boy. He was sixteen, maybe a little older. Now that he has been killed, he has become large. In our memory."

Malik notes that Marduuf's voice goes up a decibel when he speaks about his murdered brother.

Malik asks, "Do you know Fidno?"

"Yes. I worked with him several times."

"What work did you do for him?"

"I was a pirate," Marduuf says.

"And Fidno—what was he? A pirate, too?"

Malik thinks he catches a slight sneer or even a snicker. Maybe he finds the thought of Fidno becoming a pirate either ridiculous or amusing. Malik waits. Ultimately, his patience pays its dividend.

Marduuf says, "If you are educated, you do not want to become a pirate."

Now that is something new to Malik. He feels certain that it is equally new to many others: that it is the barefaced privation of opportunities, the total absence of any chance to improve your life that turns one into a pirate, especially when one's livelihood has been threatened, interrupted, and destroyed. This runs counter to the theory that the presence of a strong central state guarantees a cessation to piratical exploits. He thinks of maybe one day writing an article titled "Poverty Is the Invention of Piracy."

"What work did Fidno do?"

Finally, Marduuf is in his element, and the words pour out of him, with little stammering and fewer pauses. "Fidno is book-educated," he says. "He reads all the time. Every time we saw him he had a new book in his hands, books in the white man's language, not English. Maybe German, or so somebody said, because he lived in that country, a very powerful man there. When he talked on his mobile in one of these languages, he spoke fast, as fast as water running down a glass window after it has rained. But he is a bad man. He cheats his own pockets.

He is the kind of cheat who puts something in his shirt pocket but makes sure that the 'thief pocket' in the front of his trousers has no idea what is in the shirt pocket. Do you know what I mean? You can't trust him. He is too clever. With money, Fidno is a dangerous man."

"Did you make a lot of money from piracy?"

"Not much," Marduuf says.

"What do the pirates do with what they make?"

"Many buy Surf, a four-wheel drive."

"Did you buy one yourself?"

"I have bought a small pickup. More useful."

"Not lots of money in piracy, eh?"

"We went into piracy when we were told there was a lot of money in it," Marduuf answers. "The BBC says that people on the coast of Somalia were rich, the pirates all getting the most beautiful women, every night a wedding. But I never saw any of the money everyone was talking about, even after working as a pirate for several years. The largest share I received was seven thousand dollars."

Malik asks, "Can you name any of the ships you took hostage?"

"A Korean ship; a very, very big Saudi one, bigger than the biggest house I've seen in Mogadiscio—don't ask me to tell you their names, because I cannot remember them. There was that Spanish one, we caught the Spanish ship fishing in our waters," Marduuf says. "We used small boats to chase them and made gun noises heavier than rockets, and they stopped. We took what the ship workers had in cash, maybe three hundred dollars, we took their smart phones and expensive watches and ate their food and waited for three months. After that we received a thousand dollars each. I swear no more than that."

"What business do you do now?"

"I sell rugs straight to some of the mosques. I have a shop high up in the Bakhaaraha," Marduuf replies. "That is how my youngest brother entered his first mosque. Kaahin was with me, a young thing then, when one day I went into a mosque to conclude a sale. He said when we went out of the mosque into the sun, which beat into our eyes, that he felt comfortable inside the mosque. He left me a week or so later and joined the mosque as a pupil. He said they were teaching him to read the Koran and to write. A month and a half later, he showed me he knew how to write his name in Arabic. I was happy. Then I heard from Wiila, my sister, that someone from our family who also had a son in the mosque had heard that Kaahin had taken an oath and joined a special group inside Shabaab, very secret. He came back to see me less often after that. And then I learned he was dead, killed."

"How did you learn that he was killed?"

"I asked his *mucallim* where Kaahin was."

"What was his teacher's reply?" Malik asks.

"He said that Allah willed Kaahin to die."

"Did you ask the mentor to explain his meaning?"

"That Kaahin was in heaven," Marduuf says.

"Did you ask how he knew Kaahin was in heaven?"

"He told me that Kaahin gave his life for Islam as martyr."

Malik asks, "What did you do then?"

"I asked to see his body."

"And then what?"

"He said he would kill me if he saw me again."

"Then what did you do?"

"Nothing yet."

"What do you mean, 'nothing yet'?"

"I will take action. I will avenge my brother."

Malik is tempted to ask Marduuf if he is planning to report all that has happened to the authorities, but he checks himself. He realizes that such a question will mean nothing to someone like Marduuf, born in a lawless country and brought up in post–civil war conditions, who has never known authority in the positive sense of the term.

The tape recorder switches itself off. Marduuf is startled. He looks at the machine as if he might strike it for giving him a fright and then, for the first time, acknowledges Malik's grin with a similar one.

Qasiir shows Marduuf to his pickup truck, parked in the lot, and then returns to find Malik happy with the interview, but clearly too exhausted to stay awake.

Qasiir asks, "How early do you want me to come in the morning with Liibaan?"

Malik knows that tomorrow will be a bugger of a day, what with several important interviews and the move to Bile and Cambara's. "First thing in the morning," he says.

SAIFULLAH HAS DISAPPEARED.

No one, not least Ahl, understands how this could happen. He'd been upstairs listening to tape recordings of the Koran. Or so they believed. They trusted he was taking his time and would come down at some point, relaxed and willing to talk to them. They were trying to wait for things to be revealed—in time.

Then, at teatime, Faai, bearing a cup of tea with lots of sugar, goes upstairs and taps at his door. When he doesn't answer, she shouts his name and, for good measure, calls him by the endearments she used when he was a child. No reply. Xalan joins her, and the two women shout louder the longer they wait for him to answer their calls. Xalan wonders, What if he has jumped out of the window and is lying in the garden, unconscious? What if he has killed himself? Faai, keening, prays louder and more earnestly, "Please, God, no—please, God, no." Xalan orders her to be quiet. Faai shuffles her way downstairs and sits at the bottom of the staircase, still pleading, "Please, God, no—please, God, no." Then Ahl goes up to add his voice to the chorus, begging Saifullah to come out.

Xalan telephones Warsame and tells him to return urgently. When Ahl suggests he break down the door, Xalan collapses with nervous tension. She averts her head and presses her eyes closed with the tips of her fingers, as if attending to the self-tormenting questions that crowd one another out.

By the time Warsame arrives, Xalan is short of breath, and he worries about an asthmatic attack. He gets her inhaler from the bedside table and sits beside her, more worried about her than about Saifullah, of whom he has never been fond. He lifts her by the elbow, and together they walk toward the bedroom, their feet faltering in unison as Xalan leans on him for support. Warsame almost falls over when he misses a step.

Ahl goes in search of a hammer or something heavy with which to break the lock. It is clear that he has no idea what he is doing, because he mounts the steps again, empty-handed. Then he does what he has been wanting to do all along: he puts his shoulder to the door. He is astounded when he forces it open without much resistance. Then he announces loudly, "But he is not here."

Warsame joins him. The two men look at each other, and their eyes converge on the unused bed. They then wander in tandem toward the open window, neither speaking. Ahl turns off the tape recorder, which still blares the Koran. Xalan rushes in and stares openmouthed at the window. It is clear that she has arrived at the same conclusion: that Saifullah must have jumped out, down to the ground. Ahl, leaving nothing to chance, goes over to the window and sticks his neck out, searching the ground for a body. Finding none, he shakes his head. Then they go downstairs to contemplate their next move.

Xalan says under her breath, "At least he hasn't killed himself in our house. I don't know what I would do if he did that."

Ahl is not sure of her meaning. Does Xalan mean that she wouldn't know what to do if he had killed himself, or wouldn't know what to do if he committed suicide in a room in their house? His eyes range over the others in the no longer cheerful living room, coming to rest on Faai, who is standing in the doorway, quietly tearful.

Warsame calls in the guard and asks him if he has seen a young man leave. He doesn't give a name, but he describes Saifullah in some detail.

The guard, boasting a right cheek the size of a bird's egg from chewing leftover *qaat*, replies that he hasn't seen any young man come in or leave.

Xalan turns to her husband. "What do we do now?"

Warsame observes that it is time they zeroed in on the places he might go and the persons he is likely to seek out. Warsame asks Xalan if it is possible that Saifullah has gone to her sister's house, across the street from the main mosque. "Did he say that he had seen her on his way here?"

"Shall we go to her house and find out?" Xalan says. "A pity we were so excited at seeing him, and we forgot to ask if he had seen or visited her."

Warsame answers, "I see no harm in doing that."

"And if he isn't there?"

"More important, will she receive us or will she throw us out?" Warsame says.

Ahl doesn't want to tempt fate by saying anything. He knows of the bad blood between the two sisters, resulting from differences in character and outlook, the one very devout and uncompromising when it comes to her faith, the other of a secular cast of mind. He rises to his feet, ready to go to Zaituun's place, but not prepared to speak.

———

Xalan feels ill at ease calling on Zaituun, her elder sister. They have not exchanged visits for years, even when they have lived in the same cities—previously in Toronto, currently in Bosaso. Zaituun is prayerfully devout, expending all her energy on worship. She and Xalan fell out because Zaituun does not approve of her younger sister's lax ways, and said that she had rape and worse coming to her unless she changed. Xalan has no time for those who think she shouldn't blame Islam for what the vigilantes did to her, raping her in a mosque as three imams looked on and did nothing to stop the defilers.

A young woman lets them into the house. She informs them that Zaituun is praying. Annoyed, Xalan looks at her watch, as if to determine the name of the prayer her sister would be performing at this time of day. When Xalan wonders if it is worth asking the young woman if she has seen Saifullah, Warsame counsels patience. They take off their shoes at the door to the living room. Ahl is unprepared for this; he is wearing boots, and he knows that his socks are dirty and that one of them has a big hole in the heel.

Zaituun's house is a modest affair, with no flourish of any sort. Each room is conceived as separate from the others; it is not a house put together as one afterthought leads to another. Prayer rugs are in every corner, some standing against the walls, others laid out flat and ready for use, while others are expectantly hanging, as if awaiting a community of worshippers. The room faces the *qiblah*. The image comes to Ahl of a woman who will die praying, the words of worship stirring her lips.

And yet, Xalan has told him, as a young girl Zaituun played soccer with the boys and broke every school rule, challenging her teachers and correcting them when they were wrong. She was at loggerheads with her husband from the day they married until he died, killed in a shoot-out when armed militiamen came to loot their house in the initial stages of the civil war. Then, two years into her widowhood, the first spent at a refugee camp in Kenya, the second in a run-down two-bedroom apartment in Toronto, waiting for her Canadian refugee papers, she surprised everyone by deciding to dedicate her life to the study of the Holy Scripture. Her four daughters married and she relocated with her son to Bosaso, where she has lived ever since. Asked to explain what prompted such a sea change in her behavior, Zaituun once said to Warsame, her voice calm, her pauses well-timed, "All I recall is standing before an underground door, which opened onto a bright room awash with light from the sun. I recall going farther in until I felt totally immersed in the blessed waters of inner joy. It was only then that I realized how our daily realities are but chinks of light opening onto the darkness of our eternities."

Zaituun arrives just when the young woman has served them tea. She enters the room clear-eyed, soft-footed, a person with an inner calm. She smiles gently and nods in the direction of Warsame and Ahl and, in passing, the two sisters touch shoulders in greeting. Unable and unwilling to give themselves over to a lengthy exchange, for fear that one of them will speak out of turn, they confine themselves to this token, hastily executed salutation, the best compromise they can manage on the spot.

Xalan asks, "Have you seen Ahmed?"

Zaituun makes a "be my guest" gesture, and then takes her sweet time, pretending not to recognize the name. To draw her out, Warsame says, "Maybe you call him Ahmed-Rashid or Saifullah?"

Zaituun remains standing upright. She says, "We prayed together. I asked him where he had been, where he was going, what his plans were. He didn't answer any of my questions. We shared a meal in silence, he prayed more devotions. He kissed and hugged me, as if embarking on a journey from which he would not return, and I wished him Godspeed and God bless."

Panic sets in, Xalan straightaway displaying clear signs of agitation; this gets to Ahl and Warsame, who have equal reason to be concerned. Warsame, because he is worried Xalan might go off balance; Ahl, because he has been of the view that any possible recovery of Taxliil hinges on Saifullah providing them with up-to-date information. It takes all his energy to control himself.

Warsame, decisive, says, "Let us go."

Xalan asks, "Where are we going?"

"What are we doing here?" he counters.

Warsame hastily bids Zaituun farewell, and moves so fast that Xalan and Ahl have to scamper to their feet to catch up with him. Ahl says "God bless" to Zaituun, in an effort to soften her hard stare, which is trained on her sister. He feels the weight of defeat.

Back in the car, Xalan says, "Zaituun knows a lot more than she lets on. She is heartless, my sister. I wouldn't put it past her to know exactly what Saifullah and his mentors are up to—and I have a sinking feeling that it's nothing good. I am unsure whether to alert the authorities. Warsame, maybe you should call up one of your pals in Intelligence and share what we know with him."

Warsame says, "I don't want to rat on Zaituun. As it is, there is bad blood between us all. There is no need to make matters worse."

"What if we share our speculation with the local authorities," Xalan wonders aloud, "that an Ahmed, also known as Saifullah, may be planning an act of sabotage against the prevailing peace in Puntland?"

Ahl opposes the idea, which he feels might jeopardize any possible reunion with Taxliil. He says, "But we don't have adequate, trustworthy information to report to anyone, really."

"What an unpleasant mess!" Xalan says.

Ahl says, "Where could he have gone after he left?"

"I doubt he wants us to find him," Warsame says.

Xalan, in a mood to speak in hyperboles, says to Warsame, "Darling, why are you so terribly, so unarguably pessimistic and so unpardonably uncooperative?"

Warsame drives, unspeaking.

Meanwhile, Ahl feels as if he were standing at the center of a suspension bridge spanning a river. Every angle affords him a different perspective and points him toward a different course of action. He is sick to the core.

Xalan's hand searches for Ahl's—he is seated in the back—and, despite the awkwardness of the angle, she takes it and squeezes it. "Whatever else happens, I pray that we'll find Taxliil, safe and sound."

When they get back, they see a jalopy parked badly, at an angle. Unable to maneuver past it, Warsame honks, and the chauffeur, cheeks full to bursting with *qaat*, takes over the wheel from Warsame, suggesting they welcome their visitor. Ahl's hopes are raised afresh: he thinks maybe Saifullah is back. But his hope is dashed when he is presented to a man answering to the nickname Kala-Saar.

Kala-Saar, a professor at the newly established Puntland State University at Garowe, is a friend of Xalan's; a pleasant-looking man, gangly, plainly dressed in baggy trousers and a many-pocketed khaki shirt stuffed with cigarettes, a pipe, and accessories. He has the habit of peppering his Somali with foreign terms in Italian, Arabic, or English, depending on the tongue with which his interlocutor is comfortable. He has a doctorate from the Istituto Universitario Orientale in Naples, his dissertation on the epistemology of Islam, and is given to a natural urge to get someone's dander up. A non-cooking bachelor, Kala-Saar appreciates good tables; he is the rounder of guests at tables, invited whenever there aren't enough interesting men, or when a single woman is visiting town and there is no other man to invite.

Xalan invites him to dinner on the spot, but he announces right away that he won't stay unless he is allowed to light up at the dinner table. Then, without waiting for his hosts' approval, he lights another cigarette from the butt of the one he is about to extinguish.

Xalan values Kala-Saar's pronouncements, not his manners. She finds him inspiring to listen to when he speaks on politics or puts the actions of others under his sharp scrutiny. She says, "Wait until I return, and don't say anything of note before I get back. I want to hear everything."

Then she goes into the kitchen to attend to the meal preparation, helped by Faai. She switches off the radio Faai has been listening to in her attempt to hear snippets of their conversation from there.

Ahl senses that Warsame is less enamored of their guest as they touch base on a number of matters of common local interest. Neither has time for the president of Puntland, whom Kala-Saar describes as "highly incompetent," and Warsame labels as "a corrupt simpleton."

Kala-Saar then turns his attention to Ahl. The man is evidently well informed about Ahl's situation, thanks to Xalan. He strikes Ahl as a man who flexes his knowledge like a muscle, along the lines of the gymnasiums that train young minds for higher things.

Then Kala-Saar asks Warsame, "Why does it strike me as if Xalan has had an out-of-body experience? You don't look your usual self, either. Is there something you haven't told me?"

Ahl suspects that Kala-Saar is casting around for confirmation of something he has already picked up from talking to either the chauffeur or Faai. Warsame tells him about the appearance and disappearance of Saifullah, ending with a caveat: that Kala-Saar hold back whatever comments he is likely to make until after Xalan has returned. Kala-Saar agrees to this condition, and turns to ask Ahl if there has been any sign of Taxliil yet.

Ahl says, "Not yet, but we live in hope."

"Taxliil will be all right," Kala-Saar predicts.

They fall silent and wait for Xalan's return.

———

That there are several of them gathered at her table, eating a meal she has prepared, gives immense joy to Xalan, who constantly thinks about "family." She takes her place next to Kala-Saar, calling to Faai to lower the volume of the radio in the kitchen so that the conversation can flow.

Meanwhile, for a man who didn't want to eat, Kala-Saar is only too eager to start on the feast Xalan has prepared, with a choice of vegetables and meaty things of every variety, and fish cooked in batter. Maybe Xalan has cooked her way out of her despair.

Kala-Saar takes a sip of water and makes a face. He quotes from Yusuful Khal's "Prayers in a Temple," in which the Lebanese poet writes about a stone speaking and becoming bread, and then wine. Pressed by Xalan to explain his meaning, and egged on by Warsame, Kala-Saar looks in Ahl's direction, and quotes: "A lack, a regrettable absence from this good table, a glass of good wine."

He continues, "When you put Saifullah's and Taxliil's disappearances into the wider perspective, I can't help but conclude that it is all part of a new thinking among the young. As parents, we are at fault. As adults, we are no models to our children. As teachers, we are no example to our students. We're culpable in that we, who think of ourselves as educated secularists, have not inspired the younger generation, who are responding to our failure with rebellious rejection of everything we have so far stood for. In the early nineties, many of the young joined the clan-based militia groupings as recruits and killed and died serving the warlords who hired them. Lately, they've sought and found their role models elsewhere: imams and gurus from other places, other disciplines, and other cultures. Some have even become infatuated with dub poets of whom we may not approve. The young have marked their dissent in the strongest of terms, because we, as parents, as adults, and as teachers, have not been open with them."

Ahl asks, "But as rejectionists, what have they become?"

Kala-Saar says, "Some have become terrorists, others insurgents."

"What are the essential differences between the terrorists and the insurgents?" Ahl says.

"The terrorists massacre the innocent purposely, whereas the insurgents' resistance to the Ethiopian occupation compels their opponents, that is to say the Ethiopians or the Somalis fighting in the name of the FedForces, to kill the innocent without meaning to do so."

"I see no difference between these slaughterers," Warsame says.

Ahl asks, "How would you describe Shabaab—insurgents or terrorists?"

"Shabaab are terrorists: they aim to destroy, not to build, and as such they do not value human life, as we do," Kala-Saar says. "Even so, I would think of them as genuine insurrectionists, who oppose the occupation and fight it by all means possible. Sadly, though, it is in the nature of wars to kill the innocent."

"What about the women?" Xalan says.

"What about them?" Kala-Saar asks.

Xalan says, "Do you think that only the young form a movement of discontent?"

"They do so without a doubt," Kala-Saar says.

Ahl asks, "In your view, to what does this unhappiness lead—eventually?"

"This eventually leads to self-hate."

"Which will in turn lead to what?" Ahl asks.

Kala-Saar puts down his spoon and fork and takes his time chewing a mouthful, pondering. He stares at Ahl for a long time, and finally shifts his gaze to Xalan, smiling with the contentment of someone who has found an answer to a very tricky question. He says, "To paraphrase the French sociologist Bruno Étienne, this type of self-hate results in the nation murdering itself, and in the process of doing so, the individual committing suicide becomes a metaphor for the death culture."

The silence following this indicates to Ahl that no one has understood Kala-Saar's meaning, but no one asks him to elaborate. They all go back to their food with renewed concentration.

Xalan says, "What about us women? Don't women inveigh against the male injustices in a stronger fashion than before?"

"I don't wish to hurt your feelings, my dear Xalan, but I don't see the women in Somalia working their commitment to liberation into a viable force for change," Kala-Saar says. "They haven't shown signs of rebellion in the way the youth have done. Women in Somalia at present are no longer a force of positive, progressive change, but of retrogression. This is because the mosques serve as clubs—and you know you are hardly represented at the mosques. In my view, women have become backward-looking retrogrades, veil-wearing and submissive. Times were when Somali women were better organized—as members of political movements, as beacons of the nation. Not anymore."

Xalan studies her knuckles. "Talking about the young, what is your position on suicide bombing or self-murder—actions that are classed among their kind as martyrdom?"

Kala-Saar chews awkwardly, as though his front teeth are wobbly and of little use. He speaks with his mouth half-full and spits bits of food in all directions. "I might approve of Shabaab if their actions were likely to bring about change—a change toward a better society. They are not. They are good at disrupting, not at constructing anything. Like the Brigate Rosse. I lived in Italy when they terrorized that country. I do not approve of destructive methods. Moreover, Shabaab is a passing fad—they will go the way fireflies go."

He pauses, wipes his mouth, sips his water, and then goes on. "What is my attitude toward suicide bombing? Here is the problem. No priest is prepared to pay the ultimate price for Islam through self-sacrifice himself. Nor do any of them put forward their own children to die for the cause for which they claim to be fighting; only other people's sons and brothers. They are a dishonest lot, and I do not approve of dishonest behavior."

Kala-Saar pours more water into his glass and takes another mouthful of food before continuing. He says, "I am full of admiration for the young, because they perform sacrifice on a scale till now unknown in our part of the world. Think of Japan, of the Amhara ethnic group in Ethiopia. Two peoples with traditions in which sacrificing one's life to cause heavy damage to enemy combatants has a noble history: kamikaze pilots flying small aircraft laden with fuel, explosives, and bombs into the Allied ships; the battle of Adwa, in Ethiopia, where barefoot Takla Haymanot of Gojjam fought against the Italian invaders, who were better equipped than the Abyssinians. We in Somalia have never had a tradition of putting our lives on the line for our nation. Thomas Jefferson is worth quoting here: 'the tree of liberty must be refreshed from time to time with the blood of patriots and tyrants. It is its natural manure.'"

"So you approve of Shabaab?" asks Warsame.

"I do not approve of Shabaab's actions. They are not fighting for liberty but to gain power. They are not fighting for the national interest; they are fighting for sectional interest, insofar as they are fighting on behalf of a specific segment of Somali society, the radical fringe."

Ahl says, "What about fighting for Islam?"

Kala-Saar says, "Islam is under no threat. Nor do I think that stoning a thirteen-year-old accused of adultery and then sparing her rapist constitutes preserving the good name of Islam. Rather, it denigrates the reputation of the faith. Do you think that imposing a type of veil indigenous to other societies on Somali women is a good thing? Or banning music, disallowing sports on TV, stopping veiled women in the street on their way home or to the market and checking if they are or aren't wearing bras?"

The conversation continues along these lines, with Kala-Saar pontificating on various aspects of the same topics, or subjects related to them.

Then they hear Faai shouting from the kitchen to Xalan, "Please come and listen to this." Xalan joins Faai and then returns, slack-jawed.

"What's happened?" Ahl asks.

Xalan replies, "A suicide bomber has blown himself up in the center of Bosaso, killing at least ten people and injuring several more."

Ahl sucks in his breath, his skin loses its natural color and he sits still, unmoving. Kala-Saar, too, falls silent, seemingly shamefaced, as though he has been the cause of such terrible things. Ahl stands up and moves to the window.

His mobile phone rings. It brings him unexpected news, far beyond his expectations, news he thinks he can't cope with, his heart nearly bursting out of his chest. The phone nearly drops out of his hands. He pulls himself together to listen.

Xalan, Warsame, and Kala-Saar watch him in silence as he asks, "Where are you now?" He waits for an answer and then says, "Shall I come and get you from where you are, right now?" Then, the mobile phone almost slipping out of his hands, "If you know how to get to where I am, then I will wait." A pause. "I, too, my dearest, I am so pleased to hear your voice, so pleased to know that you are alive and well, and that I'll see you shortly." Then just before disconnecting, he adds, "Yes, of course I love you, too, my darling."

They all look in his direction, waiting to hear his news in full. But Ahl has difficulty speaking, not only because he cannot convince himself that he has just talked to Taxliil, but also because he doesn't wish to share the good news with Kala-Saar. He doesn't want to hear a man who, delighting in his superb turns of phrase, will embark on the exercise of distinguishing between a suicide bomber, whom he will cast in the vanguard of selfless young Somalis setting a new revolutionary trend, and Taxliil, a milksop unable or unwilling to bring his martyrdom to completion.

"Was that Taxliil?" Xalan asks.

By way of answer, Ahl's cheeks flow with tears that gather momentum as they pour down. He wishes he had the luxury of privacy so that he could cry his heart out with joy, alone. Just as in Somalia's civil war, the intimate affairs of this nation are fodder for gossip, shock, amazement, and newspaper headlines elsewhere, but not to the victims of the strife.

Xalan helps Ahl to his seat before his knees collapse from under him, his face and cheeks wet with tears, making him look like a child who has clumsily painted his own face. Then Xalan realizes something else: that Ahl's trousers are soaked. Has he wet himself? When? In the name of heavens, what is happening to this poor man?

Xalan, standing behind Ahl, motions to Warsame and Kala-Saar to leave the room. Then she, too, departs and joins them in the living room.

MALIK, FOR ONCE, IS UNABLE TO CONCENTRATE ON LISTENING TO the radio at news time; he has other worries on his mind. Showered and shaved, his mobile phone by his side, he is waiting for a confirmation call from Qasiir to inform him that he is on his way, bringing along the man with information about Somalis with foreign passports at the Kenyan border. But when the phone comes to life, it is Ahl, excitedly informing him that Taxliil has been in touch.

"When?" Malik asks.

"He rang me yesterday, late afternoon."

Malik takes an apprehensive glance at his watch, wishing Ahl hadn't called this instant, because he doesn't have time to talk for long. Why didn't he call right away or even late last night to let him know he had heard from Taxliil? But in their near falling-out a few days ago, Ahl accused him of caring more about his work than about anyone, so he treads with caution—let Qasiir wait, he thinks. Then he chides, as genially as he can, "You kept that secret to yourself, didn't you?"

Ahl replies, "I didn't keep it a secret intentionally. He called, saying that he would come along shortly, and then didn't do so. I've been waiting to hear from him again since then. No idea if he has changed his mind or if something has happened to him between the time he rang and now. I didn't sleep the entire night."

"If he rang you on your mobile, then you must have his number," Malik reasons. "Did you try it?"

"The readout on my phone said 'number withheld,'" Ahl explains. "I pressed the redial button but it gave me a busy signal."

"So what are you doing now?"

"Waiting," says Ahl. "What other choice do I have?"

"Ring Fidno and No-Name, see if they have news of him. It sounds like they've played a hand in his release from Shabaab's clutches," Malik says.

"No answer from either; their lines busy as well."

"I wish I could assist," Malik says.

Ahl says, "I am sure you would if you could."

"Can I call you later, then?" says Malik.

"I'll call you myself if I hear anything."

But just as Malik is ready to hang up, Ahl asks, "What would you do if you were in my place?" He sounds vulnerable, desperate not to end the conversation.

"I'd wait, just like you are doing."

"What else would you do?"

Malik reflects that he wouldn't do well as a Good Samaritan, or even as the manager of a help hotline. He has no idea how to take in hand a situation that has gone uncontrollably wrong. He hopes that his failure at rescuing Ahl from his despair won't lead his brother to do something rash.

"What do Xalan and Warsame suggest?"

"That I wait until he contacts me," Ahl says.

"Where are they now? Can I talk to them?"

"They are in their room, sleeping."

Malik says, "Why don't you do as they suggest, sleep off your exhaustion, with the phone by your side, so you can answer it immediately if he rings. Meanwhile, I will think of something and call you."

"Maybe that's what I'll do," Ahl says. "Sleep."

"Talk to you later, then."

Malik, sighing, has barely put down his phone on the worktable when it rings. Qasiir is on the line. "Uncle Liibaan and I are down at the parking lot, wondering if you are ready for us to join you."

Malik pauses, momentarily confused, then remembers that Liibaan is a former army colleague of Dajaal's, hence the term *uncle*. "Please come up," he says, and he unlocks the plate over the apartment door to welcome them.

Qasiir is the first to walk in, and he and Malik exchange a hurried greeting. Then both make room for a large man with a round belly, which he pushes ahead of himself, his feet in rubber flip-flops too small to bear his weight, the hair on his chin as sparse as the beard of a sixteen-year-old boy, and with eyes that squint into narrow slits as he concentrates.

As Malik goes off, saying, "I'll make tea," Qasiir assumes the role of a host and leads Liibaan into the living room, where they sit. Once the water is boiling, Malik joins them. He observes that Liibaan is comfortable enough to take off his flip-flops, and that the man's toenails are perilous as weapons—long, with jagged ends.

"I am glad to meet you, Liibaan."

Liibaan is silent, then he says, "Dajaal's murder saddens me so. He was very dear to me—like a brother. He was my senior in age as well as in rank. A serious, honest man, and those of us who knew him admired him; we all adored him. May God bless his soul!"

Malik contributes to the chorus of "Amen!"

Then the kettle wails, and Malik gets up, relieved to have gotten that part of the conversation out of the way. He asks his guest how he likes his tea.

"Four sugars and lots of milk," Liibaan says.

Malik says to Qasiir, "Come into the kitchen with me for a moment, please. I would like you to do something for me."

Malik sets out cups, saucers, biscuits, and a few other nibbles. Then he puts two tea bags in the teapot and pours in the water. Qasiir watches and waits in silence, noticing that Malik has set places for only two.

"I would like to conduct the interview alone," Malik says.

Qasiir says, "But of course."

Malik goes into the workroom, leaving Qasiir in the kitchen, and returns with his recording gadgets. "Give us an hour and a half."

"Okay," Qasiir says. "I'll see you in an hour and a half, unless I hear from you before then." He goes to take leave of Uncle Liibaan.

———

Liibaan, obliging Malik, gives a brief biography of himself. He says, "I was born in Jalalaqsi and brought up in Belet-Weyne, Hiiran, but schooled in Mogadiscio until my second-year secondary, when I was recruited into the National Army as a noncommissioned officer. A year later, I went to Odessa, where I trained, specializing in the tank division and taking a diploma. I returned as a second lieutenant, and soon after was sent to fight in the Ogaden War—Dajaal was my commanding officer. I served in the army until the collapse of the state structures and, having no other choice, went into the import and export business with former army colleagues, some of whom made off with money stashed away when they looted the Central Bank of Somalia. Now I run a fleet of buses on behalf of a company with large holdings, and organize the security. That is how I make my living, in the field of security."

Malik asks, "What does organizing security for a fleet of buses entail?"

"I have three dozen youths in my employ," Liibaan says, "and I put them on the buses, three to four each, as armed escorts."

"Do you go on the buses yourself sometimes?"

He replies, "Lately, I've been based in a village on the border crossing between Kenya and Somalia. It made business sense to move as soon as the men from the Courts fled. You see, I figured out that a large number of people, many of them foreigners—and these included Somalis with other nationalities—would be fleeing in the direction of the Kenyan border, aware that Somalia's border with Ethiopia was closed, thanks to the invasion."

"I presume you know how things are done at the border crossing," Malik says, "since you go back and forth yourself. I presume, as a businessman, you know some of the Kenyan immigration officers, do you?"

"I do."

"What are they like? How do they treat you?"

A knowing spark enters his eyes, as Liibaan answers, "They are easy to get along with if you are ready to part with a pocketful of cash. Then you are an instant success, their best friend, and you can come and go, no questions asked."

"Is it true that they are prone to extracting money from every Somali who presents himself at a border post, whether the Somali has the right documents or not?" Malik asks.

"The salaries of the Kenyan immigration officers are low, and you can understand their greed, if not forgive it," Liibaan says. "Besides, the Kenyans know that Somalis are by nature impatient, and do not mind paying what it takes to make their immigration problems disappear."

Malik asks Liibaan to guide him through what occurs.

"The Kenyans instruct all travelers wishing to enter Kenya to form four groups: travelers with Somali passports are told to return for the process another day; they will be told when. It was suggested that they remain on the Somali side of the border. Somalis with Kenyan nationality are to form their own line: they are dealt with right away. Somalis with foreign passports wait in their own line, as do all non-Somalis."

"Tell me about the Somalis with foreign passports," Malik says. "How are they processed?"

"These are made to fill out entry forms in triplicate," Liibaan says. "They hand these in with their passports, and they stand in line for a very long time in the sun, waiting first for their papers to be processed and then to be interviewed and have their fingerprints taken. With that exercise ended, they are taken to yet another cubicle to answer the same questions from three different officers, a Kenyan in uniform, and—according to one of the men who was refused entry, judging by their accents—an American and a Brit."

"Any idea what questions are asked?"

"From what this man told me, each officer asks a question relevant to his vantage point, and the same questions are repeated, formulated differently. Mostly about terrorism, the men from the Courts, foreign jihadis in the country, questions about funding and where it derives from—plus of course personal questions specifically geared for each traveler."

"Why was that man sent back?"

Liibaan replies, "His Dutch passport had expired six months earlier, and he couldn't remember the name of the apartment block in Amsterdam where he claimed to have lived before coming to Somalia."

"Any other unusual incidents you can recall?"

"I recall a man called Robleh talking himself into trouble earlier in the day from what a number of travelers informed me," Liibaan says. "I heard the initial part of his troubles from a reliable source, one of the drivers of the bus; and the second segment describing his troubles from the Dutch passport–carrying Somali turned back from Kenya."

"Do you know his other names?"

"His full name is Hassan Ali Robleh or maybe Hussein; I don't know and couldn't care less. And according to Dajaal, whom he made anxious, he upset Cambara and Bile. He's a nasty piece of work."

"What did he do to get himself into trouble?"

"On the way to the Kenya-Somalia border crossing, he spoke in defense of the Courts' action and described everyone who disagreed with him as traitors to Islam."

"He lived on welfare in Canada. Does anyone know why he claimed to be performing for the Courts in North America?" Malik asked.

"He was a scout for them."

"What does that mean, a scout?"

"He helped recruit young Canadians into Shabaab."

"What became of him?"

"The other Somalis on the bus who were with him and were also interviewed by the foreign officers but not detained fingered Robleh. They reported that he'd been bragging about being a scout for Shabaab. In the end, his bragging got him a ticket to Guantánamo. It's said that's where he still is."

———

The interview done, Qasiir comes and drives Liibaan home, agreeing to come back for Malik, to take him to Bakhaaraha Market.

Not a day passes now without news of armed confrontation between the insurgents and the FedForces, that is to say the interim government's forces, aided by the Ethiopians, shelling each other's positions. According to Qasiir, the market is heavily involved in selling and hiding weapons, and providing intelligence to the insurgency.

While he waits for Qasiir, Malik whips up a quick meal of spaghetti and tomato sauce, just in case Qasiir wants to eat something. Himself, he would like a salad, only he has no fresh lettuce. He packs his things, ready to be moved into the annex. But he doesn't think it wise to put his packed suitcase, computer, and cash in the trunk of the car if they are going to the Bakhaaraha, so he decides to leave his belongings in the apartment and to return for them. Then he telephones Cambara to alert her of what he is doing. After which he rings Ahl, who tells him, "No news."

When Qasiir returns, Malik serves him the spaghetti and asks him for further background on the current role of the market in the insurgency.

Qasiir takes a long time chewing a mouthful of spaghetti, then swallows noisily and replies, "There are a number of reasons why the Bakhaaraha are aiding the insurgency. You see, no businessman will show eagerness in welcoming a government that is bound to levy tax on his business. They would rather there was no government; they would rather not pay tax. The second reason is they do not like the interim president, who hails from Puntland, and whom they accuse not only of having brought along thousands of trained soldiers from the autonomous state, but also of having invited the Ethiopians to invade."

On the way to the market complex, they come upon more devastation, houses destroyed by recent bombing and families sitting out in the open or under the shade trees still standing in the rubble. Qasiir explains to Malik that many of the homeowners prefer the inconvenience of slumming it near their properties to moving out to the camps, where the homeless and the internally displaced are congregated.

They come across large groups of people moving in the opposite direction, as though they've seen enough of whatever it is they have seen. Malik reflects that in the old dispensation, when the Courts were in charge, the city was on the face of it peaceful. Now they drive through

agitated movements: of men and women running away from something and looking back, checking to see if the trouble they are fleeing
is pursuing them. They discern excitement, fear, and anger everywhere
they look. Some of them shout excitedly at each other, heatedly exchanging views.

"Do you want us to stop?" Qasiir asks, glancing at him.

Malik shakes his head and they continue. Soon the smell of burning
tires reaches them. A battery of youths and robed men charged with
the energy of foment raise their fists and chant, "Down with Ethiopia!"
Some shout, "Down with the invading Christians!" and yet others cry,
"Long live the martyrs of the faith!" Qasiir turns into a broad dirt road
and, just as he finds a parking spot, nearly runs over a man crossing
the road with feverish intent. Malik says he wishes he had brought a
camera, and then Qasiir pulls out his phone and, before Malik can say
anything, starts to take photographs of youths nearby who are setting
fire to a crudely assembled effigy of the Ethiopian premier. He and
Qasiir walk farther and farther into the heart of the chaos, watching
the goings-on with rabid interest. Despite the promise he made to
his wife not to be pulled into the abyss, Malik without regret moves in
deeper, excited to ferret about in other people's heightened emotions;
to eavesdrop on their sorrows; to listen in on their conversations and
intrude on their private and public personae. After all, when one is in
a mob, one is private in a public space.

Qasiir says, "For them, it is like theater and what they consider to
be a bit of fun. It's part of the political show, orchestrated to the smallest detail by men sympathetic to the insurgents and against the TFG.
The idea is to humiliate the interim government."

"Did you participate in the debasing of the corpse of the dead Marine in 1993, Qasiir?" Malik asks.

Qasiir doesn't answer at first.

Malik says, "I know that the chopper nearly killed your younger sister and rendered her mute and forever traumatized. But did you take part in that heinous act of self-humiliation?"

Finally Qasiir says, "Grandpa Dajaal wouldn't allow me to join them."

"Would you have joined your mates if he hadn't?"

"Yes," says Qasiir. "I would have joined my mates if he hadn't."

"I would have expected better of you," Malik says.

"The way it was put to us at the time, it was all part of a political show of solidarity to the general, an integral part of a performance. Everything pre-rehearsed, taking into account every possible detail," Qasiir explains, and then after a pause, adds, "I was young, naive."

"I've been to many of these pre-arranged demonstrations in Pakistan, in India, and in Afghanistan," Malik says. "Initially, they all appear so real. My feeling is that the performance we've just seen had a rehearsed quality to it. Although that doesn't stop many foreign journalists from being taken for a ride."

"Like hired mourners, wailing," observes Qasiir.

"I suppose nothing is free," Malik says.

He recalls the names of giants in his field, journalists and authors who pried into the deeper horrors of the universe, and who returned with all kinds of spoil. He hopes to write an article about staring into the raw truths of rage. The further he goes into the inner sanctums of the market complex, forbidden to him until then by virtue of his outsider status, the more his heart sickens, though. Qasiir, with Malik following behind, is now exchanging high fives with a mate of his who fought alongside him, now giving the thumbs-up to a former fellow militiaman who is making sure that the demonstration doesn't get out of hand and that the disorder is kept to a minimum.

Malik chokes on the smoke billowing from the effigies and other burning debris. Then he and Qasiir focus their interest on a clutch of youths in a circle clapping their hands, dancing and chanting to a chorus of protestations with the interchangeable terms—Ethiopia,

America, Christians, infidels, apostates, traitors—occurring in a discontinuous song. As Qasiir takes pictures of the youths who pose for him, the atmosphere festive, the mood buoyant, Malik realizes with shock that they are stamping on a corpse in uniform.

For Malik, this marks the moment in a people's history when sectarian rage may be portrayed as national panic. Malik thinks that a cross-section of Somalis have suspended their full membership in the human race because their behavior is unacceptable: one does not debase the dead. Nor, if one wishes to preserve the dignity of one's humanity, does one raze a house of worship to the ground, desecrate cemeteries, drag a corpse, or kick it while dancing around it. One can understand the rage that inspires a certain section of the populace to behave this way, a rage resulting from the deaths and the humiliation suffered at the hands of the Ethiopians. However, Malik condemns their conduct, because it breaks with Somali as well as Muslim tradition and departs from the norms of civilized behavior.

Too embarrassed to admit to his own fear, he walks away, sorry for the Ethiopian, killed in a war in a country about which he probably remained ignorant until the moment of his death. He feels sorry, too, for the Somali youths kicking the dead Ethiopian, an ill-educated, ill-informed lot, as unfamiliar with the concept of respect for the dead as they are with Islam. Blame it on decades of civil war, in which these youths haven't gone to schools, haven't lived in homes where there is the semblance of harmony and functionality. Blame it, too, on the current Somali political class, who are equally ill educated and equally self-centered, and who behave inhumanely toward others. Malik's sickened heart sicker than ever, he feels as if he is complicit in these terrible doings, because he cannot find a way to stop them.

Just before they leave the Bakhaaraha, there is a heavy exchange of gunfire, RPG rounds from the general direction of the presidential villa falling within a hundred yards from where Qasiir parked the car. The geography of the Bakhaaraha and the casbah make sense only to a native, he thinks. A stranger wouldn't know which alleys end in dead ends and which would lead them to safety.

They get into the car and miraculously find their way through the back streets and onto one of the city's arteries.

Malik's phone rings. Fee-Jigan is on the line, informing him that earlier, maybe two and a half hours ago, a radio journalist, whose name Malik recognizes from his impressive commentaries on HornAfrik, has been shot inside the Bakhaaraha.

"What was he doing when he was killed?" Malik asks.

"He was interviewing an insurgent."

"Where are you now?"

Fee-Jigan says he is on his way to join the funeral cortege, which is departing in half an hour from in front of Bank Tewfik. He asks Malik to put Qasiir on so that he can know how to get there.

———

Malik is the first to spot the cortege, and Qasiir pulls up at the rear. Malik then rings Fee-Jigan, who eventually joins them, and they stand beside the car, chatting. Other journalists make their appearance, and Fee-Jigan introduces them to Malik. He recognizes the names of the authors of some of the pieces he has read. Not one of the articles impressed him, he remembers, either because they lacked depth or because the author hadn't done sufficient background research before committing to a point of view. It is apparent that a number of the reporters have had no training, at least not enough to be taken seriously. Even so, he has remained in awe of their courage, their indomitable behavior.

They tell Malik more about the killing, which occurred in the Bakhaaraha market complex. Shire, the deceased journalist, was waiting for his interviewee, a top insurgent, in the back room of the computer shop. Known for his lack of fear and his outspokenness, Shire put his name to his editorials even when he knew they would upset all parties to the conflict. He had often spoken of his "foretold" death at the hands of assassins, although he couldn't predict, and didn't seem to care, whether the Ethiopians or the insurgents would get him first.

He was struck by balaclava-wearing men in the shop's back room, which was adjacent to the manager's cubicle. Three men gained access to the room, where he was waiting for the interview, and one of them shot him, using a silencer. "They emerged, waved *salaam* to the manager and the staff, and departed, having accomplished their mission," Fee-Jigan says.

"Who found the corpse?"

"The young tea boy, delivering tea to the room."

Malik thinks, What a sad way to die!

"That's the story," Fee-Jigan says, his eyebrows raised. His expression seems to suggest that there is something not right here.

"And what explanations do the manager and the staff of the shop proffer so far?" asks Malik. He thinks this must have been an inside job, and vaguely recalls an incident in Afghanistan, when a warlord was killed by Arab men posing as journalists.

Fee-Jigan replies, "Everyone in the shop claims to have been in the dark about the arrangements, because Shire had insisted that his interviewee and his escorts, who would come into the shop wearing balaclavas, be granted entry to the room in the back, where he would be waiting."

"Where is the corpse now?" Malik asks.

"At a mosque near his home."

"Are we going to the mosque or his home?"

"First the mosque, then the cemetery."

It takes the convoy of vehicles a long time to turn into a procession and get into a proper line. Malik thinks that someone with authority, in a uniform, like a traffic cop, is needed to clear the way if twenty or so cars wish to form an orderly file in a city enjoying peace. Organizing a column of cars into a well-ordered cavalcade during a civil war, however, is an impossible task.

But eventually they are under way, and Malik, while making no direct reference to their last encounter in Ma-Gabadeh's company, asks how the book Fee-Jigan has been writing is coming along.

Fee-Jigan says, "I've put it on a back burner."

"So what are you working on at present?"

"I've been working on matters closer to home."

"Such as what?"

"I've been writing pieces of great topical interest in the international media," says Fee-Jigan. "There is nothing more important these days than the targeting and killing of journalists, one dead every two days."

"Who do you think is behind the killings?"

Fee-Jigan seems unduly worried about Qasiir, whom he stares at. Malik assures him that Qasiir is trustworthy not by speaking but by nodding his head in Qasiir's direction.

Fee-Jigan says, "There are freelancing fifth columnists comprising former senior army officers, many of whom are allied to the Courts. These do the killings."

"But why would they kill Shire, who, from what I understand, was interviewing an insurgent presumably sympathetic to the Courts?"

"They kill to confuse the issue."

Malik can't follow his logic. He asks, "What issue?"

"Shire favored the truth," Fee-Jigan says. "He dared speak his mind, unafraid. At times, his hard-hitting commentaries upset Shabaab and their allies. The freelancing fifth columnists do anyone's dirty work as long as it confuses the issue."

Malik appreciates that Qasiir is doing what he can under confusing circumstances to make sure they are not left far behind, now slowing down, now going fast, and now communicating with a couple of the drivers with whom he exchanged mobile numbers before the convoy set off. They'll keep in touch in the event of a problem. When they get to the mosque and discover they are late for the funeral service, there is disagreement over where to go, some suggesting they head for Shire's family home, from which the bier will be carried on foot to the cemetery, a kilometer and a half away, others insisting they drive straight to the grave site and wait there. Malik concurs with Fee-Jigan that it is best to go to the family home and to help carry the bier.

They arrive in time to witness the bier already being carried out of the house. The street fills up with a crowd of well-wishers, passersby stopping to say, "*Allahu akbar,*" and the entire place reverberating with brief prayers of supplication addressed to the Almighty. Everyone hereabouts cuts a forlorn figure, head down in sorrow, mourning for the untimely death of a man who did no one harm and was loved by many.

The pace of the procession is quick, and a number of the journalists who arrived at the same time as Malik hurry to catch up with the coffin and help carry it, even briefly. In Islam, burial is quick, in hope that the dead will arrive at his resting place in a more contented state, with Allah's blessing.

Malik finds himself for the first and only time in his life carrying the bier of someone he didn't even know, and moved to be participating in the ritual. He gives his place over to Fee-Jigan, who in turns passes it to Qasiir, until they reach the edge of the waiting grave.

Just then Malik's mobile, which is in vibrate mode, makes a purring sound in the top of his shirt pocket. He checks most discreetly at the first opportunity, having stepped out of everybody's way. It's a text from Ahl. "Taxliil here. All well, considering. Talk when you can."

Malik recalls drafting a text message to Ahl, but not whether he sent it before the improvised roadside device struck the van he was traveling in. He remembers he'd been with others on their way back from the funeral of a journalist. Now, half-unconscious and lying on his side, in pain, he composes more text messages in his head: *Talk of the walking wounded!* But he can't press the send button. One needs hands to write a message, and Malik can't feel his hands. This does not stop him from adding a PS: *Imagine the injured working through much pain, the wounded autographing the death warrants with a great flourish.*

It is curious, he thinks, that he has not made personal acquaintance with an improvised explosive device until now.

In Somalia, IEDs did not figure much among the signatures of any of the armed factions in the Somali conflict until the Ethiopians arrived. Before, one would hear of two men on a motorbike or two or three on foot and in balaclavas, armed with pistols, hiding around a curve in the road as they waited for their victims to come out of a mosque or out of a car. The killers would ride away on their bike or they would run off, unidentified. Of late, however, roadside bombing has become the insurgents' favorite mode of operation. They study the movements of their victims and plant custom-made, pre-designed explosive devices accordingly, to pick off by remote control a government official traveling by car or an Ethiopian battalion decamping from one base to another, or journalists covering a momentous event.

Malik drafts in his head yet another text message to Ahl, informing his brother that he is now a casualty of the device, but, thank God, he is still alive. In fact, he can hear the explosion replaying in his memory, he can see the smoke it generated, he can smell the powder it emitted and he can feel in his own body the demolition of the device. He is bruised here and there and has suffered a concussion, but he senses he is regaining his ability to move some of his limbs. He moves a leg, as if to prove it to himself. Alas, the leg won't obey his command. What about his arm? His arm is more obliging, maybe because it is free from other obstructions, unlike the leg, which is bent under his body. It is in his head that the concussion has been concentrated. His neck is in some sort of a twist, and the back of his head is wet, but he cannot tell if it is blood or water that someone has spilled. He bends his knees some more and then stretches his leg, despite the impediment.

Then he opens his eyes, only to close them.

———

The device that blew up the car carrying Malik and his fellow journalists on the way back from Shire's funeral claimed the lives of three of them. Malik had chosen to ride with the other journalists instead of driving alone with Qasiir. As he replays the explosion in his memory, he is uncertain if one or two of the tires of the twelve-seater van in which they were traveling had burst, or if it had been preceded by a man on motorbike shooting at them. Anyhow, instead of the vehicle collapsing in on itself like a punctured ball, Malik sensed the minivan lifting off the ground, just as one of the journalists, now dead, was describing Shabaab as "men short on reasoning, on political cunning, and who are notorious for their doublespeak." Everyone, including the driver, also now dead, put in his word until the fragmentation grenade insinuated itself into the clamor and terminated their lively debate in instant darkness.

Even as his head hit the seat in front of him, Malik resisted dropping into the gaping dimness, remembering Amran's words—"I do not want to raise an orphan." His brief daze was replaced by a scary silence, and then he heard someone close by moaning in agony, and someone else pleading for help, saying, "I am hurt; very badly hurt." Then a sound like a goat being slaughtered.

His concussion is mild, his memory not affected; his bodily and mental reflexes are all in relatively good order. But like a newborn baby, or a dead person just interred, he is not all *there*. He is sufficiently alert to remember the unsubstantiated claim among Somalis that soon after interment, the dead hear everything, can even recognize the voices of the relatives and friends present at their burial. Malik is alive, even if he is not all *there*. He follows the protocol a person follows after a concussion; he asks himself simple questions: his own name, his wife's name, his brother's name, his date of birth, and where in the world he is now. He becomes both the asker and respondent. Only when he passes the test does he reopen his eyes. A crowd has gathered around the vehicle, some helping, some just gawking.

He has on his forehead a bump as round and big as a golf ball. His chest aches; there is someone else's blood on his clothes. Somewhere just above his groin, there are more traces of blood. He feels around and finds a fragment of glass through the rent in his trousers.

He hears Qasiir asking, "Can you hear me, Malik?" Then he feels someone hauling him out of the van the way one would heft a sleeping child out of a car.

"I am all right," he says.

"Here, take my hand," Qasiir says.

Malik does so and asks, "How about the others?"

Only when they are outside the vehicle does he see why it had taken so long for Qasiir to get to him: the dead and wounded were in Malik's way. Qasiir offers to take the wounded to hospital, and with a mosque being close by, a number of bystanders improvise coffins out of sheets and place the corpses in them to carry. Malik knows there is no point telephoning for ambulances, because they are seldom available in a city in which there are more devices blowing up than there are ambulances. No point either in taking the dead to the hospitals or bothering about postmortems; they will be buried before nightfall.

By the time Qasiir has wedged him into the back of the sedan car with two of his wounded colleagues on either side of him and the head of a third on his lap, Malik realizes that he has his responsibility cut out for him. It has fallen to him to tell the world what has occurred, how these journalists died serving the cause of their profession. Is he capable of meeting the challenge? Does he have the mettle to mourn them openly, mention names, point fingers at the culprits? In his head he drafts an obituary of "the unappreciated journalist" on the move; no time to find a desk, but he begins to debrief one of the wounded journalists who is in a fit state to answer his questions.

A twinge of regret scratches inside Malik's head, squeakily reminding him that he hasn't yet published his piece about Dajaal's murder. Then a portal of sorrow opens in the active side of his brain, and he worries that he, too, may die before he is able to write about the mobs of youth abandoning themselves to madness—and society looking on and doing nothing to stop them.

Malik and the wounded journalists are in luck. Qasiir has had the presence of mind to telephone Cambara and Bile, and Cambara has provided Qasiir with the names of doctors she knows at Medina Hospital, and mobile numbers for four medics in two of the private clinics, adding that she will try and reach them herself. Now Cambara and Bile ring Qasiir back with the message that they have reached one of the medics. He has reserved rooms in the intensive-care unit, and he and the nursing staff will be waiting for them.

And indeed they are. As the wounded are wheeled straight into surgery, Malik fills out the paperwork. He looks for the spot to provide his credit card information but learns that the clinic does not have the facility to process one. Still, he vows that he will pay if no one else does, and the administrator takes his word for it.

Now the invasive odor of chloroform sticks to his nostrils, reminding him of how close he has been to death. When the sweet smell almost knocks him out, he forces himself to sit up. He wishes he could move around, go outside for some fresh air. But he stays where he is, on a smelly, improvised camp bed with bloodstains on it. He feels a little squeamish and claustrophobic and goes out for a bit of fresh air and finds a bench in a small, untended garden. He sits down, sighing with relief.

A man approaches and asks if he may share the bench with him to rest his tired body. Malik indicates that he may. His phone rings and his editor at the daily paper is on the line, suggesting that he write a short piece about the events in Mogadiscio to go into the paper today. Malik feels his pockets, which are empty of pens and pencils. He asks the stranger if he has something with which to write. The man lends him a pencil. Malik moves a step away from the man, who seems to be eavesdropping on his conversation, to take notes on what the editor is looking for. After agreeing that he will file a story within several hours, he hangs up and returns the pencil to its owner, with thanks.

The stranger then introduces himself as Hilowleh, speaking his name in a way that makes Malik wonder if he ought to know it. His face stirs the vaguest of memories. Still, Malik can't decide if they have met before, or when or where, maybe because his brain is in too much disarray and incapable of connecting the available dots and dashes. The man's long eyelashes, his two-day-old stubble, and his ragged appearance are of no help. There is misapprehension in the man's demeanor, suggesting that talking to him is wrong. Is he embarrassed, and if so, why? Is there something weighing on the man's mind that he wishes to unload?

The man says, "I thought you were Malik."

Malik recalls watching Edward Albee's play *The Zoo Story*, in which a man sits next to another on a park bench in New York. The two men talk, and their talk leads one of them to murder the other. Anyhow, what does this man want?

"What if I were Malik?" he asks.

The stranger takes a small piece of paper out of his pocket, writes down a mobile number, gives it to Malik, and says, "Call me when you have a moment." Then he departs, without another look or word.

Malik roots in the repertoire of memories at his disposal for the right kind of reaction, but he cannot come up with a suitable one. He holds the piece of paper as if it were on fire and about to burn his fingers, and scampers after the man. He asks, "Who are you? Where have we met?"

"I was in the minivan," Hilowleh says. "My nephew is one of the three wounded journalists for whom you've offered to pay. I own a printing press, one of the largest in the city, which is why I know many of the journalists. I want first of all to thank you for your kindness."

Malik nods and waits for more.

"That is going to be a hefty bill and I am offering to share it with you, and so will others, when the clinic gets round to submitting it," Hilowleh says. "But yours is a generous gesture and it behooves us to acknowledge it, with thanks."

"I'm sure you wish to say something else besides thanking me for a bill that hasn't been submitted and which I haven't yet settled," Malik says.

Hilowleh nods and then says, "I do."

Malik thinks that Hilowleh holds his self-doubts in check the way a cardplayer with a winning hand delays revealing it.

Finally, Hilowleh says, "I happen to be privy to a few facts. I hear a lot, because I am in the printing business and my nephew has been confiding in me."

Malik feels unable to set sail in such a fog, so he waits for Hilowleh to state his real business. "What are you telling me?"

Hilowleh says, "Are you here for long?"

"I am here until I've paid the bill, for sure."

"I meant, are you in the country for long?"

"Why do you ask?"

"Because I would leave soonest if I were you."

With these new deaths, Malik is now of the same mind: he is planning to leave as soon as he has done a few more interviews.

"From what I hear you're lucky to be alive," Hilowleh affirms. "For what it is worth, it is now agreed that Gumaad has all along been the snake trailing the length of his betrayals, enviously causing their deaths, because he couldn't produce a single line good enough to be published. The advice from me is this: leave quickly, quit this accursed country while you can."

Not awaiting his reaction, Hilowleh walks off.

———

Qasiir finds Malik brooding. He has the surgeon with him. The surgeon informs Malik that the three injured journalists are now out of danger. They are, however, still under sedation in the intensive-care unit. Then the surgeon gives him a card, which has on it his full name, a home phone number, and a mobile one.

The surgeon says to Malik, "I mean what I wrote in the message on the back, thinking I might not see you. Please call whenever you want. No hour is late. I am on duty the whole week. Also, don't worry about paying the bill on a foreign credit card. Hilowleh, an uncle to one of the journalists, has agreed to settle all the charges. So if you are feeling okay yourself, be on your way. And thank you."

On their way to Cambara and Bile's, Qasiir informs Malik that on their instructions he has taken Malik's things to the annex just as he packed them.

"I wish you would have let me know before doing so."

Qasiir shrugs, as if making light of the matter.

Malik, miffed, says, "As you can see, I'm well enough to decide for myself. Nor am I dead yet. Because when I am dead, it will fall to others, like Cambara and Bile, to do what they please with my personal things."

"Just following instructions," Qasiir says.

Malik ascribes his irritability, once he has given it thought, to the fact that he doesn't wish to speak about his encounter or exchange with Hilowleh to anyone. He hates the "I told you so" posture that others would take if something terrible were to happen to him.

They listen to the news on the car radio: Nine peacekeepers from the Burundi contingent seconded to the African Union AMISOM died when a suicide bomber drove into their compound.

At Cambara and Bile's, Malik gingerly steps out of the vehicle and stands, with his hand ready to ring the outside bell; but somehow he doesn't press it. Instead, he sways this way and that, from a combination of pain and exhaustion, his head spinning, the ache in his entire body now returning, his feet feeling as heavy as lead. Qasiir rings the outside bell for him and waits until Cambara joins them. Only then does he go to take Malik's suitcase and computer to the annex.

Cambara welcomes Malik in and holds him. They walk side by side to the annex. She is too familiar with the slow pace of the invalid, and supports him well. Bile accompanies them, bringing along a pouch with painkillers and anti-inflammatory drugs, aiming to have the chance to inspect Malik thoroughly. They invite him to stay in the main house for the night, but Malik won't hear of it.

"I don't like the look of that bump on your head," Bile says. "It is pretty nasty and the swelling hasn't gone down."

"Besides, from the look of you, you seem to be running a mild fever," Cambara says. And to prove it, her cold hand touches his warm head.

Bile sits in the only easy chair in the room, Cambara on the edge of the bed, in which Malik is now lying prone. They ask him questions about the explosion. He gives the details he has already worked on in his head and which he intends to write down, just as is.

Done with his retelling, Malik points Cambara to the bag in which he has kept his soiled things. Then he goes into the bathroom to wash his face and take a look in the mirror at the bump on his forehead. Bile plies him with pills, and when Malik tells him that he is set on working on the short piece he promised his editor, Cambara prepares a couch on which to sleep and a desk on which to write.

Alone at last, Malik writes several versions of the day's events and then e-mails the short piece—a pity he has no pictures to accompany it. He postpones starting on the longer piece till the next day, but before turning in, exhausted and still in pain, he rings Ahl to let him know what has happened and to ask after Taxliil.

Ahl is eager to talk. Worn out and still in considerable pain, Malik offers to say hello to Taxliil, "just to hear my nephew's voice after such a long time."

"Taxliil is in no mood to talk to anyone."

"Says who?" Malik asks, galled.

"I say it, he says it, does it matter who says it?"

Malik tells himself that, like a contagion affecting them all, there is a lot of nervous tension going around. He is under a great deal of stress, because of the threats Hilowleh has alluded to and, more to the point, the fact that he won't speak about it to anyone—which in and of itself carries its built-in anxiety; Ahl, because of the uncertainties surrounding Taxliil; Taxliil, because of what he has just been through and the unpredictability of his future safety. Maybe it is best that they do not lose their cool at what has proved to be an ordeal for all of them. He decides that it is time to compromise.

"What will make you happy?"

"Talk to Fidno and his friend," Ahl says.

Malik asks, "Is No-Name coming along, too?"

"No-Name is not coming," Ahl says. "Instead, Fidno's associate, Il-Qayaxan, known among his friends as Isha, is joining you."

"And where does Isha fit in?" Malik says.

Ahl says, "Just talk to them, please."

"Where is Fidno now?"

"Both Fidno and Isha are in Mogadiscio waiting for your call," Ahl says. "Let me give you their respective phone numbers. Please make sure to arrange to see them tomorrow at a place and time of your choosing."

Malik takes down their phone numbers and hangs up. With the words of Hilowleh echoing in his mind, he calls up Qasiir and requests that he claim to be Malik's assistant and set up a meeting for him with Fidno and Il-Qayaxan for one in the afternoon tomorrow. "Please call me back after you've spoken to them, and I'll give you the name of the hotel and the room number, too."

Then Malik does his duty by Amran and calls her, offering her a doctored version of what he's been through, reducing the number of deaths by a third and distancing himself from their proximity.

He then speaks to Jeebleh, to whom he offers an unedited version of the day's events.

AHL HITS HURDLES AT EVERY BEND, THE MORE HE THINKS ABOUT the safest and least cumbersome way to get Taxliil out of Somalia. It is difficult enough for him to step over the threshold and doubly difficult to deal with Taxliil, who is a misguided youth because of his involvement with Shabaab. Taxliil has a way of throwing another wrench into the works every time Ahl manages to wrest one free. He finds all this exhausting, and he feels himself in danger of cracking up, never mind his stepson.

His plan was to get Taxliil to Djibouti, where they would present themselves at the U.S. embassy and explain the loss of Taxliil's passport. But the plan is so far proving to be unworkable, because they need to find a travel document of some description to leave Bosaso and enter Djibouti. No airline will accept him as passenger unless he has a valid passport. Ahl thinks that as more twists in Taxliil's tale come to light, the more numerous are the drawbacks that are bound to crop up.

Meanwhile, Ahl has been in touch with a tearful Yusur in Minneapolis, has held long brainstorming sessions with Jeebleh in Nairobi, and continues to communicate with Malik by phone and by text message. Xalan and Warsame are doing their best to help as well, but things don't look good.

When he is not thinking like a runaway, Taxliil has on several occasions apologized to his parents, admitting to his foolhardy trust in the imam back in the Twin Cities, at whose prompting he volunteered to join up with Shabaab. Now he knows better; now he knows what is what, and has learned his lesson the hard way. He wants to forgive and forget—or to be forgiven, and for the entire episode to be forgotten.

But does he realize things are not simple for him and the twenty-odd runaways? Taxliil claims he does, yet he does nothing to show this is the case. Ahl is reminded of a proverb, probably French, about the unfortunate man who falls on his back and as a result breaks his nose. Taxliil keeps doing the opposite of what he says he will do, making an already difficult situation more complicated. He falls asleep in the middle of one of Ahl's debriefing sessions. When Ahl tries to iron out the major inconsistencies in his story, Taxliil loses his cool and casts uncalled-for aspersions on his stepfather.

All the members of the household help as best they can, but keep their distance, too. Faai plies Ahl with black coffee and Taxliil with sugary drinks. Xalan gets busy organizing a Somali passport with help from a friend with access to someone working in the passports division in Bosaso. Taxliil will travel with Ahl to Djibouti, away from the ubiquitous Shabaab assassins, who if they hear about his presence in Bosaso and in this house may harm him and others as well; one never knows with them. Once Ahl has taken him to Djibouti, Ahl, Malik, and Jeebleh will work in tandem to facilitate his safe return to the United States. Of course, they can't count on criminals like Fidno and No-

Name, who appear to have had a hand in his escape, to keep quiet for long; hence Ahl's proposal that Malik "buy their silence" by granting them an interview.

Xalan telephones Ahl to confirm that she has reserved seats for him and Taxliil on tomorrow's flight to Djibouti, and that she is close to organizing the passport for Taxliil. The news has a galvanizing effect, and Taxliil knuckles down to clarifying his account to Ahl. Ahl's aim is twofold: one, to understand what happened for his own peace of mind; and to help Taxliil prepare for the grilling by the U.S. authorities that he will go through when he reenters the States.

First, though, Taxliil wants to hear, not for the first time, how they discovered he was gone from Minneapolis. It is as if he takes pleasure in having kept his parents, his friends, and the school authorities in the dark while he arranged his departure, and got away without anyone figuring it out. Ahl pampers him with answers: he and Yusur thought Taxliil was at school or at the mosque, and didn't wonder until late in the evening where he might be. Since Yusur was working the night shift, it fell to him to search Taxliil's room for evidence of his where-abouts, which is when he discovered that both his passport and his shoulder bag were missing.

"Then what did you do?"

"When we were despairing of ever finding you, because no one had seen you, we went around to the police stations and the hospitals," Ahl replies. "Petrified as we were, we were also somewhat relieved when you called two days later to say you were in Somalia."

Taxliil gloats, "But I wasn't in Somalia then."

This is the first time he has said this, and Ahl can't decide if he is lying. That's the problem with lying: one lie can make one have doubts about the truth of what has gone before or what is to come later.

"Where did you ring from, then?"

"I was in Lamu, about to travel by boat to Kismayo."

"Let's start from the beginning, before you got to Kenya. What route did you take to get to Nairobi?"

"To Abu Dhabi, with a stopover in Amsterdam. From there we flew direct to Nairobi," Taxliil says. "For company, I had another student from Jefferson High, although I hadn't known him previously."

"Did he worship at the mosque as well?"

"Yes."

"Did you know him well enough to trust him?"

"We just never connected before," Taxliil says, adding, "You know how it is. Sometimes you connect fast with some people, sometimes you don't. But during the long trip, we connected, became best buddies. And that felt good."

Ahl has a natural sympathy for this kind of attitude. He likes it when someone gets on well with others, when someone makes the effort to make others feel good. Taxliil used to have a quality that gave comfort to those in his company. He used to be easy to get along with; he was a sweet child. Spending time with Shabaab has turned him into someone else, a plaintive, fearful youth, full of misgivings about the world and its inhabitants.

"Now, tell me how you got from Nairobi to Lamu."

"Several of us flew separately to Malindi, where we eventually met up after taking different routes to Nairobi," Taxliil says, proud that he is remembering the version he has given before.

"And from Malindi?"

"From Malindi, we took a boat to Lamu."

"And from Lamu to Kismayo?"

"That's right."

Ahl is deliberately stretching their conversation a little, to give himself more time to study Taxliil's expressions. "And after arriving in Kismayo?"

"We spent a night in Kismayo before separating into small units. We gave our American passports over to the minders assigned to take us to the forest, where we would receive our training and instructions. I took ill on the second day."

"What was the nature of this sickness?"

"Malaria is endemic in the Juba Valley."

So far so good. Not a hitch or an overlong pause. Then Ahl pluckily plunges into Shabaab-infested waters, asking Taxliil to name the names of his minders and tell exactly when and where he met them.

"What was the name of the chief of the camp?"

Taxliil repeats the same response he has given several times before. "We never knew the real names of the instructors. Nor did we get to know the names of our minders, or those to whom we handed over our passports."

"Do you recall anything else about any of them?"

"Our instructor had a northern accent, and yelled at us a lot, and wouldn't tolerate any back talk; he was quite a taskmaster." Then half-laughing and half-serious, he tries to imitate his instructor. "'We are not part of history. We are *making* history, *living* history! We are not liberators, fellows,' he would chant. 'We are martyrs, through the expression of our fury, through our ambition in action, to lead this nation away from self-ruin.' Then he'd resume his chorus. 'We are not part of history. We are *making* history, *living* history!' We nicknamed him Taariikh, 'History.' It is hilarious when I look back," Taxliil says, relaxed for the moment.

"What did your training comprise?"

"It was like boot camp," Taxliil says. "A run before dawn prayer, oatmeal for breakfast, more physical training, bomb-construction training. Lunch, prayer, a half-hour break, then back at it until nightfall, no break except for prayer times." He is on a roll now, and he goes on without any prompting from Ahl. "The boy I knew from Jefferson asked to be taught not only how to build bombs but how to defuse them."

"What reaction did he get?"

"A tongue-lashing. The instructor called him a softie. He explained that Shabaab was not in the business of defusing bombs, but in the business of making them and causing as much destruction as possible, until we gained power and set up an Islamic state, the first true Islamic state not only on the continent but in the whole world. An example to others, a model and a beacon to other Muslims."

"So how did you fare there?"

"It was all fun at first."

"And then?"

Taxliil seems bewildered, as if he has gotten lost on his way to the answer. What is it that upsets him? What are the subjects about which he is not yet prepared to speak?

Ahl asks, "Did you make any friends?"

Taxliil said, "I knew I could trust Ali-Kaboole. He was more or less my age, but went to Roosevelt High, very bright, kind, always solicitous about me, generous to a fault. I found a friend in him, he was reliable. He reminded me of Samir."

"What's become of Kaboole?"

"Kaboole died—blown up by one of our own."

Ahl asks for an explanation.

Taxliil says, "One of the clan-based factions fighting Shabaab for control of the coastal city of Kismayo killed him in a clash that claimed the lives of several of our best."

"Did you take part in the fighting yourself?"

"I've never taken part in any fighting."

"Why not?"

"I couldn't fight; I had no spectacles."

"How did you cope?"

"Funny you should ask. Before he died, Kaboole took part in a fire-fight in Kismayo, and found a pair on the battlefield, a pair thick as the bottom of a bottle. They belonged to an old man, from the enemy side, killed by one of ours. Kaboole brought them to me, thinking spectacles are spectacles, and any pair would do. This became our joke."

"Nonetheless, you used them?"

"I used them. I had nothing else."

"Then what?"

"I was assigned 'civilian' duty, and after a while I proved useful as a computer programmer. I was transferred to the publications division and soon promoted. My job was mujahid liaison. I was an interpreter for the foreign contingents training the cadre in bomb building and in explosives."

"It doesn't seem that was very harsh."

Taxliil is quick to disagree. "Life *was* harsh. No TV. No fun. No games. It felt easy at first. But later, it felt like tasting a piece of hell served daily, along with your meals. We often heard the term *shahid*, martyr. When we joined, we believed in everything we heard about paradise and the houris in heaven. But eventually we realized it meant the one whose turn it is to die."

Ahl doesn't know if Taxliil's initial enthusiasm to join Shabaab is now entirely replaced by the hostile attitude he displays at present, even though this is to be expected. But will he continue vacillating between several contradictory positions until they get to Djibouti and then feel much worse at his grilling by the U.S. authorities?

"Any idea what became of your passports?"

"We heard stories. That is all."

"What kind of stories?"

"The stories contradicted one another," Taxliil says. "We heard that our American passports were being used to bring foreign fighters into Somalia, but knew this couldn't be true, because all the foreign fighters were older than us. Then we heard that some of the Shabaab leaders used them to get their sons into America," he says. "I don't know if this is true or not. I don't know."

Ahl has a glimpse, and not for the first time, of the immense difficulties Somalis are certain to face in America in the future.

"So how did you end up in the desert camp where Saifullah offered to martyr himself?" Ahl asks.

"After I got into trouble."

"What kind of trouble?"

"My instructor History, you see, had me teach English to his daughter—but only orally, as I couldn't read to her, given I had no spectacles. Then she became pregnant."

"You mean you made her pregnant?"

"I did no such thing, Dad."

"Then what happened?"

"Then History had me 'marry' her."

Ahl is furious. "He forced you to marry his daughter, even though the baby wasn't yours?"

"That's right, Dad."

Wait until Yusur hears this part, Ahl thinks. "And then what?"

"Then he had me transferred to the fighting corps."

"Do you think he wanted you out of the way, dead?"

Taxliil stares at Ahl without answering.

"What was his motive if he didn't want you killed?"

"That's what one of my friends thought."

"What did you think?"

"I was too afraid to think."

There is a pause. Then Taxliil says, "Dad I'm too tired to answer any more questions today."

"Just a couple more and then we're done."

Somewhere close by, a muezzin is calling the faithful to prayer. Taxliil seems agitated, as if debating whether to get up and answer the call or to stay seated and answer the remaining questions.

Ahl asks, "Do you remember the name of the travel agency that booked your flights?"

"I do not know the name of the travel agency that arranged our flights, or who paid for the tickets," Taxliil replies.

"Did you collect the tickets yourselves?"

"We picked them up at different airports, when we presented ourselves with our passports," Taxliil says. "They were e-tickets, every single one of them, from our starting points in the States all the way to our final destination. We did not all meet until Lamu, and then traveled together by boat."

Ahl is about to resume his questioning when he observes that Taxliil has once again retreated into the private world of which he is king.

They take a break, and Ahl tries to reach Malik to apprise him of the fresh developments. But he can only reach Malik's voice mail and doesn't bother to leave a message.

————

When they resume, Ahl explains that they'll be leaving for Djibouti the next day.

"When do we go home, to Minneapolis?"

"That we don't know," replies Ahl. "You'll have to wait and see."

Ahl is certain that Taxliil's name will be among the names the FBI have on file. The U.S. embassy will insist on debriefing Taxliil, and may even fly out an agent to talk to him in Djibouti. He is unsure if

Taxliil is the first of the twenty or so Somalis to return. After debriefing, he will most likely be flown to Stuttgart, in handcuffs, on a special military flight. But he spares Taxliil the details for now. It is one
thing to prepare him for what to expect, another to frighten him unnecessarily.

"Do you think I'll be treated as a security risk?"

"Why do you ask?"

Taxliil says, "Because Saifullah said that he preferred dying in dignity to being arrested and handcuffed by the Americans and treated
with suspicion for the rest of his days."

"There is the possibility you may be considered a security risk," Ahl
says. "But because you are still underage, they may go easy on you."

Taxliil says, "Are you trying to frighten me, Dad?"

"No, my son," Ahl says.

"I am starting to regret I didn't go on with it."

"I am glad you didn't go on with it," Ahl says.

He thinks there is no despair as profound as that of a teenager
whose innocence has led him to place his trust unwisely.

Xalan returns home with the air tickets and the passport of a boy of
similar age to Taxliil. Although it was issued months earlier, no one has
picked it up, and her friend in the passports division is prepared to take
the risk of lending it to her. He'll deny knowing anything about it if the
theft is discovered. At best, if the deceit is not discovered, the passport
is good only into Djibouti, which a Somali doesn't need a visa to enter.
To enter the United States, Taxliil needs to apply for a U.S. visa, which
is difficult to obtain at the best of times.

There is a more immediate problem: Taxliil is refusing to come
down from his room; he wants to be alone, and won't entertain the

thought of trying on the clothes Xalan has bought for him. She and Ahl try to cajole him out of his downbeat mood.

"How did your meeting go before he went up?" Xalan asks Ahl.

Ahl tells her everything.

"Maybe you scared him," says Xalan.

"I didn't mean to."

"Maybe he thinks he'll be flown to Guantánamo."

"I said nothing of the sort. I was just preparing him for what might happen."

They are silent for a long time.

Ahl telephones Malik to tell him that he and Taxliil are leaving for Djibouti the next day. He asks Malik how much longer he intends to stay on, and Malik, not for the first time, decides against telling him how deeply worried he is at present about his safety. He says only that he intends to do a few more interviews and then leave. When Ahl shares with him his good news about the tickets and the passport, Malik expresses delight and says, "Maybe I'll see you sooner than you think."

Ahl then rings Jeebleh and fills him in on the progress they have made so far. Just before they disconnect, he mentions how he inveigled Malik into agreeing to interview Fidno and one of Fidno's associates.

Jeebleh is furious with both brothers and says so. "Why do you endanger his life, cajoling him to interview two criminals at once in the same room in a hotel? This is far too risky. Do you realize what you've done?"

"I am indebted to Fidno," Ahl says.

"One is never indebted to a criminal," Jeebleh says.

"Well, I am," Ahl retorts. "His intervention has, after all, brought Taxliil home."

"What's got into you?"

Ahl says, "I love my son."

"How can you behave as carelessly as you've done towards Malik?" Jeebleh says.

"What do you want me to do?"

"I want you to think of what you've done, the danger caused to your brother."

"The matter is out of our hands," Ahl says.

Jeebleh disconnects the line in fury.

MALIK IS IN THE KITCHEN OF THE MAIN HOUSE, PREPARING BREAK-fast. He has been up almost all night—he couldn't bring himself to sleep after his exchange with Jeebleh. He won't consider calling off the interview with Fidno and Isha. It would be a cowardly thing to do, especially as he wishes to live up to the memory of those killed while performing their jobs—journalists, the Dajaals, and the large number of innocent civilians terrorized into submission by the barbarism of Ethiopians, Shabaab, and half a dozen other fifth columnists. He will do as he has agreed: conduct this one interview and then leave on the flight to Nairobi on the morrow.

The breakfast comprises greens, cheese, toast, peeled and sliced oranges, and leftovers from the night before, including lentils. Cambara is partial to caffelatte in a mug; Bile loves his with half a spoon of sugar; she likes her liver cooked rare; Bile likes his well done.

Cambara comes to the table in a tropical cotton dress and no bra, as if playing at Shabaab's recent edict that Somali woman should not wear such American-inspired, un-Islamic breast contraptions. Does she know she makes Malik pine for the company of women, especially when, as they kiss each other on the cheek, she presses her full chest against him, too?

What a pleasant surprise that Bile joins them, his complexion healthier and his appetite robust. Malik observes how Bile and Cambara take pleasure in touching, whenever a pretext permits it. Bile asks Malik how he is doing, and insists on feeling the bump on his forehead, which has gone down enough to satisfy him.

Bile says, "Have you heard about the predator attack on a human target in the town of Dhuusa Marreeb at dawn?" He tells Malik about a report on the BBC Somali service, that a Tomahawk cruise missile launched from a U.S. submarine off the coast of Somalia has killed several innocent civilians in addition to their target, a killer and one of the desecrators of the Italian burial sites in Mogadiscio. "Now my fear is that the U.S. action may lead to further protraction of the war, with more foreign jihadis volunteering to join Shabaab."

"Same old thing, dressed differently," Malik says. "Attacks by America, which are meant to tame terrorists, embolden them."

Cambara says, "You don't sound bothered by it."

He replies, "Not so much bothered as disturbed. As I said before, one must know what to expect from poorly thought-out attacks—by Ethiopians doing it at the behest of America or by America herself."

Bile picks up a cherry tomato and eats it.

Cambara says, "I'd probably be stretching it if I say that by their very nature, suicide bombers are remote-controlled. For me, however, there is no difference between the imam remote-controlling the suicide bomber and the guy orchestrating the Tomahawk launch from the safety of his Colorado base. One could be having his coffee and joking with his pals, the other could be crouched on his rug, allegedly praying."

Bile says, "It's the mindless killing of noncombatant civilians that annoys me about distance killing of any sort." Then he turns to Malik and asks, "Will you write about it?"

"No."

"Why not?"

Malik pretends not to hear the question, because he doesn't see any point in answering, and Bile doesn't press him.

Cambara asks what his plans are today.

"I have an appointment with two subjects whom I'll be interviewing in a suite I've booked in a hotel for the day."

"Who are you interviewing?" Bile asks.

And before he has answered the question, Cambara urges him to use the annex, reasoning that it is easier to monitor the movements of who is entering the compound and who is exiting. "With a hotel, it is always impossible to keep track of people's goings and comings."

When he insists on keeping the arrangements as he has made them, however, neither puts any pressure on him to reconsider.

Eating his breakfast, Malik cannot help but contrast their reaction to Jeebleh's, who said that interviewing these "criminals" was a gamble "not worth a candle." Probably because he hasn't named his interviewees or mentioned how they make their living—he doesn't actually know what Il-Qayaxan does for a living beyond being an associate of Fidno. He attributes Bile's understanding to his own obstinate loyalty to Somalia by staying on, despite all the drawbacks.

Once again, Qasiir takes Malik to his appointment. As they enter the hotel grounds, his eyes fall on BigBeard, still clean-shaven and dressed in a suit, sitting in a car with the window down and speaking on his mobile. Two unknown men sit in the car with him. Malik stops dead in his tracks, exchanges a knowing look with Qasiir, and then resumes walking into the hotel foyer. Before he gains the reception, Qasiir says, "Maybe we should consider canceling the appointment."

"Have you the requisite security in place?"

"Of course."

"Can they cope with any eventuality?"

"I can get backup, if you like."

"Do that, and let the arrangements stay."

Before he takes another step in the direction of the reception, which is farther off than he has pictured, Malik remembers Hilowleh telling him that he was lucky to be alive. Turning, he receives comfort from knowing that Qasiir is near. "Who are the two men in the car with him?"

Qasiir replies, "One of them is called Al-Xaqq."

"What deadly business is he in?"

"Explosives."

"And the other?"

"Dableh, a former colonel in the National Army," Qasiir says. "All three are suspected of being active members of Shabaab."

Malik finds it astonishing that three men known to be leading the insurgency can be sitting in a car in the parking lot of a four-star hotel, and the intelligence of the so-called Transitional Federal Government hasn't the wherewithal to apprehend them, let alone take them into detention.

"I wonder what brings all three together."

Qasiir says, "Maybe you."

"Are you trying to scare me into canceling the appointment?" Malik says.

"I want to make sure I am able to save you."

"They don't scare me. I've seen worse."

"You remind me of Grandpa—and he is dead."

Malik's insides are home to butterflies, thousands of them turning his guts into a battle zone. He is perspiring heavily as well, and continuously wipes his forehead to no avail. How sweet of Qasiir to look away, pretending not to notice.

"Maybe they are here for some other business, and not because of you," Qasiir says. "Let's hope that is the case."

"I doubt that I am that important," Malik says.

"Your security is in place anyhow."

"That'll provide me with needed comfort."

Qasiir adds. "And I'll be here, too."

"Brilliant," Malik says.

While Malik is at the reception filling in the forms and supplying the receptionist with his credit-card details, Qasiir sees two of his men in the foyer. Then he goes ahead of Malik, taking the elevator to the fourth floor, and also makes sure that the guard detail he hired are in their places. Malik crosses paths with Qasiir as he is going up, and says, "I'll call when I am done."

———

The suite has two rooms separated by a sitting place, in all probability meant for *qaat* chewers, as evidenced by the carpets and the cushions pushed against the wall. The entrance is through the middle door. It is expensively furnished, the walls embellished with photographs of Mecca and with brief Koranic verses, framed. The arrangement included plenty of Coca-Cola and bottled juices and bundles of *qaat* sufficient for three, although Malik has no intention of taking part in the chewing of the stuff, and packets of cigarettes. The air conditioner is blasting.

Il-Qayaxan, also known as Isha, is the first to arrive, right on time. He knocks on the lounge door so gently it takes Malik a long time to hear the tapping under the roar of the air conditioner. He lets him in. They shake hands, each speaks his name and mutters at the other, "My pleasure." All the while, Malik's heart is beating against his rib cage in panic, his vision fogged with fear. What a foolhardy man I've been, he tells himself, that I've allowed myself to be talked into this.

He points to where he has placed his recording devices and says to Isha, "Please take a seat." He takes his time, the better to make sense of the man at whom he now smiles. "And go ahead and help yourself to a beverage and some *qaat*."

Isha has a worry-hardened face and the muddled grin of a man awakening from a nightmare. One minute he strikes Malik as ill-humored, the next instant his expression suggests that of a guilty man. Malik's conjecture is based on his nervous, shifty body language. He is also obnoxiously smelly, and he carries a black polyethylene bag.

Malik says, "Let's begin," and switches on the tape recorder, supplementing the recording by taking notes by hand, in the event of a malfunction or mishap.

Isha has hardly spoken his first two full sentences when they hear heavy shelling in the distance, and some small gunfire close by. The sounds of fighting erupt and Malik's headache returns with a vengeance. The pain rips into him, as if his head were severed in two, as his recall revisits ancient, scabbed aches. He cannot bear it. Maybe Jeebleh was right, after all.

Malik lets the tape recorder run, registering the noise of the bombing as if for posterity. A couple of bombs fall nearby. In the pauses between the shelling and the falling of bombs, they hear a child bawling.

When the bombardments cease at last, Malik asks what business brought Isha to Mogadiscio in the first place. Isha explains that he worked as an accountant before emigrating to the United States as a refugee, in the early nineties, going first to Nashville and then moving to Minneapolis. When he couldn't find a job matching his qualifications, he set up a travel agency, and when this began to do well, he expanded the business, taking on two Indians and a Chinese from Hong Kong as his partners. In 1996, the company moved into the business of quick moneymaking, specializing in laundering dirty money from the piracy ventures. They made immense profits, as much as 25 percent. At one point, they invested some of their own money, now laundered, into funding the piracy themselves.

However, just when they expected their profits to be quintupled, the money dried up. The banks in London where all the piracy funds ended up explained that payments would be staggered, so as to deflect attention from large amounts of money changing hands in the post-9/11 world. With the passage of time, though, Isha and his partners saw no money, only numbers chasing figures. He and his Asian partners visited London to confront the bank official charged with receiving the money and distributing it among its rightful recipients, and he showed them an affidavit and a power of attorney allegedly signed by the pirates in Xarardheere, authorizing a man called Ma-Gabadeh to collect the funds on their behalf. In the attached handwritten note, the pirates swore they would kill several hostages, two of them British, unless the banks duly paid the funds into Ma-Gabadeh's accounts in Abu Dhabi. Isha explains, "It is a case of thieves situated in different dens located in different continents swindling small thieves, whose local middlemen and contacts have been bought."

Dispatched to Mogadiscio, Isha met Ma-Gabadeh with a group of clan elders, who persuaded him to pay off at least Isha to avoid their family clans declaring war on each other.

"And you accepted this deal, in which the Asians who invested in the adventure just as much as you did would get gypped?" Malik asks.

"I was buying time, since Ma-Gabadeh said in my presence to the elders of my clan and his that he needed time to pay up," Isha claims. "This was the case of a bird in hand. You take what you can get."

"Then what happened?"

"The Ethiopians invaded! And Ma-Gabadeh fled."

"Where to?"

"Where else? Eritrea."

"And where does that take us?"

"I am now penniless and stuck in Somalia."

"What if you try to leave?"

"I risk ending up in detention in the United States."

"What have you told your Asian partners?"

"They believe I've received my share and absconded. I can understand why they are baying for my blood. They are threatening to report me to the U.S. authorities, claiming they had no knowledge of any of this."

No wonder he looks angry and at the same time guilty.

———

When Fidno knocks on the door, Malik lets him into the suite, and he and Isha hug and pat each other on the back. Malik tries to take a quick reading of Fidno's face. He looks like a character out of a crime novel: deviously handsome in a Humphrey Bogart way, with a smile so captivating you have to fight to get your heart back; eyes alive with promise—a promise that will leave you cursing the day you met him. But he can't be all bad, he imagines Ahl saying. After all, he has helped to reunite him with Taxliil.

Fidno is carrying a white cotton bag with "The Body Shop" written on it in black. Begging Malik's pardon, Fidno wants to get one thing out of the way: he hands over the cash in the bag to Isha, glad to have the presence of a witness. To this end, Fidno counts out several thousand U.S. dollars and pushes the rest of what Malik presumes to be

Isha's share toward him. Isha counts the cash, putting it in the black polyethylene bag that he came in with; he has the gall to ask Malik if he is interested in having some of it. Offended, Malik declines.

Fidno picks up a bundle of *qaat* and starts to chew in silence, until his cheeks are filled with a wad of leaves the size of a lemon. His eyes are red, bulging with increased alertness. Malik smiles a makeshift grin as catharsis runs through every inch of his tense body. His head hurts, and his groin, too. He concentrates on his physical pain to the exclusion of all else, blocking out past, present, and future, and residing in a fenced-off territory of bodily agony. Unable to shut out the recent past, he sighs, sweating richly, and then breathes as unevenly as a man who has climbed a high mountain very fast without preparation. He wipes oily perspiration from his forehead, using the wet cloth that had held Fidno's bundle of *qaat*.

"I hear you were hurt yesterday," Fidno says. "Though not badly hurt, from what I can see."

Malik is in some discomfort. He does not wish to talk about how badly hurt he is—God knows he knows enough about Fidno's past not to want his medical services! And Fidno affects a harried mood, like a heckled man; he wants to get on with it, to "talk myself silly and at length."

And as he speaks, Malik is less certain why he thinks that Fidno is a dangerous man. Fidno repeats the story he has already told Ahl, with palpable insistence that no one has paid the ransom due to him and his men; that Somalis are not receiving a hearing; that the pirates are not receiving the money to which they are entitled. Most important, Fidno says, "What the rest of the world has been made to believe is untrue. Please, please write that down."

"So who is getting the money if the Somali pirates are not growing rich from their pickings?" Malik asks, trying not to provoke Fidno's ire.

"That's what I want to know," Fidno replies.

Malik says, "I understand that every criminal activity known to humankind is occurring in Somalia, from drug dealing to money laundering, people smuggling, and the importation of illegal arms. Not to mention aiding and abetting, or at a minimum endorsing, what in the West is referred to as terrorism. What do you say to that?"

Fidno stops chewing. He acknowledges Malik's go-ahead nod, but waits, then speaks with a cultivated slowness.

"In a required rhetoric class at my university in Germany, the professor spent more than half of our first class on a question an attorney put to a husband accused of beating his wife. He asked the husband when he had stopped beating his wife. The question was formulated in a way that made the husband incriminate himself regardless of what reply he gave. Now I insist that you reformulate your question so that I have a fair crack at it."

Malik says, "Does piracy work, and if so, for whom?"

"We are not sea bandits of the ilk of Captain Hook and Captain Blood. The world capital of piracy is not located in Eyl or Xarardheere, which if you visited them you would see are two of the most underdeveloped towns in the backwaters of Somalia." He pauses. "Here is the answer to your question. Piracy does not work for Somalis."

"Would you like to explain?"

"Let me try," Fidno says. "Through the combined efforts of the community and the fishermen who were affronted by the mechanized fishing that was causing not only damage to the environment but the loss of livelihood to the fishermen, the people of Puntland established a coast guard, initially with the sole aim of stopping illegal fishing in our waters. When these efforts resulted in failure, because the foreign fishing vessels employed strong-arm tactics and used guns to intimidate the communities, a handful of former fishermen resorted to 'commandeering' the fishing vessels owned by the nations fishing illegally and in an unregulated manner."

Malik has heard all this before, but he is curious about how it actually works. How, for example, can young men in twenty-foot skiffs with free boards and only seventy-five horsepower or so take ships the size of an apartment block?

"We do it with the help of *others*," says Fidno.

"Who?"

Fidno responds, "As Somali 'privateers'—we are not pirates, we insist—we avail ourselves of a network of informers of different nationalities and in disparate professions: ship brokers, marine insurance brokers, security officials with access to information about ship movements, bankers, accountants; a run of the entire gamut to do with shipping. We communicate with London on secure satellite phones; receive info from someone at the Suez Canal with the schedules of the ships, the nature of the cargo, the name of the owners, and their final destination. Dubai. London. Sana'a. The world is at our fingertips. How do you think we commandeered the ship from Ukraine carrying tanks to Mombasa, tanks meant for the regional government of the south of Sudan? How did we know about an Israeli ship carrying chemical waste? We know everything about the ships, a few days before they sail through. We have negotiators based in North America who deal with the owners of the ships. What is happening here is beyond your or anyone else's imagination."

Fidno looks at Isha, who endorses his claims with a nod.

"Here"—he points again at Isha—"is one of our negotiators. He started off as an accountant, now he is stuck here, penniless, because the due payments have not been paid."

"Where's the money?"

"In London—at a bank," Fidno says.

"Who gets paid—who has been paid, if not you?"

"Apart from the Somalis, everyone else has been paid. Our consultants in London have received their shares; the Abu Dhabi middlemen, too; ditto the Suez Canal folks. Not a cent to the Somalis. We've done the dirty work and are the 'bad guys' who are terrorizing the world's shipping lanes, but we haven't been paid."

"Can you name names, give addresses?"

"Of course."

Malik asks Fidno about the cash they've just shared out, despite the fact that he realizes he risks being told off.

"As men of all seasons, we have our fingers in different pies to survive," Fidno says. "The money we are sharing out is from a speedboat-building venture we've set up in Seychelles. I've agreed to lend half of my share to Isha, who promises to pay it back when he receives what is owed to him—eventually. And as you can see, it is not millions of dollars I am doling out; only ten thousand dollars in small denominations of ten and twenty."

Malik has no reason to disbelieve him, especially because Fidno sounds convincing, but then that is not saying much. As a journalist, he seldom trusts the truth of the version he hears until he has dug deeper and deeper and gotten to the bottom of the matter. Alas, it is not possible to do so now, as time is against him. Not to overlook the fact that his fear is making a worrying comeback, and he feels a little feverish.

Still, he won't let go. He asks, "But surely the pirates receive bagfuls of cash. We've seen pictures of these—bags delivered to the hijacked ships on TV, with the correspondent reporting a couple million dollars within."

"How can you tell from the clips you saw on your TV at home that the bags you were shown contained cash?" Fidno asks.

"So what did the bags in the pictures contain?"

"I suggest you go and ask the person who took the picture of the bags of alleged cash being delivered to the alleged hijacked ship and the correspondent who reported it. Maybe they would know. The problem with many people who are otherwise intelligent, well read, and well intentioned is that they believe what they see from the comfort of their couches, not what we here in Puntland are saying."

"The bags dangling down from a rope held by a man in a helicopter are supposed to have contained two million dollars," Malik repeats.

"Someone is lying."

"Tell me who is lying and why."

"I am not," Fidno says. "We're not."

"So who is?"

"Maybe it is all an insurance scam."

"They claimed to have paid when they didn't?"

Fidno goes on, "I bet you were also taken in by reports in the international media of the blatant lie that someone found the body of a pirate, drowned after receiving his share, that washed ashore with one hundred and fifty-three thousand dollars in cash in his pocket. Ask yourself this: what happened to the money? The author does not tell us that, does he? In the same article, there is the incredible story of five pirates drowning, reportedly carrying three million dollars: ransom from the Saudi oil tanker? Again, what has become of the money? In Somalia, there would be war between the residents of a town over a hundred dollars. Why not over one hundred and fifty-three thousand dollars or, better still, three million? Did you hear of any wars taking place because of money found on the body of a drowned pirate washed ashore?"

Malik asks, "What about the sweet life in the pirate towns of Eyl and Xarardheere I've read about in the *Guardian* in London?"

"Eyl is a run-down village, the poorest in Puntland," Fidno says. "I doubt the journalist who's written the article has been there. I have. There is nothing, nothing in Eyl."

"The BBC has aired similar pieces," Malik says.

Fidno says, "Who am I to challenge the BBC?"

Fidno's cheeks are almost empty of *qaat* now, the slim wad left no bigger than a weal raised over his cheekbone. Isha's eyes are like the eyes of a man drunk on some cheap brew, his tongue soaked in the stewed greenness of his addiction.

Malik switches the tape recorder off and says, "We're done. Thank you both."

Then they chat off the record about other matters, and Fidno inquires if Malik has been in touch with Ahl and if he can tell him how he is doing. Malik replies in general terms, without going into any specifics. In fact, he makes an effort not to mention Taxliil's name, even once. Polite to the last minute, they part in good humor, Malik promising that he will base a piece on their conversation and will send it to them if one of them provides him with an address. Fidno gives him an e-mail address.

Malik phones Qasiir to pick him up, and leaves Fidno and Isha where they are, in the suite, chewing. At the reception, he settles the bill, making sure that he is not responsible for further incidentals. Then he finds Qasiir in the car, parked where he left him.

Malik says, "Please take a different route from the one we took when we came earlier. I suggest you pretend we are going to the apartment."

Qasiir looks often in the rearview mirror, to make sure no one is following them.

Malik says, "Also I want you to book my flight."

"Your flight to where?"

"Nairobi. First thing in the morning."

AHL, READY TO DEPART FOR THE AIRPORT, TELEPHONES MALIK TO tell him how things are. Even now, Ahl does not wish to confide in Malik about Taxliil's erratic moods and behavior—let alone what is going on just now, with him having barricaded himself in the room and refusing to open the door or to communicate with anyone.

Cambara answers instead of Malik anyway. Surprised at first and wondering if he has rung the wrong number, Ahl is about to disconnect the line when she hurriedly gives her name and then says, "You have the right number, but I am afraid Malik won't be able to answer it."

Ahl offers to ring again later, and leaves her with his name and the news that he and Taxliil will be off to the airport in a short while. Or so he hopes.

Even so, she doesn't volunteer much. He wonders if Bile is in a bad way. Then he thinks about Malik's interview, at just the moment when she says, "I'm sorry to bring you bad news."

Then he knows it right away. The names Fidno and Isha join forces with his sense of guilt to choke him, rendering him speechless. His tongue feels disabled, his eyes bulge out of his face like those of one having a sudden fit.

"I am sorry, very sorry," she says.

Between sobs, she confirms almost his worst fears. Malik is in the hospital, in critical condition.

Shocked and mute as he is, he revisits his recent arguments with Malik and Jeebleh. He thinks, At least Malik's not dead. Malik is the kind not meant to die. He prays one of Malik's many lives will reclaim him from a hospital bed.

She says, "The car he was in, driving back from his interview, hit another remote-controlled roadside device. Qasiir, who was at the wheel, is dead. Malik is in the intensive-care unit. I am spending the night here by his bedside. We've organized a special plane to fly him out to Nairobi in an hour or so. I'll go with him myself."

"Is there anything I can do?"

"You have your hands full," she says.

"I meant in terms of footing the bills?"

"That's taken care of," she says. "All paid."

He can't think of what to say; not even thanks.

She goes on, "I've telephoned Jeebleh. He'll meet our flight."

"If he is in danger, Cambara, please tell me."

"He needs a hospital with better facilities than the one here," she says. "Also Jeebleh will be in Nairobi when we get there."

"What do the doctors in Mogadiscio say?"

"They are confident he won't be in danger if he is taken in good time to a Nairobi hospital with more sophisticated facilities," she assures him. And then she hangs up.

In the silence, Ahl is still for a moment. And then he breaks. He throws his mobile phone against the wall; he screams at the top of his lungs, cursing. Xalan rushes up the staircase and finds him still and silently staring at the phone, as though he has no idea what he has done and why. She follows his gaze and picks up the parts of the phone, scattered by the impact, then puts them back together, pressing the casing until the phone begins to function again. She gives it to him, and he acknowledges her with a nod of his head. She waits, ready to talk, ready to help, as his cheeks grow wet with his tears.

When his phone rings again, he moves away from it, shaking his head, so Xalan answers it, and this is how she learns what has made Ahl suffer a momentary disintegration. She takes him in her arms and the two of them rock together, as though she is helping a colicky baby to fall asleep. And as they rock, she repeats in alternation the two maledictions, "What a dastardly city!" and "What an accursed country!"

At last his features harden. He balls his fingers into a fist and remains standing, motionless, even after Taxliil joins them. Xalan doesn't tell Taxliil about what has happened to his uncle. She doesn't dare. One never knows with the young; they might say or do anything.

Of course, in the absence of an explanation, Taxliil misinterprets. Assuming that Ahl is finally showing his anger toward him, he locks himself in his room again and refuses to open the door and talk to Xalan, even after she has told him Malik's sad news. He stays on in the darkened room, feeling sorry for himself one minute as the surrogate sufferer of other people's pains, and in the next weighed down with guilt. He says loudly and repeatedly that he wishes he had finished the job in a courageous manner, as Saifullah had done, instead of chickening out at the last instant. He is in a rage, and nothing Xalan says can calm him down.

Warsame is on the phone. He has been in Garowe, the capital of Puntland, and has had a long chat with the deputy president of the region, a former classmate of Xalan's. The president's chief of staff has given assurances that the investigation into the explosion in which Saifullah died is still ongoing. Meanwhile, however, the minister of the interior has hinted to Warsame that he and Xalan may at some point be called in to answer questions. Xalan asks if Warsame has spoken to the minister about "the other matter, our young you-know-who." Yes, says Warsame. "He suggested that we clean up our house fast and make sure we remove all the dirt ensconced in the corners."

She assures her husband that she is hard at work to get Ahl and Taxliil out of Bosaso, not because they are dirty, but because their own safety depends on it; the longer they wait, the greater the chance that Shabaab will discover where they are.

Then she tells him what she knows about Malik, and everything else that entails.

She points out to him that, unfortunate as the events have been, Malik has been lucky on a number of counts: lucky that the explosion occurred close to Cambara and Bile's place; lucky that their house-keeper happened to have been on her way home as the device exploded, so that she saw the crowd gathering around the vehicle and abandoned herself to curiosity, not knowing who the victims might be until she got close enough to recognize Malik and Qasiir.

Most fortunate of all: they found a Cessna Sovereign with no cargo or passenger for its return to Nairobi. Not that this made the flight any cheaper for them, but Cambara scraped enough cash together, adding to what Malik had in his bag. With help from some of the onlookers, she eased Malik out of the vehicle, and with Bile's help, rushed Malik to a ten-bed private hospital after the housekeeper, with the help of bystanders, agreed to carry Qasiir's corpse to the annex.

Ahl rings Bile for a further update.

Bile says, "I haven't heard from her yet."

"I hope everything is well," Ahl says.

Bile asks, "When do you leave for the airport?"

Ahl doesn't tell him about Taxliil's behavior. He says only that the flight is delayed by at least an hour.

"I'll call you if I hear anything," Bile says.

"I would appreciate it very much."

Bile then asks, "How're things with Taxliil?"

"We are all jittery," Ahl says.

———

Ahl sits alone, drinking his third cup of coffee and feeling a sickness for which there is no instant cure. He is in a dilemma. He looks up when Xalan suggests that they look at the passport Taxliil will use to get him to Djibouti, but he shakes his head, resigned to the failure of his schemes. She pours more coffee into his cup.

His phone rings and he answers it. He listens for a minute or two and then puts it on speakerphone, so that Xalan can hear the barrage of accusations Yusur is leveling against him.

"Taxliil says you are scaring him," she says, "telling him that he may be flown from Djibouti straight to Guantánamo."

"I've said nothing of the sort," Ahl says.

"I can imagine you doing it," Yusur says.

"Well, I didn't."

"I am his mother and I want him back."

"But he is my son and I love him," Ahl says.

She says, "Cut the crap. You know he is not your son, and you've never loved him as a father might love a son. And I believe him. I know what you are trying to do. Scare the hell out of him."

"But Yusur, darling . . . !"

"Don't you darling me!"

He doesn't know what to do or say.

She asks, "Is Xalan anywhere near you?"

"She is."

"Can I have a word with her?"

Xalan says, "I don't wish to talk out of line, but let me tell you that you are making a grave mistake accusing Ahl of any wrongdoing. He deserves much more appreciation from you; he deserves gratitude from your son, who is being exceedingly difficult. I suggest that you hang up and call in an hour with an apology, because you don't know what we are dealing with here."

Xalan hangs up on Yusur. Then she goes upstairs and tells Taxliil that if he does not come out in half an hour and apologize, his father will take the flight to Djibouti on his own and leave him behind.

When she comes back down, she says to Ahl, "Yusur is out of line. The Yusur I heard just now is not the Yusur I've known and loved. When she called me, just before you boarded your flight, she described you as the most pleasant and caring husband any woman could have. So what has gotten into her?"

Ahl says, "Nothing new has gotten into her. This has always been there, a character trait that resurfaces when she is anxious or when she doesn't have things her way. There are a number of things about Yusur you will never know until you've shared the same space with her daily."

"What's causing the outburst, though?"

"You see Yusur's behavior replicated in Taxliil," Ahl says. "Like mother, like son; sweet one minute, poisonously bitter the next."

A frisson of doubt descends upon Xalan's features, darkening her countenance. She is sorry to have born witness to Yusuf's brazen outburst. But, knowing Yusur, Ahl is certain she will not withdraw her accusations or apologize, even if a chance presents itself. *Apology* is not a word his wife is familiar with.

Ahl, not liking the extended silence, asks Xalan if she is happy in her marriage.

"I am," she says. Then, "Actually, I've often wondered if one needs to be happy in marriage. Happiness is such an elusive thing. I've been married for a good twenty-five years, but I've found him loyal, always loyal. Many a Somali husband would've walked away after what they did to me. Even my sister turned her back on me. Not my Warsame. He didn't. That's pure love."

Ahl keeps his counsel and remains silent.

"Warsame is very unusual among his peers. He is the butt of their jokes, described as gutless, for not divorcing a wife dirtied by gang rape, and marrying another, younger woman. He is unique, because there are very few Somalis in whose blood loyalty runs."

Marveling at her courage, he kisses her wrist.

His phone rings: Cambara reporting that they are in Nairobi, stuck in traffic between the airport and the hospital. She promises to telephone him later with the Nairobi clinic number.

When it is time for Ahl to leave for the airport as well, Taxliil is there, flaunting a Lakers cap worn backward, and dark glasses, tennis shoes, no socks, a pair of baggy trousers, and, in place of a belt, a string round his waist. Faai comes out to see them off.

At the airstrip, they remain in the car with Xalan, the air conditioner on, no one talking. Taxliil hasn't spoken a word since getting into the car.

A man in a police uniform comes up, and he and Xalan exchange family news. He mentions that Warsame has called him from Garowe and has requested that he help. Xalan hands over the two passports. The man ambles away, dragging his boots on the ground and raising a cloud of dust.

Xalan asks Taxliil if he knows who he is, what his new name is in the passport that will take him to Djibouti, and where he is supposed to have been born. Taxliil has no answers to any of these questions, because he hasn't bothered to open the passport. She asks if he prefers to stay behind, in Bosaso. He shakes his head no. She asks him why not? He has nothing to say to her.

Meanwhile, the officer in uniform returns with both passports duly stamped and hands them over to Xalan, who in exchange gives him a fat envelope stuffed with Somali shillings. He toddles away quickly, and Xalan hands back the passports, giving Ahl his, and giving to Taxliil a Somali passport with an exit visa. But Taxliil is not interested in learning his new name or birthplace, even though she spells it out for him. Nothing of what she does and nothing that she says are of interest to him. Finally she puts the passport into Ahl's dependable hands. He'll keep it with his own passport until they get to Djibouti; she can rely on him to do that.

Before the passengers are to board the plane, Xalan writes down the name of a hotel in Djibouti where they can stay in the event they make it past immigration. She also copies the home telephone and mobile numbers of a very good friend of hers there, a radio journalist who, depending on how they fare, will meet them and take them to the hotel at least for the first night.

FOR THE ENTIRE FLIGHT, TAXLIIL AVOIDS MAKING EYE CONTACT with Ahl, from whom he sits as far away as possible. He acts disdainful of Ahl's suggestion, whispered in English, that he open the passport and get to know his presumed identity.

There is order in Djibouti, when they land and when they disembark. Uniformed ground personnel shepherd the passengers from the aircraft on foot to the arrivals hall. The security is competently vigilant, but without a show of naked authority. There is confidence in the organized efficiency of state power, whose trappings are evident. Given the size of the country, there are numerous aircraft on the tarmac and on the runway, with the flags of many nations on them.

Their flight has landed near the hour when many a Djiboutian loves to enjoy a sit-down chew, and a fearful slowness ensues. Ahl senses that the immigration officers on duty are eager to rush the passengers through the formalities. He is relieved not only because they are now beyond Shabaab's reach but because he derives comfort from the sense of order everywhere around them. He likes to know where he is with authority; he loves it when he can challenge the rightness or the wrongness of the actions ascribed to the state. In Bosaso, state authority was so diffuse he could not tell who was in charge. He fills in the entry forms, stating the purpose of his visit and estimating the duration of his and his son's stay at a week maximum.

He is still worried about Taxliil's mood, though, and whether he is harboring a desire to get caught, deported, or denied entry. Is Taxliil martyring himself belatedly, to make up for a previous failure? Does he, like many misguided youths, place an exalted value on obduracy? Impervious to Ahl's mild admonishments, expostulations, and appeals to get on with it, Taxliil doodles at the top and bottom of the entry form. Two different immigration officers ask Taxliil and then eventually Ahl what the problem is, and Ahl says to both, "The difficulties with teenagers."

He does his utmost not to lose his temper, and with his teeth clenched in frustration, takes the form from Taxliil's clutch and says, "Let me fill it in."

Taxliil says, "There is a problem, though."

"What's the problem?"

"I don't like something about this passport," Taxliil says.

"What don't you like about it?" Ahl asks.

"It makes me a year older. I don't like any of my aliases, either."

Who says that there is no life after death? Ahl remembers a line from Auden: that "proper names are poetry in the raw." Ahl reads the run of names to which Taxliil is supposed to answer—Mohammed Mahmoud Mohammed—and cannot help agreeing that, taken together, they sound like a made-up name. So in a moment of rare sympathy, Ahl pats him on the back and fills in the forms when Taxliil raises no objections.

They form their own line, being the only passengers left. As they approach the immigration counter, Ahl says sternly in muttered English, "Let me do the talking, if you don't mind."

Mercifully, Taxliil nods his head.

Since none of their names match and since Ahl is traveling on an American passport, which has in it a Djiboutian exit and entry stamp from less than a fortnight ago, and since Taxliil bears a Somali passport, issued a year earlier but not used up to now, they will need to give some explanation to smooth out the apparent discrepancies. Ahl feels more confident that going to the immigration counter together offers him a better chance to explain the discrepancies between the names. After all, it is not unusual in this part of the world for parents and children to bear different surnames. Besides, with any luck on their side, the immigration officer may have no way of knowing about the phoniness of Taxliil's travel document.

The immigration officer is very courteous; he welcomes them both to Djibouti. He takes a long time studying in turn the passports and their details, then looks from Ahl to Taxliil and back, and detects no family resemblance in the faces or in the sameness of the nationalities of the passports.

Ahl can see that Taxliil is nervous. He has the temperament of someone with an impulse to barrel up the stairway and run for it, or to blurt out something incriminating. Ahl volunteers, "He is my stepson," and leaves it at that.

Taxliil says, "No way will I return to Bosaso."

As with toothpaste out of the tube, no attempt to put it back in will work, despite Ahl's attempt to dismiss the disclosure as no more than a teenager's gaffe. When Ahl tries to explain, Taxliil won't let him, speaking petulantly and saying, "Leave me alone." The immigration officer takes his unrushed time to study the passports some more and to scrutinize the forms several times more. He doesn't say anything to either of them. He picks up the telephone and whispers a mere two words into the mouthpiece, in French.

Another officer, senior to the one at the desk, arrives inside a minute. He, too, peruses the passports and takes in Ahl and Taxliil's faces, as if searching for a clue. He makes a one-word phone call. A third officer, senior to both, joins them.

Ahl and Taxliil are escorted to a cubicle within the airport structure. They are put in separate rooms and are asked questions about their identities, where they were born, where they have come from, and about their final destination. New forms. New questions. Their addresses, home phone numbers, relationship, and workplace or name of school in Minneapolis. They are provided with new forms to fill in. Same questions, different officers, their conversations taped, and their fingerprints taken.

Just before nightfall, two minivans arrive to drive them out of the airport grounds to a police station a kilometer away, where they will separately undergo a longer and more detailed interrogation, first by the Djibouti authorities and then—but then, Ahl can't tell what will happen after that, can he?

———

Xalan has kept tabs on Ahl and Taxliil's movements from the moment they boarded their flight until their arrival in Djibouti. Her friend the Djiboutian radio journalist confirms to her that they are in the hands of the state security and, according to an immigration officer who has confided in him and has told him of the procedures the two have been made to go through, that the two have been taken in separate minivans to an unknown destination.

Xalan asks the journalist how he knows all this.

"The officer is my mate and we chew together," he replies.

———

Cambara shares the latest news about Malik, who is still in no state to speak, much less comprehend what is going on, with Bile, who relays it to Xalan, so that she may pass it along eventually to Yusur. Xalan, for her part, tells Bile what she knows about Ahl and Taxliil so far and all that she has learned from the radio journalist in Djibouti. Cambara shares the latest news about Ahl with Jeebleh, who met her flight in Nairobi and took them by the waiting ambulance to the clinic, where Malik is now recovering after surgery.

Cambara says, "But what will Djibouti do with them?"

"They won't slit their throats," Jeebleh says. "Whereas Shabaab would if they got a hold of either of them."

Cambara says, "That's a relief."

"That's the bright side."

"But what's their status, in Djibouti?"

Jeebleh, the student of Dante, describes Ahl and Taxliil's status as "purgatorial"—an in-between state, in which they are afforded the opportunity to gain a spiritually more satisfactory cleansing than what they would expect if they had stayed on in Somalia and been taken by Shabaab.

Cambara says, "I think I know what purgation is: the discharge of waste matter from the body, isn't that right?"

Jeebleh answers, "Yes, the discharge of waste matter in a ceremonial or ritual manner. And because Ahl and Taxliil are kept separately, each will rid himself of all defilement—especially Taxliil. Their situation is 'purgatorial' in that they may now view Bosaso as being akin to their idea of an inferno. Taxliil has his private hell to confront: a human bomber chickening out at the last minute is no easy matter for the mind to process."

Cambara asks, "Where does Djibouti come in—I mean purgatorially speaking?"

"I am convinced they are in less of a hell than the one they would be in if they had fallen straight into the hands of Shabaab, the FBI, or Homeland Security in the U.S.," Jeebleh says.

"You're saying they are in 'friendlier' custody there?"

Jeebleh says, "Djibouti will be empathic to a young Somali teenager in Taxliil's situation, caught in the politics of self-murder. The state may enter into a government-to-government deal during the extradition process. While waiting for their condition to be clarified, they will not be tortured or humiliated."

Cambara calls Bile to tell him all this, and to report on Malik's condition. The doctors in Nairobi do not consider Malik out of danger yet, but they have deemed him "lucky to be alive." His feet are up in a cast, and tubes are running into almost every orifice. His head is in a cast, too, wrapped so tight it would be uncomfortable for him to smile, even if he wanted to. He can't breathe without help: his lungs are punctured.

Journalists living in Nairobi have been coming in droves to the hospital, though. Some have even autographed Malik's cast, noting the dates and places where they worked with him on assignment and inscribing get-well messages in Dutch, French, Arabic, and English. A British female journalist and a Canadian male reporter bring flowers and keep vigil in the corridor of the clinic, waiting and chatting.

But Cambara cannot speak any longer. "Good-bye for now," she says. "Malik is waking."

ACKNOWLEDGMENTS

This is a work of fiction, set against the background of actual events whose retelling I've layered with a membrane of my own invention, and all the characters populating its pages have their origins in my imagination.

In writing it, I've borrowed from numerous sources and on occasion relied on interviews I conducted in Puntland and in Mogadiscio between the end of December 2008 and the end of February 2011. Among the many texts I've read, consulted, or borrowed from are "Nine Journalists Killed in Somalia" (Africa News, 2009); "Somali Canadian Journalist Killed" (CBS News, August 11, 2007); "Even in Exile Somali Journalists Face Death" (*The Christian Science Monitor*, August 12, 2007); "Somalia Journalist: 'I Saw My Boss Dead'" (BBC, June 19, 2009); "Gunmen Assassinate Prominent Somali Journalist" (CNN, February 4, 2009); "Fifth Journalist Killed This Year" (Committee to Protect Journalists, June 8, 2009); Eric Schmitt and Jeffery Gettleman's "U.S. Says Strike Kills Leader of a Somali Militia Suspected of Ties to Al Qaeda" (*The New York Times*, May 2, 2008); "Recruited for Jihad" (*Newsweek*, January 24, 2009); Richard Matthew's "Recruited for Jihad? What Happened to Mustafa Ali?" (Minneapolis *Star Tribune*, February 9, 2009); Abdisaid M. Ali's "The Al-Shabaab Al-Mujahidiin: A profile of the First Somali Terrorist Organization" (Institut für Stategie- Politik- Sicherheits- und Wirtschaftsberatung, Berlin, 2008); Steve Bloomfield's "Anger at U.S. 'Rendition' of Refugees Who Fled Somalia" (*The Independent*, March 23, 2007); *Muslim Human Rights Forum's Horn of Terror: Report of U.S.-Led Mass Extraordinary Renditions from Kenya to Somalia and Ethiopia and Guantánamo Bay—January to June 2007—Presented to the National Commission on Human Rights on July 2007;* Talal Asad *On Suicide Bombing* (Columbia University Press, 2007); *Somali Customary Law and Traditional Economy: Cross-Sectional, Pastoral, Frankincense and Marine Norms* (Puntland Development Research Centre, 2003); Nigel Cawthorne's *Pirates of the 21st Century: How Modern-Day Buccaneers Are Terrorising the World's Oceans* (John Blake, 2009); David Cordingly's *Under the Black Flag* (Random House, 1996); Abdirahman Jama Kulmiye's "Militia vs Trawlers: Who Is the Villain?" (*The East African*, 2001); "Speedboats v Warships: Why Piracy Works" (*The Sydney Morning Herald*, November 19, 2008); Michael Scott Moore's "What Are Those Ships Doing off the Coast of Somalia" (Miller-McCune, November 18, 2009); Clive Schofield's "Who's Plundering Who?" (*Conservengland*, November 23, 2008); Clive Schofield's *Plundered Waters: Somalia's Maritime Resource Insecurity* in *Crucible of Survival*, edited by Timothy Doyle and Melissa Risely (Rutgers University Press, 2008); "Somali Piracy Began in Response to Illegal Fishing and Toxic Dumping by Western Ships off the Somali Coast" (DemocracyNow.org, April 14, 2009); Andrew Harding's "Postcard from Somali Pirate Capital" (BBC, June 16, 2009); Mary Harper's "Life in Somalia's Piracy Town" (BBC, September 18, 2008); Najad Abdullah's "Toxic Waste Behind Somali Piracy" (Al Jazeera, October 11, 2008); Mohamed Adow's "Somalia's Trafficking Boomtown" (BBC, April 28, 2004); Robyn Hunter's "Somali

Pirates Living the High Life" (BBC, October 28, 2008) and "How Do You Pay a Pirate's Ransom" (BBC, December 3, 2008); "Pirate 'Washes Ashore with Cash'" (BBC, January 12, 2009); Daniel Heller-Roazen's *The Enemy of All: Piracy and the Law of Nations* (Zone Books, 2009); Mary Harper's "Chasing the Somali Piracy Money Trail" (BBC, May 24, 2009); "This Is London—The Capital of Somali Pirates' Secret Intelligence Operation" (*The Guardian*, unsigned, May 11, 2009); Chris Green's "Mystery of 'Hijacked' Cargo Ship Deepens" (*The Independent*, August 18, 2009); Cahal Milmo's "Insurance Firms Plan Private Navy to Take On Somali Pirates" (*The Independent*, September 28, 2010); Daniel Howden's "The Jailed Pirates That Nobody Wants" (*The Independent*, April 14, 2009).

I am grateful to many people, who, playing host to me or serving as guides or bodyguards, facilitated my travels in Somalia so that I could do my research in a secure, friendly environment. My special thanks go to the director of the Growe Puntland Development and Research Center, Abdurhman A. Shuke and his staff; to Said Farah Mahmoud and his wife, Faduma; to Hussein H. M. Boqor in Bosaso; to Hawa Aden in Galkayo; to Hussein Koronto in Eyl. In Newcastle, where I held a Leverhulme Professorship in the 2010 spring term, my thanks go to Linda Anderson, the director of the Newcastle Centre for the Literary Arts. Lastly, my thanks and love go to Anna and William Colaiace, Lois Vossen and Jay Bryon, Paula Rabinowitz, and David Bernstein.

Need I add that I alone am responsible for the opinions expressed in this novel and for any infelicities or misinterpretations?

Nuruddin Farah
March 2011